International Praise for
The House of Memories

"*The House of Memories* is a suspenseful, deeply emotional story of a woman's journey to save herself from drowning in grief. Its exploration of the depths of heartbreak is unblinkingly honest, yet ultimately it's a celebration of the power of family and connection to heal and inspire hope. An unforgettable read." —*New York Times* bestselling author Susan Wiggs

"Beautifully composed of equal parts soul and wit, *The House of Memories* is a deeply affecting novel about the anguish that breaks us and the relationships that can put us back together. Monica McInerney's tale of a family struggling to move forward in the aftermath of one terrible moment in time is everything that a powerful story of healing from grief should be. Its heart is huge, its pulse palpable, and its narrators irresistible. I read it voraciously." —Erika Marks, author of *The Guest House*

"The twists and turns of modern families are explored in this warm novel, which will have you reaching for the tissue box. This will keep Monica's longtime fans happy and make her many new ones." —*Woman's Day* (Australia)

"A compelling tale that is ultimately uplifting." —*The Sunday Mail* (Australia)

"There are two sides to every story in Monica McInerney's new heart-warming page-turner. . . . You'll laugh but you'll cry a lot more." —*Marie Claire* (Australia)

"A beautiful story about blended families and the power love possesses to hurt and to heal. A perfect weekend read." —*Grazia* (UK)

Praise for
Monica McInerney and Her Novels

"Vivid characterizations and sharply honed dialogue. . . . McInerney brings humor and insight into issues of sibling rivalry, family secrecy, and romantic betrayal."
—*The Boston Globe*

"You'll be laughing out loud one minute and crying the next."
—*Cosmopolitan* (Australia)

"One of those rare books you could recommend to anyone and know that they'll love it."
—*Australian Women's Weekly*

"A modern masterpiece . . . a wonderful, bittersweet tale that will capture your heart and imagination."
—*Ulster Tatler* (Ireland)

"Emotional and deeply moving . . . will quickly become a favorite with fans of women's fiction."
—*RT Book Reviews*

"Filled with enough heartbreak and redemption to keep even the most fickle readers swooning by story's end."
—*Minneapolis Star Tribune*

"McInerney's bewitching multigenerational saga lavishly and lovingly explores the resiliency and fragility of family bonds."
—*Booklist*

"[For] fans of Sophie Kinsella, Jennifer Weiner, Helen Fielding, and Jennifer Crusie."
—Curled Up with a Good Book

ALSO BY MONICA MCINERNEY

Lola's Secret

At Home with the Templetons

Greetings from Somewhere Else

Upside Down Inside Out

The Faraday Girls

Family Baggage

The Alphabet Sisters

MONICA McINERNEY

THE HOUSE OF MEMORIES

A Novel

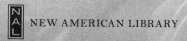

NEW AMERICAN LIBRARY

New American Library
Published by the Penguin Group
Penguin Group (USA) LLC, 375 Hudson Street,
New York, New York 10014

USA | Canada | UK | Ireland | Australia | New Zealand | India | South Africa | China
penguin.com
A Penguin Random House Company

Published by New American Library,
a division of Penguin Group (USA) LLC. Previously published by Michael Joseph,
an imprint of Penguin Group (Australia).

First New American Library Printing, February 2014

 REGISTERED TRADEMARK—MARCA REGISTRADA

LIBRARY OF CONGRESS CATALOGING-IN-PUBLICATION DATA:

McInerney, Monica.
The house of memories/Monica McInerney.
pages cm.
ISBN 978-0-451-46653-2 (pbk.)
1. Women—Fiction.   2. Grief—Fiction.   3. Family life—Fiction.   I. Title.
PR9619.4.M385M35 2013
823'.92—dc23   2013022282

Printed in the United States of America
10 9 8 7 6 5 4 3 2 1

Set in Bell MT
Designed by Spring Hoteling

For my nieces and nephews,
with lots of love

THE HOUSE OF MEMORIES

ONE

The first time I met my uncle Lucas I tried to steal something from him. It's ironic, really, considering what he would ask me to do twenty-six years later.

I was seven, on a visit to London with my mother and my father, Lucas's younger brother. We'd been traveling through my father's native England on holiday from our home in Australia. I was too young to realize the trip was a last-ditch effort to keep my parents' marriage afloat. Perhaps I should have guessed. Since we'd flown from Melbourne Airport two weeks earlier, they hadn't stopped fighting.

Lucas lived in a three-story terrace house in west London, not far from Paddington Station, two blocks in from the Bayswater Road and close to Hyde Park. Not that I knew any of those landmarks then. I remember wondering who had to mow all the grass I could see through the park gates, and thinking the houses looked like wedding cakes. I also remember running up and down the steps outside Lucas's house while we waited for him to answer our knock.

I was an only child at that stage, and was used to adult attention, but I was also used to living in the shadow of my parents' arguments. I think they were fighting when Lucas opened the door. Not physically, just the usual exchange of well-crafted, well-spoken insults. I remember Lucas running a hand through his thick mop of brown curls and saying in his lovely deep voice, "Still at it, you two?" before getting down on his haunches, looking me right in the eye and saying with a big smile, "Hello. You must be Arabella."

"Ella," I said firmly. Even at that age, I hated my full name.

"Ella," he said. "Much nicer. Do you know what that is backward?"

I nodded. "Alle."

He held out his hand. "Hello, Alle. I'm Sacul."

We followed him in, Dad and Lucas already in conversation, my mother trailing behind and complaining about her aching feet, caused by the high heels she'd insisted on wearing, though we were having a sightseeing-around-London-on-foot day. That might have been what she and my father were fighting about on the doorstep. Or it could have been any of a thousand other things. I was ignoring the adults by now, in any case. I was too busy looking around.

My parents had been here the previous year, visiting Lucas while on one of my father's many business trips abroad. I'd not gone on that trip, remaining in Australia in the care of a family friend. My father worked in the mining industry—as an accountant, not underground—often traveling to the various locations owned by his multinational employer. Sometimes during school holidays Mum and I traveled with him. So I was used to staying in big hotels and luxurious apartments. But no place I'd seen compared to this house.

It wasn't the high ceilings, the long hall, the staircase, the many doors, the fabric wallpaper or the books everywhere that grabbed my attention. It was the *mess.* The place was filthy. Not only that, there wasn't a bare surface to be seen. Boxes overflowing with paper littered the hallway, producing a kind of maze effect. One long wall was lined with bookshelves reaching from floor to ceiling. Each shelf was so jammed it would have been difficult to slide in a pamphlet, let alone another book. Perhaps it smelled musty and unclean in reality, but in my memory it smelled of paper and old books and even woodsmoke. A barbecue? I wondered. No. I could see there was an open fire in a room off the hallway. A fire in summertime!

Just before Uncle Lucas ushered my parents into what he jokingly called the withdrawing room, he turned and handed me the key of freedom.

"Go wherever you like, Ella. Touch whatever you want. Just try not to break anything."

I took off. He barely had time to offer my parents a cup of tea before I was back.

"There's someone in that room," I said, pointing across the hallway.

"Male? Red hair? Glasses?"

I nodded.

"That's Bill. One of my students."

"Is this a school?" I asked. "Are you a teacher?"

"Two excellent questions, Ella. No, not exactly. And no, not exactly."

My father explained it more later, on the way back to our hotel in a taxi. (My mother had complained so much about her feet that we'd given up the plan to go walking and sightseeing.) Lucas was the brainbox of the family, my father told me. Honors in history at Cambridge. Groundbreaking research since. He was working on a new academic study, but in the meantime, he'd also thrown open his house to bright but impoverished students to live and study in.

"*His* house?" my mother sniffed. "It should have been your house too."

"His godfather left it to *him*, Meredith, not me, as I've told you a thousand times. And as I've also told you, I never wanted it, or needed it."

"It's not about needing it. It's the *principle*. It should have been divided between you. But no, you just let him have it. Because your problem is you'll do anything to avoid confrontation."

My father ignored her and looked out the window.

"It's the *waste* of it that gets me," my mother continued. "He's sitting on a real estate fortune, and what does he turn it into? A commune for pointy-heads."

I hadn't known any of this as I'd first walked around the house that morning. All I got was a little jolt of excitement each time I opened a door to discover a student in a room. There was one in the kitchen, one in the front room, two upstairs and one on a kind of balcony at the back of the house, overlooking a small, overgrown garden. I counted five students, male and female, all either reading or scribbling or, in one case, measuring out liquid from one glass jar into another in the bathroom. If my memory serves me right, that particular student went on to work for NASA. All of them pretty much ignored me.

"I'm Lucas's niece," I said each time.

"Hi, niece," was about as interactive as one of them got.

I did as I'd been told and roamed everywhere, through all three stories. At the very top of the house I found the best room of all. It was a converted attic, with a sloping roof, bookshelves everywhere and a kind of alcove in the corner where I could see an unmade bed, a lamp and more books. On the floor, a pile of notebooks with Lucas's name scrawled on the covers confirmed that this was his part of the house. In the center of the room, not pushed against the wall like my father's desk was in our Melbourne home, was his desk. It was as large as a dining table. And it was—like the rest of the house—covered in stuff: bundles of paper, folders, boxes, books. And more books. Every surface in the room was covered in books. And in any of the gaps left, there were foxes. Dozens of foxes.

My full name back then was Arabella Louisa Fox. Mum and Dad were Meredith and Richard Fox. Which meant, of course, that my uncle was Lucas Fox. He must love his surname as much as I do, I remember thinking. I ignored the books and started counting the foxes. There were seven framed paintings of foxes on the sloping walls. Five little statues of foxes on top of the cupboards and tucked into the bookshelves. A fox pattern on a lampshade. What looked like a candleholder with a brass fox at the base. And on the desk, right at my eye level, was a real fox. A real baby fox.

There wasn't much light in the attic. None of the lamps were on, and the overhead light was turned off. The only light came in through the roof window. It seemed to shine directly on the golden brown fur of the baby fox, highlighting the glorious reds of its tail, sending a spotlight onto its little face and a gleam into its small, bright eyes. Eyes that were looking right at me.

"It's all right," I remember saying, edging toward it. "I won't hurt you."

I reached out and patted it gingerly, waiting for the snap of teeth, even while I hoped for a kind of purring sound. Did foxes purr? I wondered. The second I touched it, I knew that it wasn't real. Or at least, it *was* real, it had been alive, but it wasn't anymore. Its head was cold and still. Its back cold and hard. I ran my fingers along the fur. Several strands came off. I looked into its eyes. And whether it was because I was tired, or because my mum and dad fighting had left me jittery as it always did, I don't know; suddenly that small dead fox on the desk made me sadder than I had ever been in my life.

"You poor little thing," I whispered to it. "You shouldn't be here."

There was a piece of material on the floor, a length of curtain or an old dust sheet. I picked it up. I wrapped the baby fox in it. I put the bundle under my arm. I don't know what I thought I was going to do with it, or how I'd slip out of the house without my parents and uncle noticing. It was summer and I was in a light dress, so I couldn't even hide it under my coat. But I just remember feeling so protective and so sad, all at once. I was on a mission now. I was Ella Fox, Fox Rescuer.

I heard raised voices as I came down the stairs. My mother, then my father asking her to please mind her own business, then Lucas saying something I couldn't hear, then my mother again. I'd thought this was a friendly visit. Perhaps it had started that way. I didn't stand there, as I often did at home, eavesdropping. I slipped out through the front door. I wasn't running away, not really. I think I only wanted to give the little fox some fresh air, a brief taste of freedom.

But Uncle Lucas didn't know that as he looked out the front window. All he saw was his seven-year-old niece heading down his steps with a fabric-wrapped bundle under her left arm, the tail of a fox sticking out of it.

Afterward, Mum told me they'd thought it was very funny. "You certainly broke the tension, Ella," she'd said.

Lucas appeared at the front door just as I reached the bottom step. "Ella?" I stopped at the sudden sound of his voice, low and calm. "Are you stealing my fox?"

"No, not exactly," I said, unconsciously echoing his own words from earlier.

"No? Then what, exactly?"

"It looked lonely up there," I said. "I was taking it for a walk."

My father appeared beside his brother. "It's dead, Ella. It's a stuffed fox."

"It looked lonely," I repeated.

"Inside, Ella. Now," my mother said, appearing at Lucas's other side. "Give Lucas back his fox."

There was no more fuss made than that. In retrospect,

they probably wanted to get back to their argument. I returned the fox to its home in the attic and patted it goodbye. I was about to kiss its little snout too, but then I caught sight of its tiny sharp teeth. I still felt sorry for it, but it had also started to give me the creeps.

We said good-bye to Uncle Lucas soon after.

"Well, that was pointless," I remember my mother saying as our taxi pulled away.

"What was pointless?" I asked.

"Never mind," my parents said as one.

I thought they meant Lucas was pointless, and I didn't think that was nice. "I liked him," I said, turning to gaze out the window, more wedding-cake houses on one side, the big park on the other. "Him and his foxes."

A month later, back home in Australia, I'd received a parcel in the mail, postmarked Paddington, London. Inside was a letter from Uncle Lucas, complete with a footnote.

My dear FLN*

I'm so sorry I couldn't let you keep the fox that day. It's very precious to me. But I hope this little one will give you some pleasure. It's also a bit easier to smuggle out of people's houses.

> *Love from your London uncle,*
> *Lucas*

*Fox-Liberating Niece

It was a tiny gold fox on a key ring, just an inch long, but beautifully made, the detail of the fur and the fox's features delicately done. I called it Foxy. Foxy the Fox. At first I carried it in my pocket as a good-luck charm, whispering to it whenever I was upset or if Mum told me off about something. Once I was old enough to have keys, it turned back into a key ring. Over the years, it had held keys for many houses, in different cities of Australia, in London and in Bath. The last time I had seen it was in Canberra nearly two years ago. I'd left it, with the apartment keys, on the kitchen table beside my farewell note to Aidan—

Stop!

Change your thoughts.

Look forward.

It's always easier said than done. I've tried everything in the past twenty months—snapping an elastic band around my wrist, inhaling essential oils, meditation. I tried concentrating on my surroundings now instead, a suggestion I'd recently read in a book on managing difficult memories. *Focus. Notice. Distract. Observe.* I mentally listed everything I could see around me, forcing myself to take note of my surroundings, to be fully aware to where I was and what I was doing at this exact moment.

I was on the Heathrow Express. I had just flown twenty-two hours from Australia to London. My handbag was on my lap. The seat in front of me had a blue fabric cover. The carriage was packed with fellow travelers, some with eyes shut, others yawning, each of us recovering from our flights in different ways. I looked over at the luggage rack, checking whether my red case was still there. It was. I stared up at the small TV screen on the far wall of the carriage. It flickered from the news headlines to a weather update. The forecast for London was a cold, breezy February day. The ticket collector appeared beside me. Good, another distraction. I handed my ticket across, watched him briskly stamp it and then move on to the next passenger. I turned back to the TV. "We are now approaching London Paddington," a bright English-accented presenter announced on-screen. "Thank you for traveling with Heathrow Express."

I'd arranged to visit Lucas at two p.m., the earliest I thought I'd be able to make my way from Heathrow to his house. It wouldn't be the first time I'd seen him since the day of the fox liberation, of course. The letter he'd sent with Foxy was also just the first of hundreds—literally hundreds—of letters, faxes and e-mail messages he'd sent me in the years since. From the moment we'd met, without either of us realizing it, Lucas had become the most reliable adult in my life.

Three months after that first visit to London, my mother and father told me they were getting divorced. Irreconcilable differences. I'd had to learn how to say and spell *irreconcilable*. It was a nasty divorce. They'd fought through their marriage and they fought through their divorce: over the division of their assets, over who got the house and who got me. After legal action that lasted more than a year, Mum won most of it, our small house in East Melbourne and me included. The last time I saw Dad was the day he came to tell me that he'd been offered a job in Canada and had decided to take it.

Eight months after the divorce became final, my mother married again, to a German businessman called Walter she'd met at a garden center. They'd both reached for a large terra-cotta pot at the same time. When she would retell the story in the many magazine articles about her in later years, she would say it was Cupid at work—Walter's surname was Baum, the German for tree, and they'd met in a garden center! That terra-cotta pot led to coffee and on to a series of secret dates—she'd told me she was going to night classes. "I didn't want to get your hopes up until I knew for sure myself," she said. I hadn't had any hopes. I was still getting used to Dad being gone, not wishing for a new father.

They had a small wedding. It was my stepfather Walter's second marriage too, so neither of them wanted a big fuss, they said. Walter came complete with a large bank account, his own stockbroking business, a lot of silver hair, a beard, a big house in Richmond and a son, my instant stepbrother, Charlie. (Full name Charlemagne. Truly.) He was two years older than me, eleven to my nine. Charlie's mother had gone back to Germany to live after the marriage ended. She wasn't well, my mother told me. Certainly not well enough to look after Charlie. Mum tapped her head and did a kind of rolling thing with her eyes as she told me. It took me a while to realize she meant Walter's ex-wife wasn't well in her head. It was years later before I learned more about her. Neither Charlie nor Walter mentioned her much in the early days.

And so the two of us joined the two of them and we became four. Less than two years later, three weeks after my eleventh birthday, four turned into five, with the arrival of a baby girl called Jessica Eloise Faith Baum.

"We're a proper family now," my mother said. I remember wondering what we'd been before.

She also told me that she was changing my name by deed poll to Baum. "It's too confusing otherwise," she said. "And we should all have the same surname."

"But I like being Ella Fox," I told her.

"You can keep it as a middle name," Mum said. "You might as well have some reminder of your father. It's not as if he goes to much trouble to keep in touch any other way."

She was right, unfortunately. Dad rang only occasionally from Canada. He sent me Christmas presents and birthday cards that mentioned me visiting him in his new home, but the visits never happened. Mum didn't speak of him at all if she could help it. When she was with her friends, she referred to her first wedding day as the Big Mistake Day. None of their wedding photos were in the house. They'd somehow been left behind when we moved in with Walter and Charlie. So had all the other photos of Dad. If it hadn't been for Uncle Lucas sending me a replacement set of photos (at my request), I'd have forgotten what my father looked like. Lucas and I had become occasional pen pals since we met that day in London. I liked having a pen pal on the other side of the world, especially one who was related to me.

A month after I turned twelve, it was Lucas who rang with the news that my father had been killed in a lightplane crash in Ontario. He wrote to me afterward. *My dear Ella*, he said. *I know you hadn't seen your father in some time, and I also know he was sad about that. And I know that you have a new father and indeed a whole new family now and I hope all is well. But if you ever need some advice from your Wily Old Fox of an uncle, please send me a letter or a fax (I have just installed a very smart-looking fax machine) and I'll get back to you as quickly as I can.*

I wonder whether Lucas had any idea what he might have unleashed with that simple, kind note. From that day on, he became my combination agony uncle, imaginary friend and sounding board, all via the wonders of a fax machine.

My stepfather worked from home sometimes, and he had all the basic office equipment in his study. I'd watched him send a fax one day and thought it was the most amazing thing. He noticed my interest and let me send the next one for him, instructing me in his exact, near-perfect English. That was always when Walter and I got on best, when he was teaching me something and I was being obedient in return. Outside of those times, I think we did our best to ignore each other. It was easy enough to do without any feelings being hurt—my mother kept up such a constant stream of chatter and opinions that she papered over any silences or gaps in our relationship. And of course Walter had Charlie to talk to, in English and German, and then baby Jess as well. His real children. Looking back now, I realize it was hard for him too, and for my mum, with not only a new baby, but a new stepchild to get used to. But back then, I just felt lonely and sad a lot of the time. Like that baby fox in Lucas's office.

Two nights after I got Lucas's letter, while Mum and Walter were out at a work dinner and Charlie, Jess and I were being babysat by our middle-aged neighbor (who always turned on the TV as soon as my mother and Walter left), I tiptoed into the office and switched on the fax machine.

I decided to copy Lucas's straight-to-the-point style of communication.

Dear Uncle Lucas,

I need your advise. (Spelling wasn't my strong point back then.) *I don't feel virry happy. I have a new baby sister but she crys all the time and Mum likes her more than she likes me.*

> *What should I do?*

> > *Your neice,*
> > *Ella*

I carefully keyed in the long fax number Lucas had included with his letter, fed in the paper and watched it go, holding my breath. I sent it a second time just to be sure. And a third time. Five minutes later, I was sitting in Walter's chair, chewing the end of my ponytail and swinging my legs, when the fax machine began to make a new noise. I watched, wide-eyed, as a piece of paper started to move of its own accord, go through the roller and appear in the tray. I picked it up.

Dear Ella,

She's a baby. Babies cry. That's their job. Give her time to grow up and get interesting, then decide if you like her or not. And I'm sure your mum loves you both. That's her job.

He'd not signed it, but underneath the writing was a little drawing of a fox. A cheeky fox, with a glint in its eye.

I took out a fresh piece of paper from Walter's stationery drawer.

Thank you. I will wait.

I signed mine with a little drawing of a fox too, except my fox looked more like a skunk. I fed it into the machine and carefully pressed all the numbers again. Off it went. A few minutes later, another whirr of the machine and a new piece of paper appeared.

You're welcome. Underneath it, another fox. This one was winking.

I took all the faxes into my bedroom and read them once more before I went to sleep, feeling much better. In the morning, I put them away carefully in my treasure box.

The next day after school, Mum called me into the kitchen. "You really shouldn't use Walter's fax machine without asking, Ella." Before I had a chance to speak, she went on. "There's no need to look so cross. Lucas wasn't telling tales. He rang to ask permission to send you faxes occasionally. Walter and I have discussed it. As Walter said, he is your only uncle. So as long as you don't get too carried away, you can fax Lucas now and again and he says he'll get back to you as soon as he can. But don't annoy him, will you? He's a very busy man."

That surprised me. "Is he? Doing what?" All I could picture Lucas doing in that big London house of his was making a mess.

"I don't know exactly, Ella. Professor-y things."

"But what kind of things?"

Mum waved her hands in an "I can't even begin to explain" motion. "Ask him next time you fax him."

So I did. Lucas faxed back the very next day.

Dear Ella,

This week I am busy studying the following subjects:
Political allegiances in postwar Britain
Trends in liberal versus conservative educational policy
The rise in pro-monarchist sentiment between WWI and WWII
I also need to get the plumbing in the downstairs bathroom fixed.

I faxed back. *Thank you, Lucas. You are very busy.*

As a bee, he said in return. *Or a fox.* He signed it with that winking fox again.

It was like having a hotline to heaven. I faxed Lucas at least twice weekly and he always faxed me back. Except of course we called it foxing, not faxing. They weren't long letters. Questions or minor complaints from me, usually. Quick answers or snippets of information from Lucas, or one-liners that he called Astounding Facts of a Fox Nature. *Did you know that baby foxes are called kits, cubs or pups? Did you know that a female fox is called a vixen? Did you know that a fox's tail makes up one-third of its total length?*

Occasionally a present would arrive in the post. Not at birthdays or Christmases, but out of the blue. Always something to do with a fox, of course. A T-shirt with a fox on the front. Fox notepaper. A fox brooch once. I either used, lost or grew out of everything, except the fox key ring.

He sent books too. *I am a crime aficionado,* he said in one note, *and you seem like an inquisitive young lady, so I hope you will enjoy this genre too.* I did, reading every one that he sent—from Enid Blyton's Secret Seven, Famous Five and Five Find-Outers series, to Nancy Drew and the Hardy Boys, to Agatha Christie's novels. As I got older, Lucas sent books by Raymond Chandler, Dashiell Hammett and Arthur Conan Doyle. An Astounding Fact accompanied every one: *Did you know Enid Blyton wrote eight hundred books in just forty years? That Agatha Christie also wrote romances under the name Mary Westmacott? That Raymond Chandler only started writing detective fiction in his mid-forties?*

Jess was too young to care then, but Charlie was always curious about my faraway uncle. Not jealous. Even back then, Charlie was the most even-tempered, laid-back person I knew.

"Any new facts from the fox?" he'd ask.

I'd go to my Lucas folder and read out the latest fax. Charlie was always very impressed.

I didn't send Lucas any astounding facts in return, but I did send him regular updates on school results or any academic prizes I happened to win.

Your father would be proud of you. I'm proud of you, he'd fax back.

We didn't meet in person again until I was twenty-two. After finishing an Arts degree, I'd decided to take a gap year. I'd studied English literature; my father was English, I had a British passport—I headed straight for London. When

I e-mailed Lucas (we'd progressed from faxes) to tell him I was coming, he insisted I stay with him until I found my feet. He was still in the same house, which was still full of bright but financially impoverished student lodgers, but he was now more than their innkeeper. He'd become their employer, setting up a discreet, high-level pool of personal tutors. It worked in everyone's favor, he told me. His lodgers always needed extra money. Struggling students always needed extra tuition. Well-off parents were always happy to pay. A win-win-win situation.

I stayed for a month that first time and loved every minute—his house, the tutors, the city, Lucas himself. The following year, I returned and stayed for six weeks. After that, I visited as often as I could. I'd pay my own airfare after saving every cent I could from my new, full-time job in a Melbourne publishing house, supplemented by my evening job as an English tutor. Lucas's tutors had given me the idea. I steadily rose through the ranks at the publisher, from editorial assistant to copy editor to editor. At the age of twenty-eight, single and restless, I resigned from my job, packed up my flat, said farewell to my friends and family and flew to London yet again. I worked for Lucas as his cook and housekeeper for two months before I found a short-term job as a badly paid editor with a literary magazine in Bath. I still traveled back to London most weekends and stayed in Lucas's house each time, going to the theater or, more often, staying in and cooking dinner for him and whichever of the tutors happened to be in the house. Which was how, where and when I first met Aidan.

Two years later, on a sunny Canberra afternoon, Lucas was the witness at my registry-office wedding to Aidan

Joseph O'Hanlon, originally of Carlow, Ireland, lately of London and now of Australia. Aidan and I had moved to Canberra a year after we met, when he was offered an interpreting and translating position with the trade commission there. He was fluent in French, Italian, Spanish and German. I'd gone freelance, able to work as an editor from anywhere.

It was important to us both that Lucas was at our wedding. He'd brought us together, after all. My mother was vaguely friendly to Lucas, I think. Marriage to Walter had softened her or at least helped her forget how annoyed she'd once been with my dad and, by extension, Lucas. Walter made stilted conversation with him, as Walter tended to do with everyone. Jess pretty much ignored him. Aged eighteen, she was too busy flirting with the young guitarist we'd hired to provide background music at the reception.

Charlie was living in Boston by then, happily married and soon to become a father for the fourth time. Yet he still made the long journey to our wedding, staying for just three days. That meant so much to me.

Aidan and I didn't go on our honeymoon until Lucas returned to England. We spent the week after our wedding playing tour guide with him, visiting the galleries and museums in Canberra, driving up to Sydney and down to Melbourne. Lucas and I had been close before my wedding. We became even closer afterward. A month after Lucas went home, Aidan and I headed off on our official honeymoon— two weeks in the US, spending several days, of course, with Charlie and his family, including his new baby son. Aidan and Charlie got on so well. They were both clever, gentle men, so I'd hoped and expected it, but I was still relieved.

Back home in Canberra, work and everyday life took over from weddings and travel. I e-mailed Lucas as regularly as ever, about authors I was working with, or asking his advice about points of grammar. I told him about Aidan's job. Lucas told me he had a full house—six lodgers, the most ever. More clients than he could supply tutors to, as well. *I fear for the future of this once great country, but rejoice in my rising bank account,* he said.

Less than six months after the wedding, the news that Aidan and I were having a baby unleashed a torrent of one-line Astounding Fact e-mail from him. He continued to send them all the way through my pregnancy. *Did you know that the first sense a baby develops is hearing? That a baby is born around the world every three seconds? That a baby is born without kneecaps?*

When I e-mailed five hours after the birth (long and painful, both facts immediately forgotten) to tell him we'd decided to call our newborn son (big, healthy, so, so beautiful) Felix Lucas Fox O'Hanlon, I heard nothing back. I was too exhausted and too dizzy with love to mind, I think. Perhaps he was away. Two days later, there was a knock at our Canberra apartment door. Aidan told me the postman could barely carry the parcel inside, it was so huge. It was a five-foot-high toy fox. *Thank you,* Lucas's handwritten note said. *I am overjoyed for so many reasons.*

After that, Lucas started writing to Felix more than me. I pretended to be hurt, but I loved it.

Dear Felix, he would e-mail. *How is the sleeping going? Have you been told that Felix is the Latin word for lucky or happy?*

Felix wrote back to him too, of course, channeled through me or Aidan. He was very articulate for a baby and very appreciative of the new series of Astounding Facts for Infants.

Dear Lucas,

Yes, I am sleeping and also feeding very well, thank you for asking—I have already put on 800 grams. Thank you also for the link to the Large Hadron Collider Web site. I look forward to seeing it for myself one day.

Love for now from your grandnephew, Felix.

We sent Lucas dozens of photos of Felix. Lucas sent Felix books. Boxes of them. Not just picture books either. He sent Dickens, Tolstoy, Austen, Homer. . . . His goal, he told us, was for Felix to have a complete library of the classics by the time he started school. At the rate the books were arriving, Felix would have had a full library of the classics by the time he started kindergarten. For Felix's first birthday, Lucas sent him another five-foot-high toy fox. To keep the other fellow company, he said.

A month after that, Lucas surprised us—delighted us—with a spur-of-the-moment visit to Canberra. He stayed for less than a week, too short, but enough time for us to take dozens of photographs of him and Felix together. Serendipitously, his visit coincided with one of Charlie's trips back to Australia.

I can still picture one afternoon in particular. We were having an informal lunch at our apartment, the balcony doors wide open, the sun streaming in, a light breeze in the air. There in our small living room were my four favorite people in the world—Aidan, Lucas, Charlie and Felix. There was a moment, a beautiful, sweet moment, when I took a photograph with perfect timing: Charlie making a corny joke, Lucas throwing back his head and laughing, Aidan smiling and shaking his head, and there, in Aidan's arms, Felix, giving his big, gummy, delighted smile and kicking his legs at the same time, as if the smile alone wasn't enough to signify how much fun he was having. In the photograph, his legs are just a blur. At the time, I remember a feeling, like a dart of something, that felt like light, a warm feeling, a rush of it. I realized afterward it was joy.

After Lucas went home again, the e-mail between him and Felix increased. There were intense discussions about communism versus capitalism and the merits of cricket compared to football. The books kept arriving. Poetry from Byron, Yeats and Wordsworth. The Spot books. The Mr. Men tales. Lucas was no literary snob. Aidan had to put up another bookshelf in Felix's room. Felix e-mailed Lucas to say thank you and to remark that his bedroom looked more like a library these days.

Wonderful! Lucas e-mailed back. *A boy can never have too many books. Wait till you see what I'm sending you for your second birthday. . . .*

But then—

When—

Afterward—

After it happened, as soon as Lucas got my message in the middle of his night, he wrote to me. On paper, not by e-mail. It arrived by courier. One line of writing, on thick parchment paper, with the fox drawing on the letterhead.

My dearest Ella, I am devastated for you both. I am here if you need me. Lucas.

It said everything I needed to hear. It made me cry for hours. I had already been crying for hours.

Almost twenty months had passed since that day. I wasn't arriving in London unannounced. Lucas had e-mailed a fortnight earlier: *Where are you now, Ella?*

I was in Margaret River, in Western Australia. My contract as a casual worker at one of the largest wineries in the area was up. I'd been offered an extension but I was ready to move. Since it happened, I hadn't stayed anywhere for long. I'd left Canberra within weeks. I'd moved to Melbourne, then Sydney, before I'd heard about the winery job. I'd been there since.

I'd like to see you, Lucas had written. *Please let me buy your airfare.*

I wanted to see Lucas too, but I didn't need his help with the airfare. I'd saved every cent I'd earned. There was nothing I wanted or needed beyond the basics. I booked my ticket the next day. It felt exactly the right thing to do, after months of feeling like I was living in fog.

Even flying into London that morning had felt right. Because I thought being here again might help? Because I had loved it once, and had been happy here? I think I hoped that being back would help me or force me to feel something other than despair.

Come and see me as soon as you get here, would you? Come straight from the airport.

Lucas wasn't being mysterious. He was always matter-of-fact like that.

You do know you are welcome to stay for as long as you need to? Mi casa es su casa.

My house is your house. He had said that to me many times over the years. To his many student lodgers as well, I knew. Aidan had always laughed at his terrible Spanish pronunciation. Lucas was a genius historian but a bad linguist. *Thank you, Lucas*, I wrote back.

I walked the short distance from Paddington Station to his street. Twenty-seven years had passed since my first visit to Lucas's house. He'd been in his mid-thirties then. He was in his early sixties now. Yet he always looked the same to me. I was the one who'd changed most over the years, from that seven-year-old fox-stealing curly-haired child to the thirty-four-year-old woman I now was. I'd been a tall, skinny child. I was still skinny, still taller than average. My dark brown hair had been long until a year ago. I'd cut it two days after I arrived in Margaret River and kept it short since.

The houses on his street still reminded me of wedding cakes. His blue door was still in need of painting. There was a new door knocker, in the shape of a fox. I only had to knock once. The door opened and there he was, smiling at me. His hair was still a big mop of unruly curls, a Fox family trait. He still wore glasses that could have come from a museum. His baggy, grubby clothes might have belonged to a gardener. Seeing him standing there, so familiar and so solid, I couldn't help myself. I started to cry.

"Ella." He held me tight, waited until my tears slowed, then took a step back. "Come in."

If he was my aunt rather than my uncle, it would have been different, I'm sure. It would have been all talk, no silences. *I'm so sad for you, Ella. You poor thing. How can you even begin to get over something like that?* All the words I'd heard from so many people in the past twenty months, heard so many times that I couldn't hear them anymore. I hadn't told the people around me in the winery in Margaret River what had happened, why I was there. I didn't tell them that I was an editor, not a vineyard assistant turned restaurant kitchen hand. I could have got work in my own industry. I'd had many offers after word got around, but I needed everything to change. I couldn't have any reminders of what my life had once been like.

Time and again, people who did know what had happened suggested that keeping busy would help the healing process. It's not true, you know. Nothing helps. Because whatever I do with my body, my brain keeps ticking away, going over and over every second of that day, trying to find a new way of remembering, another way of changing what happened, winding itself into knots. That was—that is—the torture of it. Because it doesn't matter how many times I examine it, how often I try to rewrite that day in my mind; the ending is the same. And no amount of physical work helps: outside pruning grapevines, rod tying, picking grapes, or the work I did once I moved into the winery complex itself—washing floors, doing dishes, waitressing, being a kitchen assistant, working any shift on offer, doing overtime uncomplainingly, working the longest hours I could and spending any free time I had walking to tire myself out, to try to exhaust my body so my brain would have no choice but to sleep as well. . . . Nothing works.

"You look well," Lucas said.

He was being kind. I knew I looked exhausted. I probably had mascara all over my face now too. I tried to smile. "You too. Have you been working out?"

It was an old joke between us—Lucas would sooner fly to the moon than go to a gym. He grinned, running his fingers through his curls, ruffling them more than usual. He always did that when attention turned to him. I imagined he was like that at the university too, tousling his hair during his lectures, getting closer to the image of a mad history professor with every sentence.

"I like the jumper," I said. It was a jumper I'd knitted—tried to knit for him—twenty-one years ago, when I was thirteen.

I'd found the pattern in an old magazine and got our next-door neighbor to teach me how to make it. It was supposed to have a design of a fox—of course—on the front. I made a mess of it, unpicking and reknitting it so many times that each strand of wool was covered in grime from my increasingly sweaty fingers. I had trouble with the sleeves and the turndown collar, and as for the fox design . . . By the time I finished, the creature on the front looked more like E.T. than a fox. But I proudly sent it off, wrapped in Christmas paper. In return, Lucas sent me not only a fax telling me how much he loved it and how warm it was, but also a photo of him wearing it. Charlie had taken a great interest in the photo. He kindly said nothing about the jumper's design, but focused on Lucas. It was the first time he'd seen a photo of him. "Does he look like your dad? Like your dad would if he was alive, I mean."

Lucas and my dad had been very alike. Charlie was right, I realized. I now had an idea of what my dad would have looked like if he hadn't gone off to Canada and got killed.

I noticed Mum picking up the photo too, but she didn't say anything to me about Lucas's similarity to Dad. She did say something to me about the fox resembling an alien, though.

"Never mind. Practice makes perfect," Walter said. "You could try to do a jumper for Jess next."

"No thanks," I'd said. My knitting days were over.

"I get offers for it every day," Lucas said now. "It's a work of art."

"Art? That's one word for it."

I followed Lucas into his withdrawing room off the hallway. It was messier than ever.

"Drink?" he asked. "It's nighttime for you and your body clock, isn't it?"

I shook my head. I'd stopped drinking alcohol. "But tea would be great, thanks."

We went into the kitchen. It was filthy, every surface

covered in dirty dishes, saucepans and plates. I tried not to react, or wince, when he pulled out two grubby cups from the crowded sink. When he reached for a milk jug that I could see had something like gravy on the side, I couldn't stop myself.

"Sorry, Lucas." I took the cups from him and washed them out, followed by the jug, followed by the kettle, and then, for good measure, I washed out the sink too. Lucas watched it all with a half smile. He'd never taken offense when I expressed disgust or astonishment at the squalor he and his students lived in. He just took a seat at the cluttered, dirty kitchen table—my fingers itched to clean it as well—watching me with his usual amused, affectionate expression.

"It's lovely to see you, Ella. I did miss having a maid."

"This house needs a bulldozer, not a maid."

"Speaking of which, how is your mother?"

"Very well, thank you," I said, trying not to smile as I searched for a biscuit in one of the tins and found a few moldy crumbs instead.

"Still mad as ever, I suppose?"

I nodded.

"And still famous?"

"Getting more famous every day too." It was true. In the past six years, after a chance encounter with a TV crew in a Melbourne shopping center, my mother had somehow become a household name in Australia. Walter was now her full-time manager. It was unfathomable to me. My mother had barely boiled an egg during my childhood. Now she was a celebrity TV chef.

"Charlie seems as happy as ever in Boston."

I nodded again. Charlie the happy househusband, father of four and adored/adoring husband of Lucy, a sales representative for a medical company. They'd met when Charlie was seventeen and in the US as a Rotary exchange student. After becoming pen pals, they'd met again when they were both in their mid-twenties and Lucy was visiting Australia. They'd fallen in love, married and immediately begun having children. Their youngest was four years old, the oldest nearly eleven. Lucy worked full-time while Charlie stayed at home, in an arrangement that suited them both.

"I do enjoy his family reports," Lucas said. "Thank you for adding me to his mailing list. The one about the children at the dentist was like a comedy sketch."

I couldn't think of anything to say to that. I'd stopped reading Charlie's e-mail about his family. I was still in touch with Charlie about other things, of course. We e-mailed often, both of us carefully choosing our words, avoiding certain subjects. Charlie did all his communicating via computer, late at night, once the kids and Lucy were in bed. His family reports were e-mailed to only a few people—Walter, Mum, Jess, Lucas and me. They were his way of staying sane, he'd confessed to me once. They always had the same subject line, a play on words from Garrison Keillor's Lake Wobegon stories. The original began: *It's been a quiet week in Lake Wobegon.* Charlie's was: *It's been a noisy week in Boston.* I missed his stories of family life. But I couldn't read them anymore.

"And Jess?" Lucas asked. "How is she?"

At the sink, midway through pouring the boiling water, I stiffened.

He must have noticed. He waited a moment, then re-peated his question.

I turned. "Lucas, I'm sorry. I can't—"

He spoke again in the same calm tone. "Is she still writing her autobiography?"

I knew that piece of news about Jess years earlier had amused him. Jess had been writing her life story—in diary form—for the past six years, since she was sixteen years old. She'd always been convinced she'd be a musical theater star one day. "I'll be too busy when I'm famous to write anything, so I'm doing it now to save time," she'd told us all. She'd never been secretive about it either. Other teenage girls probably hid their diaries from their families. Jess did formal readings from hers. They were written as she spoke, in a stream of consciousness. The title was the first line of each day's diary entry: *Hi, it's Jess!*

"I don't know," I said, not looking at him. It was the truth. I had no idea where Jess was or what she was doing. I'd asked my mother not to mention her. She'd eventually, reluctantly, agreed.

Lucas didn't ask any more questions about her. Another reason to love him. An aunt might have kept on at me, as my mother had, many times. *Please, Ella, she's your little sister. Your family. You have to find a way to forgive her. You have to be able to move on somehow.*

But how could I move on? Where was there for me to go?

There was one other person for Lucas to ask about. As I brought over the tea, I waited for him to mention Aidan. He didn't. Not yet. But he would, I knew. I could almost feel

Aidan's presence in the kitchen between us. We'd met for the first time in here.

Lucas took a sip, pulled a face and put down his cup. "Ella, it's terrible. The cup's too clean."

I swatted his arm affectionately, glad of the change in topic. Our conversation turned to general subjects, my flight, the London weather, his own work. Yes, he was very busy, as always, he told me. Yes, the house was still full of lodgers. Four at present, with a waiting list. Yes, they were all double-jobbing: PhD students by day, tutors by night. Geniuses in the making, all four of them.

One was a literature student, he said. "You'll like her. Very cheerful girl. She has the most extraordinary hair. Bright pink one week, blue the next. You'll have lots in common too, books, words, grammar—"

It wasn't the time to tell him I'd given up editing. "She sounds great," I said.

"And you and work, Ella? Any plans yet?"

It didn't matter that I'd just stepped off a long flight. Lucas was always to the point like this. Another thing I loved about him. "No, not yet. I'll register with some temp agencies tomorrow."

"Don't."

"Don't?"

"Come and work for me again. You already know I pay well. Promptly too."

"You don't need to pay me. As soon as I finish this tea, I'm going to scrub this place from top to bottom as a service to society."

He smiled. "That's not the kind of work I meant. And

that's not why I asked you to come to see me." He stood up, walked across the room and shut the door. When he returned and sat down opposite me, his expression was serious.

"Ella, I need your help."

TWO

From: Charlie Baum
To: undisclosed recipients
Subject: It's Been a Noisy Week in Boston

The latest report from the Baum trenches is as follows:

Sophie (10): Planning eleventh birthday party. Still. The invite list has changed twenty times. She's having more fun than a nightclub doorman.

Ed (8): Maths homework last night. He counted all the way to 100 and on to 200 and beyond. He reached 253 and sighed. "Counting never stops, does it?"

Reilly (6): Teacher reported discussion in class today about religious ceremonies around the world. She asked why Easter is celebrated. Reilly's answer: "Jesus died at Easter, right? And he was on a cross. And the cross was made of wood. And the wood was brown. And chocolate is brown. So that's why we eat chocolate. And the reason the chocolate is given out by the Easter Bunny and we have chocolate bunnies is because Jesus was up on the cross, right? And below him, on the ground, running around everywhere, were rabbits. Lots and lots of rabbits."

It appears Lucy and I may need to rethink our "no religious education" policy.

Tim (4): Bathtime. Emptied entire contents of Lucy's henna shampoo into water while my back was turned for seconds. We now have one very brown son.

Lucy (36): Reaching new levels of overtime. Tired. Tired but happy. I hope.

Charlie (36): Current weight ninety-five kilos. Diet producing extraordinary results of an invisible nature. Meals cooked for the family this week: spaghetti Bolognese, spaghetti carbonara, pizza, boeuf bourguignon. Meals eaten by cook this week: salad, salad, salad, salad. Odds on cook falling asleep in next salad he is forced to eat: excellent.

Snip the cat (kitten age): Slept, played, slept, chased fly. Caught one mouse. Ate one mouse, excluding tail. Tail left on kitchen table. Children still retching. Father also.

Until next time, everyone please stay sane.

Charlie xx

From: Charlie Baum
To: Lucy Baum
Subject: re: Modern Couples

Yes, aren't we modern, sending each other e-mail rather than leaving notes on the fridge? Thank you for your probing questions. Yes, I remembered Reilly's doctor's appointment, tomorrow at four p.m. Yes, I will book Sophie in for an eye test. I wonder will she be able to find her own way there? (Hahaha. It *was* my sense of humor that first attracted you to me, wasn't it? Wasn't it??)

Two questions for you now:

Q1. Do you know how much I love you?

Answer: Lots.

Q2. Do I appreciate how hard you work?

Answer: Yes, I do.

See you tonight. I'll be the fat guy in the kitchen with all the kids.

C xx

From: Charlie Baum
To: Ella O'Hanlon
Subject: You and flight

Dear Ellamentary,

How was the flight? How is London? How is Lucas?
Thinking of you.

Charlemagne

xx

From: Charlie Baum
To: Lucas Fox
Subject: Ella

Thanks for the update. Yes, it's definitely worth a
try. Good luck.

C

From: Charlie Baum
To: Aidan O'Hanlon
Subject: Next week

Aidan, I'll take the eleven a.m. train, arriving Washington five thirty p.m. See you at the hotel bar at
six? My cell is +1 9173236740.

Charlie

THREE

Dear Diary,
Hi, it's Jess!

What an incredible day it's been! I'm sure that in years to come I'll look back at my life and be able to pinpoint today as the day it all really began. It had been a reasonably normal day (if you can call any day of my crazy life normal!!). I'd gone to the studio with Mum and Dad. Mum was taping the last of her new series of *MerryMakers*. (It really is such a clever name for a fun cooking show, isn't it?? Merry, as in short for Meredith, her name, and she makes things to eat!!) And it was so exciting. They'd given me another cameo appearance, just at the end as usual, but it was a really funny one. Mum and I had written it together last week. We taped it—in one take, as usual. That's one of the reasons the director loves me so much, he told me. He said he's worked with other girls my age (twenty-two, but I'm nearly twenty-three) and they were nightmares but I was a DREAM! So anyway, I was sitting in the green room watching clips from musicals on my iPhone when Mum came out and said, "Sorry, Jess, we need to tape that segment again."

"But I did it perfectly," I said.

"I know, darling, but there was a technical hitch—the sound dropped out. Can you come and do it again?"

So I went back onto the set. It was a skit at the end of the cooking segment, as usual. Mum had joked and cooked her way through a few recipes and then I had to turn up, make a few jokes myself and have a taste. So we went through it all again, taking the cake out of the oven, etc. etc.—luckily Mum's assistant had made several versions of the cake in question, as I really had eaten a slice of the cake in my first take! We ran through all the lines again too.

"Hi, Mum!"

"Hi, darling!"

"Wow, that smells good. What is it?"

"My perfume!" Hahaha from the canned laughter. Then me in close-up making a show of biting into the cake and really enjoying the taste of it. We'd had a letter the previous week complaining that I was being made to be too sexy. "Oh, der," as I said to Mum. That was the whole idea of me being on the program. Mum wore her tight tops and said saucy things (food joke!!—saucy as in cooking sauces and she's a TV chef!) to lure in the older guy viewers. I was there to bring in the younger guys. It wasn't exploitation. It was good business. And also, the recipes work and they are nutritionally sound.

Anyway, I was there, doing the take again, licking the cream off the cake, and I took a bite and nearly choked. There was something inside the cake. A small envelope. What the *heck*, I said. (I would have said "what the *you-know-what*" but we still aim for family ratings.) "Stop tape!" I called as I took the envelope out of my mouth and wiped off the cream. I looked at Mum. She was grinning. Dad stepped in from the side of the set. He had a big smile on his face too. The camera guys were laughing as well. I opened the envelope. Inside, all folded up, was a voucher for a plane ticket. A ticket to LONDON!!!!!!!!!!!!!!

"Surprise!" a voice sounded over the studio PA. It was the director from upstairs. I reckon my squeal nearly burst the studio lights!

I'd been begging and begging Mum and Dad for my airfare to London for YEARS. Just give me a CHANCE to make it on the West End, I'd said. I'm the right age. I've been doing all the right classes for years. I've been in youth theater since I was a little kid and done every performance class possible, tap and mime and singing and even interpretative dance. I'd been offered a couple of professional chorus roles in the past few months but I'd turned them down. They would have meant giving up work on Mum's show and what was the point? To do a six-week run in Melbourne or Sydney or Adelaide or Canberra, backwaters as far as musical theater is concerned. The West End (and Broadway of course!!) is where it's at. I have an EU passport courtesy of my German dad, so it makes sense to go to Europe—or, more specifically, London—first. That's how I always put my argument. But Mum and Dad kept saying I was too young, it was too soon, blah blah

blah, you'd be there on your own, in a big strange city. I wouldn't be on my own. As soon as I get a role, the theater company would be my family.

"Why now?" I asked when we were on our way home. "What changed your minds?"

"Because we won't be far away ourselves," Mum said.

And I said, "You're coming to London too?" To be honest, Diary, the idea of it appalled me!! How would I get to live my dream if I had to be home early each night to stop Mum and Dad from worrying? On the bright side, if they were there in London too, they'd be paying for all my food and rent, so I quickly hid my dismay and saw the sunny side of it (another of my positive personality traits, according to Mum). "Great!" I said, using my best acting skills. "We can all live together."

"Oh, aren't you a sweetie," Mum said. "I thought you'd hate it if we were there too."

That will teach me to wear my feelings on my face!

Before I had to deny it, she went on. It turned out she meant that she and Dad would be near me in Europe, not London, and not the whole time, just for a few weeks, and not until later in the year. They'd got word that the cable channel had given the green light to a new series of *Merry-Makers*. Basically it would be Mum wisecracking her way around Europe, cooking national dishes, but on the ground rather than in a studio. She was really excited about it, and started listing off all the places they'd be going: Spain, France, Italy. . . . "We'll only ever be a few hours from you, darling, and if you're not working yourself, you can fly in to us for your cameos as well. Isn't it perfect!"

I was only half listening by that stage, to tell you the

truth. I'd already taken out my iPhone and started Googling info on the current season of West End musicals and any calls for auditions. Also, of COURSE I'd be working by then and I'd hardly give up a season on the West End to play a cameo on Mum's series, even though it was very nice of her to offer, of course.

"You'll give me the money I need to set myself up, won't you?" I suddenly asked. It came out a bit bluntly, I know, but the fact was that even though I still lived at home and got paid to do Mum's show (pretty well too!!!), I didn't have any savings, and one thing I had heard many times from my singing and dance teachers was that London is very expensive.

"Of course, darling," Dad said. "We will be your devils."

It took a while to work out he meant my angels, as in my theatrical sponsors. Dad's English is very good (apart from his problem with the letter *r,* which he says as *v* sometimes, but that's a kind of speech-impediment thing, not because of his being German, and I think it's cute anyway) but it does let him down sometimes. So we had a great chat for the rest of the drive home about all the ways he and Mum could support me. It's SO exciting!! I'm going to leave as soon as I can, I've decided. No point hanging around wasting time in Australia when the real theater world awaits in London.

So, what a great day! In a few weeks' time (maybe more, maybe less, it will depend on flight availability, Dad says— he's going to take care of all of that for me too, thank you, Dad!!!!!!!), look out, West End. Here comes Jessica Baum!

Love till next time!!

Jess xxxxoooo

FOUR

It was after lunch by the time I came down for breakfast. Outside, London was bathed in soft February mist. Inside, the house was quiet and calm. Perhaps it was the mess acting as a kind of insulation. I checked in all the downstairs rooms. Empty. I stood on the first landing again and listened. No sound from any of the other bedrooms. Everyone must have gone to their lectures or tutoring jobs. I had the house to myself. I was glad of it—for now, at least.

I'd had one of the longest, deepest sleeps I could remember having. Perhaps that was all I should have been doing over the past twenty months to stop the night horrors. Kept myself permanently jet-lagged.

After our conversation the previous day, after I said I'd think about his job offer, Lucas showed me to the bedroom on the second floor that he knew was my favorite. It was luck that it happened to be empty. If my contract in Australia had ended a week earlier or a week later, I might have had to book into a local hotel or sleep on a mattress on the attic floor.

"Are you hungry, Ella? I'm sure there's probably something in one of the cupboards."

I smiled. Lucas never had a clue whether there was food in the house or not. On the positive side, he did always have plenty of good-quality stationery. "I'm fine, Lucas; thanks. And you don't need to look after me. I'm sure you've got work to do."

There was just a brief hesitation. "Actually, I am in the middle of an important paper."

Again, I felt the relief of being in his company. All the space I needed, no pressure to talk. "I can look after myself, I promise."

"Make yourself at home. There are spare keys on the hall table. And there's no rush about the job. Take your time thinking it over. The room is yours for as long as you want it, whether you take up my offer or not." He stood there for a moment. "You've got your laptop with you?"

I nodded.

"There's Wi-Fi throughout the house. High-speed. Free too."

I smiled. "Thanks, Lucas."

"Welcome back, Ella," he said, then quietly left the room.

I showered, changed and went outside. I walked all the way down Lucas's street, across Bayswater Road and into Hyde Park. I needed to stretch my limbs, breathe fresh air and try to let it sink in that I was now in London, that I wasn't in Margaret River or Australia anymore.

The last time I had taken this path had been with Aidan. We'd come here for a final walk before we left for Australia. We'd talked about all we had to look forward to, his new job, our wedding in a few months' time, a new city to get to know. How we'd be going from winter to summer. We'd felt so lucky, so—

Don't.

Observe.

Distract.

I concentrated. I looked around me. I made a mental list of the most English things I could see. Squirrels. Chestnut trees. Black taxis and red double-decker buses visible through the railings. People in scarves, boots and hats, in February . . .

I kept walking, along the path toward Marble Arch. As I came out onto Oxford Street, the crowds grew around me: tourists, shoppers, office workers, women in full burqa, teenagers in miniskirts. I passed clothes shops, department stores, newspaper sellers tidying piles of the *Times*, the *Guardian* and other papers, tourist shops selling Union Jack mugs and souvenirs of the royal wedding. I walked as far as Regent Street, up one side and down the other. Back at Marble Arch, I noticed the cinema. I went in and bought a ticket for the next film showing. I didn't mind what it was. I was just happy to have something to distract my thoughts.

It was dark by the time I returned to Lucas's house. I let myself in, hoping I wouldn't meet any of the lodgers yet. I didn't feel ready. The door to Lucas's withdrawing room on the ground floor was shut, his signal that he was reading or marking papers. I quietly went up the stairs and got to my room without seeing anyone. I fell asleep easily, for once.

The kitchen was empty, the dirty dishes on the table proof that Lucas and the tutors had been and gone. I put on some coffee, then went upstairs to fetch my laptop. The door to the bedroom on the first landing was open. I didn't look too closely. It had been Aidan's room when we both lived here. If I thought of Aidan, I would think of Felix, and if I thought of Felix—

Back in the kitchen, I poured a coffee and set up my laptop. I was online in minutes. Lucas was right—there was excellent Wi-Fi in the house.

There were two e-mail messages from Charlie. One was his family report—*It's Been a Noisy Week in Boston* in the subject line. As usual, I moved it without reading it into the folder marked *Charlie*. I opened the second one, subject *You and flight*, read it, then quickly typed a reply.

Dear Charleston. Since we were kids, we'd played around with each other's names for fun. Over the years he'd called me everything from Ellaphant, Ellavator, Ellaquent. . . . *Thanks for your e-mail. Yes, I'm here safe and sound with Lucas.*

I did a quick calculation of the time difference. Too early in Boston for Charlie to be online. But he'd worry if that was all I said; I knew that.

He's great, as ever. Very welcoming, as ever.

A new e-mail came in as I decided what to write next. It was from my mother's account. I clicked on it. It wasn't from

Mum herself. It was a general mailout from one of her production staff.

> *Missed out on* MerryMakers *this week?? Fear not!*
> *All the highlights are here, and remember, whatever*
> *you do and whenever you can—eat, drink and be*
> *merry!*

I wondered whether I was the only daughter in the
world who kept up with her mother's whereabouts via group
e-mail. I moved that into my *For later* folder and went back
to my e-mail to Charlie.

> *Lucas has made me an interesting job offer. I'm thinking*
> *about it. I'll keep you posted.*
>
> *Lots of love for now,*
> *E xxx*

The Ella of old wouldn't have signed off like that or
written such a brief e-mail. I'd have asked him about each of
his four children in turn, asked about Lucy, wanted all the
family stories and photographs. I'd have been planning a
visit too. Before . . . before everything, I'd visited Boston as
often as I could afford it. I loved seeing Charlie. I loved the
chaos of his house and life. I loved seeing him so happy with
Lucy. I loved seeing him with his children, the way they
clambered all over him, how patient he was with them, the
fun he brought into their lives, the love they had for him and
he had for them—

Do something else.

Quickly.

I finished my coffee and ate a small bowl of cereal. I didn't eat much these days. I'd lost my appetite that day and it had never really come back. I'd lost interest in everything except wishing and thinking and—

Keep busy.

I washed the dishes. There were a lot of them. The table was covered in newspapers and crumbs as well. Possibly that was one of Lucas's criteria before inviting any of his tutors to come to live and work with him. I imagined the ad pinned up at the university: *Must be clever, have a gift for teaching and love making a mess.*

I cleaned out the fridge. I swept the kitchen floor. I moved into the hall and swept that too. Next was Lucas's withdrawing room. It was hard to know where to start. I knew from experience not to touch any of the surfaces. Not that I could see any of the surfaces. They were all covered in books, papers, magazines. . . . I cleaned out the fire and emptied the ashes into the almost-full bucket. As I stood and turned around, I saw it. I hadn't noticed it the night before, too jet-lagged or sitting in the wrong seat. I dropped the bucket. Ashes went everywhere. I ignored them and walked toward the wall, holding my breath.

It was a photographic shrine to Felix.

Every photo I'd sent Lucas was here on the wall, framed. Me with Felix, minutes after he was born. Aidan with Felix. The three of us together. Felix in his Babygro. Laughing Felix. Crying Felix. Sleeping Felix. Crawling Felix. Aidan and I laughing together at him, making him wave at the camera, wave to Great-uncle Lucas in London. Everywhere I looked, there was my Felix's face, that beautiful face staring out at me, his blue-green eyes, his big, beautiful smile— the most beautiful I've ever seen. I couldn't bear to look, but I couldn't look away. Felix in the bath. Felix on a swing. Felix with Mum, with Walter. With Jess. There was a framed trio of photos of Felix with Charlie, the two of them laughing in one shot, yawning in another and, finally, both sleeping. Felix had loved sleeping on Charlie's belly. "It's a hammock built for kids," Charlie had said, patting it proudly. There was photo after photo of Aidan and Felix together, all taken by me. Aidan and Felix nose to nose. Aidan and Felix gazing up at the camera, the likeness astonishing, the same-shaped face, steady gaze, same-colored eyes. Felix on Aidan's shoulders. Felix reading *Great Expectations*, Aidan's hands clearly in shot, holding the book in place. Felix in a green jumpsuit on Aidan's lap, in honor of St. Patrick's Day. Felix and Aidan both wearing Santa hats, for Felix's first Christmas.

The punch came then. The hurt. He'd had only two Christmases.

Stop.

Quick.

Keep busy.

I swept up the spilled ash, with my back turned to the photos, wishing I hadn't seen them, wishing they weren't there.

Think of something else.

Charlie. Think of Charlie. Get out of this room and think about Charlie instead. I made it up the stairs, breathing deeply, thankful I had the house to myself.

Think of Charlie, not Felix.

Breathe.

Breathe.

I sat on my bed and I breathed, and I clenched my fists and breathed some more, forcing my thoughts in another direction. Toward Charlie.

Quickly.

Charlie was my safe haven. In the early months, when there seemed only to be sounds of terror in my mind, sounds of anguish—or even worse, silence, bleakness, like a white-out in my mind—thinking of Charlie would give me some respite, even just for a moment.

Quickly.

Fill your head with Charlie, I told myself. Go back to when you met him. Think of him. Not Felix. Not Felix, or Aidan. Or Jess. Only Charlie. Go back to the start. Right back.

Quickly.

FIVE

I think if I'd been told before we met that Charlie, my about-to-be stepbrother, would become my best friend, I wouldn't have believed it. My mother had kept the details of her new boyfriend's son sketchy.

"He's a year or two older than you, and he's very bright, I believe. Walter is very proud of him."

They didn't introduce us to each other until they were sure it was serious between them. Mum told me later that was best practice in terms of blended-family harmony. Walter was textbook like that. The German in him, Mum told me with a laugh. All she seemed to have done since she'd met Walter was laugh.

Charlie and I met for the first time over dinner. I was nine; he was eleven. It wasn't at his home or our home but on neutral ground. A family restaurant in Hawthorn. Mum and I had trouble finding a parking spot, so by the time we arrived, Walter and his son were already there. They both stood up as we entered.

My first thought when I saw Charlie wasn't complimentary. There's no way around this. Charlie was a really fat kid. I now know there are other words—plump or overweight or kilo-challenged—but back then all I saw was a fat boy with short dark hair. I was a skinny kid with long, dark hair. Somehow, straightaway, his size made him easier to talk to. I was reading a lot of Enid Blyton at the time, courtesy of Lucas's book parcels, the Five Find-Outers books especially. Charlie immediately reminded me of Fatty, the boy detective who is also a master of disguise, managing to dress as a policeman, among other things, and somehow hoodwink the adults in his life. It was all I could do not to address Charlie as Fatty when my mother and his father seated us together at the table and then pretended they weren't watching to see how we got on.

"Hi, Ella," Charlie said.

"Hello, Charlie," I said. Hello, Fatty, I thought.

"How are you?" he asked.

"Fine, thank you." Then I remembered my manners. "How are you?"

"Very well, thank you."

Our parents beamed at us as though they were the world's happiest matchmakers.

Unfortunately that brief exchange temporarily used up our conversational skills. We sat there, silently, while my mother talked to the waitress, giggling a bit too much. She was also holding Walter's hand under the table. I wondered whether she was trying to hide it from me or from Charlie. Either way, she wasn't doing a very good job.

It was an Italian restaurant. The waitress listed the specials, in a perfect Italian accent. I turned to Charlie, trying very hard to be polite and to ignore a strange, sick, sad feeling in my stomach.

"Do you like Italian food?"

"*Sì*," he said.

"See what?" I said, puzzled.

"I was being clever," he said. "*Sì* is Italian for yes. Yes, I do like Italian food."

You like food from everywhere, by the looks of things, I thought. "Can you speak Italian?"

"*Sì*," he said again. "I also speak German, English, obviously, and also a bit of French and Spanish."

Woop-de-doo, I nearly said out loud, before remembering my mother telling me off for saying it. I'd heard it on a cartoon and mistakenly thought it was a way of saying "Great, well done!"

"What's this?" I pointed to a glass, expecting the Italian, French, German or Spanish word for it.

"It's a glass," he said.

For some reason, that cracked us both up.

"And that?" I said, pointing to a fork.

"A fork."

"And this?" I said, pointing to the bread in the basket, giggling uncontrollably now.

"Bread."

It took two tellings-off from our parents before we stopped laughing that night.

The next time we met was at dinner in Charlie and Walter's big house in Richmond, a fortnight later.

"Hi, Ella."

"Hi, Charlie," I said. He was still fat but at least I was expecting it this time.

"Want to see my games room?"

"Sure."

Again, conscious of our parents watching us, obviously hoping our first successful meeting hadn't been a once-off, we went down the hall to his games room. It really was a games room. There was a table-tennis table in the middle, and shelves all around, with jigsaw puzzles neatly arranged on one shelf, board games on another, a basket of different balls—a baseball, a basketball, a football. It was like a combination sports and toy shop. It was also very tidy. That impressed me more than the games themselves. I wasn't a tidy person back then.

"Do you have a cleaner?" I asked.

He shook his head. "I do it all myself. I'm meticulous."

"Is that a kind of disease?" I wasn't even being smart.

He gave a big laugh. "You're funny," he said.

"I am?"

"Hilarious," he said.

There's something wonderful about being in the company of someone who laughs at you, when it's for all the right reasons. You feel good around them. They make you want to try harder and be funnier. Especially when the person laughs like Charlie, from his head to his toes. He literally used to shake with laughter. He still does, even though he's half as fat as he used to be. But back then, it was like watching a circus act, a boy squeezing his eyes shut and laughing with all his body at something I hadn't even realized was funny.

I wasn't feeling that funny, as it happened. I blurted out something that had been on my mind all week. "I think they're going to get married."

That sobered him up. "Your mum? My dad?"

"No, Charlie, *me* and your dad." I'd recently learned how to be sarcastic. That time he didn't laugh. I felt bad. "Yes, your dad and my mum. I think it's getting serious between them."

"I think so too," he said.

We both stood in silence for a moment, taking that in.

"Where's your mum?" I eventually asked.

"In Germany. Dad got custody of me."

"Do you mind?"

He shrugged. "Where's your dad?"

"In Canada. Mum got me."

We were both quiet again for a bit. Then Charlie spoke. "Would you live here with us if they got married?"

I shrugged too. "I guess so. Our house would be too small for four people."

"Especially me," he said, patting his stomach.

"Charlie!" It was all right for me to think of him as Fatty, but not him.

He seemed proud of it, patting his belly again. "So, do you want to see what I think would be your room?"

"Sure."

We walked down the hall into a small, bright room at the back of the house. It had inbuilt bookshelves and a big window.

"All yours," Charlie said. "Unless your mother would want it?"

"No. She'd be sleeping in the same room as your father, wouldn't she?"

We both pulled a face at each other. Charlie grinned again. I wanted to say something really funny, to make him do that shaking laugh, but I couldn't think of anything quickly enough.

We stood in the middle of the room and looked around instead. It was being used as a kind of storage room, with boxes everywhere. There was a tree outside the window. I thought it would make a very nice bedroom, but I didn't say that out loud.

"Would you go to the same school as me?" Charlie asked.

I shrugged. I liked the way shrugging felt and also I didn't have an answer for him.

"It's a good school," he said. "I think you'd like it. It's just down the road. I walk there sometimes. Mostly Dad drives me."

"Is that where you learn all your foreign languages?"

His smile broadened. *"Oui,"* he said.

"What's that?" I said, pointing to the tree outside the window.

"A tree," he said.

"And that?"

"A window."

We were nearly hysterical with laughter by the time my mother and his father came to find us.

Years later, Charlie told me that he'd thought I was

really sad when he first met me. I said that I thought he was
really fat.

"I was fat," he said.

"I was sad," I said.

We did move in with him and his father. Our parents did
get married. I did have that room as my bedroom. I did go
to the same school as Charlie. For the next year—it's funny
to say it so confidently and firmly, but it's true—I was also
very happy. I had Charlie to thank. Because as well as being
fat, and lots of fun, Charlie was also very kind. He still is one
of the kindest people I've ever met. Relaxed and kind—a
good combination in any human being, let alone a newly
acquired stepbrother.

Mum and Walter were glad we got on well, I think, but
once we all settled into the new house and the new arrangement, they let us get on with it ourselves. Perhaps they
would have paid more attention if we hadn't hit it off, but in
the first year especially, they were too busy being in love
with each other to take much notice of us. I'd hear my mother
on the phone to her friends.

"I never realized it could be like this. What was I doing
wasting my time with Richard? I must have been crazy!"

I had loved my dad. I'd have liked to talk to him more
than I did, which was once a month, sometimes less, depending on how much traveling he was doing around Canada.
Walter tried to be a kind of father to me, I think, but the
truth was I didn't really need him. Mum was always happy to
tell me what to do, and she was the person I'd go to for pocket
money or advice or if I was upset about something at school.
If I wanted to talk to someone apart from her, I had Charlie.

So Walter was just, well, there in the house, really. A nice enough man with a beard and an accent who idolized my mother, who idolized him in turn. He spent a lot of time at work—he had an office on Collins Street as well as his home office. On the weekends he would devote himself to either my mother or the garden. He liked growing roses and rhubarb.

"*R* things," Charlie said one afternoon, when we were in the games room playing Scrabble. Even though Charlie was very clever, I had a bigger vocabulary, so I usually won. Charlie had announced he was trying a different approach, and was doing his words in French, while I stayed in English. It was working surprisingly well, considering I didn't have a clue what words he was putting down. "Trust me, Ella," he'd said. "It wouldn't be in anyone's interest for me to cheat."

"What?" I said now, looking up from a rack of difficult letters. "Are things what?"

"Not the word 'are.' The letter *R*. Dad only grows things starting with the letter *R*. Have you noticed that?"

I looked out the window. Roses. Rhubarb. Rocket.

"We'll have to get him a rabbit for Christmas," I said.

"A vabbit. A vabbit called Vudolph." Charlie found it very funny to mock his father's way of speaking, especially the way Walter sometimes pronounced the letter *r* as *v*. Walter would even laugh, if he did it in front of him.

"Oh, Charlie, you are my comedian!" I still never dared to do it myself. But on our own . . .

"Not a vabbit," I said. "A veindeer. Vudolph the Ved-Nosed Veindeer."

"And a vobin—"

"A ved-ved-vobin—"

We sang together. *"The ved, ved vobin comes bob, bob, bob-bin' along!"*

We were a textbook blended family, I suppose. A child apiece, a happy second marriage, a nice house, plenty of money, holidays twice a year, both children doing well in school, Charlie in particular. He didn't just have a flair for languages; he was also a mathematical whiz kid. I was bad at maths, but good at English. I'd finally learned to spell, mastered grammar, and when I wasn't writing my own little books, I was reading other people's, still arriving regularly from Lucas. My favorite pastime was to clamber up the tree outside my window, hook a leg around the largest branch and read for hours. It was extra good if the weather was cool enough for Charlie to come outside and sit at the base of the tree doing his homework. He'd only come outside in cool weather. The sun gave him hives. But in general, we were both very content.

And then Jess arrived.

We had plenty of warning. Eight months of it, in fact. Mum and Walter brought Charlie and me together. "We won't be telling anyone outside this house yet, but we have some incredible news," she said. "Can you guess what it is?"

Charlie and I had been playing Monopoly and weren't happy about the interruption.

"We're moving?" he said, yawning.

"You're getting a divorce?" That was me trying out my new sarcasm again.

Mum reached for Walter's hand. "We're having a baby!"

We both said, "Wow!" and, "Great!" at the time, but as soon as they went out, Charlie turned to me and said, "Yuk."

"Yuk," I agreed. Yuk about the baby, about the fact that the baby meant they must have done you-know-what, and also a kind of yuk as in what-does-that-mean-for-us?

"We were here first," Charlie said, confidently. "It won't change anything. Don't worry."

He was wrong. Everything changed from the moment Jess arrived. Even before she arrived. Six weeks before Mum's due date, I was moved into the spare room, the smallest room in the house, because Mum needed my bedroom as a nursery for Jess.

"But I'll be eleven soon. The baby will be much smaller than me," I said. "Shouldn't it have the smallest room?"

"Even a small baby needs a lot of voom, Ella," Walter said.

"Voom voom," Charlie said later. "Are we getting a new baby or a new car?"

I couldn't laugh about it yet. I loved my bedroom.

Mum turned thirty-five three days before Jess was born. Walter was forty-two. They were older parents, with older-parent energy, and they needed every bit they could summon. From the second Jess was born, she needed a lot of attention. "What changed?" as Charlie said later. She was three weeks premature, and had to spend her first two weeks of life in an incubator.

We were taken into the hospital to meet her. Charlie was more interested in the technology on display than his new baby half sister. He put both hands up to the glass and peered in at the row of incubators. Mum, standing beside the one on the far left in her dressing gown and slippers, waved at us. We couldn't see our new baby sister, but we waved back, encouraged by Walter.

When Mum came out into the corridor, Charlie fired questions at her. About the incubator, not the baby. I mostly remember being amazed that Mum was a normal size again, and just as amazed that the huge bump she'd had was now out of her stomach and lying fast asleep in that glass box. The incubator kept the baby warm, Mum explained to Charlie. Walter went into a more complicated technological explanation about the importance of keeping the baby germ free while her lungs were still so fragile. Charlie listened and nodded.

"Got it," he said. "It's a combination of warmth and sterile conditions."

On the way in we'd noticed a big sign about some fundraising the hospital was doing.

"I've got a great idea," he said to me as we peered in through the glass at our new half sister. Mum and Walter were still deciding whether to call her Jessica or Molly. "They should put eggs in there to hatch at the same time. Raise money on the side as chicken farmers. It would kill two birds with one stone. Metaphorically speaking."

I got the giggles, at the mental image of hundreds of newly hatched chickens roaming the hospital as much as the "metaphorically speaking." He'd recently taken to saying it as often as possible. "Yes, thanks, Dad. I'm full, metaphorically speaking." "Yes, I'm ready for school, metaphorically speaking."

Standing beside us, Mum wasn't amused. She told us both off for being so silly.

Walter told us off again when we got home. "Your little sister is very fragile. It's veally no laughing matter."

She—Jessica, they finally decided, who quickly became

Jess—might have been fragile when she was first born, but by the time she came home, it was as if she'd been in the superstrength incubator. I'd never heard a noise like her crying. The walls seemed to shake. I also don't think she slept for more than two hours at a time in her first year. Which meant we didn't either. She needed to be held all the time, and she had her favorites. I wasn't one of them.

One Saturday afternoon, when Jess was about four months old, Charlie and I were working on a jigsaw puzzle together. Walter was at his office in town. He often worked six days a week. Mum was folding the wash while talking on the phone. Jess started to cry in her room. Mum called over to me, "Ella, darling, go in and check on her for me, would you?"

I reluctantly put down my jigsaw piece. I was just getting to the interesting corner bit. I winced at the noise as I went into Jess's room, which I secretly still thought of as my room. As I lifted her out of her crib, she started to cry more loudly. The more I jiggled her, the louder she got. I brought her into the living room. Her cry turned into a shriek. Charlie put his hands over his ears.

"I think something's wrong," I said, as loudly as I could. "Is she sick?"

Mum said something into the phone and then hung up. She was barely visible behind the piles of baby clothes. It amazed me how much laundry Jess generated. "Of course she's not sick. You're just holding her wrong. Ella, really, how many times do I have to show you?"

"I'm *not* holding her wrong. I'm doing it just like you told me to."

"You're not, Ella. Your hands are in the wrong place. You know she needs to have her head supported." Mum took Jess from me and Jess instantly stopped crying. Then, to my dismay, Mum handed her back. "I'm going to need lots of help from you over the next few years, Ella, so you need to learn how to do this properly."

The next few *years*? She instructed me again exactly how to hold Jess: a hand here, another arm there, like a cradle. I tried it. Jess was quiet for a second, another second, even a third. We all started to relax. And then she looked up at me. Her whole face seemed to scrunch in on itself. Her skin reddened. Her mouth opened. The bellowing began again, louder than before.

"Oh, *Ella*," Mum said, crossly this time. I started my Jess-jiggling again, to no avail.

"She's obviously allergic to you," Charlie said over the sound of the cries. He took in my furious expression. "Don't blame me. Don't shoot the messenger."

"Give her to me, please, Ella," Mum said. I did. Jess stopped crying immediately. Mum started cooing to her, smiling and stroking her face, speaking in the singsong voice she'd started using only since Jess had arrived.

"There we are, my Jessie. Are we all better now? Of *course* we are. You're with Mummy, darling, *aren't* you? That's my dear little baby, yes! Who's a good girl, my little Jessie? Who? You, that's right. Good *girl*, Jessie."

Jess started to gurgle, a sweet, musical sound. At that moment, I hated it even more than I hated her crying.

"She's definitely allergic to you, Ella," Charlie said. "Alternatively, she hates you."

He was joking, but it didn't matter. I felt a surge of something wild inside me—hurt, anger, jealousy, all mixed in together. To my own astonishment as much as Charlie's and Mum's, I swept the jigsaw off the table and started shouting.

"I'm allergic to *her*! I *hate* her! I hate *all* of you!" I ran out of the room and slammed the door. I heard Jess start crying again.

Right then, I really didn't care. I didn't care about any of them, or anything. Why should I? They didn't care about me. I ignored Mum calling to me to come back right now and apologize. I ran down the hall into my tiny room, threw myself onto the floor and wiggled under my bed as far as I could, until I was pressed right up against the wall, the carpet rough against my bare legs and my face. I started to cry, the tears hot on my cheeks. I heard the door open and the light being switched on. I could see Mum's feet. I shut my eyes and stayed still until I heard the door shut again. My tears kept falling but I made no sound. A few minutes later, the door opened again. I held my breath. "Ella?" It was Mum again. "Ella? I know you're there somewhere. Come back out here and apologize." I stayed where I was.

I ignored Charlie too when he came into my room soon after. I ignored Mum when she came in a third time. She had Jess in her arms, I could tell. I could hear her little hiccupy breaths. "Ella, I know you're hiding under the bed. This childish behavior has to stop; do you hear me?"

I lay there, as still as I could, until they went out again. I waited a few moments and then I really started crying, tears and loud sobs at once. I couldn't seem to stop. I cried for every sad thing I could think of, going back as far as

I could remember, finding new and old hurts. I cried about my dad, about him leaving, about the divorce. I cried about Lucas's sad little baby fox. About a bad result on a recent school test. The loss of my bedroom. But, mostly, I cried about the now obvious truth. Mum loved Jess more than she loved me.

I don't know how much time passed, how long I was under the bed—an hour, maybe more. I could hear voices outside, Walter arriving home, the sounds of dinner being prepared, the TV. I stayed where I was, on the floor, in my dark room, my face pressed against the carpet. Eventually, I got up. I didn't go to the bathroom, brush my teeth, any of it. I just put myself to bed, in my clothes. I was hungry, but there was nothing I could do about it. I wanted to keep crying but there didn't seem to be any tears left. I waited for Mum or for Walter, or even Charlie, to come in and check on me. No one did. I fell asleep and slept the whole night through.

I woke at six a.m., before anyone else was up. I dressed, made my own breakfast of cereal and toast, then quietly let myself out of the house. I was waiting at the school gate when the first teacher arrived. It wasn't until the next day that I found out Charlie had been right behind me on my walk to school, and that he had also gone back home to report to Mum and Walter that I was okay. He'd heard me get up and followed me. He didn't want them worrying about me, he told me. He'd thought I might be running away.

"And I'd miss you," he said. "Like, I don't know, a dog would miss its fleas."

That night, after Jess was fed, bathed and put to bed and

while Walter was helping Charlie with his homework, Mum called me in to her and Walter's bedroom. I knew what was coming. A telling-off. I wasn't sure I wanted to hear it. She took a seat on the bed and patted the cover beside her. I came in and sat down.

"Darling, we need to have a little chat."

I got in first. "I'm sorry," I said. I knew I'd misbehaved the night before. And I *was* sorry. I didn't like feeling this way either.

"I'm glad to hear that. Ella, you really do have to stop being so jealous."

"I'm not jealous. I'm really not. I'm just very tired."

She gave a laugh. It wasn't a nice laugh. "I think if anyone deserves to be tired around here, it's me. You just have to try harder, Ella. She's your little sister. You should love her."

My apology was forgotten. I felt that surge of crossness again, but I tried pushing it down this time. "She should be the one getting used to me. I was here first."

It was the truth, but I was also trying to be funny. I wanted to make Mum laugh. I wanted lots of things. I wanted Mum to stop telling me off and to give me a big hug, to tell me she still loved me, to tell me she was sorry that Jess, and Walter, seemed to take up so much of her time these days. I wanted her to ruffle my hair and say, of course you're tired, you poor kid, come on, an early night for you. I wanted her to tuck me into bed, and read me a story. I wanted her to thank me for being such a good girl lately, for getting on so well with Walter, and with Charlie. I wanted her to say that of course Jess wouldn't take up all her time forever, that of course she would soon be able to come into school again to listen to my reading and do tuckshop duty and all the things she used to do, and not make me take in another apologetic note to my teacher, explaining that she just didn't have the time anymore, not with a new baby in the house. I wanted her to give me another big hug, and tell me that she loved me just as much as she always had, before Walter had come along and before Jess had come along, and that, yes, she did now have another daughter, but I was absolutely right, I *had* been there first, so I would always be her special, first daughter, no matter what happened.

She didn't. She stood up, put her hands on her hips and gave me a cross look. "'I was here first'? Ella Baum, you should be ashamed of yourself. Jess is your baby sister. You should be welcoming her into our family, not being so mean to her."

I stood up too, just as crossly. I'd heard that word "should" from Mum too many times recently. *He's your new father; you* should *love him. This is your great new house; you* should *love it.* I felt the fury inside me again. This time I let it out. "I don't care! You can't make me love her!"

"Go to your room, Ella. Right now. I'm very, very disappointed in you. And Walter will be too."

My fury was running free now. "I don't care about that either! I don't care about you or Walter or Jess. And I'll never love her, no matter how much you try to make me!"

Once I'd slammed my way into my bedroom, the fury turned into tears again. I was nearly twelve, old enough to know that Mum was right. I *was* jealous. I *should* love my baby sister. But at that moment, I couldn't. It was too hard. For the second night in a row, I found myself under my bed. I cried myself to sleep.

Charlie woke me up two hours later, using my hockey stick to poke me awake. "I come bearing food," he hissed. He'd smuggled in some biscuits and chocolate (he always had a secret stash). He pushed them under the bed, reciting what was on offer as if he were a waiter, chatting to me in his usual conversational way, as if it weren't a bit strange that I was lying in my dark bedroom, under my bed, cramming biscuits into my mouth.

He waited until I'd eaten three biscuits and two chocolates before he spoke. "Are you okay?"

"No," I said, my voice muffled by the food.

"You're in the right, you know."

I swallowed. "About what?"

"Jess," he said. His voice was clear and firm in the darkness. "She is a complete nightmare. She has brought nothing but pain and suffering to this house. Not to mention a great deal of washing. She is nothing but a big, stupid, red-faced, bald crybaby. A midget, stupid, red-faced, bald crybaby."

I suddenly heard myself laugh.

He continued. "She can't feed herself, either. She dribbles. She's also incontinent. You know what that word means, don't you? Disgusting. She wears *nappies*, all day, every day. She can't string two words together. She hasn't got any teeth. Did I mention she was bald? Hairless and toothless. No wonder you hate her. She's absolutely hateful. Hideous. A blight on society. She should be banished, not just from this house, but this city, this country, thrown to the wolves, eaten alive, torn from limb to limb—"

He was going too far now. "She's not that bad. And it's not her fault she cries so much."

"It is," he said, matter-of-factly. "She is evil and she must be destroyed."

"She's not evil," I said. "She's just a little baby."

"Come out here and say that, if you're so brave," he said.

I edged out, and sat up, pushing my hair out of my eyes, feeling the imprint of the carpet on my face.

He handed me another biscuit.

"Thanks, Charlie," I said. I wasn't just thanking him for the biscuit.

"No need for thanks," he said. "Anyway, maybe your mum is right. Maybe you'll learn to love her. Like you'd learn, I don't know, to live with a wart. Or a boil. Metaphorically speaking."

He gave me one more chocolate, told me it was my turn to load the dishwasher and left the room.

I remember lying down on the carpet again for a few minutes to think his words over. Could I learn to love Jess? Like I'd learned to ride a bike, cook an omelet, climb a tree? With practice and repetition? Maybe I could at least try. I left my room, said sorry to Mum, to Walter, to Jess and to Charlie. And for the next few months, it was almost peaceful at home. If you ignored Jess's constant crying. Which I tried to do.

Life settled for all of us. I received the news about my dad's death. I was sad at first, but I also found it confusing. I'd rarely heard from him and I realized I didn't really remember him. He'd become a distant figure in my life. Mum had also made it clear she didn't like him, that he had been an error of judgment in her life. And there was always so much going on at home to distract me from any thoughts of him. Jess was starting to crawl and talk a lot. No words, just babble, a nonstop stream of nonsense words, which even I had to admit were pretty funny. I began to feel happier most of the time. Mum had started noticing me again. I had friends at school and Charlie's great company at home. Having Lucas helped too. I was still sending plenty of faxes to him, and getting plenty in return. He was my confidant and adviser and he made me feel special, something I needed whenever the jealous-of-Jess feelings started to rise. Jess might have been the apple of everyone's eye here in Melbourne, but she didn't have an uncle in London who sent her faxes and foxes and books, did she?

About a month after Jess's first birthday, I was able to repay Charlie for his kindness. He and I had recently been watching lots of American TV shows during the few hours of TV a week our parents allowed us. Copying one of them, we thought it would be funny to set up a lemonade stall down the street from our Richmond house one Saturday afternoon. We convinced ourselves we'd make a fortune. Hundreds of people walked past our gate on their way to the football at the MCG. They'd be dying of thirst, desperate for fresh lemonade.

As we set up the stall, Charlie made me laugh by giving the lemons lemony voices and getting them to talk to one another. "You give me the pip," he had one say. "Yeah?" another replied. "Well, your problem is you're too thin-skinned." "You're just a yellow-bellied coward!" "Don't think I'm going to come to your aid, lemon. Or should I say, come to your lemon-ade." It suddenly seemed urgent to let him know that, alongside Lucas, he was my favorite person in the world.

"Charlie?"

"Mmm?"

"I love you."

He swooned, clutching his chest. "Be still, my beating heart. But, Arabella, it will never work out between us. I'm sorry to break it to you, but I'm your brother."

"Stepbrother, actually," I said. "But that's what I meant. I love you in a brotherly way."

"How marvelous." Apart from using as many big words as possible, he'd also taken to occasionally speaking in an upper-class English accent. "And I, dearest Arabella, love you in return. In a sisterly way, of course."

"Good," I said.

He reverted to his very Australian accent. "Can we get back to our lemonade now?"

"Sure," I said.

Two hours later, we were packing up after a frankly disappointing afternoon. We'd made only two dollars and twenty cents and had drunk most of the lemonade ourselves. I heard a noise from down the street—shouting, and a bottle being kicked along the footpath. It was a gang of boys from one of the other schools in the area. I'd seen them now and again going past our house, and ignored them. There was an unspoken war between the two schools. They thought we were all posh brats. We thought they were all criminals.

Charlie was still very fat at this stage. It wasn't until he reached his twenties that he started to lose any weight. I could hear the gang of boys begin to taunt him as they approached. "Hey, Fatso." "Who ate all the pies?" "Someone call the RSPCA. There's a beached whale on the street."

"Come on, Charlie," I said, quickly pushing the unused cups and lemons into the packing crate we'd used as our stand. I wasn't quick enough. I was just taking down our handwritten sign when the gang stopped in front of us.

"Fatso's got a girlfriend," one of them said. The other one said something cruder in reply. I ignored them. Beside me, Charlie kept packing up too. I shot him a glance. He didn't look back.

"Give us a drink, Fatso's girlfriend."

"We're closed," I said, looking down at the footpath.

"Fatso drank it all," one said. They all laughed.

Before I could stop him, the tallest boy reached into the packing crate, grabbed one of the lemons and pelted it across the road. It narrowly missed a passing car. The driver honked his horn. Two of the boys gave him the finger.

"Ignore them," Charlie hissed at me.

I tried, but they did it again. More horns honked. The third time, they threw the lemon at Charlie, not the cars. It missed him by inches. The next one hit him on the shoulder.

"Don't do that," he said, his face turning red.

"Who's gonna stop us, Fatso? You and your girlfriend?"

The tall boy reached across and, in what seemed like slow motion to me, shoved Charlie. I watched, horrified, as Charlie stumbled back against the crate. It tilted. He lost his balance and fell heavily. Paper cups and lemons scattered onto the footpath around him.

The gang of boys laughed. I had to do something, and quickly. No one shoved my Charlie and got away with it. No one laughed at him or called him names either.

As well as the American TV shows, we'd been watching American films. One of them was *The Karate Kid.* I'd never been to a single karate class, but the boys weren't to know that. To their shock, and mine, I went into action. I leaped in between them and Charlie and made a strange high-pitched noise, a kind of "Ah-yah!" as I held up both hands at an angle.

"Watch out," I shouted as loudly as I could. It was pretty loud. "I'm a black belt."

They started laughing. One of them threw another lemon at Charlie, who was still lying on the footpath. It hit him on the head.

I shouted at them again. *"No!"*

There's something glorious about letting fury rise inside you. It's like a gas flame, a whoosh of pure emotion. I turned mine up to high and went for it. I was twelve, tall for my age, thin and fast. I seriously didn't have a clue about karate, but I knew from the films that it involved a lot of quick kicks and hand slices. As luck would have it, my first kick landed right where it would hurt, on the tallest of the four boys. He doubled up. Another kick landed behind the knee of a second boy. He crumpled. That was it in terms of my armory, but they weren't to know. I kept shouting, making so much noise that a neighbor came out to see what was happening.

"What the hell's going on here?" he said. He was more than six foot tall and very broad.

The sight of an adult was what made the boys run, not me—I know that—but I still took pleasure in seeing them run down the street, the tallest one bent over, groaning.

"Are you two okay?" the neighbor asked.

I was panting, but I nodded. Charlie nodded too.

We packed up swiftly. I looked over at Charlie. His face was red, but he was smiling.

It wasn't until we started walking that he spoke. "Wow, Ella," he said.

I smiled all the way home too. Neither of us told Mum or Walter what had happened. It was our own excellent secret.

I turned thirteen, fourteen, fifteen. I went through puberty, with some alarm at first. Charlie got taller, a bit fatter and even cleverer. He topped his class each year, became a skilled debater, applied to be a Rotary exchange student and was immediately accepted. After he passed his final-year exams, he'd be spending a year in the US. I think I was prouder of him than Walter was.

Meanwhile, Jess was growing older too. Older and bolder, as the saying goes. The house still seemed to revolve around her. When I was with her, I was often conscious of difficult, spiky feelings, not the warm, amused feeling I had when I was with Charlie. It bothered me, especially the older I got. Was it because she was only half my sister? Or was it just that I didn't actually like her very much? I couldn't work out which one.

The age difference—eleven years in my case, thirteen years in Charlie's—meant that we didn't have huge amounts to do with each other, particularly once Charlie and I went to high school. Our after-school lives became as busy as at school. I played hockey, sang in the school choir, volunteered in the local library. Charlie studied, and studied some more. In between studying, he wrote to his dozens of pen pals. The mailbox was always full, every day, with letters for him from all over the world, part of his involvement with the Rotary clubs. He'd applied for pen pals as part of his mission to be chosen as an exchange student, and then got hooked. He didn't just write one letter that did for them all, either. He would compose letters to each, carefully and considerately.

He also sent them regular photos of himself. I took the photos. He wasn't in the least bit self-conscious about his weight. He would beam at the camera, his pudgy cheeks red, his stomach round. Mum had tried sending him to dieticians and even psychologists in an attempt to find the root cause of his weight problem. Charlie sat her down one afternoon and gently asked her to leave him alone and stop worrying.

"I'm the root cause of my weight problem, Meredith. I eat too much. It's that simple."

She couldn't even try the "but you'll be so much happier if you're thinner" approach with him. Because Charlie was the happiest person any of us knew. Happy and popular, even with the girls. He didn't care that he was fat, so why should anyone else?

Walter still worked too hard. Mum worked part-time too, as an Avon lady, for the fun and the free samples rather than the money. The rest of her time was spent looking after Jess. With five of us on the move, our home life needed to be organized. Fortunately, it was. Walter was German, after all. We had rosters and timetables. Walter could easily have afforded a cleaner but he and Mum thought it more character-building if Charlie and I took on the task, in return for our pocket money.

Jess was considered too young for chores, but during our high school years, Charlie and I were given plenty to do around the house. I had to load and unload the dishwasher, make the beds and do the vacuuming every Saturday. Charlie swept the veranda, mowed the lawn and cleaned the bathroom. When we complained one month, Walter swapped the rosters so that I did the veranda and Charlie did the vacuuming.

"That should help keep it fun," Walter said as he proudly pinned up the new roster.

"It's really working," Charlie said to me the next Saturday. "I'm having so much fun with this vacuum cleaner I want to faint with excitement."

"Me too," I said, in a mock-excited voice. "Look at this dirt I've swept up. I am fascinated."

For the next week, we amused ourselves and drove our parents mad by finding everything either fascinating, wonderful or incredibly interesting.

"Stop it, you two," Mum said one night.

"We're just being enthusiastic about life," I said.

"No, you're not. You're being annoying."

But it was different for Jess. They didn't tell her to stop saying particular words, or tell her she was being annoying, or expect her to do anything but be cute. I've talked about this a lot with Charlie over the years. It was like Jess somehow bewitched our parents from the second she arrived. It was as though she was in charge of them, not the other way around. And the two of us? We were her servants.

We were told from morning till bedtime to do things around the house: tidy up, wash the car, empty the dishwasher, eat our dinner. There was no choice in the matter. From the moment Jess had any say in it, however, her answer was no.

"Jess, tidy your room."

"No."

"Jess, pick up your toys."

"No."

We would be told off if we dared to defy our parents like that. But they just smiled at Jess.

"You are such a vascal, my Jessie," Walter would say.

Charlie and I would roll our eyes at each other. "You are such a vapscallion, my Jessie," Charlie would whisper to me when we were out of Walter's earshot. "Such a vogue. Such a vatbag."

My mum was as bad. Jess could do no wrong in her eyes. A temper tantrum was a show of high spirits. A flood of tears was evidence of her emotional maturity. "She's such a character!" I'd hear her say to her friends on the phone. "Honestly, she's the light of our lives."

It helped, of course, that Jess was—is—beautiful. Physically beautiful, I mean. She was—still is—like a little doll, with a round face, rosy cheeks, big eyes and a head of golden curls. And she had a *lot* of curls as a child because she refused to let anyone cut her hair until the day she turned seven. It's true. Mum took her to the hairdresser's when she was about three and brought her back, unchanged, an hour later, both of them red-faced, Mum tearful, Jess defiant.

"She screamed bloody murder as soon as she saw the scissors," I heard Mum tell Walter. "Next time, you take her."

Walter tried. Same result. The next month, Mum tried again and came home in tears. Her, not Jess. Walter tried one more time. They eventually gave up.

One night while we were tidying up the kitchen, Charlie and I idly discussed the matter of Jess's hair. It was getting worse every week, a long, tangled mass of golden knots and snarls.

"I know," Charlie jokingly suggested. "Let's cut her hair ourselves one night while she's asleep."

Jess overheard, told on us, and we both got into trouble for being mean to her.

"It was just an idea," Charlie said to Jess later, once we'd told *her* off for being a squealer.

"A very good idea," I said. "You are looking a bit wild, Jess, if you don't mind me saying."

"It's *my* hair," Jess said, stamping her foot, like a child in a comic book. "I'll wear it the way I want." She'd have made me laugh if she didn't infuriate me so much.

One summer, the year she turned four, she refused to wear any clothes. Just point-blank refused. Fortunately for her, there was a heat wave in Melbourne at the time. Also fortunately for her, she was only in kindergarten and spent most of the time at home with Mum. After two months of nudity and wild tantrums if anyone tried to dress her or make her leave the house, she consented to wear her swimsuit, but that was it. We have a Christmas family photo from that time, the three of us kids standing in front of our tree. There's Charlie in all his gorgeous fatness, wearing his new Christmas clothes of white shirt and shorts. Skinny me beside him, giggling at something he must have just said, wearing a red shift dress and a pair of blue sandals I recall being very proud of. And there between us, like a feral Shirley Temple, is a beaming wild-haired child in a grubby swimsuit. She wore it everywhere—to restaurants, to our end-of-year school concerts, to the shops. Mum and Walter just seemed to let her do whatever she wanted.

The year she turned five, she announced she wanted a pet for her birthday. We'd been asking for years, Charlie and I. The answer was always the same.

"Not yet," our parents would say.

"When is yet?" Charlie asked once.

"We'll know when the time is right," was the answer.

"Yet" was obviously the moment Jess asked. She wanted a kitten, she told them. Really, really, really wanted a kitten. A birthday kitten.

Charlie and I were nearby, washing up or darning socks or sweeping the chimney or whatever task we'd been allocated that day in our roles as slaves in the Kingdom of Jess. At last, I remember thinking, she finally won't get her own way.

Mum smiled at Walter, then at Jess. "Do you know, a kitten around the house would be cute, wouldn't it?"

I stepped in. "But, Mum—"

"You'll all get to share it, Ella. It won't just belong to Jess."

Of course, we didn't get anywhere near it. Jess chose the kitten from the pet shop and she ruled over it like a warlord. If either Charlie or I tried to pick it up, she would roar at us. "That's my kitty!" If we put out milk for it, she'd tip the milk out of the dish and refill it. "I feed my kitty, not you!"

The kitten soon realized who was in charge. It let Jess do whatever she wanted with it. Jess carried it in a sling for the first few weeks. Not a mew of protest. For the next month, she carried it everywhere in a plastic shopping bag. Not a squeak of complaint. Mum and Walter thought it was hilarious. They took dozens of photos. Wild Jess, with her wild hair, half-naked, carrying her cat around in a plastic bag.

"That child!" they'd say. "What will she do next!"

"Run away to the jungle?" Charlie said to me. "She already looks like Mowgli."

Jungle Girl, we called her from then on. Until she told Mum and Walter, who told us off. "She's your little sister. Be kind to her."

"She's only half my sister," I remember saying.

"I'll pretend I didn't hear that, Ella. You've got very jealous again and it's not nice to see."

Charlie and I spent hours discussing the situation. *We'd* move out, we decided. They didn't want us, their two half-kids, not now that they had a full-kid in the house. That was how we thought of ourselves, full and half, as though we were cartons of milk.

Lucas tried to give me good advice via his faxes during all of this. *Try to be kind. Make your own life.*

Easier said than done. I'd asked once if I could do violin classes. "I don't think so," Mum had said. "Concentrate on your studies for now."

Jess had after-school piano, theater and dance classes.

Charlie asked if he could go on a school trip to the ski-fields. "Money's a bit tight at the moment," his dad said.

Jess got a new bike that birthday.

I know how this sounds. Jealous older siblings. Poor little Jess. But the truth is, she would drive a saint mad. Whether it was her personality or the fact she'd spent her whole short life being indulged and gazed on with endless pride, she was difficult company. It was all "me-me-me." "Look at me!" If either of us ever dared to tell her off, she'd turn into a fury in a second. "Stop ganging up on me, you two, or I'll tell!"

Charlie in particular always tried to be patient. "We're not ganging up on you, Jess. We're trying to play a complicated card game and you are too young to play it."

"Can't you play a game Jess can join in on?" Mum said. "Fish or Snap?"

"No!" Jess said. "Let's play musicals. I'll be the singer and you be the audience!"

And so the game of cards would be abandoned, and we'd find ourselves sitting beside Mum and Walter on kitchen chairs watching Jess dance, prance, jump and do somersaults, over and over again.

"It's like being on Broadway, isn't it?" Charlie said to me once in a stage whisper.

I got the giggles and was sent to my room.

Of course, the especially infuriating thing was Jess really could sing and dance. It would have been easier if she'd had two left feet, was tone-deaf and looked like a troll. But to paraphrase her favorite song of that time, "Close to You," it seemed the angels had gathered the day she was born and made a dream come true.

I still can't listen to that song. I can't think about Jess anymore. Thinking about Jess means thinking about—

Stop.

It was too late. She was in my head now. What she'd done was in my head now.

SIX

My son, Felix, died at 2:10 p.m. on Friday, 18 June 2010. He was twenty months old. He had black hair, like his dad, like a raven's wing, so black and shiny it sometimes looked blue. He had blue-green eyes, also like his father. He was tall for his age. When he was born, he was all curves and softness. Within months, he'd grown long and skinny, the skinniness from me, the height from his dad. He got his first tooth at six months. He started to crawl aged nine months.

He started speaking the day he turned one. His first words were *ta* and *bye*. His favorite toy was a blue knitted rabbit. He liked pumpkin, apples, carrots and oranges. He hated chicken, tomatoes and bananas.

His bedroom was multicolored: His cot was painted blue, his quilt was bright orange and his favorite pajamas were a rainbow-patterned flannelette pair, with a matching pair of slippers that he never wore.

He called me Mama. Aidan was Daddy. To our astonishment, and his own delight, one of the first phrases he learned was his own name. It was part toddler-babble, but we were convinced he knew what he was saying: "I'm Felix O'Hanlon!" He'd announce it out of the blue, shout it out—in a supermarket queue, at the doctor's surgery, all sorts of places. It always made me laugh, made him laugh and, mostly, made the people around us laugh.

He liked jigsaw puzzles. Blocks. Trucks. *The Wiggles. Play School.* He didn't like going to bed and he didn't seem to need much sleep. Some nights he'd go down for eight or nine hours, but more often he'd sleep in bursts of two or three hours. Each time he'd wake up and yell, literally yell, until Aidan or I came in. He'd always be in a good mood when we appeared, smiling or waving—ready for action, as Aidan put it. It was as if he'd got lonely in his room or was bored sleeping and wanted company. That was Felix. It was as if he knew—as if he had so much to do in his life he didn't want to waste time sleeping. So we would try to soothe him, talk to him, read to him. Sometimes we were successful and he'd be coaxed back to sleep, but more often he would yell again until we took him into our bed with us. If we were still up working, he'd sit on my lap as I edited or on Aidan's lap as he did some translating. He especially loved to bang our pens or pencils on the desk, laughing at the noise. It used to drive me crazy if Aidan so much as ate an apple while I was editing. Felix's pencil banging never bothered me at all.

It was wintertime, mid-June. He'd been through a stage

of being particularly energetic, even for him—waking up five or more times a night. It lasted for eight nights in a row. Aidan was very busy at work. There was an international trade conference taking place in Canberra and he was working sixteen-hour days and collapsing into bed as soon as he got home. So I got up for Felix each night. I didn't mind. The conference was a big deal for Aidan, I knew. It was a quiet time for me workwise, so I was able to cope with the lack of sleep. I caught up on an hour here or there, while Felix had his afternoon nap.

Aidan's conference was due to finish on Thursday. The delegates would be in Canberra for one more day, but Aidan's official role in their visit was over. The timing was perfect. It was Walter's birthday, and to celebrate, he, Mum and Jess were coming up to Canberra for what Mum called a cultural weekend. They weren't staying with us—our flat was too small—but in a hotel in town. They were going to have the Friday to themselves to go to the museum and galleries, and we'd all go out together that night for dinner.

There had been some recent tension between Jess and me. She had an on-again, off-again relationship with a fellow drama student, Canberra-born and now Melbourne-based, and had been up to stay with his family several times. She'd visited them—and us—most recently a month earlier. She'd arrived at the door, called out, "Hi, it's Jess!" as usual, swept in, kissed us all on both cheeks, Felix included, told us how cute he was—"He's going to break *so* many hearts when he's older!"—then spent the rest of her hour-long visit telling us about the dance award she'd won recently, the roles she'd auditioned for or planned to audition for, how much she was enjoying doing guest appearances on Mum's TV show and how great it was being stopped in the street and being asked for autographs.

I was extremely tired. Felix had barely slept the previous night. While she was talking, he started to nod off in my arms. I quietly excused myself and carried him into his room. I laid him down, stroked his cheek, relieved to see him start the slow, deep breathing that promised a few hours of sleep. Then, outside, Jess sprang up out of her chair and started showing Aidan a new tap routine she was learning. In her winter boots. On our wooden floor. The noise shocked me as much as it shocked Felix. He sat up in the cot, wailing. I went into the living room and shouted—really shouted— at Jess. I called her selfish. Self-obsessed. Self-absorbed. She burst into tears and started shouting back. Felix started crying even more loudly. Aidan tried to intervene. I shouted at him then too, telling him to keep out of my family business. "You're just jealous of me," Jess had said, as she tearfully, dramatically, gathered her bag and coat and ran for the door. "You always have been." Walter's birthday dinner would be the first time I'd seen her since that day.

On Thursday night, Aidan put down his first postconference celebratory beer, took one look at the bags under my eyes and said, "Arabella Fox Baum O'Hanlon, you are beautiful but you are exhausted. I hereby pronounce myself in charge of the world. Through the powers I've just invested in myself, I grant you a full day to yourself, starting tomorrow at eight a.m."

I remember laughing. "Sure, Aidan. I'll ask Felix to look after himself, will I?"

"Of course not. I, his loving, biological, capable father, will take care of him." He held up a hand as I started to protest. "Ella, I want to. I need him as much as you need a break from him. He won't ask me about trade tariffs, the French phrase for exclusion areas or the German word for extrapolation, will he?"

"He might. He's very advanced."

Aidan grinned. "Say yes, Ella. Leave Felix and me in peace for the day. We've got swings to swing on. Playgrounds to play in. A box set of *The Godfather* to watch."

"But your work—"

"It's finished. *Fertig. Fini.*"

"You always say that and they always call you in."

"They won't this time. They promised. But if they do, I'll bring Felix. He can take the minutes. Make the coffee. He loves making coffee. I told him that every time he pushes the plunger down, there's a huge explosion somewhere."

"Aidan, I'd love it, a whole day, but you can't. This conference, I know how important—" I was so tired I could barely make sense.

"Was that pidgin English, Ella? I'm not familiar with that dialect." He pointed to an area above his head. "Can you see that lightbulb? I've just had a brilliant idea." He took out his phone and dialed. "Meredith? It's your favorite Irish son-in-law. All set for your travels? Wonderful. I wonder if I could ask a big favor? Can I please have you on standby tomorrow, as Felix's beloved and loving grandmother, in case of any urgent babysitting?" He listened, laughed, said good-bye and hung up. "She said yes. How could she say no to a silver-tongued devil like myself? But I won't need her, of course. That ruse was just to appease you. Did it work? Are you appeased?"

I was completely appeased. I spent the rest of that evening making plans. A whole day to myself! I could go shopping, get my legs waxed, go and see three films, whatever I wanted. Aidan was amused at how often my ideas changed.

"You could make it up as you go along," he suggested. To both of our surprise, I agreed.

On Friday morning, the pair of them waved me off. Felix was on Aidan's hip, smiling and blowing kisses. He'd just learned how to do that.

"Bye," he said. "Bye, Mama. Bye, Felix."

I laughed, and repeated it. "Bye, Felix!" I kissed Aidan and I kissed Felix. Felix kissed me back, on my left cheek, then my right cheek and then on my chin, our own little ritual. I didn't know then that it would be the last time we'd ever do it.

I checked I had my phone with me.

"Leave it behind, Ella," Aidan said. "Have a proper day off."

"I'll take it, just in case. Ring if you need anything, a pint of milk, a stiff gin—"

"I won't ring. Forget about us. You've never seen us before. You are about to go back in time to your free and single days." He turned around so he and Felix were facing away from me. "Can you see her, Felix? No, me either. That's because she's disappeared. She's now invisible. You have an invisible mother. Isn't that amazing?"

I walked into the city, an easy forty minutes from home. It was a beautiful morning, crisp and bright. I went to the library, into bookshops, clothes shops. I rang Aidan at eleven.

"Who is this?" he said. "My wife? She left me this morning in a time machine. I'm not expecting her back until tonight. She may even be full of champagne by then. What am I to do?"

I laughed. "Is Felix all right?"

"Who is this stranger asking me about my own son? Are you a Russian spy? Has someone bugged this phone? But let me ask him. Felix, are you all right?"

I heard his reply through the phone. His shout. "I'm Felix O'Hanlon!"

"Did he eat his breakfast?" I asked. "There's extra juice in the freezer if you need it."

"Leave us alone or I'll call the police and report you for harassment. I'm turning off my phone. What do you say, Felix?"

I heard it again. "I'm Felix O'Hanlon!"

I was still smiling two hours later, possibly helped by the glass of very good white wine I had with my Italian lunch. I was trying to decide whether to see a film or go to the botanic gardens when I passed a beauty salon. The door was open. Classical music was playing. Inside, it looked calm and relaxing, the decor a luxurious combination of velvet and soft shades of blue. There was a price list on the window, including a special offer on massages. An hour-long massage, with scented oils and soft music, suddenly seemed to be the thing I wanted most in the world.

I was in luck. The beautician was free. "Leave your belongings in the locker. Just bring your key."

I was relaxed and obedient. I left my phone in my bag, my bag in the locker. I would be in the massage room for an hour. What could possibly happen?

Felix died in that hour.

In the treatment room, I had a brief conversation with the beautician before she began. Had I had a massage recently? she asked. I laughed and told her no, not for years. I explained that my husband had practically pushed me out the door and told me to treat myself. A husband in a million, she said. I agreed that he was.

She gave me the best massage I'd ever had. She found all the knots in my shoulders and teased them loose. She pushed deep into my back and relaxed muscles I didn't know I had. She gently excused herself toward the end of the hour, tiptoed out and then a minute or two later came back. She didn't have another client for an hour. She'd just learned a new facial technique. Could she practice it on me at no charge? I'd be her guinea pig. Did I have the time to spare?

Of course I said yes.

I came out of the treatment room forty minutes later, in a dreamlike state. I got dressed and then took out my phone. Only then. Not the moment I came out. That's how bad a mother I was. How selfish I was. In those ten minutes I could have been on my way to the hospital.

I don't care that the doctors say I would still have been too late. I might not have been. I don't care what the coroner said about the time of death. If Felix had heard my voice, if he had felt my touch, he would have done all he could to fight whatever it was that was pulling him away from me. I've relived those moments over and over. Why didn't I check my phone the moment I came out of the massage room? Why didn't I take the phone into the massage room with me? Why did I accept the invitation for the free facial? Why did I even take the day off? Why, why, why . . .

I had thirty missed calls. Three from Jess, the rest from Aidan. The phone rang even as I was registering there had been so many.

I answered. "Aidan, what is it? Is something wrong?"

"Ella—Ella, it's Felix—"

I screamed when he told me. The receptionist ran in. I was standing there with the phone.

"Miss? Are you okay?"

I couldn't speak.

She took the phone. She talked to Aidan. I don't remember it happening, but she must have called a taxi and given them the address of the hospital. She came with me. I never found out her name, and I can never go back and thank her. But she came on that taxi ride with me and held me the whole way until we arrived and she could hand me over to Aidan.

Felix was already dead. He had been dead for fifty minutes.

It was Jess's fault. It was Aidan's fault. It was my fault.

That morning, ten minutes after Aidan had joked and teased and told me to forget all about him and Felix, he'd got a phone call from his office. An emergency. Last-minute trade negotiations, a senior interpreter urgently needed. The ambassador had requested him. How quickly could he get in? He couldn't, he said. He was looking after his son. His wife was away. He was very sorry, but—

There had to be a way. They needed him now. It had to

be him. It was about contracts worth millions of dollars. Hundreds of jobs were at stake. No, he couldn't bring his son with him. It was a high-level meeting. "Can't someone in your family look after him, even for an hour? A neighbor? Anyone?"

Aidan rang my mother's number. She answered on the third ring. She, Walter and Jess had just landed, just collected their luggage, were at the taxi stand about to find their way to their hotel. Walter wasn't well. He'd got a nosebleed on the flight. He'd be fine, it wasn't serious, but he just needed to lie down for an hour or so. But of course Jess could babysit Felix. No problem at all. They'd get two separate taxis from the airport. She'd be there in ten minutes. The timing couldn't have been better, they all agreed, marveling at how wonderful fate was sometimes. What were families for, but to appear just when you needed them?

If Aidan had received that call from work an hour later, Walter's nosebleed would have been better and he and Mum could have looked after Felix. If Mum had decided to celebrate Walter's birthday in a different way, they wouldn't have been in Canberra at all. Aidan would have had to take Felix into work with him. Felix would have been spoiled and entertained by one of the secretaries or junior researchers and he would have entertained and charmed them in return.

If.

Aidan was at the front door in his suit, briefcase in hand, car keys rattling, when the taxi dropped Jess off. Felix was on the living-room floor, playing with his blocks, all smiles, waving and laughing at this surprise visitor.

"You're a lifesaver," Aidan said to Jess. "I shouldn't be

long, two hours at the most. He's had lunch, had his nap— all he'd love is some fresh air."

"Me too. That plane smelled disgusting," Jess said. "Don't worry. We'll be fine."

Aidan told Jess I was in town, that there was no need to worry me, he should be back before I was, but if he wasn't, it would be a nice surprise for me to find Jess there with Felix. Walter and Meredith might even have arrived by then too. It would be a welcoming committee, Aidan said.

Jess took Felix to the park two streets away. Felix loved the park. He loved the swings, the slippery dip, the climbing frame and the sandpit. Most of all, he loved the small nature reserve beside the playground. There was a fence running along the boundary, separating the tended trees from the bushland. If we had time, we'd lift him up, hold him tightly around the waist, and he would inch his way like a little tightrope walker along the top rail of the fence, laughing so hard that we'd soon be laughing too.

He was only twenty months old. Not big enough to climb a fence on his own. Not yet. Not without one of us holding him. He was a great walker, and he had good balance, but he was only twenty months old.

Aidan told me that Jess told him that as they were walking back toward home, Felix ran to the fence beside the nature reserve and he insisted, he yelled, until she lifted him up and walked him along the fence. She'd been with us on a previous trip, seen us do it, knew what he wanted. Three times they did it, one end of the rail to the other, back, back again.

It happened on the fourth time.

Her phone rang. It was her on-again, off-again boy-friend. They spoke. Beside her, Felix tugged at her skirt and tried to climb up the fence again. Still on the phone, Jess lifted Felix up, balanced his feet on the top of the fence and started walking. Felix laughed. She kept talking.

They were nearly at the end of the fence, two feet away at the most, when an insect flew at Jess's face. A bee, a wasp, she couldn't remember. She reacted, jumping back. She let go of Felix. Not her phone, but Felix. Felix fell. Not toward Jess. Not toward the playground. To the other side, the nature reserve, where there were tree roots, clods of earth and a large rock, hidden by leaves.

His head hit the rock at full impact.

He didn't suffer, Aidan told me, again and again. "It was instant, Ella. He died instantly."

He was falling while I was lying on a massage table, drifting to sounds of ocean music, inhaling lavender oil and thinking to myself that this was perhaps the closest I'd been to heaven. I was wrong. It was the closest I had ever been to hell.

Jess climbed over the fence, held Felix, tried to resuscitate him, phoned for an ambulance, shouted until passersby and other parents came to her. I know the details but I can't repeat them again, because all I see are strangers, dozens of strangers, leaning over my son's body, and it is too late, they are too late, and I am not there.

I wasn't there when Jess called my mobile number, three times, hysterical.

I wasn't there when she rang Aidan's mobile, interrupted his meeting and told him what had happened.

I wasn't there when Aidan arrived at the playground at the same time as the ambulance.

I wasn't in the back of the ambulance when they screamed through the city streets, the paramedics still working on my son's body.

I wasn't there until my son had been dead for nearly an hour.

I can't say what Felix looked like when I finally saw him. I don't remember what he looked like. All I remember is holding him. Holding him, tight, tightly. Aidan held me, holding Felix. The three of us. But it was now just the two of us.

I didn't see Jess. She was there at the hospital with Mum and Walter but I didn't see her or talk to her. I didn't blame her. Not then. I hadn't heard the whole story by then.

I heard it the next day.

That's when I started blaming her.

I haven't stopped.

SEVEN

Lucas's house suddenly felt too quiet.

Keep busy.

I'd already tidied the kitchen. I knew from experience not to dare tidy Lucas's withdrawing room too much, or any of the tutors' rooms at all. I'd already unpacked. Already tidied my own room.

Think of something else. Observe. Distract.

I was in London. Staying with Lucas. Lucas had offered me a job.

Think about that.

When Lucas had said that he needed my help, I'd assumed he meant as a housekeeper. He knew I'd enjoyed doing the job in the past. I think he also knew I wanted to be as physically busy as possible. That I needed to be as busy as possible.

"Let me give you a bit of background first, Ella," he'd said the night before. He had four students living with him and working as his tutors at the moment, he told me. One woman, three men.

"And there the problem lies," he said. "I don't know which one it is."

I was confused. "Which one?"

He turned and checked the door was shut. It was. "You know, Ella, that my client list has changed? Gone up a gear, in modern terms?"

I nodded. It had started to happen when I was staying with him three years earlier. Originally, his tutors had spent ninety percent of their time coaching "normal" kids—the children of eager, middle-class parents who needed private tuition on top of the generally good education they got at school. The other ten percent had been anything but normal: the children of London's super-rich—the millionaire executives, rock stars, film actors, Russian oligarchs. . . . Lucas had never advertised his services, relying on recommendations. In the past year or so, he explained, the word of mouth had increased, aided by the fact that three of his tutors' charges had scored some of the best A-level results in the country. One of them had featured on the front page of the *Times*, after perfect grades in six different subjects. The phone calls started coming in that day. Not from the "normal" parents, but from the "other" group. His clients were now almost exclusively the superrich parents.

"It's how people operate at that level of society," Lucas said. "They all want what the other has, be it a new car, a villa in Tuscany or a brainy child."

He could have taken on fifty more tutors—there was so much work on offer—but he didn't want the extra work, or the extra lodgers. The more he said no, the more money he was offered. The more he looked around his house, the more he realized what he could do with that money.

"I did my sums, Ella. This house needs urgent renovation. A lot of it. The fees I could charge would refit the entire house. Add an extension, more bedrooms, more study areas. Two years of working with those clients, difficult or demanding as they might be, would buy me and my students a renovated house and five years of research time. I decided it was worth it."

It wasn't difficult to find very bright tutors. There was a waiting list of graduates wanting to spend a year living and working with Lucas. After a week of interviews, he took in four new lodgers, all in their late twenties, experts in languages, science, mathematics and physics. All four were studying for their PhD. All four spent every free moment from their own studies working as tutors. Two of the clients' children had recently won academic awards. All of the parents reported improvements. All of the fees had been paid in full too. Lucas had already hired an architect. The renovation work was due to begin on the house at the end of summer.

It all sounded positive. I couldn't see where I fitted in. "Do you want me to manage the renovations?"

"No. The architect will do that."

"Look after the tutors' timetables?"

"No, I do that myself. With help from Henrietta. She helps me do the students' appraisals too."

Henrietta wasn't just a fellow lecturer at his university.

She was also Lucas's long-term girlfriend. I didn't pursue that subject for now. "Then how can I help?"

"Ella, I need you to play detective."

I smiled. I couldn't help myself.

"I'm serious," he said. "I have a thief in the house."

I thought of the chaos on every floor. "How can you tell?"

"Not this house. Let me explain."

He told me that the four tutors divided their time between the different clients' houses, depending on what subjects were required.

"Much as I'd like to offer one person who can teach applied physics, advanced Mandarin, French, Spanish, classic literature and algebra, it doesn't work like that. Each tutor has an area of excellence. So each of them visits different houses at different times."

I knew that from my previous stay. Back then, Aidan had been Lucas's language expert. He was fluent in French, German, Spanish and Italian, as well as his native Irish. Not that there'd been a great call for the Irish language among the upper-class children of London.

Lucas told me that two months earlier he'd received a phone call from a long-standing client. The man's two oldest children had been coached into Cambridge by Lucas's tutors. The third child, in her late teens, had her sights set on Yale. All four of Lucas's current tutors were helping her on her way. Lucas wouldn't have called the father a friend, but they had a long association.

"Your tutors haven't noticed anyone or anything unusual in the house, have they?" the father asked. "It's just that something has gone missing."

The "something" was a small but valuable eighteenth-century maritime map. Over dinner, over breakfast, in casual encounters in the house, Lucas had carefully posed the question to his four lodgers. No, no one had noticed anything untoward, Lucas reported back.

"It's just disappeared into thin air," the client said.

Three weeks later, Lucas received another phone call, a similar question from a different client. Discreet, not wanting to create alarm. A diamond necklace had disappeared. The client suspected one of their domestic staff. Had the tutors noticed or overheard anything, by chance? Lucas asked again. The tutors hadn't.

Ten days later, a third call. This time, it was a small sculpture. A valuable figurine. Once again, he asked his tutors if they'd seen or heard anything. Nothing, they assured him.

Two weeks previously, a fourth call. An antique ring was missing. No, the tutors hadn't seen a thing.

Four clients, four thefts in two months. Lucas knew that his clients didn't speak to one another. His tutors' contracts had confidentiality clauses. But it was too coincidental for all four clients to be burgled around the same time. There had to be a connection. And the only common thread was Lucas's tutors.

"Did they all call the police?" I asked.

"Two of them did, yes. The police reviewed CCTV footage where possible and interviewed everyone, including my tutors. All without result."

"And the other two clients?"

Lucas hesitated. "My understanding was they didn't want the police involved."

"The goods were already stolen property?"

"More likely bought on the black market, or undeclared taxwise. I didn't ask for more details. Where they'd come from didn't change the fact they'd all gone missing."

"And you seriously think it's one of your tutors?"

"I wanted to think it was impossible. I've been sending tutors into houses all around London for more than twenty years. Apart from one or two inappropriate love affairs, there's never been any trouble. But the more I thought about it, the more I realized the thief could be one of them. That's what I want you to find out. That's the job I'm offering you."

I still thought he was joking. "Of course, Lucas. Shall I start now? Search their rooms?"

"I've already tried that. I didn't find anything."

"You searched their rooms? Seriously? Lucas!"

"Not very seriously." A pause. "I opened their bedroom doors and looked in. Do you see my dilemma, Ella? I can't suddenly turn into a detective. Start asking them loaded questions, asking what they do in their spare time, whether they have any contacts on the black market. I've always left my tutors alone and they leave me alone. That's why it works so well. I can't call in the police myself either. If one hint gets out that my tutors are unreliable, or, worse, that they are thieves, I'll never get another client again. Which means the renovations stop before they've started, my own research finishes, the tutors' work finishes—"

"If you're sure it's one of these four, couldn't you just cancel their contracts? Get new tutors in?"

He shook his head. "We're approaching exams, a crucial time for everyone. And I don't want to cancel their contracts. These four are quite brilliant—brilliant minds and brilliant teachers. Before all this arose, I was getting only positive feedback about them from my clients."

"But if it *is* one of them, you need to know."

"Of course I do. But I can't solve it myself, Ella. Frankly, I'm too busy with my own work. I don't have time for this. I asked Henrietta if she would help but she said no. She's too busy, with her own studies, her own life—"

Her own husband, I thought.

"But you, Ella—"

We both knew what he meant. I had all the time in the world.

He placed both hands on the table, all business now. "On the surface, I'd be hiring you as my cook and housekeeper again. But mostly I want you to talk to the tutors, get to know them, ask all the questions you can. Is one of them having financial problems? Or had a sudden windfall? I need you to find out whatever you can."

"But where do I start? Mention it casually over breakfast? 'Good morning. Do any of you happen to know where I could get a cheap diamond necklace?'"

Lucas didn't even smile. "Please, Ella. You know what this house means to me."

I did know. More especially, I knew how much his research and his students meant to him. I promised I'd sleep on it. He told me he'd leave information about the four tutors in the attic. He used it as his archive room these days. I could "review their files" as a starting point, he said.

I decided to look at the files now. I needed something to do. It had started to rain outside, the dry weather short-lived.

I took the five flights of stairs up to the attic. I had to hold on tight to the banister rail; the final stairs were so steep. I wondered whether Lucas's renovations would mean changes up here. I hoped not. I'd always thought it was the most magical part of the house.

It was still a mess, of course. There were still foxes, books and paperwork everywhere. All that was missing was the bed. Lucas now slept in one of the downstairs bedrooms. I wondered whether Henrietta had insisted.

The four files were on top of a pile of folders on the desk. Before I sat down to read them, I opened the skylight window and poked my head out, breathing in the cool London air, enjoying the feel of the light mist of rain on my face. I loved the view. It was nothing spectacular, but it was so typically London: rooftops, tips of trees, brickwork and chimneys. If I leaned out as far as possible, I could even get a glimpse of Hyde Park.

"Hello, little fellow," I said to the stuffed baby fox as I took a seat at the desk. He looked even worse for wear than he had all those years ago. I gave him a gentle pat. All the fox memorabilia I remembered from my first visit was still here—the paintings, the lampshade, the candlestick. I noticed two new items—an embroidered fox-design cushion and a small porcelain fox striking an inquiring pose. Gifts from Henrietta, I presumed. Lucas had told me she was the reason the baby fox I'd tried to liberate was so precious. It was the first gift she'd given him.

I opened the files and started to read. All the information was perfectly ordered—photograph, brief biography, academic record. I shouldn't have been surprised. Young academics applying for a position like this would be sure to present themselves as impressively as possible.

I made notes as I read through the files. Forty minutes later, I was finished. I'd written four lines.

Mark, 27, maths, Brighton

Harry, 28, science, Liverpool

Peggy, 28, English literature, Newcastle

Darin, 29, languages, born Iran, raised Devon

That was it. Some detective I was. I'd gleaned basic facts and nothing more. I may as well have gone "eeny-meenymineymo" to pick my thief.

I had a moment of feeling as though I were outside myself, looking down. What was I doing, sitting up here in Lucas's attic, reading private information about four strangers, seriously considering a job like this? I could say no, of course. I knew that. I could say, I'm very sorry, Lucas; thank you for the job offer but I need to leave again.

But where would I go next? What could I do? Lucas's invitation to visit him had come at exactly the right time. I had started to feel unsettled in Western Australia. The long hours and hard work there were all I'd needed in the beginning, but recently something had changed. I'd felt a restlessness. A yearning. A subtle shift in how I was feeling.

I thought, as I had many times, of the counselor explaining the stages of grief to me. I'd had to leave, midway through our second session. I couldn't believe she was telling me that what I was feeling was something ordinary. That every single person who lost someone they loved, after an illness, in an accident, or to old age, went through exactly the same phases. It seemed impossible, I'd said to her. How could she compare what I was experiencing, this chasm, this ache, this roaring pain, to the grief someone might feel after their elderly father died, or their grandmother, after long lives, after the privilege of years with their families?

She kept her voice calm.

"It's not a grief contest, Ella. I'm not saying one is worse than the other. You've misunderstood me. What I'm saying is you all go through similar feelings, of shock and denial and—"

"Who died for you?" Afterward, I'd felt ashamed of my rudeness.

"This isn't about me, Ella. I haven't been in your situation, but—"

"Then you can't know how I feel. You can't help me. I'm sorry, but you can't." I picked up my bag.

"Ella, please—"

The words burst out of me. "My son, Felix, was just twenty months old. His whole life was ahead of him. He could have been anything, done everything. He would have had the most wonderful, joyful, action-packed, glorious life, if my half sister, if my husband hadn't—"

"Ella, sit down again, please. You must move beyond the blame. You're not only hurting yourself through your anger; you're hurting—"

I didn't hear the rest. I left and I didn't return. She was wrong; I knew that. There are no stages to grief. It's just an all-encompassing, constant, complete, irreversible feeling. It's there the moment you wake and there, right beside you, as you try to sleep. It's like being soaked in hurt and pain and sorrow, as if you have been steeped in it for days, weeks and months, so that it has infiltrated every inch of your skin, into your bones, your blood. Grief becomes you. You become the grief. That was what the counselor didn't know. I couldn't move beyond it because I had become it. All I could do now, all I had been trying to do since that day, was live with it. Live without Felix.

I don't know how much time passed, whether I sat crying at Lucas's desk for minutes or closer to an hour. I began to notice the scratching of birds' feet on the roof above me. I heard the faint sound of traffic through the open window. I felt exhausted, as I always did after tears, my chest aching, my heart aching, but even as I sat there, at Lucas's desk, trying to breathe properly, focusing on my inhalation, my exhalation, trying all the tricks I'd learned, I slowly became aware of a new feeling somewhere deep inside me. An unaccustomed one.

I felt safe.

Safer than I had felt for months. As if perhaps I could let my guard down in this house, in London, with Lucas. As if I could breathe more freely here. As if I could stay here, even for a little while.

"Stay for as long as you need, Ella," Lucas had said. "Whether you take the job or not."

If I did say yes, the job would take up thinking time. It would give me something to do. That was what I needed more than anything, every minute of every day and every night. Something to do. Something to stop me dwelling on things I couldn't bear to think about.

I opened the folders again, leafing through the pages on the tutors, trying to make a decision. If I didn't take the job, what would I do? Stay in London for a week or two? Or go back home to Australia? I imagined being back in Melbourne. I pictured visiting Mum and Walter in their new, large South Yarra house, hearing about their busy lives, the TV show, the interviews, the media attention. Mum pretending it drove her crazy, when she adored every minute of it. And before long, I knew, they'd talk about Jess, how well she was doing, what a big star she was becoming—

I couldn't hear about Jess.

Could I go somewhere else in Australia? Back to Canberra? Never. Sydney? No. Aidan was in Sydney now. He'd moved there from Canberra, after getting a job as a translator with SBS, the multicultural TV station. Charlie had told me. Charlie had sent me regular updates on him, and on Jess, until I'd asked him to stop. He hadn't been happy about it, even when I did my best to explain why. I couldn't hear about either of them. I couldn't hear that they were back at work again, leading normal lives. In Jess's case, getting more and more famous every week. I couldn't hear that they had somehow managed to piece their lives back together, rebuild, reinvent themselves. I couldn't understand how it was possible.

"Just talk to them," Charlie had begged once during one of our phone calls. In the early days, after he'd returned home from Felix's funeral, he'd rung from Boston nearly every day. I couldn't have done without his calls, but I didn't always like what he had to say. "Please, Ella. Even just speak to Jess on the phone, if it's too much to see her. She needs to talk to you."

"I can't, Charlie. I'm sorry, but I can't."

"Is this to punish her even more? You don't think she's punishing herself already?"

I didn't reply. I heard him sigh down the phone. A moment's pause, then he tried again.

"Then you have to talk to Aidan at least. You can't just leave it with him the way you did, walking out on him like that, out of the blue. You're torturing him."

"I didn't walk out. I had to leave, Charlie. He knows why. You know why."

"He was Felix's father. He loved him as much as you did. Please, just see him, talk to him—"

I couldn't. I couldn't see him or talk to him again. The more time passed, the more sure of that fact I was. "Has he asked you to call me?"

"Yes, of course he has. He's tried every way he can to get in touch with you. Because you've refused to answer any of his phone calls or letters or e-mail."

I stayed quiet again.

"Ella, please, for my sake if not his. He's not just your husband. He's my friend. It's killing me to see what's happened to you both."

His poor choice of word hung between us. I let it go. "I can't, Charlie. I'm sorry."

Over the following months, Charlie kept trying. Eventually, he stopped. He told me he wasn't happy about it, but that he wouldn't let me lock him out as well as everyone else.

That hurt. I wasn't deliberately locking anyone out. I had no choice. Surely he could see that.

Charlie stopped mentioning Aidan but the e-mail messages kept coming. So did his letters. I didn't open them. I didn't need to. I knew what they said. *Please, Ella, talk to me.* But I couldn't.

Before it happened, Aidan and I could talk for hours. We did talk for hours. After it happened, after the first few days, after the shock and the tears, after the funeral, I made him tell me, again and again, in minute detail, over and over, exactly what had happened. I had to hear it until it felt as though I'd been there myself.

With every cell in my body, I wanted to have been there myself. All I wanted, all I craved, was to somehow change the ending to the story, to stop it happening, to be there close enough to call out at the split second that Felix started to fall, "Jess, catch him!" And she would somehow hear me and she would turn in time, drop the phone and with lightning speed reach out with both hands to grab hold of Felix. "Got you!" she'd say, and he would give that little gasp he gave when he'd had a bit of a fright. Jess's eyes would open wide and she'd hold him tight and give a shaky laugh and say, "Wow, that was close!" And she'd put him carefully, gently, onto the ground, and lean and kiss his forehead or the top of his glossy black head. Or ruffle his hair, like I loved to do. Then they would walk home to the apartment, hand in hand, and she would make him a drink. Less than an hour later, Walter and Mum would get there too, and shower him with presents, and exclaim how big he'd grown in just a month or two, and wasn't his voice beautiful. Were they imagining it or did he have a bit of an Irish accent? And then Aidan would arrive back from the trade talks, and be just changing out of his suit and pouring a drink for everyone when I got home from my day in town, so relaxed, my face shining from the unexpected, wonderful facial, my body supple from the massage. As soon as he heard the door open, Felix would run to me, his arms up in the air, urging me to pick him up, shouting, "I'm Felix O'Hanlon!" in toddler-speak. We'd all laugh. I'd look around the crowded living room. "What a surprise. I thought we were meeting at the hotel!" I'd be so relaxed that Jess and I would quickly forget the argument we'd had last time she'd visited and then the six of us would go on to have a great night out together for Walter's birthday, before Aidan and I brought Felix home, still awake but falling asleep in our arms, and we'd put him to bed and then pour ourselves a drink, and talk about his work and my day and how lucky it was that Jess was able to step in to babysit, and we'd discuss the night we'd had and marvel again at Mum's growing fame, perhaps even laugh that she'd been asked for autographs twice that night in the restaurant—who would ever have believed it?—and then we'd check that Felix was fast asleep and go to bed ourselves and we would all live happily ever after.

But that was not what happened. There was no happy ending. No matter how many times I collected the details from Aidan, in fragments, tiny pieces of the puzzle, putting them together until I could replay the whole scene in the park as though I had been there, watching it unfold, I could never change it. I could never prevent it from happening.

"It was instant, Ella. He died instantly."

Aidan was wrong. The coroner's report gave me all the detail I would ever want, detail I never wanted to read again. I learned terms I still wish I didn't know. Medical names for the delicate bones in a twenty-month-old boy's skull. The injuries caused when stone meets twenty-month-old bone and skin and blood vessels and nerve endings. It wasn't instant. It took several minutes.

What did my baby feel during those minutes? Agony? Shock? Fear? Were my Felix's last moments on earth filled with the worst pain he'd ever felt? Did his life flash past him? How could it? How could it, when he'd only had such a short life, had only started his life? And I wasn't there. My baby was dying, there in the sun, on the ground, and I wasn't there. I wasn't there.

It's not just Jess and Aidan I can't forgive. I can't forgive myself.

Aidan knows how I feel. In the days before I left, I said it to him. I'm sure I said it to him. All we did was say the same things over and again, relive what had happened. It was all there was to talk about and we talked about it until we were hollowed by the words, until our apartment felt full of our own grief, the blame, the guilt, as if our pain had pushed out all the air.

I said it all to him in my note. *We can't stay together after what's happened. Good-bye.* They were the hardest and the easiest words I had ever written. They were the truth. I couldn't help him any more than he could help me.

He wouldn't accept it, though. After I left Canberra, I moved to Melbourne for a few months and then up to Sydney. It was before he moved there. I picked up any work I could, cleaning, waitressing. I didn't care what I did. I just had to keep moving. One Saturday, about four months after we had last spoken, after I'd done all I could to ignore the letters and e-mail from him, I had what I can only describe as a premonition. A feeling that Aidan was near.

I was living and working in Banksia, an outer suburb, beyond the airport, far from the harbor or the fashionable inner-city suburbs. I barely noticed my surroundings. All I did was work, walk and sleep, moving between the restaurant I worked in and my cheap flat. I'd asked Charlie not to give Aidan my new address. He didn't. He gave him the address of the restaurant instead.

That Saturday, one of the other waitresses and I were setting the tables for a birthday lunch when I suddenly felt that Aidan was nearby. I still can't explain how I knew. I put down the tray of cutlery, walked across to the large front window and peered through the wooden blinds. He was standing across the street, looking down at his phone. He was rereading the message from Charlie, I guessed afterward. The message with the address. I felt a rush of anger at Charlie, panic about seeing Aidan, then sudden anger at him too for finding me. As I watched, he put his phone into his pocket and started to cross the road.

I ran away. I'm not proud of it, but I had to. I didn't want there to be a scene. I didn't want my employers and colleagues to know anything about me, or my life before I'd started working there. I went out through the kitchen, out the back door, through the yard past the rubbish bins, out the creaking gate, and I ran, down the alleys, down the suburban streets and past a football oval. I didn't stop until I was more than a kilometer away. I wasn't sure where I was but it didn't matter. After catching my breath, after making sure my voice sounded as normal as possible, I took out my phone and dialed the restaurant. The other waitress answered. I got in first. "Mandy, it's Ella. Don't say my name. He can't know it's me. Is he still there?"

There was a cautious "Yes."

"Please, Mandy, help me. Can you talk without him hearing?"

There was a pause before she spoke in a formal voice. "I think so. I'll check in the kitchen for you." A moment later she spoke again in her normal tone. "Ella, what's going on? Who is he? He said he's not leaving until he talks to you. He says he's your husband."

I thought quickly. "Of course he's not my husband. He's an ex-boyfriend. I broke up with him a year ago and he's been stalking me ever since. Mandy, please tell him I've gone home sick. Tell him I've left for the day and you don't know how long I'll be off work."

"He doesn't seem like a stalker. He just seems very upset."

"Please, Mandy. I'll owe you."

She sighed and then told me she'd ring me back once he'd left.

Nearly an hour passed before she rang. I waited another hour before I returned to the restaurant. The birthday lunch was in full swing. Mandy wasn't happy. While we were cleaning up afterward, I invented an elaborate story. Aidan hadn't said much to her, thankfully. I told her that I'd broken up with him but he wouldn't accept it. I'd moved three times, and he'd managed to find me every time.

"You should call the police, Ella. If it's been that bad, you really should report him."

"I will when I get home," I said. Then I couldn't help myself. "How was he?"

"How was he?" She stared at me.

"I just meant, how did he seem to you?"

"Honestly?" she asked.

I nodded.

"Gorgeous," she said with a sudden grin. "Great accent. Beautiful eyes. If you don't want him, can I have him? He can stalk me anytime he wants."

I resigned the next day. Two weeks later I heard about the winery job in Western Australia. I was there a month before I told Charlie I'd left Sydney. I made him promise not to give Aidan the name of the winery, or even tell him I was now in Western Australia. Reluctantly, eventually, and only after another spirited exchange of e-mail, Charlie agreed. But he wasn't happy with me.

Neither was my mother. "You have to help us to help you, Ella, please," she'd said during one phone call. "You can't keep running away from everyone, not just Aidan and Jess, but the whole situation."

The whole "situation"? It wasn't a "situation." It was my life now. She didn't understand, I realized. I wasn't running away from anything. Everywhere I went, my pain came too.

Her voice softened. "Darling, please, talk to us. We have to get through this together. I was talking to Dr. Rob today. You know, the TV psychiatrist. I don't know if you've ever seen him. He has a slot on the network's chat show. People ring in with their problems and he's so lovely and so knowledgeable. . . . Anyway, I told him all about what had happened and he was so sad for us, and so sympathetic, and he said that what you need to do is—"

I didn't hear the rest. I said I was sorry, that I had to go. I said good-bye and I hung up.

Mum didn't leave it at that. She wrote to me, on her personalized *MerryMakers: Eat, drink and be merry!* letterhead.

Dear Ella,

I'm so sad that you won't answer my calls at the moment. I know you don't want to hear what I need to say, and I also don't know how much of this you will read, so I'll get to the point quickly. You are not alone. We all loved Felix so much. You lost your darling son but we lost our beautiful grandson, Jess lost her beloved nephew. I can't even begin to imagine the pain Aidan is feeling too. We could all see how much he adored Felix and how much he adored you as well. I know how you must be feeling, Ella. But we saw Aidan last week and I am not exaggerating when I say that all that has happened, not to mention all that has happened since with you and him, is destroying him.

My editor's trained eye wanted to underline or delete the word *destroying.* I imagined my comment beside it. *Too dramatic?* As for her phrase *I am not exaggerating* . . . My mother loved to exaggerate. It was part of her lively personality, but also what made her so difficult sometimes. It was no coincidence that Jess was theatrical, attention seeking—

the apple hadn't fallen far from the tree. Lucas had always said, with some relief I thought, that I was made up of more Fox genes than Mum's genes, that I reminded him very much of my father. I loved—I love—my mother. I do. But I've learned that loving someone doesn't mean always liking them.

I stopped reading her letter at that point. I kept thinking about it afterward, though. About being a mother, about being her daughter. I didn't want to cause her any more pain. So even when it was hard, I stayed in touch with her and Walter. I e-mailed rather than phoned. She'd have preferred long chatty phone calls, I know, but I needed some distance. I received long chatty e-mail in return from her, full of every detail of her home and working life and links to all the *MerryMakers* programs.

Sometimes, when I can't sleep, I watch them. Mum is great on-camera, natural and funny. The talent scouts in the shopping center unearthed a rough diamond and polished her until she shone. As she cooks, she jokes and flirts down the camera lens. She cracks the corniest of food puns, laughs more than the canned laughter, sings when the mood takes her, teases Walter—who never appears on-camera but is always just off set, a character on the show himself. She cooks three dishes per show. They mostly work but sometimes don't, adding to the comedy. "Whoops!" she'll laugh. "Looks like it's takeaway pizza again tonight, Walter! Good thing I have other charms!" Cue more canned laughter. Each show runs for thirty minutes, but I never watch to the end. Jess always appears in the final five minutes.

As I sat there in the attic, three stories above a London

street, the skylight now dotted with raindrops, the sound of sirens mingling with the birdsong, I realized something. My relationship with my family—with Mum, Walter and Charlie, at least—was now a virtual one, conducted via e-mail, text messages and the Internet. That wouldn't change, whether I lived in Australia or London. I no longer had any close friends back home. My former colleagues in publishing had tried their best, but one by one they'd faded away. I couldn't blame them. I hadn't made friends in any of my new workplaces. Again, no one's fault but mine.

I closed the four files and only then noticed a note from Lucas on the top one. *Dear E, Please file back in the drawer when you've read. L*

I was surprised once again by his sense of order. The true academic in him, I suppose. On the surface all mess and chaos, but underneath, a mind so sharp, able to sift through historical facts, make connections between the past and the present, make sense of the world.

There were four filing cabinets pushed against the sloping wall of the attic, each with four drawers. It took me three attempts to find the right one. Lucas's sense of order hadn't gone so far as to writing *Tutors' Records* on a label on the front. It was more organized inside, the sections divided neatly into years. I slipped my four into the front section. I'd just pushed the drawer shut when something made me open it again, and flick through the yearly sections, going back in time: 2011, 2010, 2009, 2008, 2007. . . .

I stopped there: 2007. The year Aidan applied to be one of Lucas's tutors.

Don't look.

Over the past year or more, I'd become skilled at blocking voices from my head. I did it now. I took out the folder from 2007 and returned to the desk. I leafed through the files, recognizing the names of the other tutors, until there it was. A file marked Aidan O'Hanlon.

Don't.

I justified it by saying there'd be nothing in there I didn't already know. I'd already seen what Lucas kept in these files—basic information, an academic record, a photograph. It was hardly worth reading, probably. I already knew Aidan's academic record, knew where he was from. I'd stayed in his family home, met his parents, his brother. I already knew that he could speak six languages, that he held three degrees—

His photograph was clipped to the front page. Aidan five years earlier, aged thirty-one. His hair was jet-black. His eyes that unusual blue-green, blue in sunlight, green in winter. He wasn't smiling in the photo. He never smiled in photos, not even in our wedding photo. He had a gap in his bottom teeth, a gap I'd loved, but he was self-conscious about it. His older brother had teased him about it, he'd told me. I had loved the way lines appeared around his eyes when he was amused by something, the way his eyes lit up, but he smiled properly only when his guard was down. It meant people thought he was a solemn, serious person when he was far from it.

I moved the photo to one side. Underneath was his application letter to Lucas, outlining why he needed the year's free accommodation, what skill he would bring to the team of tutors, what he planned to research in the time there.

I knew it all already. Aidan hadn't come from a wealthy background. He'd got a scholarship to Trinity College, Dublin, and then worked to support himself during his subsequent language studies in London. He'd been a barman, a cleaner, a hospital orderly, a car-park attendant, all sorts of jobs that bought him more study time. He hadn't hated or resented any of them. He'd gathered stories from each position—of funny colleagues, customers, patients. Even after four years together, he'd still sometimes surprise me with an anecdote from one of his jobs.

I kept reading, ignoring the voice inside my mind telling me to stop. I came to the section where he summarized his skills and suitability for a place in Lucas's house, with Lucas's tutors.

Language is everything, to us all. Our emotions, our thoughts, our hopes, our dreams, our worries all need words to become real. I come from a country with two languages, but that isn't enough for me. I wish I'd lived in Babel and could speak all the tongues in the world. If ever I couldn't find the exact word I needed in English, I could pause, think and find it, in Italian, French, Spanish, Arabic. . . . I already speak four languages fluently (Irish, English, French, Italian) and am learning two more (Spanish, German) but they will never be enough. I want to keep learning. I want to share all I've learned, inspire others as my own teachers inspired me, teach as I've been taught, with passion, enthusiasm, humor and love for my subject. I want to make connections through words and language. Without communication, we all

*fall silent. With it, there are no limits to what we can
express or what we can achieve.*

It took me a moment to realize my eyes had filled with
tears again. As I'd read his words, I'd heard Aidan's voice,
his soft accent, his passion for languages. He'd told the truth
in his letter to Lucas. English hadn't been enough for him.
He admired foreign words like other men admired cars,
watches. Even in Canberra, where his work often revolved
around long-winded diplomatic or trade discussions where
the aim was to not say very much at all while appearing to
say a lot, he'd return home each night with a new jewel to
share with me. A word he'd heard that day for the first time,
or a piece of slang or an unusual colloquial phrase. He wasn't
just a translator and interpreter. He was a word collector.

I turned the page. His academic record was listed, his
many years of study reduced to one page. The paper he'd
researched while he was living at Lucas's house was a study
of the English language during wartime. He wanted to find
out if language changed under times of great stress, during
war and depression. He focused on Britain during WWII,
watching hours of news footage, listening to radio recordings of interviews with soldiers, bystanders to bombings,
families in London and families in the rural, safer areas. His
bedroom was his study, and resembled a war museum when
I first met him. Before I'd learned what the subject of his
study was, I was worried he was a military buff, the kind of
man who spent his weekends building model aircraft. He'd
laughed when I admitted my fears, months later.

It fascinated me that he'd chosen to study something so

British. I knew some of Ireland's past when we met, courtesy of a book I'd edited on Irish-Australian history. The author was a fervent republican and spent many of our meetings trying to persuade me to his way of thinking. I had to become an expert on both sides of the Troubles to hold my own and bring balance to his book.

"It's the first step in bringing down the enemy," Aidan had said when I asked him about it. "Learn everything you can about them. Then infiltrate. I'm at the infiltration stage."

I hadn't been sure if he was joking. Especially after I met his father for the first time and put my foot in it politically. It wasn't just my first time meeting his family, but my first time in Ireland. It couldn't have gone worse, from the moment we arrived and I made the mistake of asking—

Clang.

It was the front door. The fox door knocker was loose and banged when the door opened, like a special fox bell. I wondered which of the tutors I was about to meet. I moved quietly down the stairs, listening, then relaxed. It was Lucas. I knew his footsteps. He'd have been out for his post-lunch walk in Hyde Park and Kensington Gardens. It was his thinking time, he'd told me years earlier. He'd walk briskly for an hour, mulling over his latest research, then come home, go straight into his withdrawing room and make notes of everything that had occurred to him. Then he'd brew a large pot of coffee, gather a handful of biscuits and return to his room to spend the rest of the day writing.

When he appeared in the kitchen twenty minutes later, I had the tray of coffee and biscuits ready.

"Ella! I'd almost forgotten you were here."

I smiled. "No, you hadn't."

"Well?"

We both knew what he was asking. Would I accept his job offer?

"Yes, please," I said.

EIGHT

From: Charlie Baum

To: undisclosed recipients

Subject: It's Been a Noisy Week in Boston

The latest report from the Baum trenches is as follows:

Sophie (now 11): Gala birthday party ended in tears. Mine. Don't children realize how long it takes to get food-coloring stains out of a carpet??

Ed (8): This morning he asked Lucy and me if we thought he should grow a beard. Not just yet, we advised.

Reilly (6): Battle continues to get him to eat anything but sausages. (It's his unhealthy German blood, I tell Lucy. What can we do? Lucy not amused. That's her healthy American blood.) In attempt to smuggle vitamins into him, I bought dried fruit biscuits. Looked like bird food, had to be good for him, surely? He had a tiny bite of one, then offered it back to me. My face crumpled in defeat (and fear. Lucy was due home soon—I needed to hide the biscuits *and* the sausages). He gave me a loving yet pitying smile. "They're nice, Dad. Really nice. I just NEVER want to have them EVER again, okay?"

Tim (4): Accompanied me on late-night car trip to supermarket. On way back, coming down a hill, the city spread out before us, lights on buildings, roadways, signs, etc. From his chair in the backseat, I heard a sigh.

"Okay, Timmy?" I asked.

"It's all so beautiful," he said.

He was right. It was.

Lucy (36): Still juggling work, overtime and study. Still tired but still happy. I hope. Constantly.

Charlie (36): Current weight ninety-five kilos plus a bit more. I blame the birthday cake. Not the one from the party, the trial one I made the day before. A disaster. I had to eat the evidence. All of it. On my own. At midnight. Delicious. Appearances aren't everything.

Snip the cat (kitten age): Sulking. I wouldn't give her any of the cake.

Until next time, everyone please stay sane.

Charlie xx

From: Charlie Baum
To: Lucy Baum
Subject: You

Here are five things I have noticed this week:

1. You are working too hard.

2. You are doing too much overtime.

3. You are studying too much.

4. You're not getting enough sleep.

5. I am missing you.

Forget the mortgage, the school fees, the medical bills. Let's take the kids out of school, you out of work. Let's go on the run, all six of us (okay, and Snip too). Let's forage for food and busk for cash. (I can see it now, the Family von Baum.) I'm only half joking.

Can you come home early tonight? Why, you ask?

6. We're all missing you.

Cxx

From: Charlie Baum
To: Ella O'Hanlon
Subject: re: You and flight

Dear Ellaborate,

Congratulations to you and Lucas on this crime-fighting partnership. Forget the Secret Seven and the Famous Five, here come the, um, Terrible Two? Please send updates. Write in code if needs be. W-ll th-y g- t- ja-l i- y-u c-tch th-m?

So good to know you're only across the pond now. Australia was too far away.

Charleston xx

From: Charlie Baum
To: Lucas Fox
Subject: A.O'H

Great news. Yes, meeting A on Tuesday. Will call or e-mail you asap afterward. Thanks again for all you're doing. C.

NINE

Dear Diary,
 Hi, it's Jess!

I'm all set! I'm leaving in three days!

I've already e-mailed all the London theater agents and have a long list of contacts to follow up. I've got all my press clippings. I've got references from my teachers. I've even downloaded a show reel onto my iPhone and I'm thinking about setting up my own YouTube channel!

I've Googled the UK weather and also all the main boutiques to see what the style is in London this time of year. It's supposed to be nearly spring there but compared to here it's COLD. And proper cold, not Melbourne-cold. But I double-checked the contents of my wardrobe against some of the other fashion sites and I think I will be right there with the look. Dad said he will give me a fashion allowance—he is SO sweet—but I said, maybe it's time we Melbourne girls taught the Londoners about real style! He's often said that if I wasn't going to be a musical theater star, I could probably be a fashion designer and I think he's right, but I'm going to give it my best shot in the West End and if it doesn't work out—no, I can't think like that, my counselor says I have to stop any negative thoughts coming into my head, because thoughts come true and affect everything in your life so you have to stay positive and keep looking forward, not dwell on the past or on things that can't be changed no matter how much you want to change them. IT WILL WORK OUT.

SO!!!! My big decision now is which of my audition pieces I want to rehearse before I leave. I talked to my teacher today and she lived in London for a bit in the nineties (ancient times!!) and she said that I have a great chance there on account of my special talents, but she does say that about everyone. Still, Mum and Dad say that I have the extra something onstage that makes people want to look at me!!! The other students are a bit jealous, I know, because I also have the extra profile from being on TV with Mum. Sometimes after our concerts, everyone else just stands around while I'm there signing autographs—for the little kids especially, or sometimes their mums or a couple of times their dads. (But between you and me, Diary, the dads can be a bit creepy. One of them said, "If I put my phone number there, would you ring me?" "Why would I ring you?" I said. I really didn't get it. "Ring me and you'll find out," he said, and he gave me THE creepiest wink. I was glad when Mum came up then. She flirted with him a bit but she does with everyone, I know it's part of her act, and then luckily Dad came up too and I was actually glad to leave.)

I broke up with my boyfriend today. Well, he wasn't really my boyfriend. We'd been out a few times and he was nice, but mostly he liked going out with me so he could tell his friends he was going out with me. I'm not being a victim here or being bigheaded, that's just the truth of it. Mum has already given me a talking-to about "sharks" in London. She actually calls them sharks! "There are sharks out there, Jess, who would like to take advantage of a pretty girl like you." Before I knew it, I'd told her the truth: "Mum, they already have! I haven't exactly been a nun, even if I was taught by them for seven years!!!!!!"

Well, that unleashed a hornet's nest, or whatever the saying is. Mum said, "Jess, I think we need to talk." So we did. I think she was actually a bit shocked to find out I'd had sex. (Mum, I'm nearly twenty-three. Get with the program!!) [Note to self—edit this from final autobiography?? Don't want to hurt Mum's feelings.] I did it for the first time when I was seventeen, ages ago now. I'd thought about it before-hand and he didn't put any pressure on me (not like Ten-nille's boyfriend who told everyone she was frigid until she would sleep with him). With us—I'll call him Mr. X (be-cause his name was Xavier, hahahaha!)—it was actually pretty romantic, especially compared to what I've heard some other girls say about their first time. He was more nervous than me, I think, till we got going.

The good thing was I've always felt pretty good about my body. You have to, if you're a dancer and looking at yourself in the mirror all the time, and the other thing was—this might sound a bit calculating—I really wanted to lose my virginity ASAP so I could play more roles. I could hardly audition for a sexy part in, like, *Chicago* or *West Side Story* if I'd never actually done it myself, could I?? I mean, of course I could, I'd act it, but I knew it would bring much more of a sense of authenticity to the role if I had actually experienced it. That's why some of the best actors in the world are old ladies like Judi Dench and Maggie Smith and Meryl Streep, my drama teacher said, because they have actually experienced life and so when they need to portray an emotion all they have to do is look back through their life to a time when they actually felt like that and just copy it! Acting is amazing! It helps of course if you like people looking at you, and I do, but I wouldn't be trying for a life on the stage as a career if I didn't think I was doing the best I could. This all hasn't been handed to me on a plate, either, no matter what some people might think. I've worked really hard for all the roles I've been given and I practice for hours every day and that's what's paying off for me now.

One of the girls at dance class was horrible today. "You're only going to London because your parents are rich and can afford it. It's nothing to do with talent." She just came up and said it to me. I couldn't believe it.

"I'll let the West End producers be the final judge of that, not you," I said, before I walked away haughtily. (I really did look haughty. I reenacted it in front of the mirror later!)

It's vicious in the theater world sometimes, it really is. I know onstage we all look like we're the best of friends and we're all smiles and dances and hugs and bows at the end of every show, but it can be really nasty and people who you think are your friends sometimes turn on you and say the meanest things about you. Last year, after Canberra, after I eventually came back to my classes, I didn't tell anyone about what had happened, but I found out a few weeks afterward that the head of the college had called everyone together to explain, and asked them to be understanding. And they were, most of them. At first, it made it worse. Everyone saying, "I'm so sorry, I'm sorry, Jess, you poor thing," and I couldn't stop myself, I kept saying, "It was an accident, it wasn't my fault, I didn't mean it to happen," and one girl said, "Of course it was an accident. Who would deliberately do something that horrible?" I took a couple of days off after that, and Mum went in to see the head again and it got a bit better then—no one talked about it at all and I was glad, I think. Except for one night when we were at a party to mark end of term and a few people were drinking, and this guy, he can be mean when he has too much to drink, he came up— and I think he used to have a bit of a crush on me, he asked me out a few times anyway and I always said no—and this night he came up and said, "You've had a pretty rough time this year, Jess," and I said, "Yes, I have," because that's one of the pieces of advice my counselor gave me as well, acknowledge what has happened, and that will help you accept it. So that's all I said to him. I thought he was being nice and sympathetic, but then he kept going on and on at me, and finally he said, "So what actually happened?"

"There was an accident," I said.

"But afterward, I mean. What did your sister say to you?"

I interrupted him there, and said, "She's my half sister." I still don't know why I had to say that. I think I just wanted to stop him saying what I knew he was going to say next.

He said, "Okay, what did your half sister say to you afterward?"

"What do you think she said?" I asked him, as calmly as I could. He wanted to upset me and I wouldn't let him. So I acted. I acted as hard as I could, pretending I wasn't bothered, trying to cover up how I actually felt, which was like crying and running out of there, but the others were looking over and whispering and I had an awful feeling someone had dared him to come over to talk to me to see if they could upset me.

Then he said, "She must really hate you."

I didn't even have to think about my reply to that. "Yes, she does."

He was a bit shocked at how cool I was being, I know. But it was easy. I was telling the truth. Ella does hate me.

He didn't stop there, though. "What about the baby's father? Does he hate you too?"

I couldn't handle any more. I told him to mind his own business. I went home early.

A week later, it all came up again. It was worse. I was in the toilet, in the cubicle, and two other girls came in and they were talking about me, saying that the gossip was I'd been having an affair with Aidan and that Ella had found out and there was a huge fight and I took their baby out in a jealous rage and—

I never knew that people could be so cruel, but they can.

I'll be glad to leave this place. Not just the college, but

Melbourne and Australia. It will do me good to have a fresh start in London. It's really exciting. Mum and I are going shopping for clothes tomorrow and tonight Dad and I are going to sit down with Google Earth and look at a few areas where I might be able to rent an apartment. He hasn't said yet that he will pay my rent while I'm in London but I have a Good Feeling that he might!! He's putting me up in a hotel first, just until I find my feet. He is so proud of me. He tells me all the time. It's SO sweet.

Time for my beauty sleep. Good night, Diary!!!

Jess xxxxoooo

TEN

I t was two degrees below freezing in Washington DC.

Aidan O'Hanlon turned up the collar of his coat as he walked out of the Washington Convention Center and up Seventh Street, avoiding a group of elderly Japanese tourists alighting from a bus. He'd been there a month, but the changeability of the weather from one day to the next still took him by surprise. Yesterday had been like Paris in the spring, the majestic buildings, boulevards and parks bathed in sunshine, the sidewalks a jostle of tourists and locals. Today the sky was slate gray, the wind like a blade, the mood on the streets brisk, not relaxed.

His head was aching, as much from the cold as from a long day of concentration. His new job in one of the city's largest translation agencies was well paid, but the hours were long. Since he'd arrived, he'd had to switch between

French, Spanish, Italian and German, interpreting for clients in conferences, trade meetings and media interviews, on subjects as diverse as cultural exchanges, import trade agreements and international road safety.

Today's client was from Milan, a representative of the Italian textile industry, in Washington to discuss tariffs and import regulations. After a successful day of negotiations, they'd gone for a drink. He'd realized midway through the first glass that the client, a woman in her late thirties, was interested in more than his language skills. He'd made his excuses and left.

It happened occasionally, not just to him, but to his colleagues too. There was something intimate about the interpreting process. Not during conference work, when it involved sitting in a booth above the conference room, providing simultaneous interpretation of the proceedings for the non-English-speaking delegates, who simply had to flick a switch on the desk in front of them to hear their own language. One-on-one interpreting like today involved hours of close contact with a client, working side by side, speaking softly into his or her ear, concentrating, listening, interpreting. Every word was important, finding the right meaning essential. There was no way of preparing beforehand either. He'd once spent a day with an Italian author on a promotional tour in the UK, the last-minute job a favor to another interpreter friend. He hadn't had time to read the book, a study of Renaissance poets, but for those eight hours and six interviews, he became an instant expert, translating thoughts and theories that the author had spent more than ten years researching. He'd forgotten it all within hours.

"You're like a butterfly," Ella had joked once. "Flitting from subject to subject, flower to flower."

Ella.

As always, his thoughts brought him back to Ella.

He kept walking until he was back at his apartment. It was small but comfortable, on the first floor of a house on P Street, near Logan Circle. He came in, threw his coat on the sofa, took off his tie, poured a beer. He lit a cigarette and slowly smoked it, standing out on the small balcony, shivering. He'd told the landlord he was a nonsmoker and he still thought of himself as one. This didn't count. It was a ritual, not a habit. There was a difference.

Afterward, he walked into the kitchen. The cupboards and the fridge were almost empty. There were too many restaurants nearby offering takeout. He already knew most of their menus by heart. He had a routine that he followed after work every night. One cigarette, one beer, dinner, an hour's writing, bed. It kept him calm. It was a way of getting through each day.

Picking up the phone to order, he noticed the light flashing on his answering machine. He wondered why the agency hadn't called him on his cell phone. Even his mother rang him on that number these days. He pressed the play button.

"Aidan, it's Lucas." A pause. "Lucas in London. Can you call me?"

It was about Ella. Something had happened to Ella. There was no other reason for Lucas to phone. Aidan reached for his address book and found Lucas's number. His hands were shaking. It took him two attempts to get the UK code right. Lucas answered on the third ring.

Aidan cut across him. "Lucas, it's Aidan. Is it Ella? Has something—"

"She's fine, Aidan. She's here with me."

"In London? She's in London?"

"She arrived three days ago. I've offered her a job and she's accepted."

"As your researcher? Your housekeeper?"

"A bit of both."

His heart rate began to slow. "And is she—" He tried again. "How is she?"

"She's fine." A pause. "No, she's not. She's just the same as you."

Aidan didn't reply. He had a thousand questions. He couldn't ask any of them.

Lucas lowered his voice. "Aidan, I know Charlie's been in touch with you. And that you're meeting up. He's going to make a suggestion, and I want to give you time to make up your mind. We both think you should come to London as soon as you can. While Ella is here."

"Lucas, I appreciate what you're both trying to do, but—"

"Think about it. Please. It might be different here, both of you away from—"

Aidan heard someone in the background. A woman. It was Ella. Ella had come into the room in London. She was a telephone line away. He could ask Lucas to hand over the phone. He could talk to her, say something to the real Ella, not the imaginary one he thought about every day—

Lucas spoke again. "Thank you for your call, but I'm not interested." His tone was formal, businesslike. The line cut out.

After a minute, Aidan put the phone back in its cradle. He changed his mind about ordering dinner. He wasn't hungry anymore. He stood for a moment, looking out the window. Then he went to his desk, opened his laptop and started writing.

ELEVEN

Dear Felix,

I miss you. You know that by now, but I want to say it again. I wish I didn't have to say it. Every day I wish everything was different. I wish I could change everything that happened.

There is no way any of us can make sense of this. There is no reason it happened. I know the circumstances—of course I know the circumstances—but it doesn't matter how many times I think it over. I cannot find a single reason to justify your being taken from our lives this soon. It was an accident. It was an accident. I hate the word accident more than I hate any word in the world.

The entire world could have continued as it was

with you in it. In the huge scheme of things, the great stage of the world, why did the universe, God, whoever is in charge, if there is anyone in charge, deem it necessary to take you out of the picture? What difference would it have made to the whole world to let you live? You weren't even two years old. I can't understand it. There are tyrants, thieves, crooks, murderers, wife-beaters, embezzlers and torturers allowed to walk on this earth every day and someone, somewhere, decides that they can keep living but that you can't. Felix, I can't bear it.

You didn't just live. You glowed. You glowed from the start to the finish of every day. There was a sparkle in your eye, a spark and a sparkle. You loved life. You did things with glee and joy. You brought glee and joy into our lives. You made us all laugh. You entertained us. You made us all realize that days can be hard but life is worth living, that the sound of a baby's laughter can feel like a big deep breath of the best air in the world.

We are all so sad. All of us. You leaving us—you being taken from us—has torn us all apart. I don't know if that will ever be fixed. How can it be, when you are gone? When each of us is hurting so much—in different ways but hurting from the same thing. Before this happened, I'd always thought something like this would bring people together, to grieve, to try to find a way of going on. Now I understand why it is the opposite. It hurts too much to be able to share it.

I miss you, Felix. I miss you every single day.

TWELVE

Since I'd got Charlie's e-mail mentioning the Famous Five and Secret Seven, I'd found myself thinking back to those detective books of my childhood. If memory served me right, the basic approach to solving a crime—in children's books at least—was to wear a disguise or hide in some bracken and wait for the suspect, or in my case suspects, to make an elementary mistake.

I wasn't sure if that would work in this instance. After three days in the house, I hadn't even met the four tutors. It didn't help that my sleep patterns were still disturbed from my flight. By the time I woke up each morning, they'd already left, a sink full of dishes the only sign they'd been there. Each night so far, they'd all been out until late, studying or tutoring, I presumed. From my bedroom, I'd hear them come in, hear murmured voices, but it didn't seem like the right time to get up and introduce myself. I finally decided the best way to meet was at a house dinner.

I'd knocked on Lucas's door the previous night. He was on the phone, but gestured for me to come in while he brought the conversation to an end.

"I do hate those cold calls," he said after he'd hung up. "Do they seriously think I'll agree to buy a new roof after one random conversation with a stranger?"

"You actually do need a new roof," I said. "I'm sure I heard water dripping last night."

"I'll add it to the list," he said. "So, Ella, how are your investigations going?"

Nowhere, I admitted. I mentioned my idea of a dinner. Lucas thought it was an excellent plan.

"What's the best way of asking them?" I asked. "Should I put notes under their doors? And do you know if any of them have any food allergies, or are vegetarians?"

To my amazement, he took out a smartphone and tapped out a message. Within two minutes, four messages came back. They were all free on Saturday and no, no allergies, no vegetarians.

"You don't have to look quite so shocked, Ella," Lucas said. "I can turn on a TV too."

On my way out, I stopped. "Lucas, your tutors . . . do they know about—"

"They know you're my niece. That you worked as an editor. That's all they needed to know."

I took my time planning the dinner. I spent Saturday shopping, cleaning and preparing the three courses: mushroom and herb soup, roast chicken with a complicated potato gratin and four other vegetable side dishes, and a twice-cooked chocolate pudding. As dusk fell, I set the table in the dining room. I lit the fire and a row of candles, set out Lucas's best china, opened bottles of wine and polished glasses. By ten to seven the room was quiet and ready, the aroma of cooking drifting across from the kitchen. By two minutes past seven, everyone was there. Lucas's tutors were not only clever but punctual.

Lucas made the introductions. "This is Ella, your new overlord, cook and housekeeper. If there's no food in the house from now on, blame her, not me."

"No more cornflakes for dinner?" the pink-haired girl said. "Three cheers for Ella!"

As I was introduced, I mentally paired each of them with their CVs. Peggy with the pink hair—the literature student from Newcastle. Harry, tall and skinny—the scientist from Liverpool. Darin, handsome, short, originally from Iran—languages. Mark, stocky, freckles and glasses—the mathematician from Brighton.

Over the next half hour, I did my best to make small talk as I topped up their predinner drinks. Lucas being there helped. It almost felt normal. I realized I'd forgotten how enjoyable it was to be in a big warm room, surrounded by the hum of conversation, wine flowing, the prospect of dinner ahead. I'd been a waitress in restaurants night after night, of course, but this was different.

At seven thirty, everyone took their seats at the long table. I brought in the first course of soup. I'd turned down all their offers of help.

"I could get used to this," Harry said.

"I already have," Mark said, shaking out his napkin.

As they ate, they talked and teased one another, and Lucas too. It was clear they had a good relationship with him. The conversation flowed around me, a discussion about a current political scandal, Britain's stance on the EU, their opinions informed and lively. I stayed quiet, watching and listening. They didn't look like thieves or criminals. They looked like exactly what they were—bright, intelligent students enjoying dinner together.

"Enough idle talk about current affairs," Lucas said, after I'd collected six soup bowls and five sets of compliments. "Why don't you all tell Ella a little about yourselves?"

"Through the medium of song?" asked Darin, the language tutor. "Let me fetch my lute."

Peggy, seated beside him, grinned. "I'll start. I'm from Newcastle, Ella, hence the amusing accent. My interests are cats, jigsaw puzzles and saving the world. When I grow up, I want to marry a footballer and never work again."

"She's lying about the footballer," Harry, the scientist from Liverpool, said. "She couldn't name a sports team if you put a starter's gun to her head. I'm the sports fan, Ella. I have a thirty-five-run average at cricket, a phenomenal memory for rugby statistics and a charming disposition."

Mark was next. "I'm an only child, a solitary being. I wander lonely as a cloud. I'm from Brighton, in the county of East Sussex. Chief attractions, a burned-out pier and a stony beach. I thoroughly recommend it for a day trip. Just be sure to buy a return ticket."

"You're sure I can't fetch my lute?" Darin said. "I'll keep it short. Ten verses max."

"Ten verses too long, Darin," Peggy said. "Your turn, Ella."

"Ella's on duty," Lucas said smoothly. "If we distract her, we'll never get our dinner."

Over the main course, they switched from scientific discussions to Greek history to Shakespearean quotes to the latest YouTube pop sensation. Perhaps they were putting it on for me, but it was like tuning into a lively radio program, all wit, banter and intelligence. I had to force myself to remember why I was here: not to enjoy their company and conversation, but to try to catch one of them out.

As I served coffee, the subject moved to their students. Not the bright, high-achieving ones. The others. Lucas had told me he insisted on confidentiality outside the house. Many of the students were the children of well-known people, after all. But here in the privacy of the dining room, it was clearly open season.

I heard about Cassandra, a fourteen-year-old student being tutored by Mark for her maths and by Darin for Spanish and Italian. She was being difficult again, they reported to Lucas. Her father—a rock star, I gathered—hadn't been home for a week and it wasn't because he was on tour. Her mother had taken to her bed, spending most of the day sleeping or smoking dope. Cassandra was texting her way through her lessons, if she deigned to turn up at all. Lucas asked questions and made notes.

Harry spoke about another student, the teenage son of a merchant banker, who had failed his most recent exams again, despite extra coaching from himself, Peggy and Darin.

"I've done all I can, Lucas," Harry said, "but the fact remains. He's thick as a plank."

"We don't use terms like that in this house," Lucas said.

"I'm sorry, but it's true, Lucas," Peggy said. "I've tried every trick I could think of to coach him through *Hamlet* but nothing seems to stick."

"He's not thick," Darin said. "He's spoiled and lazy. He told me there's no point in him studying or going to university. His father will get him a job, degree or no degree."

"That new student in Mayfair is the same," Peggy said. "I did three extra sessions with her this week, Lucas, as you suggested, but it's like pushing a boulder uphill. I know her father has won the Booker or the Pulitzer, but the sad truth is she can't string two words together. She can barely spell. She's not interested either. All she wants to do is work with horses."

"Keep at it for now," Lucas said. "I'll ask Henrietta to do another appraisal."

"It'll take more than Henrietta to fix her," Peggy said. "It doesn't help that her father is *obsessed* with her going to Cambridge. If he tells me one more time that he had the best years of his life there, I'll—"

"Tell him you went to Oxford?" Harry said.

They all laughed. I saw Lucas make another note.

After coffee, they left for their rooms. They'd offered to help tidy up, but I insisted I was happy to do it all myself. The ground floor was soon quiet again. In the kitchen on my own, I was the noisy one, working my way through the dishes. I wondered whether a dishwasher featured in Lucas's renovation plans.

As I worked, I tried to imagine one of them stealing from their clients. I couldn't. They all seemed too straightforward.

Fun, clever. Of course, they'd shown me their best sides, kept any secrets to themselves. Didn't we all? Wasn't that self-preservation? I'd done the same thing myself tonight. Pretended. Smiled, asked questions, even laughed. I realized it was the closest I'd come to feeling normal, to behaving like a normal person, in twenty months.

What if I had told them my story? What would have happened to the relaxed evening? It would have changed everything. Not just the mood in the room, but the way they treated me from then on. I knew that from experience. It was one of the many reasons I kept to myself. No one knew how to handle someone with a story like mine. I made people uncomfortable. Uneasy. I understood. Before it had happened, I wouldn't have known what to say to people like me either.

I had a sudden memory of a grief clinic I'd gone to in Melbourne, after seeing an ad for it in my local community newspaper. One-on-one counseling hadn't helped me. Perhaps this would. It was held in a room in my local library in St. Kilda. When I first walked in, I thought I'd come to the wrong place, to a book club or a music appreciation class. Everyone there looked so normal. I'd had a bad few days. It had been hard enough leaving my flat that night, let alone putting on makeup.

I stopped in the doorway. "Excuse me, but is this the—"

"Sad Room?" an old man said. They all laughed. I nearly left then.

"Come in," another said. "Make yourself at home."

They took turns sharing their stories. One after another. It was a room of pain. I stayed for the entire meeting but I didn't speak. I was already too raw. I couldn't bear to hear that so many other people were in agony too. I didn't go again.

I used to be fun. I know that's like someone describing themselves as edgy or zany. As Charlie said once, if you have to think about being cool, then you're not cool. But I used to be a happy person. I loved life. I loved Aidan and my work and our life together and our apartment, and most of all, I loved Felix. Life wasn't perfect, of course. I didn't live in a fairy tale. Aidan and I got on very well, but we did have disagreements, like any couple juggling two careers and the care of a young child. We'd argue over who was doing the most housework, whose turn it was to do the shopping, whose turn it was to get to sleep in. But our arguments didn't last long. They were passing clouds on our generally blue sky. I still thought the world was fair. I thought that if I was kind and polite, let strangers go in front of me in queues, indicated while driving and followed the rules of modern living and etiquette, only good things would happen to me. But now I know that's not true. There are no safety nets, barriers or rules. I had just been lucky. And my luck had run out.

In the first year after Felix died, all I could see were the sadnesses and injustices of the world. Not only the massive events—the tsunamis, the earthquakes, the wars and the uprisings—though they made me cry, night after night in front of the TV. The small tragedies around me broke my heart too. The sight of lonely old people. Homeless people. Drug addicts. People in hospitals. One day, out shopping, I saw an old lady pushing her elderly husband in a wheelchair. She was trying to carry a large bag of groceries and push him at the same time. I wanted to help. I even took a step toward them but then I became too overwhelmed. What good would it do? What difference would I possibly make to their lives? What was the point in even trying? Another day, I overheard a young woman on the phone. She was on her own with a baby. I didn't envy her the baby. I only wanted Felix. But I heard her fighting with the child's father and she was so upset and angry, and the baby was crying, and all I could think of was the hardship ahead for her, for the three of them.

Standing at the sink, I felt the sadness descend again. The good mood from dinner faded, like color turning to black and white in my mind. Again, all I could think of was life's dark side. The pointlessness of all we did, all our plans, our hopes. Why did any of us even bother, when in one instant, one second, it could all be taken away from us—

Stop! Stop thinking that way. Stay busy.

I decided to clean out the kitchen cupboards. They were filthy. There were more than a dozen around the room, some reaching from floor to ceiling. Some of the doors could barely close, the cupboards were so overcrowded. They probably hadn't been tidied, let alone cleaned, since I lived here last. It was suddenly very important that I start on them right away.

I was still at it two hours later when Lucas came in to say good night. I was on my knees, reaching into the tallest of the store cupboards, trying to scrape something off the back wall. It looked like spilled treacle.

He stood and watched me for a moment. "You do know it's after midnight?"

I nodded.

"Ella, they've been like that for the past three years. I'm sure they'll wait another few hours."

"I'm fine, Lucas, really. I've started, so I may as well finish."

He hesitated, and then said good night.

It was nearly two a.m. by the time I went to bed.

Three days later, I had cleaned every cupboard in the house, polished every inch of the banisters, shaken out all the rugs and filled the freezer with casseroles, soups and stews. I'd left a note asking the tutors to leave out their linen. I'd laundered it all, then delivered fresh sheets and pillowcases back to their rooms. I'd washed the curtains in all the downstairs rooms. When I wasn't working in the house, I was out walking in Hyde Park or Kensington Gardens. Even walking through the gates seemed to calm me. There were so many paths I could take, a different one each visit. I was in the center of London, but when I was walking in the park, there seemed to be nothing around me but the consolation of nature, quiet, space and light.

I hadn't spoken to the tutors since the dinner and I had barely seen Lucas. I told myself I was leaving him to his studies. The truth is I was avoiding him. He eventually cornered me in the dining room. I was on my knees polishing the fireplace tiles.

"Tea, Ella?"

I stood up immediately. "Of course. I'll put the kettle on."

"It's made. That was an invitation, not a request. Please, come and join me."

I followed him into his withdrawing room and took a seat by the fire. As he poured my tea, he smiled at me. "I'm getting worried about your cleaning. You do realize it's the dirt that's holding this house together? If you keep this up, the walls will cave in before I get a chance to start the renovations."

"You did hire me to be your housekeeper."

"No, I hired you to catch a thief."

"While undercover as a housekeeper. I'm establishing my credentials."

"You certainly are. Have you actually left the house since you arrived? Apart from what I'm guessing are your hourly visits to the supermarket for ingredients and cleaning products?"

I suddenly felt defensive. "I haven't just been cleaning. I've been doing a lot of walking too."

"Have you been like this since Felix died, Ella?"

His question shocked me.

"You never stop moving. You clean and you cook and dust and sweep from the moment you get up until the early hours. Do you ever stay still, let yourself be quiet, just think?"

He waited.

I shook my head.

"You can't keep running away from it, Ella."

"I'm not. I'm *not*, Lucas."

He raised an eyebrow.

"I'm not."

"I see. You just really like cleaning." He put down his cup, walked over and shut the door. "Ella, I had another phone call today. From another client."

"Another theft?"

"A missing watch this time. An expensive Rolex. Again, it could be a coincidence. They may have misplaced it. But perhaps not. Have you had a chance to talk to any of the tutors yet?"

I shook my head.

"I suppose not," he said. "Unless they happened to be hiding in one of the laundry baskets or at the back of the cupboards you were cleaning."

"Lucas, I don't know where to start. I've never done anything like this before."

"Didn't you read all the crime novels I used to send you?"

"Of course I did."

"What did each of the detectives have to do before they could make inroads in any of the cases?"

"Find a motive."

"Exactly. Start there. Talk to each of them. Find out what's going on in their lives. You might get a hint of financial difficulty, or perhaps even of a sudden spending spree. You're closer in age to them, new to the house. It will seem quite natural for you to ask questions."

I felt a rise of panic. "I find that hard these days, Lucas. To talk to people. To new people."

"You? Surely not? You were always so curious. So interested in everything." He smiled. "Even as a child you were always asking questions. I could barely keep up with your faxes."

I swallowed. "But I'm not that person anymore, Lucas. I'm sorry, but I—"

My tears took us both by surprise. Lucas came across and held me tight against his scratchy woolen jumper as I cried. Ten minutes passed before he gently eased me back into my chair. He reached across to the side table and rummaged in the mess of books and papers for some tissues.

I took one, embarrassed now, wiping my eyes. "I'm sorry, Lucas."

"Ella, please. You don't need to be."

"I want to be that person again too. But I can't. Everything is different now. I can't go back. I can't explain—" I felt the tears well again.

"You need to talk about it."

"I've tried. It hasn't helped. I've talked to counselors and doctors and—"

"Not with them. Not with me. You need to talk to someone who knows exactly how you're feeling. To someone who is feeling exactly the same way."

I knew who he meant.

"I can't, Lucas."

Lucas was silent for a minute. When he spoke again, his voice was soft. "I saw him last month, Ella."

I stared at him. "Aidan?"

He nodded.

"He's in London?" I got the urge to run. Now. To go, again.

Lucas shook his head. "He was passing through. He'd been in Ireland to see his parents. Ella, I barely recognized him. He's brokenhearted. Devastated. Felix was everything to—"

Keep busy. Distract yourself. I stood up. "I've had an idea about the tutors, Lucas. A way of getting them to talk to me."

"Ella—"

"It might work. I think it's worth a try. Can I tell you about it?"

He wasn't pleased. I knew that. But he listened as I

outlined my barely formed plan and agreed it was worth a try. Afterward, I left the room as soon as I could.

I made a start over breakfast the next day, getting up early, before everyone else. I cooked pancakes, a stack of them, and prepared three different fillings: fruit, spinach and cheese, lemon and sugar. Peggy was the first into the kitchen, a novel tucked under her arm. If she was surprised to see me up so early, she didn't show it. She accepted my offer of pancakes and let me pour her a coffee too.

"We'll never leave the house if you keep this up," she said, opening her book and putting her feet up on the chair opposite. "Literally. We'll be so huge we won't be able to fit through the door."

She had two large fruit pancakes. For a small woman she had a big appetite. She read as she ate. I had to pick my moment, in between her pancake eating and page turning.

"Peggy, I wonder if I could ask a favor?"

"Mmm," she said, not looking up.

"I'm writing an article about private tutors—"

"Writing?" That got her attention. "I thought Lucas said you were an editor."

"I was, yes, but I've been commissioned by an Australian education magazine to write about the world of private tutors in London. It's not something that happens much at home and—" Stop there, I thought. "I wondered if I could ask you a few questions for my article."

"Sure," she said. "I'm very boring, though. All I do is study, teach, study, teach. Oh, and eat now. Study, teach, eat."

I reached for paper and a pen. There were always

notebooks and pens lying around the house. "Could you tell me your reasons for deciding to tutor as well as study?"

"One, for the money. Two, for the money." She smiled. "But I can lie and say it's for the love of learning and to share my knowledge, if you think that would look better in print?"

I looked down at my notepad. *Money. Money.* "And what about your own background? Your own university years?"

"This is like that *Desert Island Discs* radio show, isn't it? Without the discs." She leaned back in her chair. "I grew up in Newcastle, the oldest of three. I had a teacher who noticed how much I read, who thought I had a gift for writing. He pushed me into after-school tuition, A levels, then into applying for Oxford. It was very tough. I was the first in my family to go to any university, let alone a posh one like that. But I got in and I loved it, worked hard, did well enough."

I remembered her CV. She hadn't done "well enough." She'd got first-class honors.

"In my final year, I heard about Lucas's setup here, got added to his waiting list, and now here I am"—she smiled—"doing my PhD and living rent free while the tutoring pays for the rest of my life. Thank God for Lucas. I couldn't afford to keep studying or live around here otherwise."

"So money's a problem?" *Subtle, Ella.*

"This is London. Of course money's a problem. But I'm okay. If I run short, I steal a few antiquarian books from Lucas's vast uncataloged collection and sell them at Camden Market." She laughed at my expression. "I'm joking, Ella. But I can tell you, it sticks in my throat when I go to some of my tutoring jobs. My parents had to scrimp and save to help put me through school and into university. I took any job going, cleaning and waitressing. And now I sit in expensively decorated rooms and tutor rich, spoiled children who don't want to learn and don't need to learn because their parents will be able to buy or network their way into any job or position they want, no matter what results they get. I know I have a job because of them, but by the time this year is over, I'll be a fully fledged communist marching the streets chanting, 'Share the wealth!'"

I glanced down at my notebook. It was still blank apart from the words *Money, Money*. "That's great, Peggy. Thanks very much."

"You're welcome. Any more pancakes?"

I interviewed Mark next. He ate four pancakes, asking if they were a bribe to get him to talk. I admitted that they were.

"Can you tell me what you like about tutoring?" I asked, my pen poised on the notebook.

"It's a great way to get inside rich people's houses and scope them for future burglaries."

I was starting to think they'd bugged Lucas's withdrawing room. "Seriously," I said.

He shrugged. "It's an easy way to earn good money. Money for old rope, really. Money for old algebra, in my case."

I glanced down at my notebook. *Money. Money. Money.* "And what don't you like about it?"

"On the record? Nothing. I love every single minute of it. Off the record? I don't like the students. I don't like the students' parents. I do like their houses, though."

Before I could think of another question, he spoke again. "Who did you say this article was for?"

I stumbled through my answer: an Australian magazine, different education systems, etc., etc.

"Did Saint Lucas get you that job too?"

"I'm sorry?"

"He's Mr. Fix-it, don't you think? Looking after us, looking after you. What does he get out of it? Nothing but a warm glow, as far as I can see. He's like the Mother Teresa of education. We're like members of the Cult of Lucas. Lucasians. Lucasites. Lucasades."

I wasn't sure whether he was being admiring or critical.

He was sharp enough to pick that up. "I'm not complaining. I know I'm lucky to be a chosen one. Did you know the waiting list for this house is in the hundreds? Though you got to skip the queue, of course. Three cheers for family ties."

I picked up my notebook again. "Could I ask you another few questions?"

"Sure, if you cook me another pancake. But maybe you'd answer something else for me first. What's Lucas's own story? Was he ever married? Is there something going on between him and Henrietta? Or is he gay?"

I'd liked Mark over dinner. Not now. "I'm not sure that's any of your business."

"Of course it's not. But you can't blame me for being curious. We all are. When he told us you were coming to live here, he described you as his only relative in the world. So we decided you were coming to check out your inheritance. It's true, isn't it? All this will be yours one day?"

"I've no idea."

"It must be worth a fortune."

"I don't know."

"Believe me, it would be. A place this size, this close to Hyde Park. Lucas doesn't know how lucky he is." He gave me an appraising glance. "Nor do you, by the sound of things."

I didn't like the way he was talking about Lucas or the house or me. He didn't seem to care what I thought, though, casually reaching across to pour himself more coffee.

He continued. "I thought this house was amazing when I first moved in, but you should see some of the houses we teach in. I couldn't believe it the first few times. Artwork everywhere, nannies and drivers and chefs and gardeners. And these kids—they want something, they get it. A new toy, a pony, a holiday. That's why they're so hard to teach. They're not used to working for anything. If their mummies and daddies could buy them a pill to give them extra brains, they'd do it." He glanced up at the clock. "I'd better go. Hope that's been a help for your article."

I looked down at my notes. The only words were still *Money. Money. Money.* "A great help, thanks."

The third tutor, Darin, was the opposite in manner to Mark. Charming, funny, helpful, answering anything I asked. But it soon became clear he felt exactly the same way about his students as the other two did. The children were spoiled but their parents paid well.

"It's a means to an end," he said. "I try to teach them what I can, and in return I get a place to live and study and a good wage for the year. And for all the discussions we have with Lucas and Henrietta about the students, in the end it doesn't matter what the kids learn. They'll all succeed in life anyway. We're for show, along with their paintings and jewelry and sculptures. I mean it—I've overheard them boasting to their friends. 'Our tutor speaks four languages and is a martial arts expert.' 'Oh, really? Ours climbed Everest.' 'Ours was the first man on the moon.'" He was smiling, but he was serious.

"And that bothers you?"

"It did at first. But now? I'm getting plenty out of it myself, after all."

"Plenty?"

He grinned. "Worldwide publicity. You wouldn't be interviewing me otherwise, would you?"

My final interview, with Harry the scientist, took place two days later, in front of the other three. He'd said he'd been waiting for me to ask, that he'd been feeling left out. They were all in good spirits, interrupting, teasing.

I asked him the same questions. He told me he'd been interested in science since he was a small child. Like the others, he'd come from a lower-middle-class background, the first in his family to have a university education.

Also like the other three, Harry was not just bright-eyed and quick-witted, but opinionated. He felt the same about Lucas's clients—astonished at the wealth on display and at how hard it was to get some of their clients' children to study.

Darin joined in. "We're the ones to blame. They don't take us seriously. They can tell from a mile off that we're from the lower classes, no matter how many degrees we have."

Mark interrupted. "It's not about class. It's about wealth. That rock star in Belgravia is about as upper-class as I am. All these trappings are to show off their bank accounts, not their class. Why don't they cut to the chase? Put a big neon sign on the front door with a real-life display of their bank balance? Wear T-shirts that say 'I'm Stinking Rich'?"

They all laughed, but there was a serious undertone. I could sympathize. There was no mistaking the class system here, or the chasm between those with plenty and those with little. I was always much more aware of it here than I ever was in Australia. It had been a hot topic during my visit to Aidan's parents in Ireland too. His father held very strong opinions about class divisions. He had strong opinions about everything. He'd made it clear to me that the sooner Australia voted to become a republic, the better. I didn't get much of a word in, but by the time Aidan and I left, I knew enough to head up my own republican movement.

The tutors were still arguing. "It comes down to education, not money, in the end, doesn't it?" Peggy said, earnestly. "And that's why Lucas does what he does here. He's trying to even it up. Give us the same opportunities as rich kids, a rent-free place to live and study, a good job—"

"Fattening food," Mark said, reaching for a croissant.

The other three left soon after. It was just Harry and me in the kitchen together. I gave up on my formal interview questions. "Do you know what you'll do after you've finished living here?"

He took a sip of his coffee. "A year ago, I'd have said I'd keep studying. I wanted to change the world. Cure cancer. But not anymore. I'm starting to think I should go where the money is. I'm tutoring for one family at the moment—all four of us are—that's rich from drug money. Serious drug money." He grinned. "Not street drugs. Pharmaceutical money. I met the father the other night for the first time.

When he heard I was a science PhD, he gave me his card, told me to get in touch with him as soon as I'd graduated and he'd have a job for me." He reached into his pocket and passed me a card. "Look at this. It's unbelievable. He's got six different contact numbers."

I wasn't looking at the business card. I was looking at Harry's watch. It was an enormous Rolex. He noticed and pushed his sleeve back even farther. To show it, not hide it.

"Impressive, isn't it?" he said with a grin. "Have a guess how much it's worth? Ten thousand pounds. For a watch. It's obscene. That's a year's salary. Now, guess how much I got it for."

I didn't answer.

"Twenty pounds!" He laughed. "It's a knockoff, of course. Darin's got one too. We bought them at Camden Market. But it tells the time and it fools enough people to make it fun." He looked at it again. "Speaking of which, time I left too. Thanks for breakfast. Hope I've been a help; have I?"

I glanced down. The page was blank. "A big help, thanks," I said.

THIRTEEN

An e-mail from Australia was waiting for me when I logged on to my computer the following morning. It was from a features writer at one of Australia's bestselling women's magazines.

Dear Ella,

I'm sure you'll be delighted to hear your mother, Merry, is going to be the focus of a six-page feature in our autumn issue. We can't wait to spend time with her and we know our readers will love hearing all about her amazing life and path to success too! As well as Merry and her husband, we'll be interviewing her nearest and dearest, and as her eldest daughter, that of course includes you!

We've already taken some fantastic photos of Merry and Jess together on set, and we'd love to photograph you all together. We will of course cover your costs to bring you to Melbourne. Will you please let us know some dates that might suit?

Thanks and looking forward to chatting soon!

I deleted it.

Then I rescued it. Then I deleted it again.

It wasn't Mum's fault. Mum could be self-absorbed and scatty and distracted and unthinking, but she wouldn't have done this to me a second time, surely?

I found the e-mail again and wrote back briefly, saying I was sorry but I was overseas so would be unable to take part. I hesitated, then sent another e-mail, to Mum's personal e-mail address. I should have let her and Walter know I was in London before now.

Mum, just a quick note to let you know I'm not in Margaret River anymore. I've decided to spend some time in London. I'm staying at Lucas's. I'm sorry I won't be able to take part in the magazine article. I hope it goes well.

Love to you and Walter,
Ella xx

I'd been asked to be part of one of Mum's publicity campaigns before. It was six months after Felix had died. I'd left Canberra and was working as a waitress in Melbourne. I'd been behind the front desk of a very busy pizza restaurant in St. Kilda when Mum and Walter came in.

It wasn't a surprise to see them. They'd dropped in several times before, each time saying they happened to be passing by. They greeted me with a hug. I hugged them back. They asked how I was. I asked how they were. Then I waited. I could tell they were there for a specific reason. It was before the lunchtime rush. I had a few minutes to talk. We took a seat at one of the empty tables.

Walter spoke first. "Ella, we've had some exciting news."

I listened as he told me the cable network had offered *MerryMakers* another series.

"That's great. Congratulations to you both."

"Not just us. Jess too."

I didn't answer. I waited, as they glanced at each other. Then Walter spoke again.

"Ella, there's a place on the show for you too, if you'd like to join us. We'd like you to join us."

Mum spoke in a rush. "The network loves the family aspect of it. The joking between Jess and me. You know, the way she comes into the kitchen while I'm cooking and steals bits of food and—"

"It's authentic family life," Walter said. "The viewers feel like they are there in the kitchen with Meredith and Jess."

I listened. I sat and I listened.

Mum repeated Walter's offer. "We mean it, Ella. We'd love you to be part of it. We can write you in like this." She clicked her fingers.

"How would you introduce me?"

"As my daughter, of course. My eldest daughter."

"And you'd want me to joke and stick my finger into the cake batter, and tease Jess, and it would be like a normal mum and her daughters, having lots of fun in the kitchen together?"

Walter beamed. "Exactly!"

"Messing and joking around, lots of laughs and cooking, all for a national TV audience?"

"International! More than two million and growing every week," Walter said, smiling proudly.

"And could I say during one of the shows, just casually bring it in, that I used to be married, that I used to have a baby son, but one afternoon Jess was babysitting and she chose to talk to her latest boyfriend on the phone instead of look after my son, and because of that—"

Mum interrupted. "Ella, please—"

"Would you like me to cry on-camera? Would that be great for your ratings?"

Walter stepped in. "Ella, your mother is only thinking of you, wanting to help—"

"My mother is thinking of her show and of Jess, Walter, not me."

"Ella, please." Mum, again. Her eyes filled with tears. "Darling, please. I loved Felix too. He was my grandson. You're not the only one who—"

I felt guilty. I apologized. But there was more to come. Walter glanced at my mother, put his hand on her arm and then spoke to me again, his voice even lower.

"Ella, I am sorry, this might not be the best time, but we need to ask you something else. The network publicity department has been in touch. You know they sent you some flowers, when . . . when it first happened."

There had been more than forty wreaths and bouquets sent to our Canberra apartment. I had read all the cards at the time, but I couldn't remember now who they were from.

Walter continued. "They've asked if Meredith will talk publicly about it. It would be an exclusive interview. With the most-watched current affairs show in Australia."

Mum spoke again, still tearful. "They said that so many other women would be able to relate, Ella. They said they want me to be able to show that being a celebrity doesn't make you immune to heartbreak, that there is a way forward after a family tragedy like ours, that we just need to . . ."

She kept talking but I couldn't listen. I couldn't believe someone had asked her if they could use Felix's death to promote a comedy TV cooking show.

I finally interrupted. It was hard to keep my voice level. "No, I don't think so, Mum. Could you both excuse me now? This is our busy time." I stood up.

Mum tried again. "Ella, please, don't go yet. Let us help you. Don't shut us out too."

"Too?"

Another glance passed between her and Walter.

Mum put her hand on my arm. "We spoke to Aidan again last night. He told us you still won't answer his calls or his e-mail. Darling, please talk to him. We need to stay close as a family at a time like this. Get through it together by helping each other, not hurting each other."

"Did you think of that line yourself or did the publicity department write it for you?"

This time Walter gasped. I said good-bye, turned and walked away, into the kitchen. I didn't come out again until

I was sure they'd left. I worked my shift, stayed an extra hour inventing more work and then went back to my apartment. It was only when I was in my room, the windows shut tightly and music playing loud enough to mask any noise, that I cried and cried.

I cried for Felix, as ever. But I cried for myself too. For the self that had died when Felix died. I hated what I'd said to Mum and Walter. Oh, I felt justified, angry even. What they had proposed had been so clumsy, so unfeeling. But in my heart I understood what they had been trying to do. Stay connected with me. Help me move on in the only way they could think of. I didn't regret saying no to them. Of course I had to say no. But I hated the way I'd done it. I wasn't that mean person, saying hurtful things, hitting out at people, walking away from people, was I? I'd never been like this. Yes, Jess had driven me crazy over the years, Mum had exasperated me, Walter had, well, Walter had been Walter, but I had been able to laugh about it, hadn't I? Joked with Charlie? Let Aidan tease me about my reactions to my family?

Now, though, it was like I was outside myself, saying cruel things, deliberately. It felt like it was beyond my control.

Mum rang me the next day. She apologized again. I listened, pressing my nails into my palms. I murmured that it was fine, even though I was lying. Then she hesitated and I knew she was about to mention Aidan or Jess again.

"Ella, please, can't you—"

"Mum, I'm sorry. No."

She begged me again. I said no again. Eventually, she

lost patience. I heard it in her voice. "What if it had been Charlie babysitting that day? Would you have been like this with him?"

"If it had been Charlie babysitting that day, it wouldn't have happened."

There it was, said out loud, the words that had gone unspoken until now.

"Ella, we're a family. We need to—"

Stick together? Why? I had had my own family. Now I had nothing. There was no rule that said families stayed together. I was proof of that.

I knew she was trying, as Walter tried when he rang the next day to plead Jess's case again. "She is devastated too, Ella. She cries all day and all night. You must talk to her." But I couldn't do what they wanted. I couldn't make things better for her. She had done what she had done and now we all had to live with the consequences. Jess. Aidan. Me. I couldn't go back in time. I couldn't fix the moment I most wanted to change in my life too.

Jess wrote to me then. I only got halfway through her letter.

Ella, I'm so so so so so sorry. I can't sleep for the guilt, I haven't been able to learn my lines for the new play I'm doing, or remember my steps. I think about it all the time—

Her lines. Her steps. She was back on the stage, and I could barely dress myself.

That same night I dreamed Jess, not Mum and Walter,

came into the restaurant. She was happy, laughing, dressed in a stage costume, her face made up, her curls bouncing. She'd come to tell me she'd written a musical about Felix, that she was going to star in it, that she wanted me to come to the premiere, to watch her sing and dance her way through Felix's life story. In the dream, I smiled at her, said it sounded lovely, that I couldn't wait to see it. And then I took up a knife from the kitchen bench and I stabbed her. In the heart. It happened in slow motion, and she died in front of me, in theatrical fashion, like a victim in a silent movie, mouth open, eyes wide in shock and pain, before slowly, gracefully collapsing into a bloodied heap at my feet.

I woke up at two thirty a.m. In those first moments between the dream and the real world taking over, I felt a strange, comforting calm. Jess was dead. Good. Then reality rushed in. No, Jess wasn't dead. Felix was dead. I remembered my dream and became even more upset. My wanting to kill Jess, wanting her to feel terrible pain, was dangerous and sad and I had to stop those thoughts. It was then that I knew I had to leave Melbourne. I had to get as far away from my family as I could. I had to try to outrun the pain and the anger. I got up, turned on my laptop and opened a bottle of wine.

I looked up bus timetables. Job agencies. Houses to rent. House-sitting Web sites. I took note after note. I saw job vacancies for waitresses, fruit pickers, vineyard workers, all over Australia. I worked in a kind of mania. This type of work will help me, I remember thinking as I took a sip of the wine. The more I drank, the less pain I felt.

I finished the first bottle and opened another one. I felt good. I felt great. Everything was going to be okay! My brain felt quiet, at peace, cushioned, the spikes of grief flattened. I had six glasses of wine, more than I'd had since Felix died. More than I'd had in years. I don't remember going to bed. I woke up again at five a.m., nauseous and disorientated. I couldn't work out where I was. I think I was still drunk. And there, in my dark room, lying in my bed, there was a moment—just a moment, but it felt like the longest moment of my life—when I couldn't remember what Felix looked like. I was lying there, wanting to think about him, and I couldn't picture him.

I panicked. I got up and found all the photos I had of him. I stared at each of them in turn, until his face, his beautiful, smiling, cheeky face, was imprinted on my mind again. One photograph in particular stayed with me, one I'd taken of him aged thirteen months, first thing in the morning, clambering out of his cot, one leg over the rail, both hands reaching out, ready to get going, wanting the day to start now, quickly, come on! It summed him up, his zest for life, the energy he'd had—

At the funeral, the priest had spoken of Felix's energy and of our sorrow. *When God takes a child, we are all forced to reexamine our lives. . . .* I didn't hear any of it at the time. One night, quite late, a week after I had left Canberra, I rang the priest and asked him to tell me what he had said. I needed to know it wasn't a generic speech. That he didn't have stock words of consolation. That Felix had mattered.

Mum rang me the next day. The priest had rung her, worried about my mental health.

I told her what I had told him. I needed to know what he'd said about Felix.

"Couldn't you have asked me?"

"I needed to hear it from him."

"Ella, would you like to come and stay with us for a while?"

"No." I tried to be nicer about it. "No, thank you."

The next day, Charlie e-mailed and asked me if I wanted to come and stay with him. I pictured being there in Boston, with Charlie and Lucy and their four happy, healthy, living, breathing children. Tim, the youngest, was just a year older than Felix would have been.

I rang rather than e-mailed. "Charlie, I'm sorry. I know you mean well—"

"But you can't." A long pause. "I understand."

I thought about suicide. Several times. What was the point of going on? What kind of life was this? But I couldn't go through with it. Not because of me, or my family, but for Felix's sake. I didn't want him—wherever he was, in heaven, in the galaxy somewhere—to need me, to be looking for me and me not be there for him. It made no sense, I know. I knew he wasn't coming back. I knew he was dead. The knowledge of it was like a piece of glass in my heart, throbbing every second, every minute of the day. But while I was alive, I could remember him being alive and that was the only thing, in the early months, that stopped me.

I kept moving instead. From the moment I got up until it was time for bed, I made myself stay busy. I changed cities. I changed careers. How could I be an editor anymore? How could I spend hours each day on my own in a quiet room, carefully going through lines of words on a page or on a screen, moving phrases around, asking questions, querying facts, when that was already what I was doing every single minute of every day, going over and over an afternoon in a Canberra park, wanting to change every single thing about—

I was in London, thousands of kilometers from Canberra, but the bad feelings began to rise inside me again. I had to get out of Lucas's house. Now. Be outside, be moving, be as busy as possible. Quickly.

I turned off my computer. I pulled on my walking shoes. I went down the stairs, outside, down the street, across Bayswater Road and into Hyde Park. Quickly.

It was a mistake. I'd come in near a group of children, from a nearby crèche, perhaps. They were older than Felix would have been, but it didn't matter. I had pictured Felix at all the ages he would never reach. Any child I looked at would remind me of him.

The park seemed to be filled with children.

I kept walking, moving from Hyde Park into Kensington Gardens, past the fountains, ponds and statues of the Italian Gardens and on to one of the treelined pathways.

Distract. Observe.

The sky above me was heavy with clouds. The sun was visible but it was haze rather than light. I walked, and breathed, walked and breathed. My pulse rate began to slow. In the distance, I could see the dome of the Royal Albert Hall. I passed a group of middle-aged joggers. The man at the back was very red-faced. By a small copse of trees, a woman was exercising with her personal trainer. He had a stopwatch and an American accent. I passed people walking dogs of all sizes, shapes, species and colors. It was like a mobile dog show. One young woman had five small dogs on leads and was getting into a tangle with them as she passed me. The dogs were barking and leaping. "Bloody hell!" she said as one nearly tripped her up. She was laughing.

"Bloody hell!"

Aidan and I were shocked when I got pregnant so quickly. We'd thought it could take months or years. I'd stopped taking the pill after we got married. We went back to work, Aidan to his translating job, me to my editing projects. When I started feeling nauseous four months after our wedding, I did a test.

That night, I told Aidan.

"Already?"

"Already."

"Bloody hell," he said. "Bloody hell. Bloody *hell*!"

"It's good news, isn't it?"

"It's bloody great news. It's bloody brilliant! Bloody *hell*!"

The funny thing was that Aidan never swore. His business was language. He always chose beautiful words to express his thoughts. And now, on hearing the news that he was going to be a father, all he did was swear. It made me laugh and laugh that night.

"Ella?"

I looked up. Lucas had come up beside me, so silently I hadn't heard him. It was his walking hour.

"Are you okay?"

"I'm fine." I realized he looked worried. "Why?"

"You were laughing to yourself." He smiled at me. "Please, Ella, show some restraint."

It was very good to see him. I looped my arm through his and we walked together back to the Italian Gardens, taking a seat at one of the wooden benches. The clouds had cleared above us, a weak sun now visible, adding a pale glow to the stone borders, a sheen to the water tumbling out of the fountains. The statue of the vaccination pioneer Dr. Edward Jenner across the water looked polished by the winter light. There was another famous statue not far away. A bronze of J. M. Barrie's Peter Pan. Lucas had told me all about it in one of his earliest Astounding Facts faxes. I'd been entranced that the statue had been installed secretly, in the middle of the night, as a May Day gift from Barrie himself to the children of London. I was just as entranced that the author of *Peter Pan* had lived around the corner from my uncle. Lucas sent me a photograph of the house at 100 Bayswater Road, showing the blue plaque. He'd sent me all of J. M. Barrie's books too.

In later years, I'd read about the inspiration for *Peter Pan*. I'd cried when I learned that Peter had been inspired by James Barrie's own older brother David, who died in an ice-skating accident the day before his fourteenth birthday. His mother had never got over it. James had done his best to cheer her up, even going so far as dressing as David and learning to whistle the way he had. But she never stopped mourning her first son. The boy who would not grow up. That line was written on a plaque at the base of the Peter Pan statue too.

"Shall we go back?" I said, standing up.

"Let's stay here for a minute, Ella."

I knew he was about to mention Aidan again.

"Ella, please, sit down."

After a moment, I did.

We sat beside each other looking out over the water. A minute passed before Lucas spoke.

"Ella, you're my niece and blood ties will always be stronger, but Aidan is still my friend. I can't stop caring about him even if you want me to."

"I can't talk about him."

"I'm not asking you to. But I'd like you to listen."

I concentrated on the falling drops from one of the fountains as Lucas began to speak.

"I told you he stayed with me on his way to Ireland, to see his parents."

Aidan's parents. In the past twenty months I'd barely thought of them. Their relationship with Aidan and me had been distant, physically and emotionally. Yet they of course had lost their grandson too. Had I even spoken to them afterward? I couldn't remember.

"His mother was very sick. She had an operation—her heart, I think. She's frail but recovering."

Lucas was giving me answers to questions I wasn't asking.

"Aidan went to see them on his way to America."

I looked at Lucas then. "America?"

"He's living and working in Washington DC now, with a large translating agency."

"Charlie didn't tell me."

"You told Charlie not to tell you anything. Aidan was offered the job about three months ago. The man who runs the agency is an old university friend of his."

I knew who he meant. Aidan's friend had often tried to lure him to the US. It seemed he'd finally managed it. I'd never been to Washington DC. I knew it only from news coverage and films. I did know it was where good interpreters and translators often ended up. And Aidan wasn't just good at his job; he was something special. I'd seen him in action more than once, switching between languages, interpreting simultaneously. I'd been so proud of him.

"Ella, all Aidan wanted to do was talk about you. He asked for every detail about you that I could give him. He wanted to talk about you and about Felix. That's all."

I said nothing.

"He needs to see you. He needs to talk to you. Even one phone call."

"Lucas, I can't."

"Ella, I know how you feel—"

"You don't, Lucas. You can't."

"I'm trying. I'm not a parent, but I have an imagination. I know you, and I can see how much you are hurting. I saw it in Aidan. You were inseparable once. I don't understand how you can be apart, when you are both feeling the same pain. . . . Ella, I know you think he was to blame. That he and Jess were equally to blame—"

"They were."

"Ella, it was an accident—"

"Felix died because of the two of them, Lucas. How can I ever forget that?"

This time it was Lucas who didn't answer.

We walked back to the house together in silence.

FOURTEEN

From: Charlie Baum
To: undisclosed recipients
Subject: It's Been a Noisy Week in Boston

The latest report from the Baum trenches is as follows:

Sophie (11): Sophie announced at breakfast that she has a boyfriend. "I'm not sure how long it will last, but so far, so good."

Ed (8): Skirmish in the playground. Another boy attempted to steal a football from him. "I stopped him but I had to get my temper out," Ed said.

Reilly (6): Reilly (with serious, sad look): "Dad, in my class, I'm smaller than everyone."

Me: "Yes, I guess you are."

A pause, then Reilly again (cheery now): "But I've got a smile bigger than all of them."

Me: "Have you? Who told you that?"

Reilly: "My teacher."

I like his teacher.

Tim (4): If any of you are curious about the velocity of a four-year-old's vomit following a secret but lengthy ice-cream binge, I estimate 100 kilometers per hour.

Lucy (36): Amount of overtime at work plus amount of study for her marketing degree now equals a joke. Neither of us laughing. (Fighting, but not laughing.)

Charlie (36): Doctor has suggested—let me rephrase that—doctor has insisted I get serious about my diet. I am serious, I said. Seriously good at eating, I meant. He has given me leaflets for six weight-loss organizations and two folders of dietary info. Lost nearly a kilo carrying them out to the car. This might be easier than I thought!

Snip the cat (kitten age): Another mouse. Another tail. Or worse, the same one??

Until next time, everyone please stay sane.

Charlie xx

From: Charlie Baum
To: Lucy Baum
Subject: The fight

I'm sorry.

If I was flexible enough to lie down and prostrate myself at your feet, I would.

I know you're tired. I'm tired too. But that's no excuse. It was my fault. I should have realized you were trying to study and me and the kids choosing that moment to rehearse our marching saucepan band wasn't helpful. Tim was very impressed, by the way. (So was I.) He's never heard you yell like that. (Nor have I.)

Just to recap on some of your points last night:

I promise I do know how hard you're working.

I promise I do know how much you miss seeing the kids.

I promise I do know I have it easy being home with them.

I promise I do know I never have to feel guilty about missing sports events or plays or teacher meetings. (The plays can be VERY boring, mind you. I'm not excusing myself. Just saying.)

I also know that I am the luckiest man in the world. I have you and I have Sophie, Ed, Reilly and Tim. (All right, Snip too.) I promise I never forget how lucky I am, especially when I think about Ella and Aidan and Felix.

I'm sorry, Lucy. I love you.

Yours, from the doghouse,
Charlie x

FIFTEEN

D ear Diary,
    Hi, it's Jess!

I'm on the plane! I'm on my way to London!

It felt funny saying good-bye to Mum and Dad. I've talked about going for so long, and now I'm on my way, but I'm scared.

I'm really scared, actually.

My dance teacher says you have to focus, and you have to believe in yourself.

My counselor said the same thing. I went to see her one more time before I left. I'd started having the nightmares again. She said it wasn't surprising, that a traumatic event will always rise up when your defenses are down. She said I can't demand forgiveness from Ella, or from Aidan, but I can try to forgive myself. Just say those words, over and again, she told me. I forgive myself.

But I don't. How can I?

I will think about London instead. Exciting London, center of the musical-theater world. I know I have a lot of hard work ahead of me, but I am a hard worker and I am talented and I am—

Guilty.

I am *determined*. Determined. Talented. Confident.

When I'm on the stage everything feels okay because it feels safe and I know exactly what I'll be doing next, what step I'll be taking. I've always loved it up there. I love the way I feel when there are people smiling at me and being happy for me.

I wish there was someone in London I could stay with, even just for the first few weeks. I'll find my feet after that, but it would be nice to think that I'd be with a familiar face, someone who believes in me. Mum and Dad will be cheering me on, I know, but they'll be on the other side of the world. I wish that Boston was the center of the musical world, but of course I don't have an American passport and maybe Charlie wouldn't be that glad to have me around all the time. I know he's really busy with his own family, but I'd lend a hand in between auditions. If he was around too. I haven't told my counselor this, but since it happened, I haven't been able to be around kids on my own. I'm too scared something bad might happen again. I know it was an accident, I know that, but what if something like that happened again, if I was looking after one of Charlie's kids one day and—

I can't think about it.

It's strange that Ella is in London too. It's strange that Mum didn't tell me. I forgot to recharge my phone the other day and I had to use Mum's laptop to check my e-mail. I wasn't snooping. Mum's e-mail was already open, but I saw one from Ella saying she wasn't in Western Australia anymore, that she was in London staying with her uncle in Paddington. I kept waiting for Mum to tell me, but she didn't.

Anyway, I've worked out what to do after I land in Heathrow. Dad said he'd pay for a taxi for me, but I'm going to catch the fast train, the one called the Heathrow Express that goes straight into Paddington Station. Where Ella is. But it's a huge city. I won't see her. And there's no way she will want to see me.

I've just been told to turn off my phone and any other electronic devices! I'm on my way!!!!

All for now,

Jess xxxxoooo

SIXTEEN

By the start of my second week in London, I'd found a kind of rhythm to my days. I got up early and cooked breakfast for everyone. Once they'd all left for the day or gone back to their rooms to study, I cleaned and cooked some more. In the afternoons, I made myself leave the house. I drew up a list of nearby museums and art galleries. On my way to the first of them, the Handel House Museum on Brook Street, I passed the Liberty department store. I stopped so abruptly, the person behind bumped into me. I apologized and moved out of the crowds.

A month after Felix died, Lucas had sent me a card. It wasn't a sympathy card with lilies and flowers, woodland or even a teddy bear. The image on Lucas's card was of rolls of Liberty fabric, side by side, forming a tapestry of color. The photograph and his message inside—*I am always here if you need me, Ella*—had helped me more than he could have known. I'd carried the card with me since, tucked inside the notebook I always had in my bag too. I'd started to write down all my memories of Felix, funny things he'd done, moments from his life. Lucas's card marked my page. I reached into my bag now. I'd written on so many pages the card was almost at the back of the notebook. I held it in my hand as I pushed open the heavy wooden doors of Liberty. I walked past the flowers and through the accessories and makeup sections. I didn't take the old-style elevator. I walked up the wide wooden stairs to the first floor, to the second and, finally, to the third until there I was, in the Liberty fabric department.

I'd thought the image on Lucas's card was beautiful. The real thing was even better. The walls were filled with bolts of fabric, arranged in perfect rows. It was like a wonderland of color. There were patterns and prints, pastels and bright shades. I reached out and touched them, running my finger along the cool material—

"May I help you?"

It was the assistant, all good manners and crisp dress.

"I'm fine, thank you. I'm just looking."

She gave me a nod, a quick smile. She was clearly used to people standing there just looking.

I stayed for nearly half an hour. There was so much to see. Some prints, I realized, were the trademark Liberty florals, feminine and pretty. But there were also shelves of new designs, each like a painting: tiny, delicately etched flowers, swirls of color, deep, rich shades. Beside the fabric was a display of buttons—hundreds, perhaps even thousands, of buttons—each like a small jewel. There were so many colors, shapes, designs: for heavy coats, for summer dresses, for children's clothing—teddy bears, elephants, ladybirds. There were Christmas buttons on sale still too: mistletoe, little gift-wrapped presents, Santas, candy canes, even a tiny glass button made in the shape of a delicate snowflake—

A snowflake.

I gently picked it up and turned it in my palm. It was only plastic, not glass, but it looked like a diamond to me. Lucas's present for Felix's first Christmas had been a snowflake jumper. It arrived on the twenty-third of December, as the temperature in Canberra reached thirty degrees Celsius. We managed to keep it on Felix long enough to take one photo—me holding him as we stood in front of the open refrigerator.

"Say freeze!" Aidan said as he took the shot.

That photo was on Lucas's wall too.

I bought the snowflake button. The shop assistant reached for a bag but I stopped her. I paid and put it in my pocket. I walked around the section again, drinking in the colors once more. It felt as if I was applying some kind of a balm to my eyes, simply by looking at beautiful things.

As I walked down the wooden stairs again, I recalled a woman I'd heard speak at the one grief clinic I'd attended. Her husband had died suddenly. She had never gardened in her life. That was his job. But in the months afterward she became obsessed with growing things. Not flowers, or shrubs, but vegetables. "I'd never realized how beautiful they were," she said in the meeting. "All lined up in perfect rows. The way the buds come, the color of the tomatoes, the green of the beans, the yellow of the pumpkins. I couldn't get enough of them." I now knew what she meant.

I walked from Liberty to the Handel House Museum. I stayed for more than an hour, moving from room to room, reading the information on every exhibit, talking to the volunteer guides, hearing details of the thirty-six years Handel had spent in London from 1723 to 1759. He had composed *Messiah* in this house. I also learned something surprising. In the 1960s, Jimi Hendrix had lived in the same building with his English girlfriend. One room of the museum had a joint display: Hendrix photos and memorabilia on one side of the room, Handel sheet music and memorabilia in a glass cabinet on the other. As I left the museum, I looked up. On the wall above me were two blue commemorative plaques, one for each of them. I wondered whether Lucas had known that. It would amuse him too, I knew.

I'd needed to take a tour like this. I needed to find new places to visit. I'd already discovered that my personal landscape of London—parts of Kensington Gardens and Hyde Park, the restaurants in Queensway, the pubs on Bayswater Road, even the row of seats beside Marble Arch—was too heavy with memories. Not memories of Felix. That was one consolation of this city. I'd never been here with him. The city was filled with memories of Aidan. We'd met in the final weeks of summer, when the days were still warm, the sky bright until ten o'clock. We'd fallen in love gradually, in different parts of the city, as we went out for drinks, had dinner together, went on long walks, had picnics. I could have mapped our courtship via our favorite pub, restaurant, park, cinema. I couldn't return to those places. I needed to find ones I could think of as mine, not ours.

In a café off Regent Street, I picked up a discarded brochure advertising guided walking tours that promised to show me hidden parts of London. I took out my pen and circled six of them. They would help keep me busy too.

I joined in the first walk the following day, after I'd finished my morning of housework. It was a two-hour guided tour of the grand area and houses of Mayfair. I heard historical facts and celebrity anecdotes, visited churches and Berkeley Square. The guide pointed out the Connaught Hotel, Annabel's nightclub, foreign embassies and the former residences of writers, prime ministers, scientists and scholars. In Grosvenor Square, opposite the American embassy, I stood apart from the group as the guide pointed out the memorial to the victims of 9/11. Written across the top of the simple wooden structure was a quote: *Grief is the price we pay for love.*

I walked back home through Hyde Park. The sun shone briefly as I reached Lucas's street, turning the long terrace of houses into a glow of white. As I came closer, I was struck by how run-down Lucas's house looked. Not just compared to the houses I'd seen in Mayfair, but compared to the rest of the houses in his terrace. They were all painted a rich white. His was a flaking cream. Their doors were glossy, brightly colored. His was a faded blue, the fox door knocker getting more lopsided every day. The terrace was like a row of gleaming teeth spoiled by a rotten one. Not that I dared say that to Lucas. He loved this house. And he was planning the renovations, wasn't he? As soon as he had the money to pay for them. As long as the money wasn't jeopardized by the thefts . . .

I gave him a progress report that night. It was the first time I'd seen him in two days. For a houseful of people, we all managed to successfully avoid one another. There were signs that the tutors were coming and going (mail collected, shoes left in the hallway) and even clearer signs that they were working their way through the meals I'd left for them in the freezer (a sink full of dishes). It was obvious their study and tutoring schedules kept them busy. I knew Lucas was spending hours in the British Library at present too, researching his latest paper. He was surrounded by notes when I knocked on his door. I once again declined his offer of a drink, sat opposite him in front of the fire and delivered my update.

"The good news is I've finally interviewed them all. The bad news is I think they all have a motive. Money."

"They get paid very well, Ella. Higher than average teaching rates and free accommodation too."

"Then perhaps it isn't about money."

"Why else would they do it?"

"As a kind of protest?" I told him all they'd said about their clients. That the common thread was how spoiled they thought the children were, how indulgent the parents were, how much all the clients had. Perhaps the thief was stealing simply because it was possible. Because he or she thought the clients already had too much. That they wouldn't miss the items.

"Lucas, I might be wrong. We don't have any proof they've anything to do with the thefts at all."

"No, we don't." He hesitated. "Have you had a chance to look in their rooms?"

I knew he was using the word "look" when he meant the word "search." I'd done it that morning, trying to convince myself it was part of my job as housekeeper. Accompanied by a very noisy vacuum cleaner I found at the back of the hall cupboard, I went through their rooms one by one. I found several missing cups, a surprising amount of cutlery, more than a dozen brown apple cores, some evidence that activity of a romantic nature was taking place (I felt like a prying mother as I noticed the pack of condoms on Peggy's bedside table), wineglasses, empty bottles and, in Darin's room, a bright orange traffic cone obviously taken from the roadworks nearby. I didn't find a map, a necklace, a figurine, a ring or a real Rolex watch.

"Perhaps I'm wrong," Lucas said after I'd finished my report. "I hope so. Please keep your eyes to the ground, Ella, won't you? Or do I mean ears?"

"I'll use them all," I said.

We sat in companionable silence for a moment, both of us staring into the fire. It was throwing out a gentle heat, the flames flickering rather than flaring, their light a twisting mixture of orange and red. Across from me, Lucas took out a folder of work and began to silently read.

Observe.

I made myself catalog all I could hear around me. Lucas's quiet breathing. The faint sound of traffic. A dog barking. Music from a house farther down the street. The crackle of the fire, the occasional shifting of a log. I shut my eyes to concentrate better. I heard a far-off siren. Another dog. The flick of paper as Lucas turned the page.

I used to love sitting quietly in the living room in Canberra while Aidan was working on one of his translations. I liked to watch him turn one language into another. I'd occasionally see him consult dictionaries, but mostly I'd marvel that he could have so many words in his mind, that he could without hesitation find the one he needed. Sometimes, I'd be editing too, and the room would be filled with the gentle sound of pages turning, the scratch of our pens, as we both read, made notes. When Felix was a baby, when I was on maternity leave, the happiest I ever felt was when the three of us were in a room together, Aidan reading or translating a document, me sitting in a comfortable chair, Felix sleeping on me. There is nothing to compare with the feel of a baby—your own baby—asleep on your chest. His little body would move up and down, so slowly, as I breathed. I would blow gently onto the top of his head and see the dark strands of hair lift and fall. Every now and then his eyelids would flicker or he would move, just the slightest bit. A shimmer of a dream perhaps, or an itch, or the start of growing pains, but it always made me smile. I'd press a gentle kiss on his head, or hold him that bit tighter, marveling again at how his body seemed to fit mine exactly, in the same way that he looked exactly right, the perfect fit, when Aidan was holding him. Our baby. He'd come from our bodies. He made us happier in our own skins.

Another memory came to me, of Aidan trying to bathe Felix for the first time. I'd done it at the start, Aidan declaring he was too nervous of dropping him, of him slipping through his hands like a bar of soap and flying across the room. After watching me for the first fortnight, he decided to try it for himself. I helped him set up—the plastic bath on the kitchen table, towels spread around, the water lukewarm. Aidan undressed Felix so gently, his face a picture of concentration. He carefully lifted him up and then down, slowly, slowly, into the bath, a toe, ten toes, then an ankle, another ankle, all of it in slow motion. I was watching Aidan, trying not to laugh at his serious expression or make any comment about how tightly he was holding Felix. It was a vise grip. After a minute, Felix was still barely in the water. It was going to be a long night. I glanced at Felix's face at the exact moment he looked up at Aidan. His expression was a combination of furrowed frown and a "Dad, get on with it, would you!" roll of his eyes. It was a coincidence, I know; he was probably just yawning, but it was so perfect, so exactly what he must have been thinking, that I laughed out loud—

"Ella?"

I opened my eyes, blinked and brought myself back to Lucas's living room.

"Are you okay?" he asked.

"I'm fine. Why?"

"You were laughing to yourself again."

"Was I?" I was?

He nodded. "It was nice." He went back to his reading.

Lucas was right. I had been laughing. I had been thinking about Felix and I had been laughing, not crying. For a moment, there was a glorious feeling inside me, that the pain might be fading, but even as I thought that, like a wave rushing at me, the good memory was replaced by sharp, fierce grief, like teeth, knives—

I stood up. I needed to do something. Be busy. Quickly.

"Ella?"

I stopped at the door.

"Your famous Thai curry. Do you still make it?"

It took a second for me to shift my thinking from Felix.

"Or your famous spaghetti Bolognese? Or your famous Mediterranean vegetable lasagna?"

Lucas was mocking me, but nicely. When I'd first lived here and worked as his housekeeper, I'd had to teach myself to cook. Mum had never spent much time in the kitchen and I hadn't learned more than basic kitchen skills from her. I'd tried to cover my lack of experience with flamboyant presentation, producing meals for the students with great aplomb, announcing each dish as my famous this or my famous that, as though I'd spent the past five years in a *cordon bleu* cookery school rather than university lecture halls.

"If you'd like it, of course I do."

"Not for me. Henrietta is coming over tomorrow night to go through some student appraisals with me. If her visit happened to coincide with your dinner plans, I thought she could join us."

I sat down opposite him again. "You're still carrying on with a married woman?"

"I'm not 'carrying on.'" He paused. "Actually, yes, I am."

I smiled. "Hasn't your moral compass steered you from this rocky shore by now, Uncle Lucas?"

"My soul and conscience are blameless, Ella. There's no moral ambiguity whatsoever on my side. I'm not married. I can carry on with half of London if I want to. It's Henrietta who had to make a decision. Fortunately she erred on the side of sinning." He gave a surprisingly sweet grin.

"How is she?"

"Wonderful, as ever."

"Which of my famous dishes was her favorite?"

"She did particularly like your vegetarian lasagna."

"Your wish is my command," I said.

As I shopped for the ingredients at the local supermarket the next morning, I remembered Mark the tutor asking me about Lucas's private life. I'd been as curious about Lucas when I first met him. I'd asked Mum and Dad if he was married.

"Good heavens, no," Dad had said. "Many times chased, never caught."

Mum just laughed. "What woman in her right mind would put up with that mess?"

As I grew older and no wife appeared in Lucas's life, I'd gone through a stage of wondering whether he was gay. I summoned up the courage to ask Mum about that too.

"I wondered as well, but your father said Lucas was quite the ladies' man when they were at university, apparently. Can't see the attraction myself."

But Lucas was the image of my dad, I reminded her. And she'd married *him*.

"Yes, well, at least your father used to brush his hair occasionally."

I'd remained curious but it hadn't felt right to ask Lucas that sort of question by fax or e-mail. Once I met him again as an adult, I couldn't resist. I'd been staying with him for a fortnight. He'd taken a week off from his studies and devoted his time to me. He was wonderful—there was no other word for it. He took me all over the city, turning London from a big, strange city into one filled with hidden treasures and hideaway spots. He made me feel at home but he also left me alone. He talked about my dad in a way that helped me remember him. I'd always thought Lucas was one of the kindest, funniest, nicest men in the world. I knew it for sure now. It didn't seem right that he was single, rattling around this big house on his own—the tutors aside, of course. Since I was a child, he'd always told me I could ask him anything. So I did, one night after dinner, emboldened by one too many glasses of his very good after-dinner port.

"Lucas, are you gay?"

I remember him fighting a smile. Unsurprisingly, I suppose. It probably was funny to be interrogated by your slightly drunk twenty-two-year-old niece. "No, Ella, I'm not," he said.

"Then why aren't you married? Because you're an absolute catch, in my opinion."

He thanked me, hiding another half smile. "I did want to get married. To a wonderful woman I met at university. I asked her many times. Sadly, she said no each time. And then, even more sadly, she said yes to a fellow student. I never got over her, I'm afraid, or met anyone as wonderful as her. Hence, my ongoing single status."

I remember getting quite teary on his behalf. The port, again. "Oh, Lucas! I'm so sorry!"

"Don't be upset, Ella. The story has a happy ending."

"It does? Her husband died?"

"No, he's in excellent health. As he should be. He's a doctor. But fortunately their marriage turned out to be a rocky one. I became her bit on the side."

I blinked. "You had an affair with her?"

"Still having. For more than twenty years now."

Another blink. "Here? Now?"

"Not at this minute, Ella, no. But yes, here. In this house."

"Here? She lives here?"

He laughed. "No. But she visits often. You've met her."

The only woman I could think of was one of his university colleagues, an English lecturer called Henrietta who helped with the tutors' appraisals. She was Lucas's age, much shorter than me, a little over five foot tall, with what I would describe as a sturdy build. Her clothes were well tailored and clearly expensive. She always wore her long hair—an attractive dark red—pulled up into a bun. The first time we'd met, I'd been instantly reminded of a character from childhood books, Mrs. Pepperpot. We'd spoken only briefly. She'd been blunt to the point of rudeness, asking me where Lucas was and getting impatient when I said I didn't know. The second time, I offered her a drink. She barked an order as if I were a servant, not Lucas's niece.

"You're having an affair with *Henrietta*?"

He nodded.

The port was now swirling in my head. I had a hundred questions but only managed one, sounding like a prim vicar's wife. "Does her husband know?"

"It's an affair, Ella. Affairs are secret by nature." He laughed. "Your face really is quite a picture."

I hoped he couldn't read my mind. Lucas was so kind, so good-looking, so good to be with. Henrietta—well, Henrietta wasn't.

He went across to the wall of bookshelves and returned with a small framed photograph. It was him and Henrietta together, sitting on a rug on a lawn, in what must have been their student days. I couldn't lie and say to him that she looked lovely. She looked just like she did now—plain, serious and cross—only younger.

Lucas took the photo back and gazed fondly at it. "I've never known anyone who thinks the way she does. Even back then, she could turn an argument upside down in an instant. She's so original, so clever. She's an extraordinary woman."

The next time she visited, I paid closer attention. How could I have missed it? Lucas *reveled* in her company. Not in her looks, but her mind. Appearances simply didn't matter to him, I realized. His own clothes and the mess in his house were proof of that. What he cared passionately about were ideas, arguments, discussions, original thinking. He and Henrietta connected completely on an intellectual level. I listened to them talking that night, and again on her subsequent visits. Their conversations were passionate, animated, informed. They argued, they laughed, they discussed, they argued some more. After she left each time—sometimes after an hour or so spent upstairs with him in his room, during which time I definitely didn't eavesdrop—Lucas would be so happy. Not only happy that he'd seen her, but also happy that she'd gone. She was his perfect woman. She was not just his intellectual equal and occasional sexual partner. She also gave him all the space and freedom he needed. After that, I tried my best to be friendly whenever she visited, but her manner toward me didn't change. She was only ever dismissive or brusque with me. Rude, in fact.

I told Charlie all about her. How ill-mannered she was.

How she reminded me of Mrs. Pepperpot. I e-mailed him a photo of her and Lucas. I'd taken it under the pretense I was testing my new camera.

See what I mean??? I e-mailed.

Charlie e-mailed back. *So she's no oil painting. So what? Nor am I. Lucas loves her. She must love him. That's all that counts. Anyway, no one will ever be good enough for your precious Lucas. Stop being his gatekeeper. You should be happy he's so happy.*

But she's horrible, I'd e-mailed back, resorting to childish terms to amuse him, and myself.

Maybe she's sensational in bed, he'd e-mailed back.

YUK! I'd e-mailed in return.

I was home alone when Henrietta arrived for dinner. The tutors were all out with their students. Lucas had dropped by the kitchen in the late afternoon to say he was going out for a quick meeting, but he'd be back before Henrietta arrived.

Just before seven I heard the front door open.

"In here, Lucas," I called. "Henrietta's not here yet."

"Yes, she is," a voice answered.

It was Henrietta. I hadn't realized she had her own key.

She appeared in the doorway. "I'm early," she said. "Welcome back, Ella." We briefly touched cheeks in greeting.

She hadn't changed in the years since I'd seen her. Her hair was still in the same style of bun, her eyes as blue and sharp. She was wearing an expensive-looking overcoat. She shook her head when I offered to hang it up. "I'll leave it on. This house is always freezing."

"I'm just making dinner," I said. "Lucas won't be long. Would you like to wait in the drawing room or come into the kitchen?"

"I'll watch you cook."

I asked about the weather. Yes, it was cold outside, she said. We briefly talked about the forecast, the sleet that afternoon, the prospect of snow. I offered to make her tea. She declined. A glass of wine? Later, she said. I didn't know if she'd been told why I was back in London, if Lucas told her everything about his life and his family's life, or if their conversations were based on intellectual arguments.

She watched me silently as I prepared the salad. The vegetable lasagna was already in the oven. Once, I would have tried to keep up a conversation with her, needing to fill the silence. I could go hours without speaking now. It was why the work in the vineyard had suited me so well. I'd been on my own, row after row, no chat necessary or possible with the other workers.

I was startled when Henrietta did ask a question.

"How long are you planning to stay this time?"

"I don't know yet."

She just nodded.

Another minute went by as I chopped and sliced, the sounds loud in the room.

"I'm sorry about your son."

I dropped the knife.

"Lucas told me about it. It must have been a difficult time for you."

Her words were sympathetic but her expression was clinical, watchful, as if I were an exhibit.

"Yes, it was," I said. "It still is."

"So hard for your sister. She must feel such terrible guilt."

I said nothing.

"You and your husband separated, I believe."

"Yes," I said, glad the chopping gave me an excuse not to look at her.

"I had two miscarriages myself. I know how you feel."

A shaft of feeling shot through me. It was anger. I tried to stay calm, but I had to say something. "I'm sorry, Henrietta. A miscarriage is sad, but it's not the same. Felix was nearly two years old."

She shrugged. She *shrugged*.

"Of course I recognize the distinction, Ella, but the grief that follows is the same. Hope lost. Plans dashed. I had hopes and dreams for my two miscarried children, as you had hopes and dreams for your child. What was his name?"

I wanted to throw the knife at her. I wanted to shout, "It's none of your business what his name was, you horrible, cheating—" I controlled myself. "His name was Felix. Felix Lucas Fox O'Hanlon."

"And how soon after Felix died did you and your husband separate?"

This time I put the knife down, carefully. "I don't want to talk about it, Henrietta."

"I'm sure post-trauma separation is quite common. Understandable too. People go through the stages of grief in different ways and at different times. That must cause enormous strain in a case like yours, particularly. The Swiss-American scholar Elisabeth Kübler-Ross, who is credited with identifying five distinct stages of grief, once said—"

Henrietta was lecturing me, I realized. She was talking at me as though I didn't already know everything I ever wanted to know about grief. I already knew about Ms.

Kübler-Ross. I had read her book. I could have given my own lecture on her theories. But Henrietta was oblivious to my reaction. She just kept talking.

"Did you try counseling? Cognitive behavioral therapy is quite popular in Australia, isn't it? But perhaps the old wives' tales are true in situations like this. As my grandmother liked to say, the only thing that cures grief is time. How long has it been now? Three years?"

She might have been Lucas's great love, his intellectual equal, but in that moment I hated her. I wanted her far away from me. She was still watching me as though I was a specimen under a microscope. She was waiting for an answer.

I answered, for Lucas's sake only. "Almost twenty months."

His twenty-month anniversary was just days away. It had become an important date in my mind. Soon he would be gone from us for as long as he had lived.

Henrietta nodded. "So, nearly two years. You still seem very angry. Which stage is that, the first or the second?"

I looked down at my hands. They were clenched. When I spoke again, my voice was cold, my words distinct.

"My baby son died, Henrietta. The son I carried for nine months. The son I gave birth to." I was trying to hurt her now too. The flame was inside me again, the fury, the wild feeling I thought I'd learned to control. "I nursed him for more than a year. I stayed up night after night with him when he couldn't sleep. I bathed him, dressed him, spent almost every hour of every day with him for more than six hundred days. Until my husband, my half sister—" I stopped there. I needed to breathe again. "So yes, Henrietta, I'm still in the anger stage."

I returned to my cooking, chopping the celery with fast strokes. I could feel her watching me. Studying me.

"It's true, isn't it?" she said. "Grief is the most selfish of emotions."

I ignored her. She was oblivious. She just kept talking. At me, not to me.

"Selfish in the purest meaning of the word, of course. It's all about the self. Because that's all it can be, a one-sided feeling. Only you can grieve the person who has died. They can feel nothing for you in return. You said it yourself just now—it's all about you. 'I did this with my son; I did that.' You have to believe your pain is worse than anyone else's pain. Worse than your husband's. Worse than Lucas's. Worse than your sister's. You have to believe no one has ever hurt as much as you do to make it bearable somehow."

I no longer cared that she was Lucas's friend. I threw down the knife. It skidded across the table. "My son is dead, Henrietta. My baby son. I was his mother and now he is dead. What do you expect me to do? Shrug it off? Say, 'Never mind. That was good while it lasted'?"

"I'm not suggesting anything so simplistic. You're over-reacting. What I'm saying is—"

The door opened. It was Lucas.

"Henrietta!" He kissed her cheek. "I hope Ella has been looking after you? She's made your favorite lasagna tonight; did she tell you?"

I couldn't stay. Not a second longer. I left, apologizing to Lucas. I said nothing to Henrietta.

It was past eleven o'clock when I returned to the house. I'd walked up to Marble Arch to the cinema and watched two films, one after the other. I barely noticed them. Henrietta's words kept coming back to me, the sentences in my head louder than the dialogue on the screen. *Selfish. Selfish.*

The house was quiet when I came in, the living room and kitchen in darkness. I switched on the light. The table was clean. The dishes had been done. There was a dish on the stove top. I lifted the lid. Half the lasagna. I put it into the fridge. The remaining salad was there too, covered in cling wrap. Henrietta must have done it. It wouldn't have been Lucas. Or the tutors. I had to fight an urge to throw it all in the bin.

I was in the hallway about to go up to bed when a voice made me jump.

"We left some for you if you're hungry." It was Lucas.

"I'm fine, Lucas, thanks."

"Come in and have a drink with me."

I hesitated. "No, thanks."

"Henrietta's gone home. Please, Ella."

I followed him into the withdrawing room. It was in near darkness, lit by just one standard lamp. The fire was going. There was music playing in the background, a classical piece. Lucas poured himself a whisky and gave me a glass of water.

"Why don't you drink anymore, Ella?"

"It's not good for me."

"Were you heading toward alcoholism?"

Henrietta's bluntness had obviously been rubbing off on him.

He noticed my reaction. "You don't have to answer that. It's your business. I just miss having someone to share an after-dinner whisky with."

I had a memory flash—Lucas and Aidan here sipping

whisky and trying to outdo each other quoting poetry, or was it Bob Dylan lyrics?

"Henrietta said to tell you the lasagna was delicious. Actually, she told me it was delicious, but I'm sure she won't mind me passing on the compliment."

"Lucas, I'm sorry. I hope Henrietta didn't leave early because of me. We had a . . ." A fight? "An exchange."

"She mentioned it. Don't worry about hurting her feelings. Henrietta has the hide of a rhino," he said cheerfully.

I stared at him. Hurt *her* feelings?

"Sit down, Ella, please. You're making me nervous standing there like that. Now, I need to give you an update. I discussed the entire situation with Henrietta." He noticed my blank expression. "About the thefts. She's due to go to the clients' houses next week. She does regular interviews with the students for me, formal appraisals. I'd like you to go with her."

"Me?"

"I think it could be helpful if you're familiar with each house. You can see for yourself how easy or difficult it would be for something to be stolen."

"Couldn't I go with the tutors?"

"You could. But I thought it might be a good opportunity for you and Henrietta to get to know each other. And I'd like that to happen."

"Why?" It sounded rude. It was rude. But I couldn't soften it now.

"Because you are the two most important people in my life."

That silenced me.

"Ella, I know how Henrietta can appear. But it would

make me happy if you became friends. Perhaps you could have a meal together one night first, before you visit the students."

There was nothing I wanted to do less.

"Shall I suggest some dates to Henrietta?" he said. "Would next Wednesday suit you?"

Stop being Lucas's gatekeeper, Charlie had told me. You should be happy he's so happy.

I made myself smile. "Wednesday would be great," I said.

SEVENTEEN

From: Charlie Baum
To: undisclosed recipients
Subject: It's Been a Noisy Week in Boston

The latest report from the Baum trenches is as follows:

Sophie (11): Home with a cold. Announced: "Being sick is fun because you get servants. I can boss you around all day long."

Ed (8) and Reilly (6): Overheard having conversation about birds.

"What are pigeons actually for?" Reilly asked.

"Racing, mostly," Ed said. "But also to make the sky look good."

Tim (4): Has asked me to stop playing Thomas the Tank Engine DVDs. "I don't get it. He just drives and drives and then it's finished."

Lucy (36): Exam results in. Top of the class! And verily, there was loud rejoicing in the Baum trenches. All the late nights studying instantly worthwhile. Four children and one husband very proud of their clever mother and wife.

Charlie (36): Phooey to the diet. We've been celebrating. With cake and champagne. Who eats salad to celebrate anything??

Snip the cat (kitten age): One word. Furball.

Until next time, everyone please stay sane.

Charlie xx

From: Charlie Baum
To: Lucy Baum
Subject: re: Celebrations

No, we will not stop. We are going to turn it into a yearlong festival. The Festival of We Always Knew Lucy Was Clever but Now Everyone Else Does Too. The We Can't Believe How Proud We Are of You Festival. The I Hope You Realize Now How Amazing You Are Festival. The We're So Proud I Think We're Going to Burst Festival. Okay, I may need to work on a catchier title, but the content won't change.

Yours, in awe. As always.
Your husband. xxx

To: Ella O'Hanlon
From: Charlie Baum
Subject: re: Horrid Henrietta

Horrid Henrietta indeed. Lucas's love is blind and deaf, it seems. Put her out of your mind for now. You've got crimes to solve. Thinking of you.

Charleston xx

From: Charlie Baum
To: Lucas Fox
Subject: A.O'H

He canceled. I don't know why yet. I was about to leave for the train station when I got the message. He hasn't returned my calls yet. Any clues your end?

C

From: Charlie Baum
To: Lucas Fox
Subject: re: A.O'H

Finally spoke to him. Said he "appreciated your phone call and our concern" but that the situation is between him and Ella. I said we were only trying to help. Don't feel bad about calling him. You saved me a wasted train journey. How is Ella? No luck yet with the thief-catching, I hope???

EIGHTEEN

Dear Diary,
Hi, it's Jess!!

I'm here! In London!!!!!!! It's freeeeeeezing. It's supposed to be almost spring but it feels like the middle of winter. I heard someone say it might even SNOW!! I hope it does. I've never seen snow! The sky is SO gray and everyone is wearing big black coats and they rush along the footpaths with their heads down but I don't care. It's LONDON LONDON LONDON.

At first when I landed I thought it must still be nighttime, even though I knew my flight was landing at Heathrow in the morning, because after I'd collected my bags and looked outside, it still looked dark. I got the Heathrow Express to Paddington (and yes, there were Paddington Bears for sale there!!!) and had planned to get the Tube from there to my hotel (I love that I am saying all these really London terms so casually!!) but one of the last things Dad said to me at the airport was he didn't like to think my first hours in London would be spent underground, so I took a black taxi for his sake (and yes, it felt just like in the films!!!). After we'd been stuck in traffic for half an hour I was wishing I was on the Tube. Also, not that I'll tell Mum and Dad this, but London at first looked pretty terrible. Just like anywhere. It could have been Melbourne in midwinter, houses and trees without leaves and roadworks everywhere and all in this strange half-light as if the day had decided not to be a day but wasn't sure if it was night yet either, if that makes sense. And the people just looked like people. Office people, teenagers shopping, just normal people doing normal people things, but wearing coats and scarves.

ANYWAY, I'd thought the hotel Mum and Dad booked me into for my first week might be a kind of youth-hostel place but it turns out it's a very special hotel right in the center of Covent Garden! Yes, as in *My Fair Lady*! They are SUCH sweethearts!! After I got to my room I looked in the guide and found out it's a hotel that all the big stars stay in when they are in London doing publicity tours or filming! My room is amazing. There's an actual FOUR-POSTER bed and a huge bathroom. I knew I should have gone right out and started exploring but I felt so grubby and the bath looked so inviting. So I had a one-hour bubble bath, then went for a walk.

Of course I went STRAIGHT to the West End theaters!!!! My teachers and funnily enough my counselor too said that a great way to make things happen is to visualize them happening. So I stood there in front of the theaters and I looked up at the names in lights (except they weren't in lights yet because it was still daytime) and I imagined MY name there, next to MY photo of me in costume, high up on those big posters. And then I imagined turning up for work each night and being so gracious to the doorman and the stagehands. One, because I always am anyway, it's just good manners, but also because I read once that you should always be careful of the ones you meet going up the ladder as they'll be the ones who'll catch you on the way down, or something like that. I'm a bit too jet-lagged at the moment to remember it properly.

But whatever, I stood there and looked around at all the theaters and it was incredible to see the names of all the musicals that I have spent literally the past ten years learning on the other side of the world!!

But between us, Diary, even though it was exciting to see it all for real, I was actually a bit disappointed at how ordinary it all looked in that gray kind of light. I didn't tell Mum and Dad that when I rang to say I'd arrived safely and had already been to the theaters. ("Of course you have, my Jessie!" Dad said!!) Maybe it will all look different tonight when I go back again, once the lights are on and there are people everywhere, all dressed up for their night out at the theater.

It's all about the lighting, as Mum would say. She's big on lighting. She says that the right lighting in photo shoots can take ten years off her. She's started talking about how old she is all the time lately, and she's not even that old, only fifty-five or so, but she's started telling me not to tell people her age. Also, I can put this in here, Diary, even though I've been sworn to secrecy. (Mind you, by the time this diary is published Mum will probably be giving magazine interviews about it!) Anyway, the secret is—she had Botox last week. SHE INJECTED POISON INTO HER FACE. Well, she got a doctor to do it. I noticed something was weird about her and asked her outright and she admitted it but said not to tell Dad. She'd told him she'd been to the dentist apparently. (??? How stupid does she think he is??) Anyway, she said she had to have it done because the truth was TV aged you by at least twenty years in her opinion and she had to be especially careful because on a cooking show people stop and start their DVDs or program recordings to follow the recipes. So she comes under more scrutiny than most people, she said.

I had to stop her there! I laughed and said, "Mum, nobody actually cooks anything that we make on *MerryMakers.* They just watch it and laugh at us."

She actually got upset!! "They DO follow the recipes," she said. "They are so easy and also so—"

"Yes," I said, "nutritionally sound. That's why the producers make us wear those tight tops, Mum. To show the effects of such healthy diets." I shouldn't have said that, she doesn't like being teased, but I think I was a bit mad at her for doing something as silly as POISONING herself. I am NEVER going to have plastic surgery. I told her as much and she just gave me a kind of glare and said, "You just wait. Wait and see how it feels when you get older."

Anyway, back to London! After I'd walked around the

West End it was still only three p.m. I was going to take one of the open-top bus tours but they looked a bit cold, and I thought, it's my first time in London, the first day of the rest of my incredible life, I have to mark it properly. So I hopped into another of the black taxis and I asked the driver if he would take me on a kind of tour and tell me about all the sights, like he was my own personal guide. And he didn't even hesitate and he sounded SOOOO English, like Dick Van Dyke in *Mary Poppins*, and he took me all around the city for more than an hour. It cost a fortune, but it was worth every cent—every PENNY!!

I got him to take photos of me beside his taxi and all the landmark sites too, like Big Ben (I thought it was the clock that was Big Ben but it's not, it's the bell in the tower!) and the London Eye and the River Thames. I'll put them up on Facebook later, once I've caught up on all my e-mail. I was only on the plane for less than a day and I got dozens of e-mail messages. A few spam ones, of course, but mostly from my friends and of course one of Charlie's funny family ones as well. I love them. I'd better send him an e-mail to let him know I'm here too. Dad was going to tell him but I begged him to let me, because really it was MY big news, not Dad's, but then I got so busy before I left and it all happened so quickly I didn't get the chance to tell him, so I'll do that ASAP.

I haven't had any e-mail back from the London theater agents yet, but it's only been a week since I e-mailed them and they're probably waiting until they know I'm in London before they write back to me. I gave them lots of contact details, my e-mail address, my phone number, even the name and address of my hotel—and of course THEY would have known how show-businessy it was even if I didn't, so hopefully that will have made another great impression!!

I had one strange e-mail today, actually, from my friend Jill in the *MerryMakers* production office. I don't understand it, to be honest. She was writing to say bon voyage and to say she'd be keeping an eye out for me on *The Graham Norton Show*, which was really funny, because he only interviews HUGE stars, but that's how sweet and supportive she is. She's only a junior assistant at the moment. She goes to all the meetings and takes the minutes and all of that. She's lovely but that wasn't what was strange. It was her P.S., which said—I quote—"I'm so sorry to hear it didn't work out with your own show. That would have been hilarious fun working with you, but another time, I hope."

I've written back and told her what a wonderful first day I've had here in London already, how cold it is etc. etc., and just at the end, without making much of a big deal about it, I've asked her "What do you mean my own show?" The time difference means I won't hear back from her now until tomorrow. It's a bit of a funny feeling to think that they are all fast asleep over there while I'm still up here, and I'll be asleep while they're all having their day. It's like life is happening over there without me, which it is, and I'll catch up, I know, but it also feels a bit like I'm missing out on something. But it will be great here. I really know that it will. I just need to find my own flat, and get onto the audition circuit, get offered a wonderful part and then West End, here I come!!!!!!

Love for now,

Jess xxxxoooo

NINETEEN

Two nights after Henrietta's visit, I was in the kitchen when the front door opened and someone ran in, slamming the door behind them. I heard sobs. It was Peggy. I came out into the hall in time to see her run up the stairs, crying.

"Peggy? Are you okay?"

"He's a pig," she shouted back. "A two-timing pig."

I waited for ten minutes and then came up the stairs with tea and cake on a tray. I knocked on the door. "Peggy? It's Ella."

It opened. She had mascara all over her face; her pink hair was askew. Behind her, clothes and books were flung on the floor.

"Would you like some tea?"

She gave a sobbing nod. "Come in."

I brought it in and put the tray down on her bed. There was no room anywhere else. "I'll leave you alone."

"Don't. Please. Talk to me. I need some advice."

"I'm no good at advice."

"What am I supposed to do, Ella? Darin tells me he loves me, we talk about moving in together next year, and then today I see him in the library, and he's not just kissing her, he's practically undressing her, and he saw me and he didn't even look embarrassed."

It was like listening to a teenager. Here she was, bright and intelligent, destined for greatness in academia, and as upset by a broken heart as any other girl her age.

"What do I do, Ella? And don't say it's my own fault for getting mixed up with someone I share a house with. A friend of mine said that's all it is, just proximity, that I wouldn't have had anything to do with him if he wasn't under my nose all the time, and vice versa, and maybe she's right, but I love him and I really thought he loved me and that we—" She broke off, crying. "I'm stupid, so, so stupid. Imagine falling in love with your flatmate."

I had to say something. "If it's any consolation, Peggy, I did the same thing."

"What?" She sniffed.

"Fell in love with someone living here."

"Here? When?"

"Five years ago."

She sat up straight. "What happened?"

"I met him while we were both living here. He was a tutor too."

"And?"

"We fell in love."

She waited.

"We got engaged. We moved to Australia. We got married."

"And?"

Say it. "We had a baby."

She frowned. "A baby?"

The words were caught in my throat.

"Did you get divorced? Did he get custody of your baby?"

"No." *Say it.* "Our baby died. We split up."

Tears sprang into her eyes again. "Oh, Ella, I'm so sorry. There's me upset about a stupid— Ella, I'm sorry."

"It's fine. Don't worry. It's fine."

"Why didn't Lucas tell us? We would have been—"

"Different?"

Peggy nodded.

"That's why."

"But we've just treated you like our housekeeper."

"That's what I am."

"But it's so sad. Was your baby sick? Was it leukemia or something like that?"

"No." I'd nearly gone as far as I could. "It was an accident."

Downstairs, I heard a bell. It was the oven timer. I was baking biscuits. "I'd better go."

She put her hand on my arm. "If you ever want to talk about it, I'm here, okay?"

"Thank you." I was at the door when she spoke again.

"Ella, I really hope you don't mind me asking this—"

I steeled myself for another question about Felix.

"If Lucas was to—" Peggy stopped, then started again, speaking in a rush. "If you inherited this house, would you keep it as a place for tutors too?"

I tried to hide my shock at her question. I didn't succeed.

"I'm sorry to ask. Really. I know how that must have sounded. It's just, well, I have a little sister. She's only in high school now, but she'd love to go to university—and she should; she's cleverer than I am—and after she graduated, I know she'd want to do even more study and maybe she'd get to live here too, if, you know..." She trailed off.

I told the truth. "I'm sorry, Peggy. I don't know what Lucas's plans are." The timer was still ringing. "I'd better get back to the kitchen."

"Ella, I'm sorry again. About—" She stopped there. I hadn't told her their names. She was trying; I could see that.

"My husband was Aidan. Our baby was Felix."

"I'm sorry, Ella. About Aidan and Felix."

"Thanks, Peggy."

Back in the kitchen, I took the biscuits from the oven. I felt sick that I'd told her about Felix and Aidan. I wished she hadn't asked me about Lucas's inheritance plans either. First Mark, now her. It made me wonder if she was the one who was truly money-minded, if she could be the thief. I started cleaning out the refrigerator, glad of any excuse to distract myself.

I shouldn't have been so upset. It wasn't as if it was the

first time I'd been asked about Lucas's house. Even Charlie had raised the subject when we were teenagers, after a parcel arrived from Lucas, containing more books and a photo of him standing in front of the house proudly pointing out the newly painted blue front door. It was probably still the same paint job now, I realized.

Charlie had studied the photo closely. "That is some house," he said.

"It's incredible," I agreed. I'd already told him everything I remembered from my visit as a seven-year-old: the rooms, the books, the foxes. "You should see the attic. You can see for miles."

"So who inherits it when Lucas dies? You or a fox charity?"

"Charlie!"

"I'm not being mercenary. I'm being curious. You're his only living relative, aren't you? Unless he has a few secret sons or daughters tucked away who'll insist the house is legally theirs?"

Jess came in. She was seven or eight at the time. "What secret sons or daughters? What house?"

I didn't answer. I thought Jess was developing a bad habit of wanting to know everything about everything. Charlie, however, thought curiosity was something to be celebrated.

"We're talking about Ella's uncle Lucas and his house in London, Jess," he said. "About whether he'll give it to her when he dies."

"Is he sick? A whole house? Just for her? But that's not fair! What about you and me?"

"It is fair, Jess," Charlie said. "Lucas is Ella's uncle, not ours. He's no relation to us."

"But he must be! If he's Ella's uncle and I'm Ella's sister, doesn't that make him mine too?"

I can't remember how Charlie answered that one. He probably took out pen and paper and drew a family tree, showing how we all came from different branches. One more example of the complications of blended family life. Jess was still young then, I suppose, but I was used to it. All through school there seemed to have been "Draw your family tree" projects. I'd had to stay back late once to finish mine, having added in Charlie's branch, my branch, Mum's, Dad's, Walter's. . . . Looking at the finished product, it had struck me that all the branches had led to Jess. It was as though all these people, all the different relatives, had somehow come together merely to ensure her creation.

"Do you actually like Jess?" I asked Charlie several nights later, when the two of us were alone in the kitchen washing the dishes while she did somersaults around the dining room, or trapeze acts from the light fittings or whatever her latest antic was. I knew that whatever it was, Mum and Walter would be watching on indulgently.

He shrugged.

"Charlie, you must have an opinion."

"I guess so."

"Charlie, it's important. What do you think of her?"

"She's my little sister. That kid that lives with us. Sure I like her. Anyway, it's not as if I can swap her with someone else. Remember, Ella, you can choose your friends but not your family."

"Don't use clichés."

"Then don't count your chickens before you spoil the broth."

I flicked my tea towel at him.

"Come now, Ella. Just because you're jealous of Jess doesn't mean I have to be too."

"I'm *not* jealous of her."

"No?"

"I'm not." I flicked him again. "I'm not. Besides, I was here first. She should be jealous of me."

More than a decade later, another man asked me a similar question.

"You're jealous of Jess, aren't you?"

I was shocked when Aidan asked me that. We were on what I thought of afterward as our first date. At the time it was a casual drink in our local pub, the Swan on Bayswater Road. It was summertime. I'd been in the kitchen tidying up and chatting to Lucas and one of the other tutors. Aidan had come into the room, thrown his bag onto the table and said, "I could murder a beer. Is anyone interested?" I was the only one to say yes.

I'd talked to him before, of course. We'd first met one evening when I was back from my job in Bath for the weekend. I knew his first name was Aidan and that he was about my age. I liked his voice (his Irish accent was very strong, even though Lucas had told me he'd been in London for five years), I liked his hair (he could have been Lucas's son—they shared the same mop of dark curls) and I liked the clothes he wore (as casual as Lucas's too). In the baggy blue jumper, dark jeans and runners that he favored, he looked like a roadie for a band, or a barman, not the talented language tutor I knew him to be.

He'd come into the kitchen while I was cooking dinner. It was an Italian pasta sauce that I was making for the first time. I'd fried pancetta first, then added tomatoes, red wine, garlic and chili, hoping for the richness of flavors the recipe promised. He sniffed appreciatively and looked over my shoulder at the recipe book. That was when I noticed he was slightly taller than me. I also noticed that he smelled good. Of shampoo and soap, rather than aftershave, but it was woody and, yes, sexy, especially in a kitchen already smelling of tomatoes and red wine and garlic.

"That smells great," he said. *"Bucatini all'Amatriciana? Grande! Il mio preferito."* He sounded like an Italian native.

"Have you just complimented me or told me off?" I asked.

He smiled. That was when I first noticed the gap between his bottom teeth. Standing that close to him, I also noticed that his eyes were slightly different colors. Months later, when we'd be in bed together, I loved to lie with my head on his chest and make him shut one eye and then the other, as I tried to decide exactly what color they were. "They're both just boring blue," he'd say, shutting his eyes.

"They're not," I'd say, lifting his eyelids, peering in, making him laugh. And they weren't. One was bluey green and the other was greeny blue.

"Here, taste it," I said, giving him a spoonful. I cared what he thought of it. I took my cooking duties in Lucas's house very seriously.

"Nice," he said, putting the spoon in the sink.

"*Nice?* The most boring word in the English language?"

"It is, Ella. It's very nice. Very good, in fact. But I've been spoiled. I grew up eating that particular sauce. It's my mother's specialty. People come from far and wide to try it. There's some secret ingredient she puts into it. She says she'll take it to her grave. I think she means it."

"Your mother's Italian?"

He nodded. "When my father was in his twenties, he went to Rome on an exchange trip. He was staying with an Italian family, a well-known restaurant family, and he fell instantly in love with the youngest daughter. Their families were against it, so they eloped. As they fled in the middle of the night, she took her grandmother's recipe book with her, so she would always have something of home to cling to, no matter where they ended up."

One of the other tutors came into the kitchen then. "Don't believe a word he tells you, Ella. His name is Aidan Joseph O'Hanlon and he's about as Italian as the Queen."

Aidan grinned. "She's got Italian blood, hasn't she? Or is it German?"

The other tutor left and I went back to my stirring. Aidan stayed. I realized I liked having him there. Usually I became uncomfortable if anyone watched me cook. "So none of that was true?"

"Sorry, no." He smiled again, looked at his watch and pulled a face. "I'm late for a class. I'd better go." At the door, he stopped. "I was wrong, Ella. I'm sorry. Your sauce isn't nice. It's fantastic."

He wasn't there for dinner that night. A week passed without me seeing him again. I knew from casual questions posed to Lucas that Aidan was one of his busiest tutors, his skill with languages very much in demand. I was at the stove again the next time we spoke. This time, I was trying to master a French recipe.

I heard his voice first. "Ella, hello."

I turned and was surprised to feel a tiny jolt at the sight of him, like a little electric charge. "Hi, Aidan."

"I'm ravenous. I haven't eaten since we last spoke."

"Not since that one spoonful of my pasta sauce?"

He shook his head. "Not even a crust of bread."

"You must be very hungry."

"Very," he said solemnly. "What culinary delight is this?" Again, he leaned past me to see the recipe book. Again, I smelled the soap and the shampoo. Again, it mingled too well with the herbs, the white wine, the garlic. I felt another of those jolts.

"Entrecôte à la bordelaise?" he said, saying the name of the dish in what I knew had to be perfect French. "May I taste?"

"Of course," I said, handing him a spoon, trying not to smile.

He tasted it. "Very nice," he said. "But sadly, not a patch on my mother's version. You see, when my father was young, he moved to Paris and stayed with—"

I laughed and ordered him out of my kitchen. He gave me one more grin and then he left. I hoped he'd be back for dinner but he wasn't. I didn't see him again for three more days. Until he casually issued that invitation to go for a beer and I just as casually accepted.

"Have fun, kids," Lucas called after us.

Over the first beer we talked about London, about his work, my work in Bath. Over the second he talked about Ireland; I talked about Australia. During the third we talked about my family. He laughed when I told him stories about Charlie, about his regular e-mail reports. I told him about Jess too, my all-singing, all-dancing half sister. I also told him how much Mum and Walter adored her. Doted on her. Spoiled her. Which was when he accused me of being jealous of her.

"Of course I'm not jealous of her. She's just my little sister."

"Half sister."

"Sister, half sister. Tomahto, tomayto."

"Does Charlie get on better with her than you do?"

"Are you a language expert or a trainee psychologist?"

"I just wondered."

"He feels the same way about her as I do."

"Conflicted and jealous?"

"I'm not. Really, I'm not."

"The lady doth protest too much, methinks."

"The man is a Shakespearean show-off, methinks."

He smiled. "I can do Yeats, Heaney and Hardy too, if you like. Laurel and Hardy, even. I'm like a literary jukebox."

I took a sip of my drink, thought about it, looked across at Aidan and decided to tell the truth. The truth that had just become blindingly clear to me in that moment.

"You're right. I am extremely jealous of Jess. She drives me absolutely crazy. She always has."

Aidan laughed. And so did I. It felt brilliant, so wonderful, to say it, to admit it to someone. For as long as I could

remember, I'd felt bad for not instantly loving Jess, for finding her annoying, for not responding to her in the same
joyous, admiring way as everyone else. And yes, I'd felt hurt
that Mum and Walter showered her with so much attention,
and I felt bad that I couldn't sing or dance or enchant people
like she could. I could read a lot, and I liked cooking, but
they were all dull pursuits compared to the fireworks she
could produce. She was much more beautiful than I was too,
all dimples and curls and cuteness. I was like Pippi Long-
stocking next to her Shirley Temple. But I'd never said it
out loud before, not even to my friends at school, at university. I'd hoped that if I kept agreeing with everyone when
they said "Isn't she adorable?" I would start to believe it
myself.

But not now. Here, in this London beer garden, I told
the truth. "I'm insanely jealous of her."

Another smile from Aidan.

"She ruined my life."

An eyebrow lift.

"She's the most spoiled, overindulged, cosseted—"

"Don't hold back, will you?"

"Infuriating, attention-seeking, self-absorbed—" I was
laughing now. "I mean it."

"I can see that," Aidan said. "So, in a nutshell—you
hate her."

I nodded, happily. "I really hate her."

"Despise her?"

"Completely."

"Grand. Let's kill her, so."

"Great idea. Thank you. Would you do it?"

"Of course. Do you want me to take Charlie out at the same time? Two for the price of one?"

"Not Charlie. I love Charlie. But Jess, yes. Did you mention price? You'll charge me?"

"It's murder. Of course I'll charge you. What do you think this is, a charity? I'm an impecunious student, remember. Now, do you want her to suffer or will I make it quick?"

I pretended to give it some thought. "Quick but very painful would be good."

"A poison-tipped arrow?"

"Perfect, thank you. How do I repay you?"

"With a kiss," he said. Just like that.

I felt that unsteady feeling again, a kind of swirl, up and down my body. It wasn't the alcohol.

"Before or after you murder her?" I asked.

"Where is she?"

"Australia. Melbourne."

"And we're in London. A geographical obstacle. Let's do the kiss now, and I'll do the murder next time I'm in Australia."

So we kissed. Across the table. For a few seconds, which became a minute, which was the most extraordinary minute of my life. Until someone shouted, "Get a room!" and Aidan laughed and I felt the laugh against my lips. If it was possible, I would have kept kissing him for the rest of that night. But we stopped and I blinked and he did too, as though we were coming out of a kind of trance. Months later, when we talked about when and how we knew, about when we'd first realized that this was going to be serious between us, we both said that kiss.

We had one more drink that night. Then his mobile rang. It was Lucas, not checking up on us, but to say there'd been a call to the house from a client in "something of a state." One of the students was having a pre-exam meltdown. Was there any chance at all that Aidan could—

"I've had three drinks, Lucas. Your niece has led me astray."

I held up four fingers.

"Sorry, Lucas. Four drinks. But I can still stand, if that's helpful." *Do you mind?* he mouthed at me.

Of course not, I mouthed back. *Go.*

I was glad of a chance to stop and think about what had happened between us.

He told Lucas he was on his way and hung up. I watched as he switched straight back into work mode, all serious where he had been playful. "I'm sorry, Ella. I don't want to go."

"I don't want you to go."

"This is just intermission, then? Part two tomorrow? Same place. Eight?"

"Same place, eight," I said.

He smiled. Then he leaned over and he touched my cheek and he left. He didn't kiss me again. If he had, I don't think I would have let him leave.

That was how it started. Easily, warmly, quickly. That was how it kept going. I'd had boyfriends before, but they'd always been short-term relationships, generally beginning at uni parties when we were both a bit drunk and then petering out before they properly started. There was one relationship in Melbourne that began in a more promising way—we were match-made by friends—but that soon became uncomfortable too, as if we were both wearing the wrong size shoes.

I'd always felt I was to blame. I'd never known how to behave, how to be a girlfriend. I'd read somewhere that you learn how to be a woman from watching your mother, but that was no help to me. I was the complete opposite of my mother. I was tall; she was small. She wore bright colors; I liked dark shades. Her way with Walter was giggles, flirting, big eyes and helplessness. Her way with my father had only seemed to be arguing. As a teenager, I'd talked about it with Charlie. We were both children of broken marriages. How were we going to get it right ourselves?

"Don't ask me for advice," he said. "I'm just a fat kid. No one will ever fall in love with me. I'll be lucky if I get even the scrapings."

"But what do men like in a girlfriend?"

"I told you, I haven't a clue." After more prodding he told me he thought what he would like was someone who would be like his best friend, but added, "It would also help if she was hot, so I could show her off to my friends. If I had any friends."

Charlie had heaps of friends. I wasn't the only one who found him great company. He was also very popular with the girls. He just hadn't told me in case I "got a complex," he admitted later.

But when I was with Aidan, I didn't feel like I was trying to be anything. I was just me. I talked to him like I talked to Charlie, except the difference was I never wanted to kiss Charlie. I wanted to kiss Aidan all the time. Make

love with him all the time. We slept together two weeks after our first date. In his room the first time, my room the
second. Lucas gave us knowing glances when we came down
for breakfast, the other tutors teased and made racy remarks, but we didn't mind. We laughed. We loved it. For the
first three months of our relationship, we couldn't physically
get enough of each other. I'd never felt anything like it. If he
touched my hand, I'd want to go to bed with him. It was as
if every cell came alive when he was around. It wasn't just
physical. There didn't seem to be enough time to say everything I wanted to say to him, or enough time to hear all his
stories. I wanted to look at him all the time. I thought he
was the most handsome—no, the most *beautiful*—man I had
ever seen. He wasn't a male model. Far from it. His face was
a bit wonky, really, his nose a little big, his hair unruly, but
when he smiled at me, it was as if something magical happened. I thought he had the most perfect face I'd ever seen.

He felt the same way about me. That was the incredible
thing. He thought I was beautiful, sexy, clever, funny. He
asked me question after question and listened so intently to
my answers. He remembered everything I told him. He
drew stories out of me—about Lucas, my dad, about Walter.
He thought the story of Mum being discovered in a shopping center was hilarious. He insisted on sitting down with
me one day to watch all the *MerryMakers* DVDs she'd sent.

"She's funny," he said at the end. "A complete head case,
obviously, but she's really funny."

She was, I agreed. "And what did you think of Jess?
Adorable? Talented? Funny too?"

"Absolutely," he said. "Much more adorable and talented

and funny than you. And it's obvious your mum loves her much more than she loves you. I'd say Charlie does too. And Walter. It is Walter, isn't it? Or Wolfgang? Werner? Whichever one, I'd say he thinks she is *wunderbar*."

"I should have kept you to our murder pact."

"Oh, no. I couldn't do it now," he said. "Not now I've seen her in action on your mother's show. A nation would go into mourning. Can I start her fan club or has someone beaten me to it?"

I poked my tongue out at him and then I laughed. He made me laugh a lot.

I was already booked to go back to Australia for Christmas. Aidan came with me. "You don't want to be in Ireland for Christmas?"

"Let me think. Gray skies and freezing temperatures. Sunshine and warmth. How can I choose?"

"You won't miss your own family too much?"

"I'll battle on bravely without them."

We'd been together for six months by then, but I still hadn't met his family. It was the one subject we didn't speak about much. I knew the details, of course—he had one older brother, his parents were now in their early sixties, they lived in Carlow, a county to the south of Dublin, still in Aidan's childhood home. It wasn't that he'd had a tragic *Angela's Ashes*–style Irish upbringing, or a battered-by-the-priest one either. He said it had been happy enough. Not much money, but he'd had good teachers at school who recognized he had a gift for languages, first in Irish, then in French. He was the first in his family to go to university. His father had worked in a drapery; his mother had stayed at home. No, neither was an alcoholic, he assured me. They were just ordinary, hardworking, regular parents. His brother, Rory, was a self-made success story, managing director of a car-hire company that was now one of the best known in Ireland.

"I'd really like to meet them," I said one afternoon.

"They'd like to meet you too. My mother especially."

"Do your parents know about us? About me?"

He nodded. "I record all our conversations and send them the tapes each Friday."

He always deflected questions about his family with a joke. "I mean it, Aidan. I really would like to meet them. I'd like to see Ireland too."

"And so you will, Arabella, so you will," he said. "If I survive meeting your family first."

We had two weeks in Melbourne together. He loved Australia: the warmth, the big sky, the sounds of the birds, the relaxed people, the casual turns of phrase, especially the way shop assistants farewelled him with "See you later." Where were we going to meet up again? he wondered. He and Walter got on well, especially when Aidan spoke in German. Mum flirted with him and made lots of bad Irish jokes that he pretended to laugh at. Jess welcomed him as a new member of her audience. She'd even prepared a performance especially for our arrival. We were barely in the door from the airport, still getting to grips with the bright light and summer heat, when she'd ushered us all into the kitchen where she'd arranged a row of chairs. First she danced an Irish jig. Then she sang a soulful version of "Danny Boy." As she took a dramatic bow and we applauded, Aidan leaned across to me and whispered, "Does she do children's parties too?"

I loved him even more in that moment.

We rented a car after Christmas and drove up the coast to Sydney. On New Year's Eve, we stayed in a cheap hotel without even the hint of a harbor view. On New Year's Day we took the coast road back to Melbourne. He asked me to marry him when we were halfway there. While he was driving. I had to ask him to pull over.

"Did you just ask me to marry you?"

He nodded.

"Just like that?"

Another nod.

"Yes, please," I said.

"You can change it," he said later that night as we lay in bed in an ordinary roadside motel. "If you want to make it more romantic when you're telling your friends and family. You can say we were climbing the Harbour Bridge and I threw myself off and as my parachute opened, you could see I'd hand stitched the words 'Will You Marry Me, Ella?' onto it."

"I'm not telling anyone anything."

"Because it was too ordinary? Because you regret saying yes? Because I turn your stomach?"

"Because it was too good."

I met his parents a month after we returned to London. We flew to Dublin, rented a car and drove down to Carlow, two hours away. Aidan laughed when I kept saying how green the fields were. But it looks just like Ireland should, I said. I was amazed to see road signs and place-names in

English and Irish. Aidan pronounced each of the Irish words for me. I loved the sound of them. We passed a thatched cottage with whitewashed walls and he patiently took photographs of me in front of it.

His own family house was an ordinary bungalow on an ordinary suburban estate outside the town of Carlow. His mother was quiet, welcoming, kind. His father was more difficult to like. He barely drew breath from the moment we arrived. I put my foot in it almost immediately, purely through nerves, by making the mistake of saying the south of Ireland was part of the UK.

"We fought for that term 'republic' and you Australians should do the same thing," he said to me.

I knew Aidan's mother's name was Deirdre and his father's was Eamon, but I called them Mrs. and Mr. O'Hanlon. Aidan apologized for the formality, but I liked it. The formal terms matched their house. It was so orderly compared to my own family's and to Lucas's house in London. There was a formal sitting room, which they called "the good room." Meals took place at specific hours. Mr. O'Hanlon sat at the table while Mrs. O'Hanlon fetched and carried. There was no grace before meals—Mr. O'Hanlon had very strong views about the Catholic Church too. He listened to the radio news on the hour, turning up the radio until it was finished, regardless of whether there was a conversation in progress or not. Over the weekend I heard a lot about British imperialism, Australian republicanism, American conservatism, German efficiency, the incompetence of the Irish government, the foolishness of the local council and the shocking state of the roads. They were lectures, not discussions. He didn't seem to care what his wife or Aidan thought, let alone what I thought. We were just his audience.

I also heard a lot from him about Aidan's brother, Rory. About the number of people he employed. His head office in Dublin. How much he'd contributed to the Irish economy. His big house. His big car. His success with women. "He's a catch—I'll give you that. The one who finally snares him will be one lucky woman. But she'll have to be pretty special." I didn't hear Mr. O'Hanlon ask Aidan anything about his studies or work.

Aidan seemed different there. He was quieter. Distracted. We slept in separate rooms. I reached for his hand once as we sat watching the TV news with his parents and he moved away. We had our first moment of tension that night as we walked down to the local pub.

"Aidan, is something wrong?"

"No."

"Do you want to break up?"

"Of course not."

"Are you ashamed of me?"

"Never."

I stopped walking. "Aidan, please, what is it? It's like you're a different person here."

"I know," he said, after a few moments. "That's why I left."

I felt him relax as soon as we got in the car to drive to Dublin Airport. By the time we boarded our flight he was the Aidan I knew once again. He held my hand the whole way. I was happy, but I was also confused. It wasn't that I expected everyone to play Happy Families. God knows my own background was complicated enough. Back in London, I asked more questions and got some answers.

"Why didn't your brother come down on the weekend to see you too?"

"He was busy, I guess. He's very successful. You might have gathered that from my father."

"I'd like to meet your brother," I said.

"No, you wouldn't," Aidan answered.

Three weeks later, Aidan mentioned his brother was going to be in London for a work trip. At my insistence, the three of us had dinner together. Rory chose the venue, a Michelin-starred restaurant in Knightsbridge.

"I'll pay tonight," he said almost as soon as we walked in. "I know you student types. You're always skint."

He was the opposite of Aidan in every way. Well-groomed, dressed in expensive clothes. Loud, his accent a kind of affected American twang compared to Aidan's soft Irish accent. Confident. Sexist. Dismissive. Opinionated. His father's son in every way. I tried my best to be friendly but after his fifth joke about Australians, the fourth time he talked over me, and the third time he spoke to the waitress's chest rather than her face, I gave up. When Rory suggested he and Aidan "party on"—"You can work out the Tube home for yourself, Ella, can't you?"—I was grateful and relieved when Aidan said no, that we both had to work early in the morning.

"Work!" Rory laughed. "Is that what you call it?"

"Arrivederci!" he said, too loudly, as we said good-bye in front of the restaurant. "That's Italian, isn't it?"

"Was he like that when you were growing up?" I asked as Aidan and I walked to the Tube station.

"Worse."

But he was still Mr. O'Hanlon's favorite son. I'd seen that when I was in the house. It wasn't said, but the intimation was there. Rory's got a proper job. You just spend your time speaking foreign languages. His mother loved Aidan; I'd seen that. But she was overshadowed by her husband. I imagined most people were.

"I'm sorry, Ella," Aidan said out of the blue later that night. We were in bed. The lamps were off, the light coming in through the curtain soft, the noise of the traffic a steady, comforting hum.

"What for?"

"My brother. My father. What I was like when we were in Ireland. I'm sorry my family isn't one of those warm, welcoming, musical, storytelling Irish ones you were probably expecting."

I laughed. I couldn't help myself. "Aidan, I'm sorry my mother couldn't stop flirting with you. I'm sorry my stepfather only wanted to discuss German tenses. I'm sorry my half sister kept up a one-woman show. I'm especially sorry you didn't get to meet Charlie. He's the only normal one. That's why he lives thousands of kilometers from us all."

He turned over in the bed so he was facing me. He sounded so vulnerable, his voice quiet in the darkness. "I had to get away, Ella. Not from my mother. From my brother, my father. They've always been like that. Life's about money, opinions, prestige, possessions, status. I don't care about any of those things. Rory thinks it's hilarious to call me the eternal student; Dad just thinks I'm a waster, that studying for studying's sake is pointless, that I should come home, cap in hand, and beg Rory for a job. He said I should ask him if I can work at his company's airport desk, that at least my languages would be useful there, all the foreign tourists—"

It was the most he'd ever talked about his family. Afterward, I told him the truth. I said it didn't matter to me at all what his father and brother were like. That I loved the fact languages were his life's work. That I loved him, I wanted to marry him, live with him, spend the rest of my life with him, not with his brother or his parents. I curled in around him and kissed him and told him we'd just have to make our own family, a great big family. We'd have a dozen kids, maybe more, and we would be the most perfect, well-balanced, un-messed-up family in the whole world.

I heard a soft laugh, felt a kiss against the top of my head. "Ah, now, Ella. We don't want to bring up a tribe of goody-two-shoes kids who never put a foot wrong, do we?"

"They won't be goody-goodies. Our children will be perfect and we'll be the perfect parents."

"Of course we will. The ideal parents."

"With ideal children. They'll be delightful, quirky, intelligent, well behaved—"

"Grow up speaking ten languages each—"

"They'll spell before they can walk—"

"We'll never argue in their presence—"

"Never," I agreed. "We'll stay together, devoted to each other, until we are both one hundred—"

"Our children and our children's many friends will love us for our independent spirit and our open-house policy—"

"They'll come to us with any problems, secure in the knowledge our advice will be helpful, heartfelt and hands-off."

"We'll embrace their partners, their choice of occupations, their lifestyles, their hairstyles and their fashion styles," he said.

"We'll be babysitters on demand but we'll never once be a burden or source of guilt," I added.

"We will conveniently die on the same day to save them any excess trouble and expense."

"Having won the lottery when they are all in their thirties, we'll also have ensured they are secure for life but only once they're settled in their respective careers and with down-to-earth values."

We would be everything our parents hadn't been, we agreed. Of course we would. And then we had kissed and made love and then we had slept. And from that night, that whispered conversation became the secret blueprint for our life together.

We'd had so many plans. So many hopes and dreams. We'd been joking that night, but not completely. That was what we had wanted. Our own big family. Our chance to reverse what had happened to us. We wanted to give our children a happy, secure home. Encouragement. Love. Constant love.

We'd already made a start on our big plan with Felix. We loved being parents so much that we'd been trying for a second child. We couldn't wait to give him a little brother or sister. We'd been trying for a baby the same month that he died. The same month that everything changed.

The same month our marriage ended.

Standing there in Lucas's kitchen, I shivered. It wasn't cold, but I felt like I was surrounded by ghosts.

I thought of Aidan going back to Ireland for the first time since Felix died. Of his mother being in hospital, being sick, and Aidan going to visit her. I tried to imagine Aidan with his father. Would Mr. O'Hanlon have been sympathetic about Felix? Would his brother have made the trip from Dublin to see him? Or would it have been left to his mother to say all that Aidan needed to hear from his family?

I suddenly remembered something. I'd convinced myself that I'd had no contact with them since it happened. But I had. I'd spoken to Mrs. O'Hanlon the morning I left Aidan.

I'd been in our Canberra apartment. My suitcases were at my feet. I had just finished writing my farewell note to Aidan when the phone rang. I wouldn't have answered but I'd thought it might be Charlie. He usually rang around that time. But it was Mrs. O'Hanlon.

It was the first time she and I had spoken since it happened. Aidan had rung her the day after Felix died. He called from our bedroom. I was in the living room, with Mum and the priest, or perhaps it was the funeral director. Aidan had asked me if I wanted to speak to his mother, but I wasn't able to.

She had never met Felix. We'd sent her photographs and promised to bring him over to Ireland when he was a bit older, and she had sent cards and presents on his first birthday. But I wasn't able to talk to her that day. I could barely speak to my own mother.

Since my first visit to Ireland, I'd met Mrs. O'Hanlon again just twice. She'd come to London with a friend to see a musical and we had met for afternoon tea. It had been stilted but nice. Her friend did most of the talking. Aidan and I had also flown back to Ireland for a final weekend before we moved to Australia. Rory had been there that weekend too. It had mostly been about him.

We'd invited the three of them to Canberra for our wedding, of course, but Mr. O'Hanlon didn't like air travel and Mrs. O'Hanlon didn't want to leave him on his own. Rory accepted. "Someone has to fly the flag for Ireland!" he e-mailed. He sent a stream of e-mail in the weeks beforehand, asking us to book him into the best hotel, asking for the names of the top car-rental companies in Australia, telling us he was going to use the trip as a tax write-off. The week beforehand, he canceled, citing work pressures. "No recession in my business!" he e-mailed. He sent a dozen bottles of Moët & Chandon champagne as an apology.

After Felix was born, Mrs. O'Hanlon and I had more contact. Aidan and I phoned her once a month or more. Aidan would do most of the talking and then I would have a few minutes speaking to her too. We talked about what Felix was up to developmentally, anything funny he had done, but mostly we seemed to talk about the weather in Canberra compared to the weather in Carlow. Perhaps if she had met Felix, if she and I had spent more time together in person, we would have had more to talk about, but we never got beyond pleasantries. One of us invariably made the remark that it was a shame we couldn't swap some of that Irish rain for some of our Australian sunshine. We'd laugh, as if we had just thought of the idea, and then I would put Aidan back on.

The O'Hanlons sent flowers to Felix's funeral. A huge bouquet, with a card from the three of them. *Our prayers are with you.* Mrs. O'Hanlon had also had a mass said for Felix in their local church. I heard that from Aidan. She had phoned several times, but I still hadn't spoken to her myself.

Until that morning when I was leaving. After an awkward minute of weather conversation we both fell silent. It was as if neither of us could bear to mention Felix first. As the quiet stretched out, I realized I wanted to tell her the truth.

Mrs. O'Hanlon, I'm leaving Aidan today. I have to. We're destroying each other. I'm so sorry.

I imagined trying to explain to her why. How there wasn't enough room in this small apartment for all our pain, for the guilt, the blame, how our sadness was pressing against the walls, how his tears, my tears, were like poison, that we couldn't console each other, couldn't even begin to console each other, when all we could feel ourselves was such sadness, such—

I took the coward's way out. I said nothing. I pretended someone was at the door. I said good-bye, telling her in a strangely bright voice that I'd be sure to tell Aidan she'd rung. As if it was a normal day, we were a normal couple, that we did normal things like tell each other about missed phone calls.

But I didn't tell him. I'd already written my farewell note. How could I add a P.S. now? *Your mother rang. Please call her back.*

I left with one suitcase. I took some clothes, some books, my share of photos of Felix, and that was all. I knew I had to keep moving, I couldn't carry much with me. And in the first days and weeks afterward, whenever I would wake in the middle of the night, I would tell myself it wasn't because I'd left Aidan that I felt so bad. I somehow managed to convince myself that the reason I was feeling so guilty was because I hadn't told him his mother had rung.

TWENTY

Dear Felix,

So many things happen that I wish I could show you. Not just normal things, like dogs and cats and cars and trains. I'd have shown you all of those things, but I'd also have taken you to galleries. Museums. Even really boring ones, with steam engines and old cars, if that's what you'd have liked. Today I was out walking and I saw a little boy about your age, on a kind of a tricycle thing with a long stick attached. His mother was pushing it along, so she was doing all the work, but the little boy either didn't know that or didn't care. He was smiling so widely, with such a look of triumph as though he was Evel Knievel, a stuntman, a daredevil, not a little boy being pushed along a city street on a plastic bike by his mother. And I realized in his head he was that stuntman. You could see it in his eyes, in his expression, in his smile.

And I had to forget my walk and go home and I cried like I haven't cried since the early days. It's not going to get better, is it? I thought it might, that time would eventually help me, help us all, but now, today, I am frightened that it won't. Because there will always be a hole your exact size in our lives, and we can never fill it because you are not here anymore.

I miss you so much, Felix. I loved you so much and I miss you so much every single day.

TWENTY-ONE

From: Charlie Baum
To: undisclosed recipients
Subject: It's Been a Noisy Week in Boston

The latest report from the Baum trenches is postponed. All troops are down with stomach bugs. Trust me, you DON'T want the details.

Normal transmission will resume as soon as possible.

In the meantime, stay sane. We're staying close to the bathroom.

Charlie xx

From: Charlie Baum
To: Jessica Baum
Subject: re: I'm in LONDON!!!!!!!!!!!!!!!!!!!!!!!!!!!!!!!!!!!!!

London!! Wow. Big news indeed. Excuse this hasty
one, down with a stomach bug here, will write again
properly soon as have recovered. Give Buckingham
Palace a pat from me.

Love Charlie xx

From: Charlie Baum
To: Lucas Fox
Subject: unexpected development

L, Jess is in London. I don't know all the details,
why or for how long. Just got one line from her,
mostly squeals. Have e-mailed Dad for more info.
It's a big city. I hope it won't affect us. I'll let you
know if I hear any more. C

From: Charlie Baum
To: Lucas Fox
Subject: re: unexpected development

You'll recognize her. Small, lots of hair, singing,
dancing. We might need to move faster on the A
question. If E knows she's here, she might take off
again.

From: Charlie Baum
To: Lucas Fox
Subject: Update on J

Spoke to Dad. Jess in London funded by him. She's
wanted to go for years, auditions, West End etc.,
long as I can remember in fact. Dad & M gave in,
felt she was in need of change of scene. Many ups
and downs recently. More downs. Understandable.
They've given her credit card, hotel etc., to find her
feet, but expect her back within a month or two. Hotel is in Covent Garden. Dad says she has been very
fragile, but they hope this will give her a lift. I've
e-mailed her again but no word back yet.

From: Charlie Baum
To: Lucas Fox
Subject: re: Update on J

No, don't think she has your address. More asap.

TWENTY-TWO

Getting ready for my dinner with Henrietta was like preparing myself for a trip to the gallows. It didn't help that Lucas was so excited. He was like a matchmaker, checking what time we were meeting, if I was sure I knew how to get there. Our reservation was for eight and yes, I was, I told him each time.

"Is there anything I should know before I meet her?" I asked. "Any subjects I shouldn't mention?"

"Heavens, no. Ask her anything. I'm sure she'll tell you if you stray into choppy waters. I'm so glad you're having dinner with her, Ella. I know you'll enjoy each other's company."

I wished I was as sure.

That morning I'd e-mailed Charlie for advice. He'd been very unhelpful.

Just stay calm. Lucas asked you to have dinner, not elope
with her. If she gets too personal, give her a couple of
karate chops (or lamb chops). That should shut her up.
Alternatively, ask her the most insensitive questions you
can and see how SHE likes it.

Henrietta was waiting in the restaurant foyer when I
arrived. She looked cross. I checked the time. I was early.
That must have just been her natural expression. She took
charge from the moment we sat down. It was a formal room,
with white tablecloths, suited waiters, classical music and
leather-bound menus. She briskly called the waiter over and
ordered a large predinner gin for herself. I ordered sparkling
water.

"White or red wine with your meal, Ella?" she asked.
When I said I was happy with water, she swiftly read the
wine list, ordered a bottle of expensive burgundy and told
the waiter we'd give him our food order in ten minutes.

"Yes, ma'am," he said. I half expected him to click his
heels and salute her.

We'd barely taken a sip of our drinks before her questions began. "So you don't drink alcohol?"

"Not anymore, no."

"Do you have a problem with it?"

"I don't like the taste."

"Imagine." She took a large swallow of her gin, then set
it down. "It seems I may have upset you with my questions
the other night. I apologize."

I was surprised. "Thank you."

"It's obviously a very sensitive issue with you. Is what

Lucas told me true? You've had no contact at all with your husband since you left him?"

I thought of Charlie's advice. I forced myself to think of Lucas. "No, I haven't," I said, as politely as I could.

"That's been your choice, not his? You didn't try to work through it with him?"

I realized my hands were already starting to clench. "It wasn't that simple, Henrietta."

"No. Lucas told me the circumstances. Such a tragic accident. So much guilt for you all, for so many reasons. How is your poor sister? She's probably the one you should really be worried about. Her guilt must be particularly horrendous."

I answered with difficulty. "She's fine. She's back starring on a weekly TV show with my mother. She's come through it without any problems."

"Fine? I don't believe that for a minute. She was looking after her little nephew, he dies and she bounces right back? She'd have to be inhuman not to be affected by that. Where is she?"

"In Melbourne."

"What kind of a TV show is it?"

At last, safe ground. I seized on her question, answering in great detail. I didn't care that she didn't seem that interested at first, fiddling with her bread roll, glancing around. I just continued to talk and talk until she had no choice but to listen.

I started from the very beginning, telling her that Mum had been in a suburban shopping center one afternoon when she noticed a commotion on one side of the food hall. It was a TV crew inviting people to take part in what they called Speed-Cooking—the hasty assembling of six ingredients to make a two-course meal. The prize was a food processor and a guest appearance on one of the midmorning cable network chat shows. Mum put her name down. Why was a mystery. She hated cooking. She said it was because she had an hour to fill. She was on her way to meet a friend, all dressed up, her hair done, looking great, lively and bright, as always.

By the time her name was called, she'd had a bit too much of the free wine on offer. She was also a bit nervous. When Mum is tipsy and when she is nervous, she talks. And talks. And so the second she got up there on the stage with the TV crew filming and a crowd gathered, she started talking. She didn't stop. She said whatever came to mind as she picked up each ingredient: "This spaghetti looks like a plate of carsick worms." She put on a pirate voice and kept saying, "Sugar me timbers!" when she was measuring icing sugar for the cake decoration. The crowd started laughing. The louder they laughed, the giddier Mum got. I've seen the footage. She was on the manic side of funny, overwrought almost, but you couldn't look away or not laugh. Somehow she kept cooking, making a complete mess of the spaghetti sauce and an even bigger mess of icing the cake. The woman competing against her seemed drab and dull in comparison, even though she was obviously the better cook. A producer stepped in and offered more wine. Mum practically snatched it out of his hand, held it up to the camera, winked, said, "Cheers everyone!" drank it in one swallow, gave a big smile, and then started singing "Food, Glorious Food," from the musical *Oliver!* She was not only word perfect but note perfect, helped I'm sure by hearing Jess sing it a million times around the house. And then she sang "My Favorite Things" from *The Sound of Music*, changing the words to include all the German and Austrian food she could think of, not just apple strudel, but Wiener schnitzel, sauerkraut and pretzels. The cameras kept rolling and the crowd kept growing.

She lost the competition. The crowd booed. Two days later the network called her in for a meeting. Less than six weeks later the first episode of *MerryMakers* went to air. One of the production team coined the name. Mum had never called herself Merry—she was always Meredith—but she became Merry in public from that day on. Her personality seemed to change to suit. She became merry Merry, in and out of the studio. The show was something of a cult hit at first, particularly with hungover students: a rapid combination of recipes, gags, wine and food tips, with Mum saying whatever came to mind and singing whenever the mood took her. It went up a gear when a food stylist joined the team, and up another gear when Jess joined the show. The network put advertising and publicity behind it. Ratings improved and kept rising. A TV star—two stars, Mum and Jess, with Walter on the sidelines—was born.

I finally stopped talking, waiting for Henrietta to pour scorn on the idea of something so frivolous. She didn't. She seemed genuinely interested. She asked me all the usual questions people asked. I gave the usual answers. Where was the program shown? Australia, New Zealand and on cable TV food networks in the US, Canada and Spain. Was Mum now famous enough to be stopped in the street? Yes.

Did she actually cook the dishes beforehand or did she have people who did that for her? She had people. That was the real joke of the show. Mum still couldn't cook.

"And do her recipes work?" Henrietta asked finally.

"If you follow the steps properly, yes. They're nutritionally sound too," I said. I'd heard those lines a hundred times.

"I love cooking shows," Henrietta said as she took a final large swallow of her gin. "I can't cook but I like watching other people do it. Your lasagna was good the other night, by the way. Thank you."

I was more unsettled by her compliments than by her bluntness. "You're welcome," I said.

The waiter came back to our table. I watched Henrietta as she asked detailed questions about the sauces, the origin of the meat and vegetables, taking a long time over her choices. I ordered simply: the soup, a salad. I could feel her eyes on me, could imagine her next question—about my appetite, probably, or a comment that I was too thin. I decided to take Charlie's advice and get in first with my personal questions.

I began as soon as the waiter left. "What does your husband do, Henrietta?"

"He's a doctor. A specialist in immunology."

"Have you been married long?"

"Thirty-two years."

"And having an affair with Lucas for most of that?" This was fun, I realized. Tact was overrated.

"Yes," she said, glancing over her shoulder for the waiter. "I wonder where he is with that wine."

"Do you ever feel guilty?"

"At times, yes."

"So you didn't have children?"

"No, it didn't turn out to be possible."

"Why did you stay with your husband?" I genuinely wanted to know the answer.

"Because I loved him. I still love him."

"But you love Lucas too?"

She reached for her glass of water, took a sip, put it down with precision and then gave me a long look. "I know what you're doing, Ella. You didn't like the questions I asked you last week, so you are asking me the most uncomfortable questions you can in return."

"Yes, I am." I felt a blush rising. "But I still hope you'll answer them."

My honesty seemed to surprise her. Her honesty surprised me, in turn.

"The answer is yes, I love them both, even though the two of them couldn't be more different. My husband is obsessively tidy. Lucas, as you know, isn't. My husband is a workaholic, driven, committed to scientific facts and deadlines. Lucas is all thought and discussion, content to spend weeks, months even, searching for one historical detail. My husband is wealthy. Lucas has nothing to his name, his house aside. I get to take wonderful holidays with my husband. Live in a fine house. Work as much or as little as I please. Life is comfortable, easy. But when I'm with Lucas, my mind is fully stimulated. Not just my mind. In marriage— I don't know if you were with your husband long enough to find this, Ella—but sex can become mundane. It's never been like that with Lucas."

I didn't particularly want to hear those details. "But if Lucas is your soul mate—"

"I didn't say that."

"That's how he describes you."

"Yes, I know."

She said it so confidently. I wondered what that would feel like, to know you had that much power over another human being. I realized I did. Aidan had had that power over me. I'd had that power over him. If you loved someone, your happiness was in their hands.

The wine arrived. We fell silent as the waiter uncorked it. Henrietta tasted it and he filled her glass halfway. After he'd left, she filled it to the top, took a sip and then gave me another long look.

"You're a romantic, Ella, I can tell. I'm a practical woman. Lucas had nothing when we met at university. I looked ahead. I knew then what I know now. Love doesn't pay the bills."

"But then his godfather left him the house. Didn't that change things between you?"

"That wasn't a house. It was a life sentence. Lucas insisted on following his godfather's wishes to help those less fortunate. The place was overrun with students within weeks of Lucas taking ownership. The last thing I wanted to do was live there with him. I'd had enough of communal living at university. Lucas and I argued constantly about it."

"About the students?"

"The students. The mess. The chaos. The impact on Lucas's own study. His ridiculous selflessness. A house full of rooms and where did he choose to sleep? In the attic. An attic so small it was barely possible to stand upright in. That was about the only battle I won and only because I started refusing to go up there. Even so, it took years to get him to move downstairs."

So I was right. Henrietta had been responsible for Lucas's relocation into a "proper" bedroom.

Our starters arrived. The conversation turned to general subjects. A play she had seen. The guided walks I'd been taking. Since my tour of Mayfair, I'd seen Charles Dickens's London, Jack the Ripper's London, and walked in the footsteps of Sherlock Holmes. Over our main course, Henrietta told me about her own studies in great detail. A punishment for my detailed telling of my mother's TV story? She specialized in Victorian literature. Again, it felt more like a lecture than a conversation, but I was happy to stay silent, nod where appropriate and feel relieved that she wasn't interrogating me about my own life anymore. I surreptitiously glanced at my watch. Two hours had passed. I could go home soon.

We had just finished our dessert when Henrietta put down her spoon with an air of purpose.

"Ella, this dinner is opportune. I intended to speak to you privately and here is our chance. It's regarding Lucas. Lucas and the house. I need your help in regard to a very sensitive matter."

I noticed her voice was slightly slurred. She'd had a lot to drink tonight. "The thefts, you mean?"

"Forget those." She waved her hand dismissively. "I still can't understand why Lucas cares so much. A few trinkets here and there, taken from people who can easily afford a loss. You're coming with me next time I do appraisals, aren't you? You'll see for yourself. More money than sense or taste, most of them."

"But if word got out, it could be the end of not just his clients but all of his renovation plans too. He could end up having to sell his house just to make ends meet."

"Exactly!" she said. "And the sooner it happens, the better."

"The better?"

We were interrupted again by the waiter, offering coffee. She waited until he had gone and then leaned forward. Her gaze was intense.

"Ella, I'll be blunt. I *want* Lucas to sell the house. I want him to sell it as soon as possible and the two of us to go and live in France together on the proceeds." She sat back, an oddly defiant expression on her face.

"But he can't sell it. He loves that house. It's his life."

"It was his life. He's nearly sixty-five, for God's sake. That house has been falling down around his ears for years. If he cared so much about it, he would have fixed it up long ago. The only sensible option is to sell it. The market is down, but he'd still get a very good price. More than enough for the two of us to set ourselves up. I'm about to retire myself. So should he. No more lecturing, no more research papers, no more students."

"But he loves the lectures, the study. He cares about the students."

She gave another dismissive wave of her hand. "Students come, students go. He'd realize that soon enough. He needs a new direction in his life and I need your help convincing him, Ella. You're his only relative. Of course I realize this impacts you to some degree. Perhaps you were expecting to inherit the house, though whether you'd want a millstone like that around your neck is another question. That's immaterial now, anyway. The point is, I want you to help me convince him to sell up and retire. I've already made enquiries. It's an excellent time to buy in France. If we moved quickly, he and I could be living there by the summer."

"But what about your husband?"

"I've decided the time has come to choose between them. I've chosen Lucas."

I was having difficulty taking this in. "But why does that mean Lucas has to sell his house? When you and your husband get divorced, won't you come to some financial agreement?"

She called the waiter over again and ordered a port. She stayed silent until it was in front of her, took a sip and then fixed me with what might have been an unsettling look if she had been sober.

"It's a complicated situation, Ella. Let me explain. My husband is not just wealthy. He's extremely wealthy. And when we got married, his parents deemed it necessary to protect that wealth. So I found myself signing what is now called a prenuptial agreement. I must confess I'd forgotten all about it. Until my husband announced less than a week ago that he wanted to end our marriage—"

"He announced? I thought you said you'd made the decision to leave him."

She waved her hand again. "It was just a matter of timing. It transpires he's been busy extracurricularly himself. What it boils down to, if you'll pardon the colloquialism, is that my marriage is over and I can now live openly with Lucas. But I refuse to do it in that house. So, as I have explained, the most obvious solution is for him to sell it and we start fresh somewhere else. France, preferably, but elsewhere if need be. But I know Lucas won't think about selling while you're there. So that's my next question. How long do you plan to stay?"

"Pardon?"

"You weren't planning on living with Lucas forever, were you? Playing housekeeper for squatting students for the rest of your life?"

"I don't know, Henrietta. I've only just arrived."

"No need to be upset. I'm sure this has come as a shock. But I hope you will put his happiness ahead of yours and see that selling is the best possible option in these new circumstances."

Henrietta's phone rang before I could answer. She glanced down. "It's my husband. Excuse me."

She moved to a corner of the restaurant to take the call. I now knew why she'd accepted Lucas's suggestion to have this dinner. It wasn't to get to know me better. It was to give me notice to vacate.

When she returned, I pleaded a sudden headache. If she guessed I was pretending, she let me get away with it. We briefly brushed cheeks as we said good-bye. "We'll talk further, Ella," she said as she hailed a taxi. I walked home. I needed all the thinking time I could get.

The house was lit up when I arrived. A student in every room. Before I lost my nerve, I knocked at Lucas's door and went in. As usual, he was by the fire, papers and books strewn around him. He looked up and smiled, so familiar, so welcoming. My spirits fell even further when I realized it wasn't lecture notes or research papers he was looking at. It was architectural drawings. His renovation plans for the house.

"Ella! How was dinner?"

On the walk home, I'd decided to tell him everything. Now, in front of him, I lost my nerve. I needed to wait until I'd quelled my own feelings about Henrietta. I needed to remind myself that she was Lucas's great love. I also needed to quieten another voice in my head. The one that had started whispering to me, like a child, *What about me? If Lucas sells, where will I go?*

I told him it had been very nice. I told him about the restaurant, the food, the other diners. He nodded and looked so pleased.

"She's wonderful company, isn't she?" he said.

She is, I agreed. I felt like Judas. After ten minutes, I repeated my headache charade and said I was going to bed. He was disappointed, I could tell. He was obviously in the mood to talk. Perhaps he could show me some of the renovation plans in the morning, he suggested. We could even go out for coffee together. That would be great, I said.

At three a.m., I was still lying in my bed, staring at the ceiling. For the first time in twenty months, it wasn't thoughts of Felix and Aidan that were keeping me awake.

TWENTY-THREE

From: Charlie Baum
To: undisclosed recipients
Subject: It's Been a Noisy Week in Boston

The latest report from the Baum trenches is as follows:

Sophie (11): Reported current state of play with her group of friends at school. "Kayleigh isn't talking to Rumer, because Rumer sat next to Lindsay at lunch and told her that Kayleigh was in love with Oscar, but Collette and Katie said that it's Billie's fault, not Rumer's, that she even knew about Oscar."

"And what about you, Sophie?" I asked, after the dizziness passed.

She lowered her voice and said, "I keep my lips sealed."

Ed (8): Came across a mention of the *Titanic* in a book and asked me about it. I explained in detail: a big ship from long ago, supposed to be special because it was unsinkable but on its very first trip, it hit an iceberg and nearly everyone drowned etc., etc. His only comment? "They should have gone in summer."

Reilly (6): International food week at school. Told me that for lunch today "we had special rice called puss-puss."

Tim (4): "Dad, can we play a game?"

"Sure," I say, thinking of Fish, Guess Who?, Snap. . . .

"Okay, here's how it goes. You speak animal language and I come to your ship."

WT?

Lucy (36): Still bathed in her top-of-the-class glow. Just as well. We had a power outage this week. Only lasted a few hours, fortunately. We ate dinner in her reflected brilliance.

Charlie (36): Diet backward is Teid. Sounds like tired. I am tired of diets. Isn't that a coincidence?

Snip the cat (kitten age): Worryingly cute all week. Purred. Chased own tail. Fell asleep in odd but funny places, e.g., towel cupboard, small cardboard box. Has she been taking "How to Make Your Human Family Love You" classes??

Until next time, everyone please stay sane.

Charlie xx

From: Charlie Baum
To: Lucy Baum
Subject: You. Again.

You are still amazing. Just saying.

To: Jessica Baum
From: Charlie Baum
Subject: you

You've organized auditions already?? Congratulations! I can't walk after a long flight let alone dance or sing. Are you warm enough? Speaking of which, don't drink the beer. Break a leg at the auditions. Not literally. I'm being artistic. Love C xx

TWENTY-FOUR

Dear Diary,
Hi, it's Jess!

This has been the worst week of my life. SERIOUSLY. That's why I haven't been able to write until now. It started badly enough, but because I am optimistic by nature, I decided to take it in my stride and used all my affirmations: "What doesn't kill you makes you stronger," "The darkest moment is before the dawn," etc., but they didn't do any good. It just got worse and worse as the week went on and now I don't know what to do. My counselor used to tell me to try to isolate my feelings, to give the emotions words and try to take charge of them that way, so here is how I am feeling right at this minute. ANGRY SCARED FURIOUS DISAPPOINTED.

I will start at the beginning. My first audition. HID
EOUS. There is no other word for it. If I hadn't come top of
my classes in Melbourne year after year and had fantastic
acclaim and feedback all my life from my dance and voice
coaches, I would seriously be having some self-doubt about
my abilities as a performer right about now. The people at
the audition could not have been more horrible if they tried.
They were the witches and warlocks of the theater world
and if I ever get famous—WHEN I get famous—they are
SO going to regret being that mean because I am going to
remember their names and I will refuse ever to perform in a
show that they have anything to do with. Even if they beg
and offer me a million pounds.

What happened was, I had been on all the Web sites and
got the trade papers and made a note of all the open casting
calls. I hadn't heard back from any of the agencies I e-mailed,
so I decided to keep myself busy in the meantime and also I
figured that it would probably be easier to get an agent if I
had already been offered a role, as that would show not just
my talent but also my get-up-and-go. There were three auditions taking place on the same day but I decided that if I
got to the first one early, maybe I would be seen quickly and
then I could make it to the other two as well.

I asked my new friend Ben for some advice. He's a porter
at the hotel. (He's delivered my room-service meals each day
and we've had such a great chat each time—I've given him
big tips too!!) He's an aspiring actor. Most of the staff are, as
far as I can tell. I suppose it makes sense because it is such
an artistic hotel and that way the staff can tell almost without thinking what the needs of the stars and other people

like me (future stars!!) might be. Anyway, I went downstairs and showed Ben the ads for the auditions and he said he had never done musical theater, he's more into serious acting (!!!!), but he would ring a friend of his.

My ears pricked up at that. Perhaps the friend could help me, but it turns out the friend is a lighting technician, not a performer, so no use to me really, but he told me which of the three shows was getting the most industry buzz and that made it easier to decide which audition I would go to first. I suppose I should have gone back to my room and done a bit of research on the three shows, but Ben was finishing his shift and he said he and a couple of his friends were going out for a few drinks, did I want to come?

The truth was I was a bit lonely in my room on my own, so I said yes. I don't like drinking that much, but I felt a bit nervous with three basically strange men, so I had two vodka and tonics pretty quickly, actually. I practically drank them both in one swallow, which was my first mistake. Or mistakes. The guys were drinking fast too and they were getting a bit stupid, to be honest—juvenile really, teasing me about being Australian—and I said, "I don't sound Australian when I sing; nor does Kylie, and anyway, what about Cate Blanchett? No one ever tells her off for being too Australian, do they?" And one of them, his name is Zach, he's an old school friend of Ben's, said no, but Cate Blanchett doesn't sound like a dingo pup like you do. And I DON'T sound like a dingo pup, but even so it made me feel a bit stupid, so I went quiet and they didn't seem to care and so just to give me something to do I drank another two vodkas and I started to feel a bit sick and dizzy then, but luckily Ben helped get me home to the hotel and I was in bed (ON MY OWN) before midnight and I woke up in time for the first audition and I felt fine.

But now I wish I hadn't woken up and that I had slept through the whole audition; it was so horrible. Back in Melbourne, I know all the other dancers and singers, and people know me, especially now because of the TV show. Sometimes the people casting the shows call me by name before I even get a chance to introduce myself. Not here. They didn't even give me a MINUTE to prove myself. I was given about EIGHT seconds to introduce myself and tell them what experience I'd had and one of them said "Are you Australian?" as if she was asking "Are you a terrorist?" I started to sing my audition song, "Memories," which is my trademark song, really (the review in the college magazine said it was "thrilling in its emotional dexterity"), but they stopped me after ten seconds, saying I wasn't right for the part, but thank you anyway. And I said, "But what about my dancing?" And they said, "That's fine, thank you. You're not what we're looking for."

I made it to the door before I started crying and I know it's only jet lag and of course they'll regret it and it will take a little while before I get used to a new way of auditioning, but they could have been nicer. The worst thing was that I had no one to ring. Usually Mum or Dad come along to the auditions with me, as much as there are any in Melbourne—it's not exactly a hotbed of musical theater—but the time difference meant I couldn't ring and I didn't even have Ben's number and he was the only person I knew in London, really. Apart from Ella, but of course I couldn't ring her.

Anyway, things got worse. I should have said in that bit above that I didn't make it to the other two auditions that afternoon. I was on my way to the second audition when I realized I'd left my phone back at the first one and of course it's my lifeline and also it's one of the latest ones, so I couldn't leave it there for long, someone would definitely nick it, so I had to go BACK to the audition studio, and they were still seeing people and all these girls were coming out smiling and ringing their friends and families and I had to wait until the room was empty and go in, and thank God my phone was there. "You're a lucky girl," one of the assistants said. Oh, yes, the luckiest girl in the world, I thought, but I didn't say that, of course. I just put on a bright smile and said "Hope to see you again" to the casting directors, who were still there behind the table, and I turned back at the door and they weren't even LOOKING at me. I had made no impression on them whatsoever.

I was too late for the second audition by then and I realized I'd lost the address for the third one. I'd written it down but left it in my hotel room. I remembered what Tube stop it was (Goodge Street), so I went there, but all the streets and the buildings looked the same and I couldn't see any signs for dance studios anywhere. I asked three people and no one knew what I was talking about. Two of them were tourists lost like me. It all felt so hopeless and I was suddenly really starving too. All I wanted to do was go and eat a big piece of cake but I thought, sure, that'll really help matters. I apparently already sound like a dingo pup. The last thing I want to look like is a fat dingo pup.

So instead I ate two bananas and decided not to take the

Tube back. I'd walk to the hotel instead and of course I got lost again and all of London looked the same, just more of those crowded streets and so much traffic and it started to rain, so long story short, I caught a black cab (I still really like them—I feel like I'm in a film every time I get into one), but I KNOW the driver ripped me off. I had only been two Tube stops from the hotel, hadn't I? How could it possibly take him half an hour and twenty pounds to get me back there, regardless of one-way systems or whatever his excuse was? I couldn't really understand him. He had the thickest Cockney accent. Thankfully Dad had given me petty cash for emergencies like this. So I got back and had a long bath and then did some stretching exercises and a bit of singing practice, which went well until the porter (not Ben) knocked at the door and asked if I could please keep my voice down, as my neighbor was an actor filming night scenes and he needed some peace and quiet. The porter wouldn't tell me who it was but I'm going to sit in the foyer with my laptop tonight and pretend to be working until the actor comes down.

Ben started work at six p.m. and I went down to say hello to him and he asked, "Are you okay?" in a strange kind of way and I said, "Sure, why wouldn't I be?" And he said, "You seemed a bit drunk last night. I practically had to carry you back here," and I said of course I wasn't drunk, it was jet lag, and so he said, "Well, we're all going out again tonight if you'd like to come," but I decided an early night would be better. Now, of course, I wish I had gone out because if I had, then I wouldn't have just got the e-mail from my friend Jill in the *MerryMakers* production office, which is what has made me SO upset now.

She'd written to me a few days ago to say she was sorry she wouldn't get to work with me on my new show, and I didn't know what she meant, so I e-mailed her back and hadn't heard anything because it turned out she had a few days off, but then she wrote back tonight (tomorrow her time) but I just don't understand it. She said—and I quote—"I hope I'm not interfering or getting anyone into trouble, and maybe I have it wrong, but I was in a couple of meetings and the producers here said that they were hoping to give you your own show, that they had the format and the title all finalized, they'd done market research and audience-testing and all this other stuff, and apparently you [as in me, Jess] really appeal to prepubescent young boys AND their dads."

Me again now. Anyway, apparently that is a really good thing and also VERY lucrative from an advertising point of view, so according to Jill what they were hoping to do was to give me my OWN show, working title *Mess with Jess*, which would be me cooking and basically flirting with a male guest every week (the stars from the TV soaps, mostly, as well as a couple of the hot footballers) AND singing a song AND dancing, basically using ALL my talents. But then Jill said that it was about to get the green light and they'd even talked about it with Mum and Dad when next everyone heard I was going to live in London. Jill finished her e-mail by saying, "I'm really sorry it didn't work out. It would have been great fun!"

She's right. It would have been REALLY great fun. But the thing is, Diary, I knew NOTHING about it. Not a single word. Of course if I had been offered my own show, I wouldn't have upped and gone to London. I know I'd been begging to go for years, even though Mum and Dad kept saying I was too young. But that's not the point now. The point is, why wasn't I told about MY OWN SHOW???

I've just e-mailed Mum and Dad and asked them about it outright. I've also told them I'm really upset and also feeling betrayed. Mum usually checks her e-mail first thing in the morning, even before she's out of bed, so she should be ringing me back soon.

Hang on, my phone is ringing, back in a sec.

I CANNOT believe it. I've just hung up from talking to Mum. Actually, I hung up on her. Then Dad rang back and I hung up on him too.

Mum and Dad knew all about the show and THEY CHOSE NOT TO TELL ME.

"You weren't ready for it," Dad said. "It didn't feel right," Mum said. They have got NO idea what I am ready for, or any idea what is right for me. It is MY career and this was MY opportunity and now they have blown it.

I'm going to e-mail my friend Jill and ask her if she thinks it's too late about the new show. I don't know what I'll do if she says it's NOT too late. Can I go back to Australia after only a week here?? But I have to know one way or another. I just cannot believe Mum and Dad. My phone's ringing again now. Dad again. I'm not going to answer it. I am VERY VERY upset.

It's four hours later. I've just been out with Ben and his friends again and everything makes more sense now after talking to them about it, except now I'm even more unhappy and also a bit dizzy. I don't think vodka agrees with me. I told them about what had happened. They were so nice and they got me to show them the kind of things I would have done on the show, just a quick song and a bit of a dance—we were in a pub after all and I didn't want to draw too much attention to myself—but they liked it so much I took out my phone and showed them a few videos from my show reel, including me doing that Rihanna song about umbrellas. "Wow, sexy, Jess," one of them said. "I'd like to mess with Jess myself!" And they all laughed a bit too loudly. I just tried to ignore that. I know they were being supportive but I didn't like the way one kept trying to look down my top. Not Ben. He's nice. He's also gay, he told me. I'd kind of guessed.

Anyway, we got another round of drinks (well, I did—I seem to be the only one who has any money, and I felt a bit guilty about that but then I realized I was still mad with Dad and it was *his* money I was spending, so it was kind of karma in a way) and when I came back from the bar, they'd changed seats and I had to sit next to Zach, who I don't really like much. There's something kind of arrogant about him, even if he is the best-looking of them all (kind of like Robert Pattinson but not as good). The others were all talking about football or something and Zach leaned in to me and said, "You do realize your mum is jealous of you?" He's not only arrogant, by the way; he's got a really upper-class kind of voice, as if he is Prince William or someone. Mind you, Ben told me Zach had had elocution lessons to sound like that. He also told me Zach had been trying to get a good theater role for years but kept getting passed over and that he was getting a bit bitter.

I said that of course my mum wasn't jealous of me. She

was my *mother*. And Zach shook his head and gave me a really pitying look and said, "Jess, I'm sorry, but it's obvious. The TV people recognized that you were the one with the sex appeal, so they were going to ditch your mother and sign you up. Your mother gets wind of it and what does she do? Ships you off to London."

She wouldn't do that, I said to him.

He shrugged and said, "Hell hath no fury like a woman scorned. And that's not Shakespeare, by the way; it's William Congreve. The actual quote is, 'Heaven has no rage like love to hatred turned / Nor hell a fury like a woman scorned.'"

I didn't care about the stupid quote. I didn't know what he was talking about. I tried to ignore him, and tried to stop thinking about what he'd said about Mum being jealous. I was glad when Ben suggested we all go to another bar in Soho where there was room to dance, but as soon as we'd found a table in the new place, the others all went straight to the dance floor and I was left with Zach again. I would have got up to dance myself, just to get away from him, but it was one of those techno songs that I hate, and also I was in the corner and Zach had kind of hemmed me in. He was pretty drunk by now.

"You're staying at Ben's hotel, aren't you? For how long?"

"As long as I need to. Till I find my feet," I said, not that it was any of his business.

"Have you got any idea how much it costs there a night?"

I didn't have a clue. Dad set it all up from Australia, using his credit card. So I said, no, I didn't know.

That was when Zach told me it's at least four hundred quid a night. He got all worked up about it. "A *night*. I have to live off less than that a fortnight."

Four hundred pounds a night! I did a quick calculation myself and worked out it was nearly six hundred dollars!!!! I didn't let on to Zach that I was shocked, though. Anyway, Dad might have negotiated a better deal for me. He's really good at making deals. That's why he's so good at being Mum's manager. And my manager.

"You're just a trust-fund kid, aren't you?" he said, shouting into my ear over the music.

I said I didn't know what that was. I wasn't going to play his stupid name-calling games.

Zach just kept talking. He didn't seem to care whether I answered him or not. "You are, Jess. I'm sorry to be so honest, but don't give us your poor little rich girl whining and complaining—oh, poor beautiful me, oh, the auditions were horrible, oh, Mummy's jealous of me and wouldn't give me my own show to play with. I'll give you another quote—" He leaned right in to my ear as if he was about to KISS me or something. "'He who pays the piper calls the tune.' It means the person who pays gets to call the shots. You take Mummy and Daddy's money, you have to do whatever they tell you. Even if it is just spare change to them."

I got really angry then. How DARE he say those kind of things? He didn't know how hard I'd been working for years and what a lifelong dream appearing on the West End was to me. "Sure, Zach. So what am I supposed to do? Try to hold down a job while I go from audition to audition?"

"Like the rest of us have to? Of course not. No, Princess

Jessica, you do it your way. But stop complaining about mean Mummy and mean Daddy when they're bankrolling every second of your day, would you? When you wouldn't last an hour if you were doing it on your own."

Thank God Ben and the others came back then. I pretended I had to go to the bathroom and by the time I came back everyone had shifted seats and I didn't have to sit next to Zach again.

I'm not going to think about him anymore, Diary. I've written it down now so it's out of my system, just like my counselor advised me to do whenever I found myself feeling sad or scared or anything. Ben's right. Zach's just bitter because his own career hasn't taken off.

I'm going to go to sleep now. Tomorrow is a brand-new day.

Bye, Diary. Love for now,

Jess xxxxoooo

TWENTY-FIVE

I'd thought the tutors were exaggerating when they told me about the opulence of the homes they visited each week. An hour into my rounds with Henrietta, I realized they'd been telling the truth. Outside of the pages of glossy interiors magazines, I had never seen houses like these.

We'd be visiting five students tonight, Henrietta told me. She had another four to visit the next evening too, but as there'd been no thefts from their homes, Lucas felt I didn't need to see them.

"We'll give you a cover story," Henrietta said. "I'll explain you're Lucas's niece and you're training to be my assistant in regard to the appraisals."

"Feel free to ask them as many questions as you like, Ella," Lucas said.

In the taxi on the way, I waited for Henrietta to raise the subject of Lucas and the house. Remembering how much she'd drunk that night, I wondered hopefully whether she'd forgotten the entire conversation. The whole idea. Then it was as if she read my mind.

"Have you had a chance to speak to Lucas about selling the house yet?"

I shook my head.

She made a *tsk* sound. "Please do it soon," she said. "I don't want to end up sleeping on the street."

Lucas's attic is free, I wanted to say.

The first home was in Fulham, a three-story house in the middle of a curving row that looked onto a private, gated garden. The trees were lush and green, even in winter. Before we went inside, Henrietta reached into her large leather bag and consulted a folder. "The student's name is Antoinette. She's ten years old. We tutor her in French, algebra and classics."

I knew from Lucas that the item stolen from here was the antique map.

A housekeeper let us in. Another member of the staff took us up two flights of stairs to a luxurious sitting room, which was obviously being used as a study area. It was as big as my entire Canberra apartment. As well as a desk, a computer and a filing cabinet, there were two large sofas and a coffee table. The walls were covered in framed paintings, landscapes, portraits, abstracts. Two large windows looked over the park. I glanced out of the window and noticed a sign on the iron fence. I could just make out the wording: *No bicycles or balls allowed.*

There was the sound of light footsteps and Antoinette appeared. She was small for a ten-year-old, beautifully dressed in a red pullover and matching corduroy skirt, shiny black boots, her dark hair in a bouncy ponytail, her eyes bright. Behind her was her mother, about thirty-five, also beautifully dressed in wool and cashmere, high boots, glossy hair, not so bright-eyed.

Henrietta introduced me as Lucas's niece and her tutoring assistant. They barely noticed me, immediately falling into a discussion about a recent exam result. I listened but I mostly looked. At the mother's jewelry. She was wearing rings on each finger. Eight large diamond rings. She had an emerald necklace around her neck. She also smelled extraordinary, of lilies and lemon and something else. Wealth, I suppose.

Henrietta was brisk and formal. We took seats on the sofas and she fired questions at mother and daughter, making notes in her folder. Antoinette was doing very well, getting ninety-plus scores on all her tests. She'd had some difficulty with aspects of the algebra course recently but the additional tutoring sessions with Mark had proved very helpful.

Henrietta turned to me. "Ella, any questions?"

I was put on the spot. "How are you, Antoinette?"

"Good, thank you." Her voice was like a bell, clear, high.

I had to do better than that. "Is this where you always study? And where the tutors take their break?"

Antoinette and her mother both frowned. "Why do you need to know?" the mother asked.

"We're reviewing our insurance policy," Henrietta said.

"We need to be specific about where each tutor works in each of our clients' houses."

I sent her a silent thank-you.

Most of the study took place in here, they told us. The breaks were also taken here, though occasionally in the kitchen downstairs.

"I showed Peggy my bedroom once," Antoinette said. "She said it was the most beautiful bedroom she's ever seen, like a princess's. Would you like to see it too?"

"Go ahead, Ella," Henrietta said, turning to the mother and opening her folder again.

I followed Antoinette up another flight of stairs. She was very chatty away from Henrietta and her mother. "Are you a tutor too, Ella? I'd like to be a tutor when I grow up. Tutors know everything. Mark says it's because they read all the time. He says I should try to read at least two books a week."

I told her I wasn't a tutor, but I did like to read. "I hope your tutors are nice to you. Are they?"

"Yes, very," she said. She told me Peggy was her favorite, then Mark, then Darin. "I like Peggy's funny voice. She says it's because she's from a far-off land."

A far-off land called Newcastle.

"Is your name short for Cinderella?" she asked as we climbed the last few stairs.

"Not quite," I said. "Arabella. But I've always hated it. I prefer Ella."

"Yes, that's much nicer," she said solemnly. "My bedroom's just down here."

We walked down a corridor at a leisurely pace. I counted at least six rooms running off it.

"Do you have brothers and sisters, Antoinette?"

"No. Mummy says she and Daddy got it so right with me there was no point in trying again. Are you married, Ella?"

I hesitated for only a moment. "Yes, I am."

"Do you have children?"

"No. No, I don't."

"I'm going to marry Justin Bieber."

"Are you? Congratulations."

She stopped at the doorway to what was obviously her bedroom and nodded. "Daddy said he can arrange for me to meet him. I know every single thing there is to know about Justin Bieber. Daddy says I could win a Justin Bieber *Mastermind* quiz. Mummy says my room is like a Justin Bieber museum."

She opened the door. Her room may have been in a city mansion, but it was the replica of ten-year-old girls' rooms the world over, I was sure of it—a bright pink bedspread, soft toys in rows on the shelves and all four walls plastered in posters of bands, actors, cartoon characters, models, but mostly of Justin Bieber.

"He's gorgeous, isn't he?" she said, sighing.

"He's got very nice hair," I replied.

"He's only eight years older than me. I don't think that's too much of an age difference, but Mummy does. What's your favorite animal?"

"A fox. What's yours?"

"A giraffe." She opened a wardrobe door. There was an enormous giraffe toy standing there. It was like a giraffe stable. I immediately thought of the two giant fox toys Lucas had sent Felix. Where were they now? I realized I had no idea.

"Wow," I said.

"I asked for a real one but I got this instead. I like sliding down its neck. Have you seen enough?"

"Yes, thank you," I said.

She walked me back down to the study, still chattering about Justin. I pretended I had a problem with my boot, asking her to wait, hoping to slow our pace down. As I fiddled with the lace, I glanced around. The house was like a combined museum and art gallery. The walls were covered in framed prints, maps and paintings of different sizes. Lucas had told me the stolen map was only small, but very valuable. As I stood up straight again, I reached and touched the nearest framed print. It wasn't secured. If I'd wanted to, I could probably have taken one myself.

Henrietta was ready to leave. "Did you see all you needed to?" she asked me as we left the house, shown out by the housekeeper.

"It was very helpful," I said.

The second house was within walking distance. Henrietta and I didn't speak on the way. I didn't mind. We were met at the door by the student's mother. She was eerily similar to the first mother in appearance. The interior of the house was also similar—luxurious carpets, curtains, furnishings and decorative features. I met the student, a thirteen-year-old boy: polite, groomed, confident and, again, clearly very bright. Henrietta got right down to business. Yes, his results were excellent. No, they had no complaints about the tutors—Darin and Peggy in this case.

As Henrietta moved into a detailed discussion about a new teaching method Peggy was trialing, I asked if I could use the bathroom. A housekeeper appeared and showed me the way. I was led down to the next floor, without conversation. It was from this house that the figurine had gone missing. Again, the thief had been spoiled for choice. The house was filled with what my mum would call "knickknacks," and what a fine-art expert would call *objets d'art*. Again, it was obvious how easy it would have been to lift something from one of the tables or shelves, put it into a bag or a pocket and leave, undetected. The study area was one of the three living rooms, the one closest to the front door. If I'd been so inclined, I could have easily left that house with more than my purse, notebook and keys in my handbag.

The third house was a ten-minute taxi ride away. I expected Henrietta to bring up the subject of Lucas's house as we sat in the back, but she took another large folder out of her bag and started to read its contents. I followed her lead, taking out my notebook and writing details about the houses. We were in a traffic jam, still a mile from our next stop, when her phone rang.

She glanced at it. "Excuse me. My solicitor. I need to take this. He's impossible to get hold of."

I didn't mean to listen. It was a private conversation. But she was right beside me. She was also soon so agitated it was if she'd forgotten I was there.

"How can that be the case? It can't *all* be in his name. Sue him? No, of course I can't. I'll be lucky if I can afford to pay *you*, the fees you charge."

She didn't refer to it when she hung up. We continued on the journey, once again in silence.

In the next house, I met the rock star and his daughter.

On the way into their four-story mansion, I saw a gold Mercedes, a vintage BMW and what I think was a Rolls-Royce in the long drive. Inside I noticed jewelry lying on a table, original paintings leaning against walls and bottles of dusty, expensive-looking French wine in a cupboard. I asked to go to the bathroom and wandered through the house afterward on my own for five minutes. I had an "I'm sorry, I'm lost" line ready if anyone came looking for me, but no one did.

It was after eight by the time we left the final client—the Booker Prize winner with the horse-mad daughter. All Peggy had said was true. The daughter, fifteen years old, didn't care about university, literature or studying. All she wanted to do was talk about horses and show me her horse-riding DVDs. After twenty minutes, I was relieved when Henrietta came to get me.

I didn't need to visit any more houses to make my conclusions about the thefts. It was clear how easy they would have been. The tutors—and by extension Henrietta and I—were considered part of the family. Above reproach. They had the run of each house, the trust of the parents and the friendship of the children. They could have loaded their bags with goodies and walked out. Someone would probably have held the door open for them or called for a taxi.

I'd expected Henrietta to come back to Lucas's house with me, but she announced a change in plan.

"Something's come up, Ella," Henrietta said as we waited for a taxi. "I'll ring Lucas with my report. Please don't mention the house matter to him yet." With that, she walked away.

I arrived back home to a full house and a crowded kitchen. Unusually, all four tutors were home and eating together. They'd assembled a hotchpotch of my frozen dinners—Peggy was eating a Tuscan bean casserole; Darin had a big bowl of minestrone soup; Mark and Harry were sharing a beef, leek and mushroom stew. The mood was festive.

Lucas came into the kitchen behind me, carrying two bottles of wine. "Ella, welcome back! What a shame Henrietta had to go on to that meeting. You'll have to give us the eyewitness report instead." He smiled at his tutors. "They all seem confident on the surface, I know, but deep down they are terribly insecure. If you have any praise for them at all, please don't hold back."

I passed on what I could. Lucas seemed pleased with all the positive feedback. Afterward, the tutors wanted to know what I thought of their clients.

"Isn't the rock star ridiculous?" Peggy said. "I'm sure he looks good onstage, but, God, close up, he's like a walking corpse. I'll never be able to listen to his songs again."

"What about Pony Girl? Did you get the full horse-riding DVD extravaganza?" Mark asked.

"She's getting worse each week," Darin said. "I keep expecting her to hop on my back and make me gallop around the room."

"In your dreams," Harry said.

After dinner, the gathering broke up. I started doing the dishes, once again turning down any offers of help. I'd just finished when Mark came in, sifting through the large collection of mail that had been left piled on the hall table. In my first days here I'd sorted the post each day, leaving the tutors' letters, magazines or circulars under their door. I'd eventually stopped. The house seemed to operate best in a certain degree of chaos.

"One for you, Ella," he said. "Nice stamp. George Washington. Can I have it when you're done? My nephew's a philatelist."

Even before he passed it over, I knew who it was from.

Aidan.

TWENTY-SIX

From: Charlie Baum
To: undisclosed recipients
Subject: It's Been a Noisy Week in Boston

The latest report from the Baum trenches is as follows:

Sophie (11): Sophie has two soccer coaches, Jenny and Rick. She sent Rick a card for his birthday, on which she wrote: "You are my favorite coach." I explained that it was nice to have a favorite coach, but that Jenny, her other coach, might be hurt if she was to see the card. Sophie nodded wisely, picked up her pencil and wrote on the bottom, "Don't show Jenny."

Ed (8): Lucy and I were talking about our next-door neighbor's new daughter being adopted. Ed overheard. "That little girl's a doctor? Wow! She's only six years old!"

Reilly (6): Doing sums. "Dad, twelve is a dozen."

"Yes, it is," I said.

Pause while he finishes another sum.

"Dad, you know how twelve is a dozen?"

"Yes?"

"Well, what is nine?"

Good point.

Tim (4): In the car with me. He puts his fingers and thumbs together to make a triangle.

"Look, Dad," he says. "A triangle."

"Mmm," I say.

"An isosceles triangle," he adds.

I nearly crash the car.

Lucy (36): Long days on the road may be coming to an end. Interesting office-based job has come up in her company. She's applying. I'm wishing and hoping and thinking and praying, channeling my inner Dusty Springfield.

Charlie (36): A glorious moment at this week's weigh-in. I'd lost four kilos! In one week! Very cruel of Lucy to remind me that Tim had dropped the scales into the bath.

Snip the cat (kitten age): Days of cuteness short-lived. Life of a small bird in our garden nearly short-lived. Snip now wearing a bell around her neck that wouldn't look out of place on an alpine cow. (I've told her it's her German heritage.)

Until next time, everyone please stay sane.

Charlie xx

From: Charlie Baum
To: Lucy Baum
Subject: re: New Job????

Yes, of course you should apply for it.

Yes, of course you will get it.

Yes, it would change everything—yes, for the better.

Not that I want to change anything.

I am the luckiest man in the world as it is.

C xx

From: Charlie Baum
To: Lucas Fox
Subject: re: Jess

No, I don't think so. Haven't heard from her for a few days but I looked her up on Facebook. She seems to be busy sightseeing and using exclamation marks. Dad told me he's loaded up her credit card so I'd say she's also going to see every musical London has to offer. Don't worry. Chances are slim she and Ella will run into each other.

C

From: Charlie Baum
To: Aidan O'Hanlon
Subject: (no subject)

Hope all is okay. Have left a couple of messages for you at home and work. Would be good to talk.

C

From: Charlie Baum
To: Walter Baum
Subject: Meredith

Is Meredith okay? Watched the latest video link of her on that chat show and barely recognized her.

From: Charlie Baum
To: Ella O'Hanlon
Subject: You

You've gone quiet on me. All okay over there?

TWENTY-SEVEN

D ear Diary,
    Hi, it's Jess!

I'm not going to talk about what is happening here in London because it's too awful. Instead, I am going to work on the chapters about my childhood.

I have to just say one thing first. I hope I haven't made a big mistake, but the more I thought about what Zach said, about me not really being independent while Mum and Dad are paying for me here, the more I realized he was right. Once I thought that, I couldn't stop thinking about the other comments those people in my dance classes had made. That I was only here because my parents were rich and paying my way. And then I couldn't stop thinking about what Mum and Dad had done—not told me about the TV show, basically shipping me off to London, out of the way—and I got so mad, it was like a storm in my head, and I did a stupid thing. I cut up the credit card Dad gave me. The one I could use as a credit card and a cash card. And I did it before I looked in my purse and I only have one hundred pounds left in there. I should have taken some money out before I cut up the card. It was so stupid of me. What on earth can I do now??? It's not as if I can ring Dad up and say, "I'm going to stand on my own two feet but before I do, can you give me another few hundred pounds?"

I've just rung downstairs and the receptionist said she's very sorry but she can't extend my room booking without authorization from the credit-card holder who originally made the reservation. Which is Dad. Who I am not talking to. Which means that in one day's time I won't have any-where to live and I haven't got any money. I am really scared.

I'll write about my childhood instead.

I was born on 5 April 1989, to a mother called Meredith Baum and a father called Walter Baum. Dad is German by birth but has lived in Australia for nearly forty years. I have a half sister called Ella, from my mother's first marriage, and a half brother called Charlie, from my father's first mar-riage. Ella is eleven years older than me, and Charlie is thir-teen years older than me.

I am going to write this next bit honestly. When the time comes to publish my autobiography I will probably have to edit out a lot of this so that no one's feelings get hurt, but I have resolved to make the first draft as honest as I can. So here goes. . . .

I had a very happy childhood. I knew from the moment

I was born (well, as much as I can remember of it) that I was very loved and also very wanted. To this day, my mum and dad are the most in-love couple I have ever met. They are very affectionate with each other, and while I don't know all the details of their first marriages, it's pretty clear from what they have both hinted that things weren't good for either of them, which makes sense, of course; otherwise why would they have got divorced? Mum and Dad met in very romantic circumstances, in a garden center of all places (and *baum* is German for tree, how cool is that!!), fell in love instantly and were married within a year. I came along soon after—I was always an impatient child, Mum said!!!

We lived in Melbourne in a very nice house in Richmond, which is a cosmopolitan inner-eastern suburb. Mum looked after me while Dad worked full-time but I can honestly say that I never felt he was an absent father. He was always there for me and to this day is very generous and loving.

~~My half sister Ella and my half brother Charlie were always very nice to me.~~

~~My half sister Ella and my half brother Charlie were very welcoming and were the best big brother and sister any little girl could have.~~

~~Charlie tried his best but I know my half sister Ella always hated me.~~

I will have to edit this out at the end but for now I am going to write down the truth. For as long as I can remember, it was always the two of them against me. There was a big age difference, but I can remember so clearly wanting to do things with them and them always saying, "No, Jess, leave us alone. No, Jess, you're too young." It was just as well I liked to spend time in my own company, practicing my dancing and singing, or I would have been a very lonely and sad little girl. The two of them were always giggling and whispering to each other, and if Mum and Dad asked them to include me, they would say no at first, or if they did eventually say yes, they would make such a fuss that it wasn't fun anymore. Mum noticed. It was hard not to, but even if she pleaded with them to be kind to me, often they still wouldn't be and I would feel very left out.

"They're just a bit jealous of you," Mum would say to me sometimes, and I didn't understand when I was young but now that I have met a lot of other kids who have divorced parents and stepsiblings or half siblings, I understand that it can be tricky to feel like you only half belong to a family, whereas for me I was always with my mum *and* my dad and I knew they loved each other and me, so that was a very secure environment to grow up in.

Ella's biological dad is dead. (He died in a plane accident in Canada when I was just a baby so I never met him.) Mum said he was nice at first but very argumentative in the latter years of their marriage. Charlie's mum, Dad's first wife, was mentally unstable and went back to Germany after their divorce and there was hardly any contact, and then she died the year Charlie turned sixteen. I never met her either. He and Dad went back for the funeral, which must have been very difficult, I suppose, even though Charlie didn't really ever know his mother and in a way he was abandoned by her. I have to try to be understanding of Charlie and Ella, only having one parent each, even if sometimes I think they are the ones who should be more understanding of me, as the youngest in the family.

It's like when I started in a new school after we moved from Richmond to a bigger house in Malvern. By the time I started in the middle of the first term, all the kids had already made friends and it took me ages, nearly a week, to make some really good friends. It was the same for me in my family, if you look at it. By the time I was born, Ella and Charlie had been brother and sister for more than a year and had all sorts of in-jokes and so I had to try to break into that, which was tricky when I was only just born and couldn't even speak yet!

I can't write about them anymore. I can't stop thinking about what I should do next here in London. I should just say sorry to Mum and Dad, and ask Dad to send me a new credit card and book me in for another week here. But I'm too angry at them. I really am. I'm angry and hurt.

I'll ask Ben for help. He might let me sleep at his flat even for a few nights, until I get a job somewhere. I might have been a bit optimistic that I would get a part in a musical so soon.

I can't sleep now. I have to be so careful not to start worrying too much because when I do, everything I've been taught by my counselor seems to fall away and all I do is go over that terrible day again and again, and all I seem to be able to feel is Felix, the weight of him in my arms, and how it felt to have his hand in mine and then that horrible moment when he started to slip and I saw it. It was as if I knew something really bad was going to happen and I couldn't stop it and I screamed and I screamed and I heard it. I heard the noise when his head hit the rock. I never told Ella or Aidan that—how could I?—but I heard it that day and I've remembered it so many times since, and if I could give him my life, if I could swap it, I would. I would do whatever I could to fix that day. He was such a beautiful baby. He wasn't a baby, he was a little boy. He called me Ess. He didn't seem to be able to say the letter *J* yet, even though he was a really good talker for his age. It used to make me laugh so much. When he'd see me he'd hold up his arms and shout, "Ess! Ess!" So I called him Elix. His favorite game was peekaboo. He could play it for hours and he would get this sort of gurgling laugh when I played it with him and it was impossible not to laugh too.

I still can't understand it. How can God let something like that happen? I'm not sure I even believe in God anyway. No proper god would let a little boy die.

I wish I hadn't started remembering it all. Not when I'm here on my own like this. Once I begin thinking about it, it's really hard to stop, and all the bad thoughts come rushing at me again. Mum always helps me when it happens at home. She holds me tight until I feel better, and she says the same things. "It was a terrible accident, Jessie, an accident," and I know that, but even knowing it doesn't ever help, not really. I just keep thinking about the day it happened, and the days afterward. It all becomes a big horrible blur in my head. I just remember crying so much and wanting to see Ella but she wouldn't see me. Of course I can't blame her, but she still won't see me or talk to me. She never will and I just have to come to terms with that, my counselor said. I did see Aidan. He came to the hotel the next day. I was in shock, I know I was, and he came into our room and he hugged me and he said, "It was an accident, Jess. I know it was an accident," and I cried and he cried so much, both of us, and I asked him if Ella was coming too and he said no. I saw her at the funeral but she wouldn't look at me. I don't know if she saw anyone that day. I watched her. I was watching her in the hope that she would turn around even for a second and see me and I could say sorry to her, but she didn't turn. She just stared straight ahead the whole time. I could hear her crying. I've never heard anything like it. Dad took me outside, before they carried Felix's coffin out of the church, but I still saw Ella stand up and really start to cry and then she—

I'm sorry. I have to stop now.

TWENTY-EIGHT

I hadn't read Aidan's letter.

I'd had it for twenty-four hours. The envelope was still unopened.

Aidan hadn't written to me or e-mailed me in months. I'd wanted it that way. I'd needed it to be that way. But now he had written again, out of the blue. Why? I'd been awake most of last night thinking about it. I'd thought about it all day today. I knew I couldn't open it without preparing myself as much as possible. His letter could only be about one of two things, I'd finally decided.

It would be about Felix. About the anniversary that was now just days away. I tried to picture what Aidan might have written.

Ella, I know that next week is Felix's twenty-month anniversary—

The idea of it being an important date had come from Mum. Someone in the early days had tried to give her some solace by saying the pain became more bearable once you passed the anniversary of the age the child was when he or she died. It had seemed impossible to me at the time. It still was. How could the pain ever be bearable? But for Mum especially, it had become a summit we needed to reach. Mum had told Charlie about it too. He'd mentioned it to me himself. Had she talked about it with Aidan as well? Was that why he was writing? To say that he too was thinking of that date?

Or was he writing about something else?

Something quite different?

Ella, I've met someone else. I want a divorce.

All day, my mind had flicked from one possibility to the other. I wasn't ready to read either of them. Not yet. I'd open his letter tomorrow. Yes. Tomorrow. For now, not knowing what it said was easier to deal with than knowing.

Distract.

Observe.

It was ten o'clock at night. I was in my bedroom. There was nothing in here for me to do. It was already spotlessly tidy. It was too late to go downstairs and start cooking or cleaning. I turned on my laptop instead. I hadn't checked my e-mail for a few days. There were two new ones from

Charlie, one of his family reports and one asking how I was, saying that I'd gone quiet.

I'd e-mail him now. Nighttime in London was the afternoon in Boston. It was coming up to what he called Hell Hour, feeding time at the family zoo. There was no way he'd be online at the moment, but I had an urge to talk to him.

I quickly wrote an e-mail. I didn't mention Aidan's letter.

Sorry for silence. News in brief: Henrietta wants me to get Lucas to sell house. She and her husband are divorcing. She wants to move to France with Lucas. Needs house money to fund new setup.

I sent it.

A moment later, there was a reply from him.

WTF??

I typed back quickly. *How can you be online now? Isn't it Hell Hour?*

Forget Hell Hour. Am in Hell on Earth aka neighbor's child's birthday party. Am barricaded in laundry with my iPhone. Sound of multiple hot dogs being devoured frightening to the human ear. Of course Lucas won't sell. He loves the house. Anyway, it's your inheritance. Tell her to keep her dirty mitts off it.

Before I had a chance to write back, another one arrived

from him. *Did you say Horrid Henrietta said she needs the money? Maybe she's the thief??*

Very funny, I wrote.

I'm not joking.

Stop it, Charlie.

I'm NOT joking. Back soon. Wailing child banging on door.

It wasn't Henrietta I wanted to talk to Charlie about. Now was a good time to ask him. He was online. He could write straight back. I wrote the e-mail.

Charlie, I know that Aidan is in Washington. Have you seen him?

I deleted it. I tried again.

Charlie, have you had any contact with Aidan recently? Lucas told me

I deleted that too. Just say it, I told myself. Just ask him.

Charlie, do you know if Aidan is seeing anyone? If he is, is it serious?

I deleted that as well.

Another e-mail came in from him before I had a chance to write a fourth version.

COULD it be Henrietta?? She's often in the houses too, isn't she? Maybe she's like those movie stars who shoplift for kicks. Not sure how you'll break that news to Lucas though . . .

I wrote straight back. I still didn't mention Aidan.

Of course it's not Henrietta. She's too busy researching French properties to be a thief.

I hope you're right. Yikes, sound of breaking window outside. Better go. C x

Charlie might have gone off-line again, but he had planted a seed. Could it be Henrietta?

Could it?

Of course it couldn't, I told myself. Just because she was planning to leave her husband and set up house with Lucas and didn't have any money of her own but urgently needed lots of it and had plenty of access to those houses . . . It didn't mean anything. It couldn't be her.

I returned to my e-mail, scrolling down through the in-box. Amid the spam, there was one from my mother. She'd written twice since I'd told her I was in London, cheerful e-mail messages thanking me for letting her know where I was, telling me a couple of stories from her filming days, an update on Walter's plans for his new garden. I expected more of the same this time.

My breath caught as I read it.

Darling Ella,

You are always in our thoughts, I hope you know that, but especially so this month. It is barely possible that Felix has been gone from us for almost twenty months. I thought you might like to know we are having a mass said for his anniversary. I hope you don't mind. I haven't converted, I promise, but it gives me great peace.

Love from Walter and from me, darling.
Mum xxx

I wrote back immediately.

Dear Mum and Walter,

Thank you very much. That means a lot.

E xxx

I blinked back sudden tears. As I sat there, another e-mail came in from the *MerryMakers* address. An answer from her already? It was barely seven a.m. in Australia. I clicked it open. It wasn't from her personally, but from her production team. A link to an interview Mum had done on one of the main TV channels. I read the accompanying note, working my way through the exclamation marks that littered any message from the *MerryMakers* team. They were especially excited this time. An interview like this was a big step, I knew. There wasn't usually much crossover between cable TV stars and what people thought of as "real" network television.

I opened the link and pressed play. The clip began. The tanned host began his introduction, calling her "Australia's wackiest mum," "the kooky cook," "the madcap, mischievous mistress of the mixing bowl and masterchef of mirth, Merry of *MerryMakers* herself!"

Mum appeared at the top of some flimsy-looking stairs and practically ran down. How she managed it in high shoes and a short skirt, I didn't know. Her hair was styled into bouncy blond curls. She was wearing her usual bright colors. She sat down and waved enthusiastically at the camera. The interview began.

At first I thought there was something wrong with the connection. I stopped it, started again. I put it in wide screen, then back to small. I wasn't mistaken. Something was definitely different about her. It wasn't what she was saying. She was being as funny as ever. She sang as well as ever too, bursting into a chorus of "Food, Glorious Food" midinterview. She crossed the studio and did a demonstration at a mini kitchen setup. Her cooking was as chaotic as ever. What was different was her face, I realized. Mum had had Botox. A lot of Botox.

I was shocked. Why on earth would she have done that? Everyone knew she was in her fifties. She'd never hidden her age. It was part of her appeal. I was sad and disappointed all at once. I started to write her an e-mail, not editing myself, telling the truth.

Mum, please tell me I'm imagining it? Botox?? I've just seen you on that chat show and you were brilliant but your forehead didn't move once. You were

beautiful the way you were. That's why everyone loves
you, because you are yourself. You won't seem like my
mum if you don't look like my mum. I really wish you
hadn't done it.

I couldn't send it, of course. I was thirty-four years old,
not fourteen. If she wanted to have full-scale plastic surgery,
then that was her choice, whether I liked it or not. I pressed
delete. I looked again. I'd pressed send. I tried to stop it but
I was too late. My e-mail was on its way to Australia.

I hurriedly wrote another one. *Mum, I'm sorry. I didn't*
mean to send that.

I checked a minute later. No answer yet. I pressed re-
fresh. Still no answer.

I rang her instead. It was the first time I'd rung her in
over a year. She answered immediately.

"Ella! Darling, what time is it there? How are you? Is
everything all right?"

"Mum, I'm fine. I'm sorry to worry you. I'm ringing
about my e-mail. I shouldn't have sent it—"

"The one saying thank you? I just got it. Thank you,
darling. I'm so glad you didn't mind me having the mass
said for Felix. I wasn't sure if it was my place—"

"Your place?"

"You know, whether it should be me who has the mass
said—"

"But Felix was your grandson. Of course you can have a
mass said for him."

"Are you sure? I just didn't know if I should have checked
with you beforehand." Before I had a chance to answer, she

spoke again. "Oh, another e-mail from you. You have been busy. Isn't the world amazing? I'm talking to you on the phone and getting e-mail from you on my laptop, all at once." There was a moment's silence as she read it and then I heard her laughing. "Is this the one you shouldn't have sent? Your e-mail about the Botox?"

"Mum, I'm sorry. It's none of my business. I—"

She laughed again. "Oh, don't worry, Ella. Everyone has told me off about that. Walter is horrified. I'll let it ooze out or wear off or whatever it does. And I won't do it again, I promise. It's hideous. I look the same no matter how I feel. What was I thinking? But don't you worry about me and my silly Botox. How are *you*, darling? How is London?"

"It's still very cold. It snowed last week. Just a few flakes, but—"

"I know! Jess was so excited to see it. She rang especially to say—" She stopped abruptly.

"Mum?"

"I'd better go, darling. I'm late for the studio. Thanks so much for ringing. It's wonderful to hear your voice."

"Mum, please wait. Did you say Jess—"

She'd hung up. When I rang again she didn't answer. I didn't leave a message. I didn't call again. Instead, I did something I hadn't done in a long time. I went onto Facebook.

I'd banned myself from looking at it. Now, despite a voice telling me not to, I keyed in Jess's name. I knew there wouldn't be any privacy measures in place.

Her page appeared. She had updated it in the past week. There were dozens of photographs with dozens of exclamation-mark-laden captions. Jess in front of Buckingham Palace.

Jess beside a black taxi. Jess in front of the London Eye, the Houses of Parliament, a red phone box. Jess in the West End, pointing up at the billboards of different theaters.

Jess was in London. And by the look of the photos, she was having the time of her life.

TWENTY-NINE

Dear Felix,

Next week is the twenty-month anniversary of your death. We all hoped it would be significant in some way, help us in some way, I think, but I can't imagine a day when I am not devastated that you died. A day when I won't wish time and again that I'd made a different decision that afternoon. That I had somehow been able to stop it happening. I have relived that day over and over so many times, wishing I could change the ending. I still wish it.

 But I've also made a decision. I will always be sad when I think about you but I am going to try to remember something happy too. Every time I feel sad I want to have a good memory ready to try to cancel it out. I am going to make myself remember all the beautiful things that happened while you were in our lives, not just the sad way you left us. Because there are so many wonderful memories, Felix. I don't know how you did it, but from the moment you arrived, you filled all our lives with happiness, just by being you.

Here are just two of my favorite memories for now:

The way you looked the day you were born. Felix, you had so much hair. Even the nurses remarked on it. I'm sorry to put it so bluntly, but you looked like a monkey.

One day when you were about four months old I was trying to put your nappy on. You didn't want me to do it. Every time I tried, you struggled. I left you alone, then tried again. No, you still struggled and squirmed and kept trying to sit up. I wasn't cross, just tired, but I said, a bit sharply, "Fine, Felix. Don't wear one." And you got upset. It was as if you understood what I'd said. Your bottom lip quivered and you looked up at me as if you were sorry to cause trouble, and then, the funniest thing of all, you lay down flat again and stretched out your legs, stiff as can be, as if to say, "Go on, then. If you're going to get so worked up about it, put the bloody nappy on." I know you were probably just stretching but I don't think I've ever laughed so much. I still didn't get the nappy on you in time, by the way. You got it all over me. My own fault.

I miss you so much, Felix. It's still so hard.

THIRTY

From: Charlie Baum
To: Ella O'Hanlon
Subject: Meredith

Yes, I saw it. Not so much *MerryMakers* as *Merry-Can't-Make-a-Muscle-Move-in-Her-Forehead*. Glad to hear she's laughing about it. Not that we'd be able to tell if we were looking at her. How long does it take for that stuff to wear off??

From: Charlie Baum
To: Ella O'Hanlon
Subject: On a different subject

E, I know the anniversary is coming up soon. I just want you to know we are all thinking of you. Stay strong and brave and know how much we all love you and how much we all loved Felix too. C xx

From: Charlie Baum
To: Walter Baum
Subject: Jess

Just got your message. No, I agree, that's not like her. Will call you first thing your morning. Don't worry yet. Maybe she's just lost her phone. C

THIRTY-ONE

D ear Diary,
    Hi, it's Jess.

I am so scared. I've made a huge mistake. I'm in trouble.

I should never have come here. I'm not good enough. I was a big fish in a small pond in Australia and I'm a tiny fish in a huge, huge pond here but that's not what I mean about being in trouble. It's just a part of it.

I've moved out of the hotel and into Ben's flat. It's in Barons Court, about eight Tube stops from Covent Garden. It's above a laundrette, so it smells good, like washing powder, but it's so small, just two bedrooms and a tiny kitchen and a pretty small living room. He said it belongs to his aunt and she rents it to him cheaply, that he's actually really lucky, a place like this would normally cost a fortune. But between us, it's really ordinary and really crowded. Zach has been staying here too, so his stuff was in the spare bedroom but Ben said that he'll get Zach to move out into the living room on the sofa, and I can have the bedroom. I don't know what Zach will have to say about that. He wasn't there today. He was out leaving his CV at all the agents again, Ben said.

I went to another two auditions today. I won't even tell you how I got on. Yes, I will. They were terrible. I knew within seconds that they didn't want me. I was too upset and I couldn't seem to get the beat and I was out of tune and they wouldn't give me a second chance. Only one person was kind and explained to me they have to go on first impressions at the audition, because if you don't get it right under pressure then, how can they have faith that you'll get it right on the night?

After the second audition (worse than the first), I gave myself a good talking-to. I pretended I was talking about everything with my counselor and she was urging me on. Usually I try to imagine Mum and Dad urging me on and telling me not to worry, that everything will get better, that the day will come when everything won't feel as bad as it does now, but I couldn't think about them because I'm not talking to them at the moment. I'm trying to stand on my own two feet. I imagined the counselor asking me how I was and what was worrying me the most at the moment. And my answer to her was "Money." My lack of it. And my imaginary counselor said, "What about trying to get a job?"

So after the auditions I went into every restaurant and café near Ben's flat but there were no jobs going. I even went into a temp agency but I didn't have any qualifications. I can type but not as fast as I need to be able to, and they said there's not that much work going anyway.

I've only got sixty pounds left. When I counted it, I nearly decided to throw my pride out of the window and ring Mum and Dad and beg them to send me money, but something stopped me. I realized I am still really actually mad at them. Then I thought, I'll just go home and stay with some friends in Melbourne, not go back to Mum and Dad's, not until I calm down and also not until they apologize. So I rang the airline and I had to hold for so long I was worried my phone battery would go flat and then the woman who eventually answered said it would cost me one hundred pounds to change my ticket!! That's outrageous, even if I did have it. Which I don't. So I can't go back home yet. Anyway, I could just imagine the people in the TV studio laughing at me, "Oh, Jess, you're back. We only just tidied up after your farewell party." And as for everyone at the dance classes, I just know how it would be. "Wow, Jess, welcome back. Your West End career went so well! How long did it last, a week?"

What can I do?????? I'll go for a walk. That might make me feel better. I'll pretend I have some money and go window-shopping for clothes.

It's three hours later. I'm in a café not far from Oxford Street trying to make a cup of tea last for as long as I can but the waitress is starting to give me death glares AND she's Australian. I thought she'd be nicer. Maybe she's from New Zealand. I've only been here for an hour and there are plenty of empty tables around me now so I don't know what her problem is. I am still really worried and scared. I wish I knew someone here apart from Ben. I know Ella is here in London. I know she's here at her uncle Lucas's house. But I have to put that out of my mind.

Ben said he won't be home until later. I don't want to be at his flat on my own with Zach, so I said I'd meet him back there at nine p.m. That only leaves five more hours to kill. I'd go to the cinema except that would use up money that I don't have to spare.

I'll go for another walk instead. It's really cold. What I thought was a heavy coat in Melbourne isn't really heavy enough in London. Hopefully walking will warm me up.

It's an hour later. I'm in a café in Paddington now. I didn't mean to come here, I really didn't. But I was walking and I got so cold and a bus went past and I just got on and it was only afterward that I realized where it was going. I don't even know where Ella's uncle lives. I never had the address. And I can't ask Mum for it. And what would I do if I had it anyway?

Charlie might know it.

But he won't give it to me. Ella would have told him not to.

But I can ask him anyway. He might.

No, he won't.

The café I'm in is near a big road called Baywatch Road or something like that. I didn't realize Paddington was near Hyde Park or maybe it's Kensington Gardens. I can't work out where one finishes and the other starts. The houses are nice around here. Big, and all painted white. I saw a blue plaque on one of them saying that the man who wrote *Peter Pan* used to live there. I looked him up in my online guidebook, and it turns out there are hundreds of those blue plaques around the whole city about all the famous people who lived here and there. If the weather was warmer, I would walk around and see some of them, except what's the point? It's not like you get to go inside the houses.

London is so huge. I wish again I knew someone here who could show me around, even for a few days.

Now the waiter HERE is starting to give me death glares too. What is it with people who run cafés in London?? It's not as if anyone has come in and wants to sit exactly where I'm sitting. I'll go to Paddington Station instead. There are lots of cafés there.

I'm at the station now. I walked up a long street on the way here, past loads of those big white houses, and I could see into a few of them because people's lights were on in their living rooms and I could see they were watching TV and reading and starting to make their dinner, all these happy people with their safe lovely houses, and I couldn't help it. I started to cry as I was walking along.

I'm having a really terrible day. I've still got two hours to fill until Ben finishes work and I'm hungry so I bought a banana but I'm so worried about spending any more in case what I have has to last me for another week. I called into every café, hotel and restaurant I passed on the walk here too but none of them had any job vacancies either. I even called into two hairdressers' to ask if they needed anyone to sweep up the hair, or to be hair models, but they all said no. I'm not sure how much longer I can last on my money.

I still can't believe Mum and Dad didn't tell me about the show. Is that really why Mum had the Botox? Because she was feeling threatened by me?

It's now eight o'clock. I'm still in Paddington Station, in a café in a sort of shopping area. Only half an hour to go before I can start making my way to Ben's flat. I found a Tube ticket in my bag and thank God I realized I'd bought a monthly pass when I got here, so at least I can use that without breaking into my last pounds. I'll catch the Tube to Ben's. I'll have to change lines but I think I've worked out how to do it. There are birds everywhere here, even though the station is under a roof. It's kind of disgusting actually. What else is disgusting is how much food people leave. If I was really, really starving, that's what I'd do. I'd come to this café and wait until I saw someone get up and leave half a sandwich or most of their cake behind and I'd get it before the birds got to it, or the waitresses.

I just saw a waitress chase a homeless guy away who was trying to do exactly that.

I just realized I'm like him. I don't have a home either. I'm really scared.

THIRTY-TWO

I woke up feeling as if I hadn't slept. I barely had. I'd dreamed of Jess in London. Of Aidan and his letter. I'd relived the dinner with Henrietta. When I rang Charlie in my dream to ask his advice, he'd hung up, laughing. Lucas disappeared. I ran from room to room trying to find him but it didn't matter how many doors I opened—he was nowhere to be found.

This house had been my safe haven. It felt different now. I felt different. My heart felt fluttery in my chest. My bedroom suddenly felt too small. It was the beginning of a panic attack. I knew the feeling. I couldn't let it happen. The key was to do something definite, focus my mind, concentrate on something real, something present, something nearby.

All I could think of was Aidan's letter.

I couldn't open it now. Not when I was feeling like this.

I got up. I got dressed. I wanted to run away. Leave London, today, now. But I couldn't. Not yet. I couldn't do it to Lucas. He needed my help.

I was now pacing the room. My mind was racing, leaping from thought to thought. I hated the idea of Lucas leaving London. How could I possibly ask him to sell his house? I hated that Henrietta had asked for my help. If she wanted him to sell, then she could ask him herself. I wanted nothing to do with it. I didn't want to help her.

I didn't *have* to help her.

Why hadn't I thought of that before? Why had I been agonizing over how and when to ask him? I didn't have to obey her. She wasn't my aunt. Even if they did get married, I could never think of her as my aunt. I would still see Lucas—I would make sure of that—but away from her. Somehow. We could meet in Paris, perhaps, if I was still living in Europe.

Where would I go next? Where else could I live? I had some savings, enough to do some traveling. That was it. I'd go traveling. The first thing I would do if and when Lucas sold the house and moved to France would be to go and see Charlie in Boston. I hadn't seen him in almost two years. After that? Could I come back to London? Could I look up some of my old publishing contacts from my time in Bath? Could I even consider taking on an editing project or two in London? I could rent a cheap flat somewhere, not here, not in the same area as this, that would be too hard, but somewhere new. Yes, in a brand-new part of the city—

I suddenly felt energized. I was making plans. I wanted to be on the move now, today, this morning. Yes. I would go and see Henrietta today. Now. Tell her that I was sorry, but she would have to talk to Lucas about selling his house herself.

The tutors had already left for the day. Lucas was in his withdrawing room. I knocked on the door, said good morning, kept my voice casual. I made the idea of me dropping over to visit Henrietta sound normal. He was distracted with his work but pleased at my idea, I could see. I mentioned something about a book she'd talked about lending me. What was her address? Her house was within walking distance, wasn't it?

"Anywhere is within walking distance if you've got the time," he said, smiling.

He gave me her address and directions to get there. It was in Kensington, about forty minutes on foot. I decided against ringing first. I'd let fate take over. If she wasn't home, I'd go another day.

"Everyone's in tonight, Ella," Lucas said as I put on my coat and scarf in the hallway. "Would it suit you to prepare dinner for us all?"

"Perfectly," I said, surprised at how relaxed I sounded. "Will I do my famous Thai curry?"

"Lovely," he said. "Enjoy Henrietta. Give her my love."

"Of course," I said.

It was a cool, misty day. It felt good to be outside. I walked into Kensington Gardens and took the path that led across to Kensington High Street. I followed Lucas's directions from there. I walked past long rows of houses with entrances on the street like Lucas's, many divided into flats, obvious from the number of bells in the doorway. The closer

I came to Henrietta's street, the farther back from the foot-path the houses went. Steps gave way to small front gardens. I turned into a very grand street, the houses barely visible through large hedges or over tall stone walls. They were mansions now, rather than houses. I saw security cameras. Sculptures visible over walls or through fences. A fountain in one front garden. A gardener sweeping up leaves in another.

Henrietta's house was one of the largest on her street. There was a discreetly designed intercom in the wall and, on a post nearby, a camera trained on the spot where I was standing.

I pressed the button. A moment later, a voice. A male voice. Henrietta's husband? I hadn't expected that.

"Yes?" So much came across in that one word. Confidence. Intelligence. Impatience.

"Hello. My name is Ella." Did Henrietta know me as Ella Fox, Ella Baum or Ella O'Hanlon? I didn't know. I left it at that. "Is Henrietta in, please?"

"Are you one of her students?"

"No." How did I describe myself? I wasn't her student or her friend. "I'm Lucas Fox's niece."

"Just a moment."

I waited for the gate to open. It didn't. I stood there, unsure. A minute later, Henrietta's voice sounded down the intercom. "Ella? What on earth are you doing here?"

"I need to talk to you."

"Couldn't you have rung first? I'm busy." She sighed, the sound noisy through the small speaker. "Come in, then. Go to the side door. The front door's just been painted."

The gate slowly opened, revealing a landscaped front garden, white gravel, two cars and stone steps going up to, yes, a freshly painted yellow door. I made my way around to the side of the house. Henrietta was there waiting for me. I'd expected a maid or a housekeeper.

"Why didn't you ring?" she said again. There was no greeting.

"Is it a bad time?"

"Yes. Come in anyway."

She took me through the kitchen, a long room with gleaming appliances and uncluttered shelves, through a kind of scullery and up a flight of stairs into a living room on the first floor. The walls were painted a soft cream. The carpet was a deep blue. The furniture was highly polished. The contrast between her house and Lucas's was striking.

"Tea? Coffee?"

"Tea, please." I didn't really want it, but I was glad of a chance to gather my thoughts. Now that I was here, on her territory, in the shadow of her strong personality, my nerves were failing me. I expected her to ring for someone to make the tea, but she went downstairs.

I heard a phone ring. A minute later, she was back. "Ella, you'll have to wait for the tea. I need to deal with this call. I'll be at least fifteen minutes. Do you want to stay or come back?"

If I left now, I knew I'd never come back again. "I'll stay," I said.

I took a seat at the large bay window. It was a beautiful room. The furniture was antique. There were china ornaments on the marble fireplace. The walls were covered in portraits and landscapes, arranged by someone with an eye for color and symmetry. I mentally compared it to Lucas's house again, with his books piled ten high in the hall, dozens of unframed prints and paintings leaning against walls—

How could the two of them ever live together? They were so different in every way. Perhaps that worked well in an affair—clearly it had worked for them—but as a permanent arrangement? Lucas couldn't make her happy. He would drive her mad. It would never work between them. I hoped it wasn't just wishful thinking on my part.

"You're Lucas Fox's niece, did you say?"

I jumped at the sound of the voice. A man in his sixties was standing in the doorway. I didn't know what I had expected Henrietta's husband to look like but it wasn't this. He was as tall as she was short, and very thin. He was bald. His clothes were crisp, tailored. He might have been handsome in his youth but now he was florid. His eyes were sharp. He struck me immediately as the male equivalent of Henrietta— clever, confident and not to be crossed. I had a split-screen moment, imagining Lucas standing beside him, all disheveled curls, warm smile and baggy clothes. I had to blink it away.

"I am, yes," I said. I held out my hand. "Ella Fox." I surprised myself with my surname. I hadn't been called Ella Fox since I was a child.

"Dr. Samson," he said, briskly. He didn't tell me his first name. "You're Australian?"

I nodded. "Lucas's brother married my mother. She's Australian. I grew up there."

"I see. Do you tutor as well?"

He knew about Lucas's tutors? Of course he did, I realized. Henrietta's work appraising Lucas's tutors had been their cover story for years.

"No," I said. "I'm an editor, but at the moment I'm working as Lucas's hou—"

"What kind of editor? Which publishing houses?"

He was Henrietta's equal when it came to blunt questions too. I named the publishers I had worked for in Australia and England. He asked for more details. I named some of my authors, the titles of their books—some fiction but mostly nonfiction. I was talking too fast, saying too much, but he had that effect on me.

He nodded. "I'm looking for an editor. What do you charge?"

"I'm sorry, but I'm not an ed—" I stopped. I was still an editor, wasn't I? I still had the skills. I still had my experience. I could soon be leaving Lucas's house. I would need a new job.

"It's difficult to quote a fee without knowing more about the project," I said, noticing my accent become more refined. "Could you give me some more details?"

"I'm drowning in details. I've been working on this for twenty years." He smiled and took a seat in the armchair opposite me. He was instantly less intimidating.

I didn't feel like Ella the housekeeper now. I was Ella the editor. I reached into my bag for my notebook and uncapped my pen. It felt strange, yet so familiar. I'd had introductory meetings like this with many authors over the years.

He leaned forward, clasping his hands, his expression different now, less imperious—eager even. He told me the project was a history of his family. A memoir told over three generations. It was an absolutely fascinating story, he told me.

I stayed quiet. Family histories were often notoriously dull for everyone except the family in question. But as he continued, I became interested. His father had been a renowned biologist. His grandfather had also been a doctor. They had both kept detailed diaries throughout their careers. Henrietta's husband—I still didn't know his first name—planned to use extracts from both. The final book would be part family story, part social history, part scientific journal, a record of the changes in medical knowledge in England over a century.

"It sounds fascinating," I said. I meant it.

"It's a bloody nightmare," he said. "I've got boxes of material, diaries, letters, old editions of the *British Medical Journal*, photographs, patients' records—"

"Is it cataloged?"

"Perfectly. Indexed too. My section is written. My father and grandfather's diaries are transcribed. All I need now is someone to pull it together, give it shape, structure, a narrative."

To my own surprise, I was suddenly interested. "When would you need that someone to start?"

"Whenever that someone was able to start. Do you have references?"

"Many, yes." It would take me only an e-mail or two to gather them. The hardest thing would be composing the e-mail. My publishing colleagues hadn't heard from me in nearly two years.

"I'd need to see those. And examples of your work, of course."

"I have copies of everything here in London." Lucas had shelves full of the books I'd edited. I'd always sent him a copy at the end of each project.

"I'd pay an hourly rate." He named a figure. It was three times what I'd been paid in Australia. "You'd work for it. It will be a long job. I'd also need you to sign a contract promising you won't leave midstream if the going gets too hard." He was talking as if I had already accepted the offer. "You'd also have to work from here. The material is too precious to leave the house. You could use Henrietta's office. She won't be needing it anymore, after all."

He'd raised the subject of her leaving. I had to acknowledge it. "No. I'm sorry."

"You're sorry? Why?"

I felt myself go red. But I couldn't stop now, not when he was looking at me in that imperious way again. I apologized once more. "I shouldn't have mentioned it."

"I'm intrigued now. Why are you sorry, Miss Fox?"

I felt like I was six and in the headmaster's office. I stammered my answer. "Because you're getting divorced, aren't you? She's going to live in France with Lucas—"

"Really? And there I was thinking she was simply retiring." He stood up, walked to the door and shouted—literally shouted—Henrietta's name. I didn't move. I couldn't speak. He stood by the door and waited.

After several minutes of excruciating silence, she appeared.

"For God's sake, Claude. I was on the phone. What do you want?"

He nodded toward me. "This young lady has just informed me you and I are getting a divorce because you and Lucas Fox are going to live in France together. How marvelous for you both. Were you planning on telling me at any stage?"

THIRTY-THREE

From: Charlie Baum
To: Walter Baum
Subject: Jess

No luck yet. I couldn't find out any more than you did. Hotel manager said she had checked out, all paid up. Don't worry about her not using bank card. Could be very simple explanation. And no, don't ask Lucas for help. He's busy with Ella. I'll look into flights to London today myself. I can be there in seven hours. Stay where you are for now. Try not to worry. Tell Meredith not to worry either. Jess has probably landed a big role and is out celebrating.

THIRTY-FOUR

Dear Diary,
Something terrible's happened. I don't know what to do.

I can't write it down.

I want my mum.

THIRTY-FIVE

I ran out of Henrietta's house. I had trouble opening the gate.

"You stupid, stupid, idiot girl," Henrietta had said to me. "You've ruined everything."

I'd tried to find my voice. "But you told me, you said—"

"That's enough, Miss Fox, thank you," Dr. Samson added. "You've done your dirty work on behalf of your uncle. Leave us now, would you?"

"I didn't realize. I'm sor—"

"Get out, Ella," Henrietta said. "Now!"

I finally got out onto the street, and stood there, disoriented, on the verge of tears. I hadn't imagined Henrietta telling me they were getting divorced, had I? She *had* asked me to convince Lucas to sell the house, hadn't she? I was suddenly unsure. My mind had been racing so fast this morning, my brain still full of the troubling dreams. Had I somehow managed to imagine it all?

No, I hadn't. Henrietta *had* told me that she was getting divorced. That her husband had asked for the divorce, that he'd confessed he'd been having an affair. I'd heard her talking to the solicitor in the back of the taxi. I hadn't imagined that. I'd heard her discussing financial arrangements.

I felt sick inside. What would Lucas do when he heard what I'd done? I had to get back to his house as quickly as possible. I ran to the nearest main road, praying for a taxi to appear. Like a miracle, one did. I hailed it, climbed in, gave Lucas's address and sat back, my heart beating fast. I knew Henrietta would ring him as soon as she stopped arguing with her husband. I'd have to try to ring him first.

I reached into my bag for my phone. It was then I realized I'd left my notebook in Henrietta's house. My notebook containing not just all my memories of Felix, but also Aidan's letter.

I leaned forward, urgently. "Can you stop the cab, please?"

The driver pulled over.

I didn't know what to do. I couldn't go back there. I had to see Lucas. But I couldn't leave my notebook behind. It was too precious. It had—

My phone rang. It was Lucas. Henrietta must have already rung him.

I answered. "Lucas, I'm sorry. I'm so sorry. I've done something terrible—"

"Where are you, Ella?"

"In a taxi. On my way home."

"Good. See you soon."

My decision was made. I asked the driver to keep going.

I had never been frightened of Lucas. I had never dreaded visiting him. I had walked up those steps hundreds of times in my life, always sure of my welcome, sure that I could knock on that door, call out his name, and he would greet me with a smile, with warmth, with love. Not now. I had ruined it. I had ruined his life, his plans, his relationship with Henrietta.

The door to the house opened as I got out of the taxi. Lucas stood there.

I wouldn't cry. I couldn't cry. "I'm so sorry, Lucas."

"Come and tell me what happened, Ella."

We went into his withdrawing room. The fire was lit. The photos of Felix were on the wall. It was all so familiar and now it was all so forbidding. I told him everything. From my conversation with Henrietta over dinner, what she had asked me to do on her behalf. Why I had gone to see her this morning. What had happened with her husband, how he had come in, our conversation about the editing. And then, what I had said about the divorce, about him and Henrietta going to live in France.

"I'm so sorry, Lucas. She's so angry with me. I can't blame her."

"She is a little upset, yes."

"But she *is* going to leave him, isn't she? She told me. She wants to go and live in France with you. She wants you to sell this house—"

"She's been asking me to do that for years, Ella. I've always said no. I said no this time too."

I stared at him. "You don't want to sell the house?"

"Of course not."

"You're not moving to France?"

"No. I like London too much."

"But she said—"

"I'm sure she did. But that doesn't necessarily mean it was true. Ella, please, sit down. Calm down. Everything's fine."

"How can it be? Haven't I ruined everything?"

"Of course not. Let me go and make some tea. And while I'm doing that, I want you to take a look at this." He handed me a folder of paperwork.

"What is it?"

"Take a look and you'll see."

He left the room. I opened the folder. It was the architect's drawings for his renovations. I couldn't understand it. I'd just ruined his decades-long love affair and he wanted me to look at renovation plans?

I went out into the kitchen with them. "Lucas, we can't talk about this now."

He looked up from the kettle. "Why not? I've been trying to get you to talk about it with me since you got here. Now seems as good a time as any."

"Lucas, don't you realize what happened today? I made a mess of everything for you with Henrietta and her husband."

"No, you didn't."

"Lucas, I did. And I've done the same thing with the job you gave me. I'm still no closer to finding out who's behind the thefts. I know how important it is. I'll keep trying, I promise—"

"Ella, forget about the thefts."

"I won't. I promise I'll work out which of the tutors it is, even if—"

"You won't be able to."

"I will. I just haven't concentrated enough on it yet."

"Ella, listen to me, please. You won't be able to find out which tutor is to blame because none of them are. Because nothing was stolen."

"Pardon?"

He repeated it.

"But you said—"

"Yes."

"You e-mailed me. You asked me to come to London—"

"To give you something to do. To stop you running."

I could only look at him.

"It was my idea and then Charlie backed me up. We thought if I said I needed your help, if I gave you a job, you would stay here out of loyalty—"

"But why?"

"Because one of us had to try something."

"Why?"

"To stop you tormenting yourself and the rest of us with you."

I shook my head. "I'm sorry, Lucas. I can't listen to this."

"Ella, you have to. We need you to stop running. Not just from Aidan, not just from Jess. From all of us."

"That's not fair, Lucas. It's not true."

"It is true. When I saw Aidan a month ago, I realized I couldn't stand back any longer. I had to do something."

"That's why you asked me here?"

He nodded. "We tried to get Aidan here too. We haven't managed it yet."

"Here to London?"

"Yes. But he's stopped answering Charlie's messages. He's gone quiet on us."

I hesitated. "No, he hasn't."

"What?"

Tell him. "I've had a letter."

"From Aidan? Sent to this house?"

I nodded. "I got it two days ago."

"What does it say?"

"I don't know."

"You don't *know?*"

"I haven't read it yet."

An unreadable expression crossed Lucas's face. I couldn't tell if it was anger or disappointment or something else. "What a surprise."

"Lucas, I couldn't—"

"Ella, you could have. But you chose not to. You could have opened all of his letters. You could have stayed with him and helped him at any stage over the past twenty months. You chose not to. You chose to punish him for something that wasn't his fault. As you've done to Jess. Punished her for something she must have wished again and again had never happened."

I couldn't believe what he was saying to me. I ignored what he said about Aidan. I focused on Jess instead. "How can you know that? Have you talked to her?"

"I didn't need to. I could imagine how she feels."

"Lucas, no—"

"Yes, Ella." He paused. "Because what happened to Jess with Felix nearly happened to me too."

I shook my head. I couldn't speak.

"You need to hear this, Ella. It happened the night I was looking after him in Canberra. Do you remember? The night before I left? When I insisted you and Aidan go out for a drink together on your own, for an hour?"

I nodded.

"Something happened that night."

I could only stare mutely at him.

"He loves fruit, you said. Oranges especially. Just give him small pieces, though, won't you? So I did. I put him into his high chair, just as you'd shown me. I put the cut orange in a bowl and I gave him one segment. He loved it. I gave him another. He loved that too. I went back out into the kitchen to get more. And in the five seconds I was gone, he started choking. He'd put another whole piece in his mouth. When I came back in, his face was blue. I panicked. I pulled him out of the chair and I turned him upside down and I hit his back and reached into his mouth until the orange came out, until he started crying and I knew, thank God, I knew he was okay."

I didn't move. I didn't say a word.

"Twenty minutes later you and Aidan came back home."

I remembered. We had the glow of two drinks and an hour in each other's company on us. We walked in and there was Lucas on the sofa, Felix happy and sleepy on his lap. Lucas was reading to him. I could even remember the book. It was *Madame Bovary* by Gustave Flaubert.

I found my voice at last. "Why didn't you tell me?"

"I was too shocked that night. I was leaving the next day. I decided you and Aidan didn't need to know. But that's why I know how Jess feels. Because I was five seconds from feeling it myself."

Behind us, the phone rang. We ignored it. The answering machine clicked on. It was one of Lucas's clients, wanting an extra tutoring session.

The room was too quiet afterward. I didn't know how I felt. Shocked. Exhausted.

"Lucas—"

He held up his hand. "Let's stop there for now, Ella. It's been a difficult morning for us all."

"I have to tell you this. Jess is in London."

"I know. Charlie told me."

"Charlie knew? And he didn't tell me?"

Lucas didn't answer. He didn't need to. I'd told Charlie not to tell me anything about Jess or Aidan.

"Lucas, is Aidan—" I stopped.

He waited.

"Has Aidan—" I couldn't say the words. *Has Aidan met someone new?*

"Has Aidan recovered? Is that what you want to know?"

I nodded.

"Aidan is brokenhearted. From what I could tell, he has no life beyond his work and his guilt."

"Why has he written to me again?"

"I don't know."

"Has he met someone? Does he want a divorce? Is that why he's writing to me?"

"I don't know, Ella. Aidan is your husband. Ask him yourself. Read his letter. Please. Now."

If I'd had it, I would have taken it out then, read it in front of Lucas. I told him where it was. In my notebook, on the table in Henrietta's living room.

To my astonishment, he started to laugh. Not just chuckle. He roared laughing.

"It's not funny, Lucas."

"Oh, it is, Ella. It is." He reached for his coat, picked up his glasses. "Come on. Put on your coat."

"Where are we going?"

"Where do you think? To visit Dr. and Mrs. Samson, of course."

THIRTY-SIX

From: Charlie Baum
To: Walter Baum
Subject: re: Jess

Dad, am writing from Logan Airport. Got the last seat on a flight leaving Boston this morning. Will be in London by late afternoon UK time. Will go straight to Jess's hotel. I'll ring you from there. She'll be fine. Don't worry.

From: Charlie Baum
To: Lucy Baum
Subject: re: Thank you

On board, about to switch phone off. I'll call from London as soon as I can, hopefully with good news.

Thank you. For everything. Please thank your boss from me for giving you the time off as well. I'll be back as soon as I can.

Please kiss the kids good night from me. And good morning too.

I love you, Lucy.

C xx

THIRTY-SEVEN

We hailed a taxi on Bayswater Road. "This is a bad idea, Lucas."

"It's an excellent idea."

"They'll kill us."

"They can't kill us, Ella. It's illegal. Who are you so frightened of? Henrietta or her husband?"

"Both of them."

"There's no need. I've known Henrietta since she was eighteen years old, remember. We met on our first day at university. I've known Claude since he was twenty. He was an old bore at that age and he still is. Don't tell me—the editing project he mentioned was about his family?"

"Yes, his father and—"

"His grandfather, who revolutionized medical science in

Britain, blah blah blah? He's been going on about that for as long as I've known him. I could write that book myself, I've heard the stories so often. Many a good dinner party has been ruined by his ancestors."

"You socialize with him?"

"Of course. He's one of my oldest friends. A bore, as I said, but good company if you can keep him off the subject of his family. And cricket. He's very widely read. That's one of the reasons he and Henrietta have managed to stay together for so long."

"Because they like discussing books?"

"No, they both like to read. Which means they don't have to talk to each other."

"Lucas, I am very confused."

"Let me explain, Ella. Henrietta is wonderful in many ways, but she has an unfortunate weakness for the finer things in life. Good food, expensive wine, luxury holidays. That's one of the reasons she never wanted to leave Claude for me. I couldn't offer the same things."

She'd said as much to me, I remembered.

"She stayed with me one weekend when he was away, at some tedious family history conference probably, thousands of people droning on about Great-uncle Sylvester or some such thing. I can't imagine anything worse. Anyway, Henrietta came to stay. Ella, I thought you were obsessive about cleaning. She was worse. I'd had visions of a weekend in bed together—"

"Lucas—"

"Ella, are you embarrassed? You really are sweet. I was alive and kicking in the swinging sixties, remember." He dropped his voice to a whisper. "I've even taken drugs."

"I don't want to hear." I was only half joking.

He smiled. "I didn't inhale, of course. Or did I? I can't remember. I was probably drunk at the time. The fact is, Henrietta refused to sleep with me that weekend. She said the bed was too small and the attic made her claustrophobic. We moved downstairs to another bedroom. She said there were spiderwebs. I got rid of the spiderwebs. She said the sheets weren't clean enough. I changed them. It was like having Mrs. Beeton to stay. We did nothing but discuss household maintenance. Eventually we booked into a hotel. She only agreed to stay with me again if I promised to make the bed with her sheets." He laughed again. "She'd always arrive with new ones, fresh from the shop. It must have cost her a fortune over the years." He leaned forward. "Ah, here we are."

I tensed.

"Don't be frightened, Ella. They're just people. Old people, at that."

We got out. I stood back as he pressed the intercom. A male voice answered. "Get lost."

"Let us in, Claude. You've already frightened one Fox away today. It won't work with two."

"You've done enough damage—"

"I'll do more if you don't let me in."

The buzz sounded. The gate opened. Lucas started to walk up the steps.

I took his sleeve. "They've just painted the front door. We have to go around the side."

"The servants' entrance? How apt." He let himself in and called out. "Henrietta? Claude? Are you lying in a bloodied mess somewhere or having an early G and T?"

"I told you on the phone I never wanted to see you again, Lucas."

I spun around. It was Henrietta's voice. I couldn't tell where it was coming from.

"So you did," Lucas called back. "I must have forgotten. In the conservatory, then?"

I hadn't noticed the door when I'd been there earlier. Lucas opened it. It was a large conservatory, old-style, filled with plants. At the end was a glass table with four chairs. Henrietta and Claude were sitting there, both with drinks in their hands. It wasn't noon yet.

"Now, who will apologize to Ella first?" Lucas said. "Henrietta? Claude? Or shall we go in alphabetical order?"

"Fuck off, Fox," Dr. Samson said. His tone was mild.

I couldn't believe it. Where was the shouting? The anger? The talk of divorce?

"We'd both love a drink; thanks so much for asking," Lucas said. "But actually we've dropped by to collect something Ella left behind this morning, when the two of you rudely chased her out."

Henrietta rolled her eyes. "We didn't chase her out. Frankly, Lucas, she ran."

"Your word against hers. We'll have to review the security footage. So, her notebook? Have you seen it?"

"It's upstairs still, I imagine," Henrietta said. "Wherever she left it."

I spoke for the first time. "May I—"

"Of course, Ella." It was Lucas who gave me permission. "Can you find your way? I'll wait here."

I ran upstairs. The notebook was there, on the table. It

was still open at the same page. I picked it up and quickly checked inside. Aidan's letter was there. I stood in the middle of the room, counted to twenty and then went back downstairs again.

Lucas was sitting down now too. It all looked so social, so friendly. "All fine, Ella?"

I nodded. I had to ask. Him, not them. "Lucas, is everything okay? I haven't ruined everything?"

Dr. Samson answered me. "Everything's fine, Ella. I must apologize. Lucas tells me you were very upset about this morning. Don't be. Henrietta and I are constantly divorcing. She takes a notion, rings her solicitor, he reminds her that she won't get a bean if she leaves me, so she stays. Isn't that right, darling?"

Darling?

Henrietta nodded. Sulkily, like a child.

Dr. Samson smiled at her. "Why do we put up with her, Lucas?"

"God only knows," Lucas said. "You found your notebook, Ella? Ready for home?"

"Yes, please," I said.

We were at the door when Dr. Samson called my name. I turned around.

"I would still like to see samples of your editorial work, Ella. And your references. If you're still interested, of course."

"For God's sake, Claude," Lucas said. "Ella's my niece, remember. You think I'd let her work for you? That project of yours is so dull it would take years off her life. Find some other poor sap to do it. Lovely to see you both. Goodbye, now."

We were barely out of earshot before he spoke.

"You didn't mind me turning down that job on your behalf, Ella, did you? Trust me, he would have driven you demented."

I didn't mind at all, I told him. I'd already decided I wanted as little as possible to do with Henrietta or her husband.

It wasn't until we were walking down their street that I started asking more questions. Lucas was very relaxed and very forthcoming. Yes, Dr. Samson had always known about their affair. Yes, since the beginning. Yes, he had had affairs of his own too. No, it wasn't a conventional situation, but it worked for the three of them. Yes, Lucas agreed, he'd been flexible about the truth with me over the years, but it was for the tutors' sake more than anyone's. Henrietta had felt it was better if they didn't know the extent of her relationship with Lucas. She only ever stayed the night at Lucas's house when the tutors were away, for that reason too. He hadn't deliberately hidden it from me either. He'd simply felt it didn't matter if I knew the whole story or not. His private life was his private life.

He glanced at me. "So, Ella, are you shocked? Or disappointed?"

"Astonished?" I said.

"That people our age can get up to these shenanigans?"

That was partly it, I said. But mostly, I realized I was relieved. Lucas wouldn't be moving to France. He wouldn't be selling the house. As for whether he was leaving it to me or not, I didn't care. He could leave it to the university, if he wanted. To a dogs' home. I told him as much.

"Dogs?" he said. "A foxes' home, surely?"

"To whichever you want. It's your house. But I don't want to think about it yet. You're not going anywhere for a long while."

"I'm sixty-three, Ella. I will be going somewhere, some-day. And the house will be yours, whether you like it or not. I couldn't hand it over to any dogs or foxes. Imagine the mess they might make. How could I bear that?" He glanced across at me. "Do you know, that's the first time I've seen you smile today? You haven't done nearly enough smiling since you got here."

The noise of the traffic on Kensington High Street made it difficult to talk. We kept walking, finally reaching Kensington Gardens. I expected him to take the path that would lead across to his house. Instead, he turned right.

We were silent at first. The trees around us were bare, not even the smallest of buds evident. Far off in the distance I could hear the sound of a saw or a lawn mower. Ahead, there were dogs barking. Behind us, traffic. We walked until we reached the Serpentine, the stretch of water that marked the border between Kensington Gardens and Hyde Park. Only a few other people were around. The wind was cold. I turned up the collar on my coat and pushed my hands deep into my pockets. The breeze was whipping the surface of the water. I watched a ripple make its way right across, a duck bobbing up and down in its wake.

Lucas broke the silence. "Tell me about *your* married life, Ella. Was it as complicated as Henrietta and Claude's? I hope not. Because I always thought the two of you had something special. You and Aidan were great friends, as well as everything else. You used to laugh so much when you were with him. Do you remember?"

"Lucas—"

"You changed him too. In so many ways, all for the better. You gave him confidence in himself. I could see that you understood him, got his humor, got his intelligence. You were a great match for each other."

I hadn't realized Lucas had noticed so much about the two of us. But I couldn't talk about it. Not when I had Aidan's letter in my bag. Lucas wasn't waiting for an answer. He kept talking.

"So tell me, Ella, what did you expect would happen when you married Aidan? That you would both live happily ever after? That the two of you would somehow escape all the trials and tribulations of life now that you'd found each other? That you would right all the wrongs that had happened to you both in your own childhoods?"

I couldn't stop the question. "How did you know?"

"I could see it. It made sense, from what I knew about the two of you, your own families. But no one is bulletproof, Ella. There's no equality rule for heartbreak or pain. All you can do is decide how to cope with what life throws at you. Some people get through it together. Others don't."

I felt like he was criticizing me. I had to make him understand. "Lucas, our baby died. Felix died. We didn't separate over who did the dishes or who left their towels on the floor."

"I know that, Ella."

"I thought you of all people would be on my side. But you're not, are you? Not anymore."

"I've always been on your side."

"But you're not anymore. Since I got here, you've kept asking me, Why wouldn't I talk to Aidan? Why wouldn't I read his letters? Why couldn't I see him?"

"And you still haven't answered me."

"Because I *couldn't*." I was almost shouting now.

"Why not?"

"Because it would hurt too much." The truth was roaring in at me. "I had to leave him, Lucas. I had to go. We couldn't be in the same room. We couldn't even look at each other."

The words poured out as I tried to explain to Lucas how I had felt, all that had happened in the first weeks after Felix died. How once I'd left Aidan, once I had grown used to being on my own, with only my own pain to feel, I'd known I could never see him again. Because if I did, if I even heard his voice, I knew I would be right back at the start, right back to how I felt the day Felix died. I had spent every day of the past twenty months trying to build a wall between me and that pain. Every day I'd discovered how transparent and flimsy the wall was. Even a photo of Felix could smash a hole through it, pull me back through time, make the grief as raw as if it had just happened. What would talking to Aidan again, seeing Aidan again, do to me?

"I can't risk it, Lucas. I can't feel that bad again. It would kill me second time around."

"It's already killing you. It's killing Aidan. You need to help each other."

I shook my head.

"So that's it? That's your vows put to one side? For better or for worse? Too hard, was it?"

"You can't talk to me about vows. Look at you and Henrietta and her husband. What kind of mockery of marriage is that?"

"It's our arrangement, Ella. Our choice. It suits the three of us. There's no comparison with you and Aidan. He had no choice in it at all. You abandoned him when he needed you the most. As you abandoned Jess, and your mother and Walter."

"I'm not listening to this anymore. You can't say these things to me."

"Then who will, if I don't? Charlie's tried everything he could. But he has to step on eggshells with you too, in case you freeze him out of your life. Everyone does. Did you know your mother has rung me twice a week since you got here to ask me how you are?"

"I don't believe you."

"She has. Because she doesn't dare ring you herself in case she happens to say something that turns you away from her. All she wants to do is talk to you. All she especially wants to do is talk to you about Felix. She wants to share memories of her grandson with you, his mother, but you won't let her do that either."

"That's not true. She—" I stopped. I remembered something she'd said the day before. *I wasn't sure if it was my place to have a mass said for him.*

Lucas kept talking. "Felix was your son, Ella, but we all loved him too. You're not the only one who's hurting. You're not the only one who misses him. Do you know you've never once asked me how I am? How I felt to lose my beautiful grandnephew?"

I tried to think back. I must have asked him. I must have.

His voice softened. "You're like a daughter to me, Ella. You know that. I didn't want children of my own, but then I got you and I got all the best parts. Your curiosity, your friendship, your faxes and letters. I got to see you grow from childhood to adulthood, to share in your life, to be proud of you. You met your husband through me. I was at your wedding. I was godfather to your first baby. You gave me so much. But you wouldn't let me grieve for Felix either. Only you were allowed to."

I was crying now. "Lucas, I didn't—"

He opened his arms. I moved into them. I pressed my face against his jumper and I cried until I had no more tears. He waited. When he spoke his voice was gentle.

"Ella, you've been like this all your life—do you know that? Expecting everyone around you to be perfect. Getting so upset when they weren't. I blame my brother. If he hadn't divorced Meredith, if you'd grown up in a happy home, perhaps you would have been different too."

I stepped back then, roughly wiped my eyes. "I had a very happy childhood."

"Did you? I always thought otherwise. I used to worry about you a lot. But obviously I was wrong. You had a very happy childhood. Good."

We started walking again. I told the truth. "I found it hard at times. Especially when Mum got married again. When she had Jess."

"You never did get over that, did you?"

I stopped. "Over what?"

"Being jealous of Jess. I must have had hundreds of faxes from you about her."

"I can't talk about Jess, Lucas."

"You could. You should. You should talk about her until there is nothing left for you to say."

I kept walking. Behind me, Lucas spoke, his voice clear in the misty air.

"Ella, I can't stop you running away again. You're free to go anytime you like. You probably will, now that I've foolishly told you there were no thefts."

I stopped and turned. "I don't want to go yet."

"Good. Because I don't want you to go yet."

I came back to where he was standing.

He smiled. "You weren't a very good detective, by the way, if you don't mind me saying."

"And your tutors could sue you for libel, if you don't mind me saying."

"The tutors knew nothing about it. They believed you were actually interviewing them for a magazine. They've asked me about it since, by the way. You might need to write that article."

"You even convinced Henrietta, didn't you? Lied to her too."

"She didn't care about the thefts. She'll care even less that there weren't any."

He held out his arm. I looped my hand through it. We began walking back toward his house.

"So what are you going to do about Jess being here?" he asked.

"Nothing." My tone was too sharp again. But I meant it.

"I know you think it's simple, Lucas, but it's not. I know you think that all I need to do is talk to her and Aidan, cry together, and life will go on. It won't. Can't you see that? How can I forget that Felix died because of them?"

"He didn't."

"He did, Lucas."

"Felix died because he hit his head on a rock, Ella. Because he fell off a fence in an accident that tragically happened while Jess was babysitting him. And she was babysitting because Aidan had been called into work. That's what happened. That's exactly what happened. And hating Jess and hating Aidan for the rest of your life is never going to change that."

"I don't hate them. I don't." *Didn't I?*

"No? So what has been fueling you these past twenty months, Ella? What's kept you running and running? If it wasn't hatred, what was it?"

Fear. The word appeared in my head in block letters. *I've been so scared.*

We reached his house. We climbed the steps. I waited for him to unlock the door. Instead, he turned and stood in front of it.

"You can't come in yet, Ella."

"But I have to cook dinner for everyone. I need to make a list, go shopping."

"Forget dinner. We've done enough talking too. You are going back across to the park and you are going to open Aidan's letter. And you're not allowed back in here until you've read it."

He meant it. I could see that.

"Fine," I said.

THIRTY-EIGHT

I took a seat at what I had now started to think of as my bench, in the Italian Gardens. I reached into my bag for the notebook and took out Aidan's letter.

I looked at the envelope, putting off the moment of opening it for as long as I could. I knew his handwriting so well. He'd left me dozens of notes in our years together, from the earliest days in London.

We'd kept our separate rooms in Lucas's house at first. One afternoon I came back upstairs to find a note pushed under my door. *Dear Ella, You are beautiful. Signed, A Secret Admirer.*

"Thank you for the note," I said later that night.

He'd smiled. "Note? What note?"

It continued in Australia. He worked very long hours in

his trade job. I'd wake up to find he'd already left for work. I'd see a note on the pillow beside me, or beside the toaster.

Fresh juice in the fridge. You are gorgeous.

If I was out late at a work dinner myself, I'd return home to notes on the kitchen table.

Charlie rang to say hello. Sends his love. I love you more.

Welcome home. Have decided to write in code from now on. I L Y. Can you decipher?

In the first weeks after Felix was born, when our son seemed to want to be up all night and sleep all day, I snatched my own sleep whenever I could, often as soon as Aidan came in the door. There was one week when we barely spoke to each other. We said everything via notes.

E, have sterilized the bottles. Also had a word with Felix about his nocturnal behavior. He said to say thanks for being up all night with him. Says you're great company. W L Y.

E, spoke to your mother tonight. Sorry, correction, listened to your mother tonight. She is very excited. Arriving six p.m. flight on Friday. Insists she'll get a taxi. I L Y, by the way. So does Felix. (Evidence points to the fact your mother does too.)

After Felix was born, Mum used to come up to Canberra

to see him often, every second or third weekend at least. Why hadn't I remembered that? My memories over the past twenty months had only been of her visit that final weekend. But there had been so many other visits too.

She'd also insisted early on, even before he was born, that she wanted our baby to call her Granny. I was amazed. "Don't you want to be called Meredith?" It was what Charlie and Lucy's four children called her, I knew. Charlie had always called her Meredith too, never Mum. They had a good, if not close, relationship, but he was always her stepson and she always seemed conscious that Charlie's children were her step-grandchildren, not full grandchildren. The complications of a blended family, yet again. Walter was Papa, a nod to their German background.

It was different with Felix. Mum was emphatic about it. "I'm his granny so I want him to call me Granny." Felix did. It was one of his first clear words.

She and I spoke often during my pregnancy. "Don't worry," she told me when I rang her after our first alarming appointment at the birth clinic. We'd been shown a graphic video of childbirth. Aidan had gone pale while he watched it. So had I. "You're doing what your body was born to do. Just let it happen," she said.

She told me to ignore all the medical advice I was getting. Her own source of information was Dr. Rob, her network's resident expert. She sent me e-mail messages with links to all his segments. Aidan and I watched them together. Her technological skills sometimes let her down.

"She's so thoughtful," Aidan said after we watched one clip. "If you don't mind me saying, you have had something of a wart outbreak since you got pregnant."

The next day, there was another e-mail from her. *Whoops, sorry about the warts! Here's the one I meant to send.* It was Dr. Rob on nappy rash.

"I preferred the warts," Aidan said.

She decided to fill our freezer with home-cooked meals, so we wouldn't have to worry about cooking for the first month or two after the baby arrived. She came up one week-end to do it, three weeks before Felix was born. She wouldn't let me help. After a full day and a lot of mess in the kitchen there was one shaky-looking quiche on the counter. It didn't look like it would survive a day, let alone a few months in the freezer. We had it for dinner that night.

Two days later, after Mum had returned home, there was a knock at the door. It was a delivery van from one of Canberra's best-known restaurants. She'd ordered dozens of gourmet meals for us, each of them labeled and freezer-ready. *No quiches, I hope!* Mum's accompanying note said. We lived off those meals for the first two months.

She, Walter and Jess flew up to Canberra the day after Felix was born. They came into my hospital room laden with presents. Mum carried flowers, Walter carried cham-pagne, Jess carried her laptop. She set it up as we took turns holding Felix, all of us marveling at his shock of black hair, all trying to decide who he looked like the most, me or Aidan. No, he definitely had Aidan's ears. Yes, but he had my nose. All the while, Jess was there with her computer, plug-ging in cables and pressing buttons. Suddenly, there on her laptop screen via the wonder of Skype was Charlie and his family in Boston, crowded around their computer, waving at us. Jess had arranged it all. She did the same thing with Lucas, as soon as the time was right for her to call London.

He'd used one of his student's laptops, up in his attic. I'd been able to see the fox paintings on the wall behind him as we spoke, as we held Felix up for him to see.

I had forgotten all of this.

Lucas's words came to mind. *We all loved him too.*

I thought of the photos of Felix I carried with me. Felix and I. Aidan and Felix. The three of us together. The beautiful photo of Lucas, Charlie, Aidan and Felix. But there had been other photos too, photos that I hadn't taken with me when I left Canberra. Dozens of photos of Mum with Felix, cheek to cheek, reading to him, walking with him. Laughing with him. Holding him. A photo of Felix sitting on the cushion Mum had made for him, a bright green square with his name embroidered on it in yellow wool. Mum hated sewing but she'd found the time to embroider his name and date of birth. Felix had loved that cushion.

There had been photos of Walter and Felix too. Not many. Usually, Walter was the one who took photos of the rest of us. But there was one special photo, a funny one, of Walter holding Felix, bouncing him on his knee, a little awkwardly, and laughing as Felix reached up and tugged at his beard. Where was that photo? Had I left that behind for Aidan? Or just left it behind?

Another memory flashed into my mind. Walter crying at the funeral. Holding Mum, holding her as she sobbed and sobbed. Tears on his face too. I remembered him standing behind Mum the times they visited me in the restaurant, holding her. Supporting her. Literally supporting her.

I couldn't stop the memories coming now.

I remembered Jess with Felix. Ess and Elix. Their pet

names for each other. She had come up to Canberra as often as she could too. Whenever Aidan and I drove down to Melbourne, every couple of months or so, she'd be the first to run out to the car, the first to get Felix out of his baby seat in the back, the first to offer to babysit. "Come to Auntie Ess, Elix," she'd say. And he'd hold out his arms, impatient to get out of his seat after the eight-hour drive, calling, "Ess! Ess!" And we would all laugh. And Walter would say, "She's a natural with babies, isn't she?" "Everyone loves Jess," Mum would say.

And I would get a flash of jealousy. Even though we were the center of attention, even though we were all in a circle looking at my baby, even though the whole gathering was to welcome us back to Melbourne, to coo over Felix, I would still feel jealous of Jess. I wouldn't like it when she took him into the back garden to play. I'd leave her with him for five minutes and then I would go out there and bring him back in. He was my baby, not hers.

But as the months went by, Felix became something of a bridge between us. He gave Jess and me something to share, to talk and laugh about that wasn't complicated by tricky childhood memories. She loved him. Really loved him. She was so good with him, too—endlessly patient, happy to sit on the floor with him and play peekaboo or build castles out of blocks for hours. For longer than I could. He loved her singing and dancing. He would laugh, really laugh, while she clowned around in front of him. She would do that for hours too. It was the perfect setup. He loved watching her. She loved having an audience. Elix and Ess.

She was at the funeral. I didn't see her. I didn't want to see her. I don't remember seeing anyone. It was the hardest day of my life, to stand there in that church, in the row of seats beside that small white coffin, to think that inside it, that inside was—

Two weeks after the funeral, I went to the doctor. Aidan begged me to go, telling me he was so worried, would I please just go and talk to someone. The doctor wanted to give me antidepressants and sleeping tablets. I refused them. I didn't know what they'd do to me. I was scared they'd affect the part of my brain that held my memories of Felix. The doctor said I needed something, that medication would help get me through these early days. I walked out. I couldn't risk blocking out even one thought of Felix. They were all I had of him now.

As I came into our apartment after my appointment, I heard a noise in Felix's bedroom. Aidan was in there, sitting on the floor, a box beside him. He was putting Felix's toys into it. He'd been trying to, at least. The box was empty. He was on the floor surrounded by Felix's toys and books, crying so hard he didn't hear me come in. He didn't know I was there until I started shouting.

I see now what he'd been trying to do. I didn't see it then. I shouted at him to leave Felix's things alone. I wouldn't listen when he said he thought it would help me, that he was just trying to—

"*Help* me? How can you help me? It's all your fault— don't you realize that? This is your fault."

It was the first time I'd said it out loud. I'd thought it but I hadn't said it. It was said now. Jess was the one who'd been in the park, but if Aidan hadn't agreed to go into work and asked her to babysit, it wouldn't have happened.

That was when it changed between us. At that moment, with that sentence. We stayed together for another month, but what had been said couldn't be unsaid. I blamed Aidan every time I looked at him. He blamed himself. If I looked at him, I could see only guilt. We slept in the same bed but we didn't touch. He moved to hug me once, and he took me by surprise and I jumped back. I flinched. That was the last time we'd touched.

Now, here I was in London, many months later, holding something that he had touched recently. An envelope he had sealed. In it, a piece of paper on which he had written—

Ella, I want a divorce.

I could see the words so clearly it was as if I had opened the letter. I shut my eyes as tightly as possible. There was one word in my head.

No.

No.

I didn't want to divorce Aidan? Was that what I was thinking? I didn't want him to divorce me?

You abandoned him, Ella. Lucas's words.

Suddenly all I could think of was Aidan in Felix's bedroom that day. On the floor, crying. I had stopped him cleaning out the room. I had ordered him out. I'd shut the door. I'd left the apartment without going in there again. So who had finally tidied it? Who had packed away Felix's toys, his books, his clothes? Who had taken down all the pictures? Aidan? On his own?

Another memory, long pushed away, came to me. A

message from Mum on my voice mail. A short message, softly spoken, telling me she was on her way to Canberra to help Aidan pack up. They were the words she used. Two days later, another message. She was back home. She'd brought everything back to Melbourne. "I'll keep it all here, Ella. It's safe, I promise."

I hadn't called her back. I hadn't called her back even after she'd rung me to tell me what she and my husband had done with my son's toys and clothes.

"Is this seat taken?"

It was an elderly woman, an umbrella in one hand, a small dog at her feet.

I stood up. "Please, have it. I was about to leave."

"Are you sure? I don't want to hurry you."

"I'm sure," I said.

I went straight to Lucas's house. I was going to read Aidan's letter now, but not on my own. I wanted Lucas to do it with me. Be beside me as I read it. Help me cope with whatever it said.

His door opened before I had a chance to use my key. He must have been watching for me.

"Lucas, I haven't read it yet. I need you—" I stopped. "What is it? What's wrong?"

"Your mother's just rung. Charlie's on his way to London. Jess has gone missing."

THIRTY-NINE

I rang Mum back immediately. Lucas had given me the basics, but I needed to hear all the details from her.

She was crying. It took a minute or two to get her to stop. "We didn't want to tell you, Ella. We didn't want you to know that she was even in London. But she needed a change of scene so badly. We've been worried sick about her, and we thought a new city, a few auditions, might help her, give her something to be excited about. It's so cutthroat over there, but we thought it might do her some good, even to be away for just a few weeks. She's a great singer and dancer, she really is, but she needs more experience. We wanted her to try it, so she would feel that she'd achieved something, that she could still do something. It's been so hard to keep her spirits up. We've been so worried about her. She took herself off her medication, and—"

"What medication?"

"She's been on antidepressants on and off since it happened. And then I got so worried that she might start to hurt herself again. I know she'd stopped doing it but we were so—"

"She'd done what?"

"She was self-harming. Ella, I don't want to talk about this with you. Not this week. I know what date is coming up—"

"Mum, please."

She told me everything. Jess had been under psychiatric care for the past twenty months. She'd been on different types of medication. She'd been unable to stop crying for weeks after it happened. Eventually she managed to go back to college for occasional classes, and to do her slot on Mum's show, but it was often the only thing she could do all week. They'd had to script it to the last word and she'd become so nervy that if she got it wrong, she'd be depressed for days afterward.

"All she seemed to be able to do was write in her diary," Mum said. "I know I shouldn't have, but I read it. It was the only way to find out how she really was. And it just made me cry and cry for her. She was pretending to herself that everything was okay, that her career was going well, that she was so happy. But it wasn't true. She could barely get out of bed some days. And I read about what had been happening at college. Some of the other students were kind to her but the others have been so mean, so cruel, Ella. Walter and I thought she needed time away from there as well. She'd talked about going to London for years—you know that—so we thought, even if she only stays a month, it might build up her confidence, make her feel independent again. Even though we helped her, of course. We paid for her hotel and gave her a credit card. We were even thinking about surprising her with a visit, especially once we knew you were there too, but then she rang and we had an argument and since then—"

"How long has she been here?"

"Ten days. We put her up in a lovely hotel in Covent Garden for a week, and the plan was for her to find a flat after that, perhaps with some other performers, to help her make friends. She never goes out with her old friends here anymore. And of course we were happy to pay her rent until she got a part. But then there was a big misunderstanding about her getting her own TV show. She was told something that wasn't completely true and we tried to explain, but she wouldn't listen and that's the last time we—"

I made Mum slow down and explain it all. It seemed that the cable network had done market research and discovered Jess was very popular with male audiences, young and old. They'd proposed a new weekly show for her, provisionally titled *Mess with Jess*.

"And of course we said no to it, Ella. You should have seen the script. Frankly, it was soft porn. We didn't bother even telling her about it. We didn't tell her when we got approached by one of the men's magazines either. It was the last thing we wanted her to do, pose topless, no matter how tasteful they said the shots would be. And the show would have been the same—not topless, but all about sex. But she didn't let us explain. She thought it was her own comedy cooking show, a showcase of her singing and dancing. And she got so furious and said we'd let her down. She thought we'd said no because I was jealous of her and she hung up on us. We thought she'd calm down and ring back again but she didn't. And she hasn't used Walter's credit card since and she's moved out of the hotel and she hasn't e-mailed or texted us or posted anything on Facebook. There's just been nothing. We didn't do anything for a few days. Walter said perhaps what she needed was her freedom, time to think and be on her own without us watching her every move. But she still won't answer our calls and no one at the hotel knows where she went and she hasn't got any money." She gave a shuddering breath. "We're so worried, Ella. We couldn't ask you or Lucas to help—we knew that—so Charlie's on his way to London now. I only rang Lucas to ask if—"

"I'll meet Charlie at the airport," I said.

"Ella, we don't expect you to. We know—"

"I want to. Please." I asked for the flight details. Charlie was due to land in four hours' time. "You've got my mobile number too, haven't you?"

"Of course."

"Mum, don't worry. She'll be all right."

"But what if she isn't, Ella? What if she isn't?"

She was still crying as we said good-bye.

Lucas had heard everything. He explained she'd rung him to ask if he could book Charlie into a hotel. "I insisted he stay here with us, of course."

He told me Mum had also asked him if he would go into Jess's Covent Garden hotel to speak to the manager and find out what he could before Charlie arrived.

"I'll come with you," I said. As Lucas fetched his coat, I thought of Aidan's letter in my bag. Now wasn't the time.

We took the Tube, changing lines once, coming up and out of the cramped elevator into the center of Covent Garden. We went straight to Jess's hotel. It was well-known, Lucas told me, frequented by actors and film stars. It was sleekly designed, darkly lit. All the staff looked like models. We spoke to the receptionist. Five minutes later, we were sitting opposite the manager, a young, elegant woman. She'd already spoken on the phone to Charlie in Boston and to Walter in Melbourne. No, she assured us, of course she didn't mind talking to us too. She clicked her long-nailed fingers on the notebook computer in front of her. Yes, she could confirm Jess had checked out of the hotel four days earlier. No, she hadn't left a forwarding address. Yes, there was CCTV footage. If we really did feel it was necessary, yes, of course she could arrange for us to see it.

She was skeptical underneath her businesslike courtesy. Jess was twenty-two, an aspiring performer in London for the first time. If she couldn't go wild now, when could she?

Lucas seemed to guess her thoughts. Without going into detail, he explained that Jess had had personal difficulties. He used the term "at risk." The woman's attitude changed for the better.

"She was here for a week," I said. "Would there be any staff members she'd have had regular contact with?"

"Our staff are friendly and helpful to all our guests," she said. "We pride ourselves on that. But I'll ask around, certainly. Do you have a photo of her I can show them?"

We didn't. Instead, we brought up her Facebook page on the manager's computer. There were dozens of photos there.

"She's beautiful, isn't she?" the woman said. "I'm sure people will remember her."

We thanked her and left our phone numbers.

We tried the theaters next. We spoke to three box-office managers before realizing it was pointless without a photo of Jess to leave with them. Even as I described her—small, pretty, lots of hair, an Australian accent—I knew I was describing hundreds of young women in London.

As we walked back into Covent Garden, I thought I saw her, walking across the cobblestones with that confident dancer's walk. I even called her name. The girl turned, not in response to my voice, but to change direction. It wasn't Jess.

Lucas and I parted at Paddington Station. While I went to Heathrow to meet Charlie, he was going home to phone the theater companies about their audition schedules. He was going to print off some flyers. He was also going to phone the police.

It wasn't until I was on the train, halfway to the airport, that I took Aidan's letter out of my bag. I slit open the envelope. There was only one sheet of paper inside. I unfolded it.

I had to read it three times before the words sank in.

FORTY

Dear Diary,
    This isn't a diary entry. I'm writing this so I have a record if I decide to go to the police. I would ring Mum but I don't even know what her number is. It was in my phone and my phone is gone and so is my money, and worst of all I might even be pregnant or have some STD. I don't know what to do.

I'm going to write it all down exactly as it happened.

I got back to Ben's at nine p.m. He'd just got home himself. If I'd had the money I would have bought him a bottle of wine but I couldn't afford it, so I bought a bottle of cider. It was the cheapest thing I could see in the bottle shop or off-license or whatever it's called here. But Ben said it didn't matter and he produced two bottles of champagne, actual champagne, and Zach (he was there too) laughed and said, "You've found the key to that magic cave again, I see." And I said, "What magic cave?" and Zach laughed and said, "A long, long time ago, Jessica, there was a magic land and in it there was a magic cave and in it were the most wondrous things anybody could want or need, from the creamiest soaps to the softest towels, sheets and pillowcases to the most expensive champagne and—"

"Shut up, Zach," Ben said. "Ask no questions and we'll tell you no lies, Jess, okay?"

I realized then what he meant, of course. The champagne was stolen from the hotel. And then I remembered his bathroom. All the nice towels. The nice soap. I thought of the biscuits and chocolate in the kitchen. The flat was full of things from the hotel. "But that's stealing," I said.

"No, it's not," Ben said. "It's supplementing my below-par wage."

"But that champagne costs about fifty pounds a bottle."

"Says the little princess," Zach said. "Have a bath in it, Jess, did you? When you were still on Daddy's payroll?"

I didn't answer him. I'd decided the only way to handle him was to ignore him.

"You can have water, then, Jess," Ben said. "If the idea of stolen champagne is so appalling."

I nearly did but then I thought there's no way I can sit here sober while they get drunk. So I had a glass of it. And it was beautiful, it really was, all tiny fizzy bubbles, and it tasted like honey and flowers and it was just delicious. And it made me feel happier, even for a little while. It made us all get really relaxed, and Zach stopped picking on me and I made a couple of jokes and the two of them laughed, especially Zach, and I started to think, maybe he's not so bad, maybe it was because I was so tense and upset when I first met him that I didn't get on with him. And it was all fine, it was even good fun and we put music on and I sang along and they said, "Wow, Jess, you've got a really good voice. Do another one," and they weren't being sarcastic. So I stood up and sang a proper song and they applauded and it felt so good and I thought, I *can* make it here. I can't let a few bad auditions put me off. I really do want this to be my career.

Then Zach opened a second bottle of champagne and Ben brought in a basket of food, and it was all stuff from the hotel too, minibar things like chocolates and wasabi-flavored snacks and peanuts, but I was really hungry, so I had a bit of everything even though it was stolen. And we were talking and drinking and it felt great, fun almost, but then I said something about my counselor and it all went funny after that. Zach jumped on the word counselor—"Oh, so Mummy and Daddy sent their little princess off to a psychiatrist, did they? Why? Because you weren't happy with the pony they bought you for your birthday? Or your tree house was too small? You'd wanted one with ten rooms, not eight—"

I never talk about that time; I don't. I get too upset, but the champagne and the week I'd had and his mocking face just all got too much and so I said it, in a horrible way. I just said the truth. "No, Zach. I had to see a counselor because I killed my nephew."

And he shut up and Ben said, "That's not funny, Jess," and I should have stopped there. I should have pretended I was making a bad joke and changed the subject but I'd said it and it was the first time I'd said it out loud in such a long time that I just started telling them what had happened and I couldn't stop.

It was as if all the times I hadn't been able to speak about it had saved themselves up and were there in my head. It came out in a rush, every detail of what had happened that afternoon in the park. I could see Ben and Zach were shocked, really shocked, but I could also see they were really listening. So I just kept on talking. I told them everything, about Felix walking on the fence, the horrible moment when he fell, about ringing Aidan and the ambulance coming, but all of us knowing that it was too late. And I told them about the funeral, how Ella had started crying as they were taking the coffin out of the church, the saddest noise I have ever heard, like a wail, and how she couldn't seem to stop herself—she stepped out into the aisle and she kind of put her arms around the coffin, and it was just so sad. I started crying too and then I couldn't stop. I couldn't stop for days. I couldn't sleep. All that kept happening was the picture of Felix falling and me not being able to stop him. It just went round and round in my head and it didn't matter what anyone said to me—that it was an accident; over and over again Mum and Dad said it to me. Aidan had said it to me too but it didn't help. How could it help when it still meant Felix was dead, and he was dead because of me?

I told Ben and Zach all of this last night. They just kept staring at me, as if they couldn't believe what they were hearing me say.

"Why didn't you tell me this before?" Ben asked, and I said, "Sure, Ben, when we were out having that first drink: 'By the way, I killed my nephew.'"

"You shouldn't say that," Ben said, and he was angry about it. "You didn't kill him. It was an accident."

"It was an accident that happened because I was looking after him. I killed him. If it wasn't for me, he'd be alive now."

"But you didn't do it deliberately. You didn't want to kill him. It was fate."

They started talking about fate then, about preordained paths in life, saying that perhaps Felix was destined to have a short life. That if it hadn't happened when I was looking after him that day, then maybe it would have happened another time. He might have been hit by a car, or got sick with leukemia. I know they were drunk, I know they were trying to make me feel better, but I couldn't bear to hear those things. They were talking about Felix, my little Elix.

I had to stop them somehow and so I stood up and I showed them my tattoo. I had never shown anyone voluntarily before. It was in the smallest letters the tattooist had been able to do, but I had needed to mark Felix's life somehow, and I had needed to feel pain for Felix. I know that sounds so stupid—as if it would change anything—but it hurt so much when the tattooist was doing it and I was glad it hurt, because I had hurt Felix. I had made him die and I needed to hurt in return.

I got the man to put Felix's name, in lowercase letters, exactly where Felix came up to on me when we used to play our measuring game. We had this game where whenever I first saw him, if I was up in Canberra visiting him or if Ella and Aidan brought him down to Melbourne, I would always say, "Wow, Elix! You've grown so much since I saw you last! Soon you'll be taller than me!" And I'd lift him up and hold him above my head and he would laugh and laugh. And I'd done it that day in the flat when I first saw him, and then again on the way to the park. He'd been walking beside me, holding my hand, and I'd lifted him up and then put him down again and said, "Let's measure you again, Elix, because I think you might even have grown since we left home five minutes ago, don't you?" And so we'd stood side by side again, and I'd measured where his head went up to on me and I said, "You have grown! You're like the beanstalk in 'Jack and the Beanstalk'! You go up to here now, look!" And I'd shown him the spot by pointing to a flower on my skirt and I had worn that skirt when I went into the tattoo parlor so the man was able to put Felix's name in exactly the right spot.

That's how it started, I think. The hurting. It made me feel better just for a little while when the tattooist was using the needles. Two nights after I'd had the tattoo done, I woke up with the nightmares again and I went out to the kitchen to get some water. I saw Mum's sewing basket on the shelf, not that she uses it much—she isn't really the sewing type—but I knew there'd be needles in there. So I took one and I brought it back into my bedroom and sat on the bed in the dark and I started pushing it into my skin, on my waist, where the skin was soft. It hurt so much but I knew it could never hurt as much as I had hurt Felix and Ella and Aidan. So I kept doing it and I could feel the blood but I didn't stop until I had done it a hundred times. I counted as I did it. In the morning I got a fright because the bed had blood on it and the skin on my side was all bloody and starting to bruise but I just washed my sheets myself the next day and any other time I needed to.

It was the wardrobe lady at work who told Mum about it. She'd been doing a fitting and I'd been in the dressing room in my underwear. I hadn't done it for a couple of weeks so it wasn't as raw as usual. I had almost forgotten about it; I really had. But she must have noticed something because that night Mum came into my bedroom and said, "Jess, I need you to show me your side." And I didn't want to at first but then I started to cry and so I showed her and she started to cry too and she said, "Why, Jess? Why are you doing it?" And I told her the truth—because it made me feel better, even just for a minute.

That's when they took me back to the doctor and got me in to a counselor three times a week. And I went to her for the next year. I only told Ben and Zach a bit of what went on in those sessions, even though they asked me heaps of questions. Did I have to lie on a couch? Did she shine a light on me? Those kinds of things. I told them a bit of it but not much, because it was hard and it was horrible and I don't like remembering it. She wasn't always kind but she helped me, I think. She taught me how to put other pictures in my head when the bad images came in, and she made me promise to myself and my body that I wouldn't hurt it anymore. She kept saying to me, "Your body is a precious thing, Jess. You have to love it and look after it. Hurting it won't bring Felix back. You have to accept that."

Ben wanted to see the marks. Zach told him off. He was being so kind to me now, but the funny thing was I didn't mind Ben asking. I had never shown them to anyone but Mum, but I'd had a lot to drink and it felt like it was helping me to talk about it and they were so interested. So I lifted my T-shirt up a bit to show my waist. There are still some scars but most of them have faded by now. It's two months since I last did it. I've wanted to, I've even got as far as getting a needle a couple of times, but I've learned to stop it by thinking about Felix being upset at my doing it. That was my counselor's idea. She was right. He would have hated my doing something like that.

After I'd shown them, Ben came over and he kissed the top of my head and it was so sweet I started to cry a bit. And then Zach said, "I'm really sorry, Jess. Is that why your mum and dad sent you here?" And I said yes. And I told them the rest too, that it was especially hard around now, because of the twenty-month anniversary coming up.

It still feels almost unbelievable that it's only twenty months ago. Sometimes it feels like ten years ago. Sometimes it's like it only happened a week ago. Time has gone all funny since it happened. But all of us, Mum and Dad and I think Aidan too and Charlie, and I don't know about Ella, but her too, I'm sure, we've all had the twenty-month anniversary in our heads as being a big thing, an important date. I'm not sure why. I think it was a card someone sent or maybe something someone said at the funeral. My memory from that time is all a bit confused. But Mum and I kept kind of saying it to ourselves, that if we managed to make it to the twenty-month anniversary somehow, then we would be okay. But it's not true; I know that now. It's only a few days away and I know Ella will never be able to talk to me and Aidan has left Australia and I don't know if Mum or Dad are in touch with him. If they are, they don't tell me, but I haven't talked to him for months. I've tried e-mailing him but I was never able to finish writing the message. What could I say? It's like he left our family too. I heard Dad talking to Charlie on the phone one night and I was sure they were talking about Aidan but Dad never brought up the subject again, so perhaps I was mistaken.

I'm meant to be writing about what happened last night. I'd told Ben and Zach about the anniversary coming up and then Ben's phone rang and it was a friend of his in London just for the night, and he said, "Do you mind if I head out and meet him for a few drinks, Jess?" I said of course not, even though I didn't really want to be there with Zach on my own, but he had been so nice and I was a bit drunk and I had also already made up my bed in Ben's tiny spare room with lovely sheets that he'd stolen from the hotel, so I knew I could go to bed soon anyway. Ben asked Zach if he wanted to go out drinking too but he said no, he had to catch an early train the next day. He'd behave himself and have a quiet night too.

But after Ben left, Zach opened another bottle of champagne and he asked me more about Felix. Not about how he had died, but what he was like. So I told him a few of the stories, especially the one about how obsessed Felix always was with brooms and vacuum cleaners. Felix used to make us laugh so much with the expression he'd get when he was pushing the broom around Ella and Aidan's flat. He always looked SO determined. I hadn't thought about that for so long and it all welled up inside me again, how funny he had been and how much we'd all loved to just sit and watch him do ANYTHING. He just had to stand there and we'd all laugh at him.

I started crying again. Some of it was because of the champagne but then I couldn't stop. I hadn't cried properly since I got to London and I think it had all built up and once I started I couldn't stop. Then Zach came over to where I was sitting and put his arms around me and before I knew it we were kissing. I wasn't that attracted to him—he was good-looking but not my type—but it felt so good to be that close to someone and to be kissing and he was a good kisser. And then he put his hand under my T-shirt and touched the scars and he said, "You shouldn't have done that to your beautiful body, Jess. You have such a beautiful body," and he kept saying it and touching me.

I knew why he was saying it. I knew what he was doing but I didn't care. I wanted it. I wanted to feel beautiful again and he was touching me so slowly and he knew what he was doing, and so I took my clothes off and he took his off and there was a moment when I wanted to stop him. I knew I was drunk but it was too late by then. I didn't want him to be mad at me and I was enjoying it. I was. I didn't fight him off. It wasn't rape. I said "yes" when he asked, "Are you sure you want to do this, Jess?" and I kissed him and I said, "Yes, I'm really sure," because anything was better than being on my own and feeling so scared, and he said, "Have you got a condom, by any chance?" and I didn't and he said, "Hang on. I'll look in Ben's room," and I could have stopped at that moment but I didn't. I lay on the sofa and when he came back and said, "I can't find any but I'll be careful, I promise," I just let him do it. I let him and I can't lie—I enjoyed it too. It was really good. It was actually nicer than it had been with any of my boyfriends in Australia—the champagne and everything, I suppose. And we actually did it a second time. This time we did use a condom. Zach got up and got dressed and said he'd be back in a minute and he was back in about fifteen minutes and he had bought some chocolate and a bunch of really cheap-looking flowers as well as the condoms.

We went into the spare bedroom then, my bedroom, and we did it again and it was even better that time. And we both fell asleep and he stayed in my room and then I was woken up when Ben came back with his friend and a few other people. He must have wondered where Zach was because he was supposed to be sleeping on the sofa, and he turned on the light in my room and Zach kept sleeping but I woke up and Ben was drunk, or stoned or on something else, I could see. And he just kind of laughed and said, "Well, I see the two of you are getting on much better," and turned the light out again. I lay there and I could hear them all drinking and talking but I stayed where I was and eventually went back to sleep, and it was nice, it was really nice, to be in bed with someone. I felt safe for the first time since I'd got to London. And I actually slept and it was a good sleep, for about six hours, but when I woke up this morning it was a nightmare again.

Zach was gone, but I'd expected that because of his train, and he left a note (*Take care of yourself xx*) but when I went out into the living room, Ben had already gone to work and not only that—and this is what I will have to call the police about—my purse and my phone were missing. I'd left my handbag in the living room when Zach and I went to bed. I didn't even think about it, and one of the people who came back with Ben must have seen it and taken out my purse and my phone. All they left was my diary and my tissues and makeup.

I panicked. It was so horrible. I was really thirsty and my head hurt from the champagne and the place was such a mess, glasses and ashtrays everywhere and a bong too. It really stank. I kept thinking, I'm jumping to conclusions. My phone and my purse will be here somewhere. I must have taken them out of my bag the night before and put them down somewhere. But they weren't anywhere. I looked in the living room as well as Ben's room and the room I'd slept in, in case I'd brought them in when I went in there with Zach. I even looked in the toilet and bathroom, but they were gone. It was the most horrible feeling. I've never been robbed before. I thought, I'll have to ring Ben at the hotel, but there wasn't a phone in his flat, because everyone has mobiles these days after all. And I couldn't ring him on my mobile because it had been stolen.

I didn't know what to do, and I didn't have any money to use in a public phone. I didn't even know if there was a public phone nearby. It just all started to pile in on me. It was the most terrible feeling and I could feel my breathing going funny. But there was nothing I could do. I was there on my own; I had to handle it. I made myself calm down. I had to use everything the counselor had taught me.

I went back into Ben's room and I found a pile of change on the dressing table and I went downstairs. I had to leave the flat door propped open with some shoes because I didn't have a key, and I ran down the road until I found a phone box. I had trouble getting the number for the hotel and then the girl on reception wouldn't get Ben until I started crying and crying (real crying, not acting-crying) and saying it was an emergency because it was. He eventually came on, and I told him what had happened and for a minute he thought I was accusing him, but it wasn't him. I knew that. Ben is kind, and I had to ask, did he think Zach would have taken it? He said of course not. He could be a pain sometimes but he wasn't a thief. It must have been one of the other guys who'd come back for a drink and a smoke.

Ben was really apologetic, asking me how much was in the purse and was it a valuable phone, but he didn't really understand how bad it was. He said to just stay there until he got back from work and he'd help me, but I could hear it in his voice, that he thought I should just ring my parents and get them to sort everything out. I asked him did he think I should call the police and he said "No!" really firmly. "What, Jess—have them come and search the flat?" and I realized he meant all the stolen stuff from the hotel, not to mention the bong. And then he said he didn't even know the guys who came back, they'd all just met at some club, but it must have been one of them who took my stuff. "But what can I do?" I kept saying, and he said, "Just stay there. I'll help you sort it out when I get back," and then I heard a voice in the background and he said, "Sorry, Jess. I have to go. I'll be back as soon as I can after my shift."

And that was an hour ago. I can't ring the police. What could they do anyway? The first thing they would probably say is for me to ring my parents but I'm not doing that. I'm not. I don't know what to do now. I can't ring anyone else because there isn't anyone for me to ring. I don't know what to do. I want to do it again. I want to hurt myself again. But I can't. I won't. But I don't know what else to do.

FORTY-ONE

I was waiting at Charlie's gate thirty minutes before his flight landed. I saw him before he saw me. I had to stop myself running past the barrier to hug him. Then he saw me too and he started walking quickly and then his bag was on the ground and we were hugging. I had forgotten what a fantastic hugger Charlie was. No one hugged as well as he did.

"Don't cry," he said.

"I'm not."

"Nor am I," he said.

I stepped back. It was nearly two years since I'd seen him. He looked just the same. He hadn't lost any weight. He had the same big smile, the same mop of black hair. I hugged him again.

"It's been too long, Ella," he said. "I've missed you."

"I've missed you too. How's Lucy?" *Ask him.* "How are the kids?"

"They've all missed you too."

The arrivals area of Heathrow wasn't the place for all we wanted to say. We switched into business mode. No, he had no luggage, just his cabin bag. We could go straight into London.

Did he need a cup of tea, something to eat? He must be starving, I said.

"I'm just off a flight, the first time you've seen me in years, and already you're making remarks about my weight? Ella, I'm like a camel. I could live off my own body fat for months."

I could hear the American twang in his accent. "I've some snacks in my handbag if you need them."

"I'll gnaw on my own arm if I get hungry. Thanks anyway. Let's go straight to Lucas's, drop off my bag and get to work."

We joined the stream of people walking toward the platform for the Heathrow Express.

"Are you okay, Ella?" he said. "Are you sure you can do this?"

Lucas had asked me the same question. I nodded.

It felt so good to be sitting there on the train beside him. I wanted to hug him again. I remembered telling him for the first time that I loved him, when we were kids.

I said it again now. "I love you, Charlie."

I thought he'd make a joke. He didn't. "I love you too, Ella."

He asked for an update on Jess. I told him all that Lucas and I had done that day. He'd checked his e-mail as soon as he'd landed. Walter and Mum still hadn't heard from her. They were packed and ready to get on a plane to London themselves, just as soon as Charlie gave the word.

"Do you think she's okay?" I asked him.

"Of course she is. Of course."

He sounded confident, but how could he be? Jess was just a kid, alone in a huge city. What had Mum and Walter been thinking, letting her come here? I ignored the voice reminding me I was twenty-two when I came here on my own. It was different for me. I had Lucas. Jess had nobody.

I'd made this happen to her. I didn't say it out loud, but the thought wouldn't go away. I'd wished bad things on her for twenty months and now something had happened.

"You're not responsible for this, Ella."

I turned. "You're mind-reading now?"

"I don't need to. Ella, she's nearly twenty-three years old. Having an adventure in London. Dad and Meredith are just overreacting. She's probably just lost her phone. And the credit card. You know how careless she is with her belongings."

Jess wasn't careless with her belongings. She never had been. I let the lie go. It soothed me.

"Besides," Charlie added, "I've been waiting for an excuse to come over to see you. I'm glad she's gone missing. Walter wouldn't have paid for my airfare otherwise."

"Charlie!"

"I'm joking. I paid for my own airfare. I like your new do, by the way. I've never seen you with short hair. It suits you."

I pulled at the short strands. "It's easier like this."

"Very now. Very gamine." He said it in an exaggerated French accent. "Very chic."

"*Merci*," I said.

"What about me? Do I look any skinnier?" he asked.

"No."

"Good. Because I'm not. I don't want to be. As I keep telling the doctor, being this fat means there's more of me to love."

I smiled. I wanted to tell him again that I loved him. I didn't need to. He knew.

We were both quiet for a few minutes, watching the weather forecast on the carriage's small TV screen. There was more cold weather ahead, even sleet, a forecast of four degrees Celsius.

Charlie broke the silence. "Do you remember that time you met me and Dad at the airport, Ella? After we'd been in Germany?"

I nodded. Of course I remembered. They had been in Germany for his mother's funeral.

"That was really nice of you. What you did. I don't know if I ever thanked you."

"You did."

"Thanks again."

"You're welcome."

I'd made a banner. I'd needed to do something to mark his homecoming. He and Walter had been gone for a fortnight. It was Charlie's first trip to Germany, to bury the mother he hadn't seen for more than ten years. We'd never talked about her much at home. If I asked Charlie, he just shrugged and said he didn't really remember her. I never dared ask Walter for any details. It wasn't until Mum and I were on the way back from dropping them at the airport that Mum told me the whole story. I was just old enough to take it all in. Old enough, too, to feel sad not just for Walter and Charlie but for Birgitte, Charlie's mother, as well. She'd had addiction problems, Mum told me. Not alcohol or hard drugs, but prescription tablets—Valium and painkillers. She'd had difficulties before she and Walter left Germany. They'd got worse once they came to Australia. There was a good period while she was pregnant with Charlie, and during the first year of his life. But then she started taking the tablets again. In secret at first. Soon there had been no hiding what she was doing. Walter did what he could. He stayed with her until Charlie started school, but her problems became more serious. She'd been in and out of treatment centers. She told Walter repeatedly that she hated him. She had no real relationship with Charlie. Eventually, her older sister came out from Munich and took her back home. Walter filed for divorce and was granted custody of Charlie. He met Mum in the garden center the year Charlie turned eleven.

While he and Charlie were away for Birgitte's funeral, Walter rang home every day, but not for long. I didn't speak to Charlie for the entire two weeks. I really missed him. So did his friends at school. Throughout that fortnight I was stopped at least once a day by one of Charlie's friends. Had I heard from him? How was he?

"Fine," I told them all. "Fine. Very sad, though, of course."

I was lying. I'd talked about it with him before he left,

after his aunt had rung with the news that his mother had died, and to say they would delay the funeral until Charlie and Walter could get there if they wanted to come.

"Do you want to go?" I asked Charlie.

"*Ja, natürlich,*" he said.

He was trying to joke. I wasn't in a joking mood.

"Do you remember her?"

"Not much."

"Are you sad?"

"Not really."

"But she's your mother, Charlie."

He shrugged. "I didn't know her, Ella. I can't miss someone I didn't know."

The night before they arrived home, I spent hours on my banner. When they came out into the arrivals hall, I was there holding it up. *Welcome home Charlie (and Walter)! I missed you (both)! xxxx* I'd originally only had Charlie on it but Mum told me to add Walter in case his feelings were hurt.

Charlie burst into tears when he saw it. He cried for hours afterward.

"Are you cross that I didn't make you a banner today?" I said.

"No. I just wanted another excuse to cry. I've really missed you, Ella."

"I've really missed you too."

"We all have. Me. Lucy. The kids."

"I'm sorry, Charlie."

I couldn't say more than that, not in public. I hoped he knew what I meant. I was sorry for not reading his family reports. For not coming to see him. For not sending his four children birthday presents or Christmas presents. For having nothing to do with his family for the past twenty months.

"You know you're welcome anytime. Whenever you're ready."

"I know."

"Maybe you'll come and see us when you've finished your detective work with Lucas?"

"I have. Didn't Lucas tell you? It was Colonel Mustard in the ballroom with the candlestick."

"Oh." He gave a sheepish smile. "You know?"

"Lucas confessed."

"Lucas has a big mouth. Are you angry with us?"

"For bringing me all the way to London under false pretenses? For putting four innocent tutors under suspicion?"

He nodded.

"No."

"I'm sorry, Ella. We were so worried about you. We wanted you to stay still, even for a month or two, to see if—"

"Lucas explained, Charlie. It's okay."

We were approaching Paddington. The woman on TV was thanking us for traveling with her. I needed to tell Charlie something else. Now.

I reached into my bag, took out Aidan's letter and handed it to him. I watched as he read it. I didn't need to read it again. I already knew it by heart.

Dear Ella,

I'm working in London next week. If you'd like to see me, I'm staying at the Paddington Hilton.

Underneath he'd listed his dates. He was here now. He'd arrived yesterday and was staying for two more nights. He'd signed his name under that. Just his name, not *Love, Aidan,* or *All the best, Aidan.* Just *Aidan.*

Charlie read it, returned it to the envelope and handed it back.

"Did you know?" I asked him.

He shook his head. "I talked to him recently but he didn't mention any work in London. What are you going to do? Are you going to see him?"

"You talked to him recently?"

"Ella—"

"Charlie, please. I need to know."

Charlie hesitated. "I'd arranged to meet him in Washington. We wanted to convince him to come see you while you were staying at Lucas's house."

"We?"

"Lucas and I. But Aidan canceled at the last minute. Lucas told him what my visit was about and he canceled. He told me he appreciated our concern but that it was between you and him."

"Were you going to tell me any of this?"

"Eventually." He paused. "Actually, no."

"Charlie, is Aidan seeing anyone?"

"What?"

"When I got the letter . . . Charlie, I haven't heard from him in months. Nearly a year. I think he wants to tell me he's met someone else. He wants to ask for a divorce."

"Ella, I'm sorry. I don't know. We've spoken on the phone a few times since he came to Washington but he only ever asked about you. He didn't mention anyone else."

The train pulled into Paddington Station. I knew the Hilton was close by. As we walked along the platform I could see it through the glass roof of the station.

Charlie saw it too. "Go, Ella. I can find Lucas's house on my own."

This wasn't the right time. He was here until the end of the week. I had two more days.

"I'm coming with you," I said.

Lucas greeted Charlie with a hug. I was struck by how close they seemed. How easy their conversation was. I remembered Lucas saying he had talked to my mother regularly. It seemed he had talked regularly to Charlie too.

Lucas had been busy. He'd phoned the police and reported Jess missing. The policewoman had taken all the details, but she'd been skeptical, he reported. "She said she'd put out a bulletin about it, but it sounded to her like Jess was off having either a big love affair, a sulk or an adventure."

Lucas had also printed some simple flyers, using a photo of Jess from her Facebook page, and adding our contact numbers. We decided to take them to as many places in the West End we could think of. We'd just put on our coats to leave when Charlie turned to Lucas.

"Did Ella tell you Aidan's in London, Lucas?"

I passed the letter to him. He read it. "Go, Ella. Charlie and I can look for Jess on our own."

"I want to help."

"Ella—"

"Please, Lucas."

He didn't look happy. But he let me come with them.

———

Six hours later, we were back, cold, tired and footsore. Our mood was grim. We had passed out nearly a hundred flyers, but we had no leads and no news. We'd called in to theatrical agents, casting agents and cafés all around the West End. No one remembered seeing Jess.

We called in to other hotels in the area, in case she had booked in there. Nothing. We waited until the theaters began to open for business, watched as the crowds gathered outside. Jess wasn't among them. We showed her photo to ushers after most of the crowds had taken their seats inside. No one knew her.

It had been very cold walking around the West End. We'd seen homeless people huddling for warmth in doorways; others, some of them just kids, begging for change. We'd walked through Soho, where many of the theatrical agencies had their offices. I'd seen the lap-dancing clubs, the strip clubs. Could Jess have ended up in one of those? On the Tube on the way home, Charlie raised the same theory. We'd agreed to return to Soho tomorrow with more flyers.

It was nearly eleven. Charlie wanted to phone Walter and Mum. Lucas thought it was better to wait until there was something definite to report. He phoned the police for an update. They had no news either. Charlie compromised by sending an e-mail: *No news yet, but we'll find her. Don't worry,* he wrote.

There was nothing more we could do tonight. We turned to practical issues. Charlie offered to cook some pasta. Lucas lit the fire. I made up Charlie's bed. I'd given him my room and moved a mattress up to the attic for myself. Of the four tutors, only Darin was in the house. The others had gone home for midterm break. He came into the kitchen just after we arrived home, met Charlie, took a handful of biscuits out of the tin and went to his room. We didn't see him again.

We ate in front of the fire, in Lucas's withdrawing room. I let Charlie and Lucas do the talking. Neither of them mentioned Felix, or Aidan. I was relieved.

Just after dinner, Charlie started to yawn. We were all tired. We agreed to meet again for breakfast at eight a.m. Lucas would call the police for an update and then we would go out with the flyers again.

The attic was warm and dark. The mattress was small but comfortable. I didn't read or turn on the lamp. I looked up at the sky through the roof window, listening to the sounds of London: sirens, voices, music from somewhere, buses, taxis—a city switching into night mode. I tried to imagine Jess, out there somewhere.

Let her be all right.

I wasn't praying. I didn't pray anymore. But something must have happened to her. It must have. Something that was stopping her from ringing home, using her credit card, sending an e-mail. Young girls could drink too much, take drugs, meet people they shouldn't trust, get into cars they thought were minicabs—

Stop.

Distract.

I thought of Charlie downstairs. I thought of the three of us, Charlie, Lucas and I, there by the fire this evening.

They had talked mostly about Jess. Charlie had known it all, about her medication, the counseling, the self-harming.

I stayed quiet. I stayed silent when their conversation moved to other subjects too. Charlie's kids. Life in Boston. His e-mail reports. Lucas asked Charlie to tell him the story about the family's visit to the dentist again. Charlie had smiled. "Please, don't remind me." It had been pandemonium, he said. Sophie had fainted. Reilly leaped out of the chair and ran screaming through the waiting room. Ed pocketed some false teeth he found on a shelf. Tim, the youngest, somehow managed to turn on the drill. They'd been ordered out and politely asked never to return. Charlie smiled again as he told the story. Lucas did too, enjoying every detail.

I hadn't heard it before.

"That was great news about Lucy's results, too," Lucas said.

"She's brilliant," Charlie said. "Two more semesters and she'll have her marketing degree."

I hadn't known she was studying for a marketing degree.

I turned over in the bed. I'd been exhausted, but now I couldn't sleep. I replayed every moment from the day. The morning at Henrietta's house. My conversation with Lucas. My phone call with Mum. Aidan's letter. Looking for Jess. Charlie's arrival at the same time as Aidan was in London.

Something Charlie said on the train came back to me.

I've been waiting for an excuse to come over to see you. I'm glad she's gone missing.

Missing.

As the map, necklace, figurine, ring and watch had apparently gone missing.

I sat up. Jess wasn't missing. Lucas and Charlie were

behind this as well. They must have known Aidan was going to be here for work. They must have decided this was
their best chance to get Aidan and me talking. Was Mum in
on it too? Jess? Had they asked her to stop posting anything
on Facebook, just for the time being? My mind made connection after connection. It all made sense.

I pulled on my dressing gown and went downstairs.
Charlie's bedroom door was open, his bed empty. I could
hear the shower running. I went down to the ground floor.
Lucas was still up, in his withdrawing room, putting the
screen in front of the fire.

He turned as I came in. "You couldn't sleep? I'm not
surprised."

"Jess isn't missing, Lucas, is she? This is you and Charlie
pretending again. Lucas, I appreciate it, I do, but you have to
let me—"

"Ella, I'm sorry, but you're wrong."

"Lucas, please, tell the truth. Charlie arrives just as
Aidan happens to be in London for a conference? Jess happens to go missing? I know what you're trying to do. But
please, won't you just—"

"No, Ella." Lucas ran his fingers through his hair. He
looked very tired. "I wish we were behind this. I wish Jess
wasn't missing. But I wouldn't put Meredith and Walter
through this, even if I did hope it would bring you to your
senses and make you start thinking about other people as
well as yourself."

I went still.

"I'm sorry to be so blunt. I also know it's Felix's twenty-
month anniversary soon. I know what that means to you.

But you are not the only person in your family hurting at the moment."

"Lucas—"

He held up his hand. "I know. I know what you're going to say. You have all the excuses in the world to do whatever you want to do. But everyone has been through hell these past twenty months. Everyone has had to try to remake their lives. Charlie has tried harder than everyone, to keep us entertained, to keep up his family e-mail, to cheer your mother up as much as he can. But he barely dared to mention his children around you tonight. Did you notice that? When are you going to stop punishing him for still having four children, for having a happy family?"

I couldn't believe what he was saying. "It's only been twenty months, Lucas. Not even two years."

"It's been twenty months for all of us, Ella. For all of us. But one day soon you are going to have to make a decision about the rest of your life. Whether you are going to open yourself up to all of us again, or stay locked in your own prison of grief."

He came across to me. He put his hand on my shoulder, pressed a kiss on top of my head. He looked tired. More than tired. He looked disappointed. In me.

"Go to bed, Ella. We're going to be busy tomorrow."

I walked back up the stairs to the attic. I felt like I'd been winded. I sat on the mattress, in the darkness. I felt as if Lucas had given up on me. As if I wasn't the person he'd thought I was. Of all the people in the world, I couldn't bear to let Lucas down.

You didn't let us grieve with you, Ella.

But Felix was my son. My baby.

We all loved him, Ella.

I remembered Henrietta's words to me that night in the kitchen.

Grief is selfish.

I didn't want to think about her.

I'd thought staying away from everyone was the only way to go on. I had never thought I was causing more hurt myself.

I wanted to go downstairs again. I wanted to talk to Lucas, to say sorry to him, to beg his forgiveness. I hated what he'd said to me, but I knew he was telling me the truth. If I had grown up believing he was on my side, all my life, I had to believe it now.

Was everything he'd said about Charlie true? It was, I realized. I'd been punishing Charlie for having four children. I'd punished him by ignoring them, even when I knew they were everything in the world to him. But he never said anything to me. He kept e-mailing, kept cheering me up, listening to me, phoning me, being kind to me, when all the time I was being so hurtful to him.

So much must have happened to him and his family that I knew nothing about, because I had chosen not to know. I'd heard just two stories tonight. What else had happened to Lucy, to Sophie, Ed, Reilly and Tim, over the past twenty months?

I could find out, I realized. I could find out, right now.

I got up, switched on my laptop and logged on to my e-mail account. I went straight to a file of e-mail that had been sitting, unread, for months. Charlie's family reports. I pulled up a chair, wrapped a blanket around myself, opened the first one and started to read.

It was nearly two a.m. by the time I finished. I walked quietly down the stairs. Charlie's light was on. I could hear voices. The radio? I knocked softly.

"Charlie? Are you awake?"

I heard his voice. "Enter at your own risk." He'd used to say that when we were kids.

I opened the door. He was sitting up in bed, the laptop on a pillow on his knees. He smiled. "I couldn't sleep. Just talking to the kids. Hold on, kids. It's Auntie Ella."

Charlie beckoned me closer. I stayed where I was.

"Poor Auntie Ella's a bit shy," he said into the camera. "You need to coax her to you, as if she's a wild animal that needs to be tamed."

I could hear their different voices. "Come here, Ella!" "Don't be shy, Auntie Ella!" "We won't bite, Auntie Ella!" "Ed *might* bite, Sophie. Put your hand over his mouth in case."

Charlie turned the laptop around so the camera was pointing at me, not him. I appeared in a small box in the right-hand corner. The rest of the screen was like an aquarium filled with Charlie's children: Sophie, Ed, Reilly and Tim, smiling and waving out at me.

They were even more beautiful than I remembered. Reilly and Ed were like mini Lucys, blond and blue-eyed. Sophie was the image of her mother too, but with Charlie's black hair. Tim was like Charlie shrunk to miniature size—cheeky grin, chubby cheeks and all.

Before Felix died, I'd talked to them at least once a week. I'd listened to their tales from school, heard songs they were learning for concerts, praised paintings they held up to the camera for me to see. They'd met and got to know Felix over Skype. They'd seen him the day after he was born. They'd seen his first tooth, in close-up. They'd watched him crawl across our apartment floor. They'd watched him eat, and laughed as he ended up with most of the food on his face. They'd seen him take his earliest steps. They'd sent clothes and cheered to see him on the screen wearing them. They'd sung songs to him. They'd laughed and laughed one afternoon when Felix stood in front of my laptop camera and shouted, five times in a row, at the top of his voice, "I'm Felix O'Hanlon!"

They waved at me now, as if it had been just last week we had spoken to one another.

I came closer. "Hi, kids," I called.

"Look at this, Ella!" It was Ed. He leaned right into the camera so his face filled the screen and then smiled. He was missing the two front teeth. "One was coming out anyway but I pulled the other one out. It really hurt."

"Ouch," I said. "Did you tell the Tooth Fairy? You might get paid danger money."

Ed sat back. Beside him, Sophie gave me a big wink. "That's a great idea, Ella. I'll help him write to the Tooth Fairy tonight." She put a lot of emphasis on the words *tooth* and *fairy*.

Reilly held up a book. "I'm reading this, Ella. Back to front. It's harder but it means I know what's going to happen."

"That's a great approach, Reilly. No surprises that way. How are you, Tim?" I asked. I steeled myself as I looked at him. Tim, the youngest, the closest in age to Felix.

"Good," he said. "Look." He bared his teeth at me. He wasn't missing any. They were all there, like a little row of dolphin teeth, sharp and pointy.

I laughed. "Wow. What fantastic teeth. You must really look after them, do you?"

He nodded.

He'd been a toddler last time I saw him. He was four now. I had missed nearly two years of his childhood. Of all their childhoods.

I needed to leave now. I said good night to each of them by name. There was a chorus of good-byes in return. "Bye, Ella!" "Talk to you soon, Ella!" "Bye, Ella!" "So long, Ella!"

"Do you want to wait?" Charlie said to me. "I'll only be a few minutes. Did you need to talk?"

I shook my head. "I'm fine. Don't worry. I'll see you tomorrow."

I called out good night to the kids again. Four cheery American-accented good nights sounded behind me as I carefully shut Charlie's door.

FORTY-TWO

Dear Diary,
Hi, it's Jess!

Everything's okay again!!!!! I've got two places to stay and I've even got a job offer! Thank God, thank God, thank God for that Australian waitress. I know I said she was horrible before but she isn't. She was just having a bad day. Let me start at the beginning, back to yesterday morning.

After I'd spoken to Ben while he was at work and he wasn't that nice, I got very upset and I came really close to hurting myself again. It all just rushed at me again, like a wave, and I was even looking for something to do it with. But then something stopped me. I don't know what it was. Suddenly I just thought, no, I don't want to start doing that again. And the more I thought about it, the more I knew I wouldn't. I made myself remember things the counselor said to me. "You will get through this, Jess, because you are special and wonderful and you have to keep telling yourself that. You loved Felix. You would never have hurt him deliberately." The more I said that, the more I reminded myself that Felix wouldn't have liked me hurting myself either. And that's what really stopped me. The thought of him seeing me do it. I've always secretly hoped he is an angel somewhere, watching all of us (but I hope he wasn't watching while I was in bed with Zach). I wouldn't want to make him unhappy.

The counselor always said to me, "You can control your thoughts, Jess. You can't change what happened, but you can change the way you think about things." And so I kept saying that to myself, especially after I had my shower and came out into Ben's filthy living room again. At first, seeing the mess only reminded me that one of the horrible guys who'd been there had taken my phone and purse. But then I looked around and I just decided, "I'm not going to let them or this beat me. I'm *not*." And I know it sounds so corny and stupid but I made myself imagine I was playing a role in a musical, that all of this was just a part I was playing. And I realized I needed to actually do something if I was playing a part, so I decided to do a big cleanup. The place was a pigsty and that was making me feel worse, so I thought, I'll fix it up and that will make me feel better and it will also be a way of paying my way because Ben has been nice to me and it wasn't his fault his friends were thieving creeps.

So I just got really stuck in and I decided to sing as I worked. I sang and I sang and this time there was no porter to come and tell me to shut up. I sang all the big cheery songs we always keep for the finales: "There's No Business Like Show Business" from *Annie Get Your Gun* and "Don't Rain on My Parade" from *Funny Girl* and "I Feel Pretty" from *West Side Story* and then most of the ABBA songs from *Mamma Mia!* as well. I cleaned the whole place up, every room except for Ben's, and I bet it has never been cleaned so well. The furniture was still pretty battered but it all looked so much better than it had. And then I felt so good I didn't want to sit in and spend the day waiting for Ben to come home. He'd told me there was a spare key in the teapot, so I got it and I kept talking to myself. "Treat this like a day off, Jess. Go exploring. You're in London, after all. Pretend you're in a film now and just ACT as if you're carefree."

So I did and that REALLY helped too. It kind of made it fun—whatever I did, I just imagined there was a camera crew following me. So I did things like swing around a lamppost and sniff flowers outside florists' and all the stuff people do in films when they are exploring a city, and even though it was freezing cold I walked alongside the Thames for a bit, with my collar up and smiling at complete strangers, because you always see people in films doing that too. Unfortunately I didn't have any money apart from a few coins left over from Ben's spare change—I'd used most of it on my phone call to him at the hotel—so that was a big drawback, but I kept telling myself not to worry about that yet either, something would turn up. I even kept looking down at the ground as I walked along because in a film the girl would probably find a twenty-pound note or something. I'd also taken the precaution of bringing a packed lunch. I didn't think Ben would mind. It was all stuff he'd stolen from the hotel anyway, so strictly speaking it didn't belong to him either. And it was really nice, like a picnic! I sat on a bench and I had peanuts and then biscuits, and then for dessert three chocolates, really nice ones, the ones that maids put on the pillow when they turn down your bed at nighttime. I recognized them from when I was staying in the hotel myself.

After lunch I still had a whole afternoon to fill, but the sun was actually out—there was even a bit of blue sky, enough to make a sailor a pair of pants, as my mum would say. So I went walking all the way to Oxford Street and Regent Street again to look at the shops. On the way, I saw a bus going to Paddington. I got a bit sad then, thinking about Ella and Felix, but I kept reminding myself of what the counselor used to say to me, "You *will* get through this, Jess. It has been a terrible tragedy for you and your family, but you will all come through it if you let it happen, if you all allow yourselves time to grieve and be kind to yourselves, because none of you wanted that terrible and sad thing to happen to Felix." And I also remembered something else the counselor said: "You'll never get over it, Jess. You won't. You'll learn to live with it. That's a very different thing." I hope I will learn that one day.

I did a bit of window-shopping and even tried on a few outfits, but then as I was walking down some back streets I saw the café where I'd spent that hour and I don't know what, but something made me go in there. I checked my coins first and decided I had enough money for a cup of tea, at least. So I went into the café and the Australian lady was there on her own behind the counter.

She wasn't very friendly at first to me this time either. She must have remembered I'd been there for ages the other day but I just took a deep breath and before I knew what I was saying, I basically threw myself on her mercy and begged her for some work, peeling potatoes or cleaning the toilets, anything she could offer me for even a few pounds. I said that basically I didn't have any money and I wasn't a druggie or anything, I promised, I was just a young Australian like she must have been once too, needing some assistance from a Good Samaritan. It really helped that I kept thinking I was in a film. It made everything less scary because I just told myself I was playing a role, that it wasn't really me, Jessica Baum, saying all this stuff.

And she said, "What, no money at all?" And I said I'd had some but it had been stolen. And she said, "Were you mugged?" and before I knew it, I'd told her EVERYTHING that had happened, about staying in a hotel when I first got here (I didn't say which one) but then having a fight with my mum and dad (though I didn't tell her what the fight was about) and being stupid and cutting up the credit card and Ben taking pity and letting me stay in his flat and then his friend being there too (though I didn't tell her I'd had sex with him) and then waking up and hearing Ben with his friends from the club and then waking up again and my bag being there but my phone and my purse gone.

"You didn't know any of these guys? You'd just met one of them in the hostel you were staying in?"

I didn't correct her that it was a hotel, not a hostel. I just nodded. And she lost it! She said, "You're bloody lucky you weren't raped and murdered. What a stupid thing to do, to go and stay with a bunch of strange men. Bloody hell. Didn't your mother teach you anything?"

And I suddenly wanted to cry then, because of COURSE my mum wouldn't have wanted me to get into a mess like this but I made myself NOT cry and made myself try to joke about it instead. I said, "All she's taught me is how to cook. And she's a useless cook."

And then, I couldn't believe it, the lady kind of took a step back and said, "I know you, don't I? You're from that TV show, that ridiculous cooking one with the mother and the daughter. Mad Mary or something."

"*MerryMakers.*"

"*MerryMakers,* that's it! Am I right? Is Merry your mum?"

I have never ever EVER been so grateful for the fact that Mum is a cult TV star! It turns out the lady—her name is Angela—had been home to visit her family in Sydney for Christmas and had stumbled across *MerryMakers* on the cable network one afternoon and got hooked and had watched loads of episodes, even the reruns. She changed completely toward me after that. She called out to the guy in the kitchen. He was Iranian or Russian or something. It turns out he's her husband, not her boss. His name is Victor, and she said, "Can we give this kid a job for the afternoon? She's in a bit of trouble."

He came out and said, "Why don't your family help you?"

"I'm trying to stand on my own two feet," I said. I didn't want to go into all the details again.

I started work there and then! I was only there for three hours, but I worked really hard. I washed dishes and peeled potatoes and filled up about a hundred plastic bottles with tomato sauce and mustard. They got really busy in the late afternoon, when the workers at a construction site down the road finished for the day and they all came in, and they knew Angela and Victor's names and they all ordered huge plates of basically breakfast food in the middle of the afternoon! Sausages and beans and eggs and—worst of all—liver. I've never seen or smelled anything more disgusting. How can anyone eat liver?? I even had to cook some of it when it got really busy and Victor had to run out and get more eggs and I nearly threw up in the pan at the smell. Then I did all the washing up again, and there was a lot of it and not even a dishwasher, but one thing I am really good at is washing up. I decided to keep pretending I was in a film, so I sang loads of songs too until Angela asked me to shut up. She said the customers preferred the radio.

The other kitchen hand is back tomorrow. I was just lucky he was off sick today, so that was it for me employment-wise there but they still paid me TWENTY POUNDS!! I felt really rich when they gave it to me. Not that it's that much really and it wouldn't pay for a hotel room or anything, but luckily I had Ben's place anyway.

Angela asked me all about his flat. I think she had it in her head that it was like a crack den or something with needles on the floor and boards on the windows, but I explained that it was actually pretty nice, and smelled like washing powder, but that I didn't plan to be there forever, because I didn't want to overstay my welcome. And she said that if things got really hairy for me at Ben's, I could sleep on their floor (as in her and Victor's flat, not in the café!!!) and I thought that was really nice of her because she had only just met me, and I said that to her and she said I reminded her a bit of her little sister and then she said, had I ever heard the saying "a babe in the woods," because I reminded her of that too. And I said, well, I'd heard of that pantomime *Babes in the Wood*, of course, but I'm not sure what that had to do with me right there at the moment. I'm an adult, not a baby, and in London, not a forest.

But then Angela also said—actually she INSISTED— that I ring Mum. I thought at first it was because she wanted to talk to her herself, Mum being a celebrity, but then she went on and on and said, "Mothers really worry about their kids. Have you talked to her since that fight?" and I said "No" and then I confessed I hadn't e-mailed her or Dad either. And she said, "So how long since your mother has heard from you?" And I said, "Five days, I think," and she said, "She must be worried sick. You need to send her a message right NOW." She got really bossy, as if SHE was my mother, and I said, "But my phone was stolen," and she said, "Here, use my phone. Do it now. Your mum won't mind being woken up, I can assure you." But then, it was really embarrassing. I had a complete blank about our home number and Mum and Dad's mobile numbers too. They were all just stored in my contacts list; who ever needs to memorize anything anymore? So then Angela said, "What about e-mail? Can you remember her e-mail address?" and I could. It's Merry@MerryMakers.com.au. So I sent a quick note. *Hi Mum and Dad, Jess here, sorry for hanging up on you, everything's great, I'll ring soon, love Jess xxoo. P.S. Have lost my phone and am borrowing a friend's to send this so please don't worry about trying my old number.* And I did feel a lot better afterward. I'd been feeling a bit guilty that I hadn't been in touch with them. I'm still upset that they didn't tell me about my being offered my own show but they did fly me here and put me up in the lovely hotel and I'm not being avaricious (right spelling?) or anything, but the truth is if I want to stay on here in London, and I think I do, I probably will need to get financial assistance from them because it doesn't sound like kitchen work pays very much and also, how will I get time to go to auditions if I'm working all the time?? Zach is right. Maybe I am a bit of a princess but I'm just lucky to have parents that support me and my dreams.

So I will definitely ring her and Dad tomorrow (just quickly; I don't want to use up all my twenty pounds on a phone call!!). I would have rung home soon anyway. I know Mum will be thinking about Felix's anniversary.

I didn't tell Angela about that part of things. I was going to, but I remembered what happened with Ben and Zach, and I realized I wanted to keep it to myself. I'd been drunk when I told them everything, and afterward I'd wished I hadn't. I want to do some private thinking about Felix, and if I told Angela, it would feel like I'd shared him again and I didn't really want to do that.

As I was leaving, Angela even gave me a hug and told me to come back again if I wanted, and then her husband said his cousin has a restaurant and the chef was so horrible they are always going through staff but if I was prepared to work hard I could probably get a job there. He told me the chef would shout at me a lot, but it would be in Russian and he could teach me some stuff to shout back if I wanted. I said I'd think about it. And maybe I will. But the more I thought about it as I was in the Tube going back to Ben's, the more I realized I really just wanted to talk to Mum and Dad again and say sorry and get things back to the way they were before, with them helping me, not just financially, but giving me lots of encouragement and kind of protecting me, even from the other side of the world.

I think I might put the auditions on hold for a while too. I haven't given up on that yet, but I just wonder if I maybe threw myself into it all a bit too quickly, before I was ready, which might have been why I didn't get through to the next stage. I might sign up for a few dance and singing classes here, just to keep everything in proper working order. And also maybe look around London a bit more too. I can hear Ben coming up the stairs, so I'd better go!! I hope he notices how clean the flat is!!!!

Love for now,

Jess xxxxoooo

P.S. It's an hour later. Ben was THRILLED with the clean flat. And he said sorry if he'd sounded a bit weird on the phone earlier, his supervisor was listening. He also said that I can stay here for as long as I want, especially if I'm going to clean up like that!! (He's obviously feeling REALLY guilty about my stuff being stolen!) So now I basically have TWO places to choose from, here and Angela's floor. And guess what? He said that someone was in the hotel looking for me today!! He doesn't know more than that, because he was so hungover he spent most of the day hiding and sleeping in the linen room and so didn't talk to the manager like all the other porters did, but apparently two people were in asking about me, a man and a woman. I think they must have been agents!!! I gave the hotel as my contact details in my first e-mail messages to everyone in the theater world, and maybe they tried to phone me but when they couldn't get an answer on account of my phone being stolen they came to the hotel instead to meet me in person!! I begged Ben to ring the manager to ask who they were but he said he needs to lie low with her at the moment (he's worried someone told her he spent the day in the linen room) but he'll ask tomorrow. He's on the breakfast shift so he'll be in there bright and early. Am Very Hopeful and Excited!!

FORTY-THREE

The phone woke us all up. It was just after five thirty a.m. Lucas answered it. I heard him coming up the stairs calling to Charlie and me. In seconds, both of us were out of our beds. We met Lucas on the landing. He was in his pajamas, holding the phone. "It's Walter. They've had an e-mail from Jess. She's lost her phone but she's alive and well."

"That's it? Where is she?" I asked.

"She didn't say. They don't know."

"She disappears for five days and then doesn't say where she's been? The selfish—"

Charlie put his hand on my arm. "Ella—"

I let the rush of temper pass. I let myself feel relief instead. "Sorry," I said.

Charlie took the phone and had a brief conversation with

Walter and then with Mum. I couldn't hear what they were saying, but I could guess. Charlie soothed them both, gave them my love too, promised to e-mail Jess himself and meet up with her as soon as possible. When he hung up, I could see the relief on his face as well.

We stayed up. Charlie brought his laptop down to the kitchen and wrote Jess an e-mail while Lucas brewed coffee. He read it out to us before he pressed send. He hadn't held back.

"Jessica Baum, you are in BIG trouble. I'm in London because your parents have been so worried. You can't just disappear like that. AS SOON AS YOU GET THIS E-MAIL ring your mum and dad and then ring me. I'm at Lucas's." He typed in the number and pressed send.

We'd just finished our breakfast when there was a pinging noise from his laptop. An incoming e-mail. It was from Jess. Charlie read it out loud.

"Charlie!!! I'm up early too! Are you really in London????? FANTASTIC!!! I'd love to see you!! I'll ring Mum and Dad first and then I'll ring you, promise. I've got a bit of a problem phonewise. (I'm sending this from my new friend and flatmate Ben's phone. He works at the hotel I stayed at. I'd ring on his phone but he has to go in early today to find out if there were agents in looking for me yesterday—it's a long story!!!) So I need to go to the phone box down the road but I'll call you as soon as I can, I promise! CAN'T WAIT to see you!!!! Jess xxxxoooo." Charlie looked up. "Fifty exclamation marks. I think she's okay."

He turned back to his laptop again, rapidly keying in words, bringing up an airline Web site. He was checking for flights back to Boston, I realized.

"Are you going straight back home?" I asked.

"I need to. Lucy's had to take time off work to look after the kids. But I won't go until I've seen Jess in person. Told her off in person. Can you both come with me? I might need a bodyguard. Or Jess might, at least."

"I'll come," Lucas said. "I'd like to meet Jessica again. Ella, will you come too?" There was a challenge in his voice. But I couldn't join them. In the middle of the night, I'd made a decision about what I would do once we knew Jess was safe.

I told them I was going to see Aidan.

Lucas offered to accompany me to the hotel. Charlie offered to call me a taxi. It was less than ten minutes' walk away. I thanked them and said I was happy to go on my own.

I showered. I changed my clothes three times. I pulled at the short strands of my hair, as though that would make it long again, as though that would turn me back into the person who had last seen Aidan, all those months ago in Canberra. I wanted to go back even further, to the woman I had been before everything happened. I put makeup on, then I took it off. I put lipstick on. I wiped that off as well.

"Have you rung him?" Lucas asked when I came downstairs.

I shook my head.

"But he's here for work, isn't he?" Charlie said. "He might be in a conference room somewhere. Wouldn't it be better to make a time with him?"

I knew they were right. But I didn't want our first conversation to be over the phone. I needed to see his face, his eyes.

"I'd rather just turn up," I said.

When it was finally time for me to go, they both came to the door to say good-bye. They both hugged me too.

"Good girl," Lucas said quietly.

I walked along the street, joining the flow of morning commuters, as if I were going to my ordinary office job, on an ordinary morning. I glanced at my watch. It wasn't even nine. It was bitterly cold. The wind was like ice. I pulled my coat in tighter around me, tugged my scarf up higher. I wished I'd worn my hat. It had been a moment of vanity as I left. I hadn't wanted to spoil my hair. It would be enough of a shock for Aidan to see it so short. He'd only ever known me with long hair.

It was barely nine when I arrived at the hotel. It seemed too early. I walked around the block twice, glad of the traffic noise. It made it hard to think. It was nine thirty when I came into the Art Deco–style lobby.

There was a large group of people checking in or checking out; I couldn't tell which. They were speaking different languages, French, German, Italian. A tour group or a company delegation? The delegation Aidan was here interpreting for? I turned, expecting to see him in the middle of the group. No, they were tourists, holding maps and brochures. They were all checking in. I was in for a long wait.

Observe.

I walked around the lobby. There was a lounge area with a piano and a restaurant full of people having breakfast. I didn't want to look too closely in case Aidan was there, finishing his coffee. He always had two large cups of coffee in the morning. There were three elevators to my right, their doors opening and shutting constantly, the hotel at its morning busiest. I didn't want to watch them in case the doors opened and Aidan walked out. Not on his own. With someone.

With his new girlfriend?

Distract.

I'd traveled with him on several work trips over the years. The farthest had been to Bangkok, when we were first living in Canberra. I spent the days visiting temples and markets, joining him in the evenings for the formal gatherings with the rest of the trade delegation. He kept apologizing for having to work so much.

I'd laughed. "It's so rude of you to work on a work trip. I'm fine, Aidan. It's fun. I get to see you in action."

I'd felt so proud watching him at those dinners and cocktail parties. I stood with the other partners, making small talk about the weather, the food, the sights, while the real business was done around us in six different languages, four of which Aidan spoke. The conference had lasted for three days. I expected to fly home on the Thursday with everyone else, but he surprised me. He'd booked us in for three more days and upgraded us to a suite. It was a five-star hotel.

"Aidan, we can't," I'd said. "It's fantastic but we can't afford it." We were saving for a house. It was before we were married, before Felix.

He lowered his voice. "Don't call the police, but I've raided the curtains money."

It was a joke between us. Aidan had discovered my

long-term house savings plan consisted of emptying my purse of any spare change at the end of each day and putting it into a biscuit tin. He said I reminded him of being a kid back home in Ireland, saving for the foreign church missions. But he joined in all the same. Our two sets of change started to fill the tin. I made a label for it—*House Money*—but then got worried it would be too obvious if we were ever burgled. I put a new label on instead: *Curtains.*

"Curtains?" Aidan said when he saw it.

"It was the first thing I thought of."

"Excellent decoy. Burglars will never look in there. Unless they're after very tiny curtains."

From then on, our spare money was called our curtains money. If we were exhausted at the end of a week's work and didn't feel like cooking, we'd raid the tin and go out to a local restaurant.

"Thanks, curtains," Aidan would say as he paid the bill.

It wasn't the curtains that had paid for our surprise holiday, though. Aidan confessed he'd taken on two freelance projects to pay for it. He'd told me he was just doing overtime.

I rejoined the queue in the hotel lobby. Fifteen minutes later, one of the three receptionists smiled over at me. "Good morning, ma'am. I'm sorry to keep you waiting. Are you checking in?"

I stepped forward. "I'd like to see one of your guests, please. Mr. Aidan O'Hanlon."

I heard the click of computer keys. "Your name, please."

"Ella. Ella O'Hanlon. Arabella Fox Baum O'Hanlon." I'd given my full name as if I were at a security checkpoint.

"One moment, please." Another click of the keys. He picked up the phone and dialed Aidan's room. After a minute, he replaced the receiver. "I'm sorry, Ms. O'Hanlon. Mr. O'Hanlon's not in his room. May I leave a message?"

I breathed out. Tension, relief, I wasn't sure which. I'd have to come back. I'd be more prepared next time. As I tried to decide what message to leave, I noticed the receptionist lean forward to look at his screen. "Excuse me, ma'am. One moment, please."

He went into an adjoining office. Behind me I heard a sigh, an impatient guest waiting her turn to check in. The receptionist at the next terminal called her over. I stayed where I was.

The man returned, holding a yellow envelope. "My apologies, Ms. O'Hanlon. I didn't see the note on my computer straightaway. Mr. O'Hanlon left this package for you. Could you sign here, please?"

It was A4-sized, about an inch thick. "What is it?"

"I'm afraid I don't know. If you could sign here to confirm you've received it?"

"Is there any other message? Will he be back later?"

He made a point of smiling at the person in the queue behind me, a smile to say he'd be with them soon. "I'm presuming any message is in the envelope, Ms. O'Hanlon. Could I ask you to please sign here?"

I turned. More than a dozen people were waiting behind me. "Of course. I'm sorry."

I signed my name. I wanted to ask more—what time Aidan had left the envelope, what he'd said when he left it there, how he had looked—but the receptionist was already dealing with the next guest. I took a step to the side, trying to decide what to do.

Another tour group came in. The noise level rose. I moved farther back, to a corner of the now-crowded foyer. It had taken me four days to open Aidan's letter. I couldn't take that long this time. I would go straight back to Lucas's and—

Jess might be there. Jess might have already rung Charlie, got into a taxi and come to visit. She could be sitting at the kitchen table right now, drinking tea with Charlie and Lucas—

I couldn't go back there. Not yet.

There was an empty armchair in the far corner of the lounge area. Just one, pushed into a corner, as if it had been moved out of the way by a cleaner. That would do.

I walked across the foyer, holding the envelope tightly. The contents felt familiar, like a manuscript, one hundred pages or more. What would it be? Legal letters? Divorce papers? A statement of our assets to be divided?

We had no shared assets. We never had bought that house. We'd decided to keep renting. There had been a car but I'd left it in Canberra for him. What else had we owned together? Books? Some furniture? Kitchenware? I didn't even know where any of those things were now.

You just ran away and left him, Ella.

If it was a legal letter, I'd agree to everything. I'd give Aidan everything. Whatever he wanted. Wherever it all was, I'd pay to ship it all across to Washington, if he hadn't already done it. I'd make this as simple as possible for him, so he could make a new life for himself. I would sign whatever he needed me to sign and give it back to the receptionist. We wouldn't even need to see each other again.

The armchair was as private as it was possible to be in a crowded hotel lounge. There was a large potted plant to one side, a small table on the other. Before I had a chance to open the envelope, a waitress appeared. "Can I get you anything, ma'am?"

I wasn't a hotel guest. I couldn't just sit here. "A pot of tea, please."

I decided to wait until she came back before I opened the envelope. I sat with it on my lap, forcing myself to stay calm. To breathe. Observe.

I glanced across at the elevators. The doors of the middle one opened. Aidan walked out.

It couldn't be Aidan.

It was Aidan.

It was Aidan.

He was with two women. Women in suits. They stopped in front of the elevators. One was talking. Aidan listened, spoke. The other talked; Aidan listened, spoke. Back and forth it went. He was working, interpreting. I shrank down into the chair. My heart started beating more rapidly. I waited for him to go to the desk, to ask if his parcel had been collected. He didn't. He didn't look back at the desk, or around the foyer or in my direction. He and his two companions simply walked out through the main doors, out onto the concourse. A uniformed porter lifted his hand. A black taxi appeared. All three of them got in. The taxi pulled away.

"Your tea, ma'am?" The waitress placed the tray down. She poured my tea. I thanked her and asked to pay my bill straightaway. I gave her a tip. More thanks. Then, finally, I was alone.

I wanted to rewind that scene at the elevator. I wanted to see him again. I wanted a freeze-frame of my husband. It had been too quick, but he hadn't looked any different. He had looked like Aidan. Dressed in a dark suit. His hair still so dark. He hadn't been smiling. He'd looked very serious. It was a serious discussion. A work discussion. Perhaps I was wrong, but I didn't think either of those women was his new girlfriend.

I wanted to know why he was here. I wanted to know everything about him, right now. I wished I had Googled conferences in London, Googled his company in Washington, found out who his clients might be, what might have brought him to London. Because I now knew he hadn't come here to see me. It was simply convenient that I was here too, that he could leave this envelope for me. Civilized. The way it would be between us from now on.

I opened the envelope.

It wasn't divorce papers. It had felt like a manuscript, because it was a manuscript. There were nearly one hundred pages, bound with two elastic bands, just like all the manuscripts I used to receive at work. I glanced at a page inside, at random. The lines were double-spaced, numbered at the bottom.

There was no note attached. I checked inside the envelope again to be sure. It was empty. I took off the rubber bands and removed the top page. Underneath was a cover sheet, laid out like hundreds of other manuscripts I'd seen in my working life. The title. Author. Date. Word count. Contact details.

US
Aidan O'Hanlon
February 2012
50,000 words
+ 1 9123997899

I thought at first the title was *US*—United States. Had Aidan written a nonfiction book about his work in America? A novel about life in Washington? Was this why he'd got in touch? To ask me to edit his book? I looked at the title again. I was mistaken. It wasn't *US*. The word was *us*.

I turned to the first page. I began to read.

FORTY-FOUR

D ear Diary!
   Hi, it's Jess!

Someday someone will make a musical of my life and today's happenings will be one of the BEST parts of it! Talk about action-packed! It's like that famous story—when a butterfly flaps its wings in the forest, something else happens hundreds of kilometers away. And me cutting up Dad's credit card was the butterfly flapping its wings and making all these other things happen and people getting all mixed up, but it's okay now, it really is. In fact, it couldn't be better!

I've seen Charlie and I've been to Lucas's HOUSE! At last! I was always a bit jealous of Ella and her London uncle and his amazing house. I'd met Lucas at Ella and Aidan's wedding, of course, but only briefly. This was different. He looked better in

London, somehow, all kind of shaggy-haired and in a big jumper, between us a bit mad-looking but also really clever-looking. And he has the most wonderful voice. He sounds like Kenneth Branagh. Actually, he even sounds a bit like the captain in *The Sound of Music*, that nice deep voice (even though the captain is supposed to be Austrian but is actually played by a Canadian actor called Christopher Plummer).

Anyway, I'd better go back to the start!! What happened was after I got Charlie's e-mail and e-mailed him back, I took all the change Ben had given me (he had heaps of it—he said people always give him handfuls of coins as tips when he delivers their room service) and I went down to the phone box. (Which stank. Seriously, it was disgusting.) I rang Mum and Dad first, because I'd promised in my e-mail that I would. And Mum started crying as soon as she heard my voice and kept saying she'd been so worried and was I okay, and Dad came on too and said the same things. He even sounded like he was crying.

I felt a bit bad. I'd just been trying to find my own feet and be independent (and all right, also teach them a bit of a lesson) and it seems they thought I'd been kidnapped by an ax murderer or something. And Mum kept apologizing (when I suppose it should have been me apologizing really but I was happy to let her go first) and she told me everything about the TV show that I'd got upset about. She said that it wouldn't have been good for me because basically it was going to be R-rated, and the network wanted me to wear low-cut tops and little skirts and flirt with special guests, and Mum and Dad didn't mean to upset me by not telling me about it, but they really thought it wasn't right for me, and then I finally got it—when they'd said it would be called *Mess with Jess*, the network people had meant it in a sexual way, not make a mess as in be untidy around the kitchen. Yuk, I said. No thanks. I wouldn't have liked to do that.

And I meant it. One of my goals in life is to play the role of Maria in a stage version of *The Sound of Music* either in Melbourne or on the West End or basically wherever it happens first, and no one would believe I could be a nun if I'd appeared on a TV show like that, would they?

I told Mum and Dad all about what had happened since we'd talked last, how I'd managed to live on just a few pounds as well as some food from the hotel. (I nearly said "food that Ben had stolen from the hotel" but stopped in time. Dad wouldn't have approved of that kind of behavior.) And I said I'd been offered two places to stay AND a job in a kitchen and that I had spent the previous day cooking liver (still disgusting to think about) and that I had a possible job in a Russian restaurant too!!

"But what about the auditions?" Dad said. And I told the truth, that I didn't think I was ready for more of them just yet, that I needed to go to lots more dance classes and singing lessons first, that the standard was so high. "But how will you be able to practice or go to classes if you are working in a kitchen?" he said. And I said, "Well, I won't be able to, I suppose. I'll just have to work to earn some money and worry about my performing career later."

And Dad really is SO sweet. He said straightaway, "No daughter of mine is going to waste her talents in a restaurant kitchen when she could be onstage," and Mum came on and said, "Darling, you can work in a restaurant anytime. There are hundreds of restaurants in Melbourne but you're in London now. If you're not in the mood for the auditions, why don't you just have a holiday for a couple of weeks, move back into that nice hotel if you want, or pick another one if you'd prefer, and go to see as many musicals and plays as you can, soak them all up. That will be as good for you as a hundred auditions, surely. And then if you want to come home after that, you can. Or you can stay there and then meet up with us in Europe in a few months' time on our filming trip. It's up to you, Jess. You're an adult now. You can decide for yourself."

What fantastic parents!! Seriously. I said I'd think it over even though I didn't need to. I'd LOVE to move back into the hotel again. It would be so hilarious to have Ben bringing me my room-service dinners—I'd give him really big tips from now on, of course! And I'd LOVE to have a couple of weeks of just seeing musicals and forget about auditions for now. And I'd LOVE to go home for a bit and then come back with Mum and Dad on the European filming trip. But I said I'd call them back later with my answer.

"Later? Does that mean tomorrow or later today?" Mum said.

"After I've been to talk to the people in the restaurant," I said. But then I thought about having to go into a kitchen and be shouted at by a bad-tempered Russian chef and I realized I really wasn't in the mood for that either. I'd much rather get started on moving back into the hotel and booking to see some shows, so I said, "Actually, I don't need to think about it. I'd love to do all of those things. Where should I get a new credit card from?"

Dad said he'd work it all out with the hotel and that he'd

talk to Charlie about giving me some money and organizing a new credit card, and that reminded me I needed to call Charlie next, so I said good-bye to Mum and Dad and told them I loved them and then I rang Charlie at Lucas's number. And it was brilliant to talk to him. He told me off a bit at first but that didn't last long and then we got talking and he said, "Just get over here, Jess. We'll talk more in person." Before I had a chance to ask, he said, "Ella isn't here at the moment. I'm not sure when she'll be back." So I went over to the address in Paddington he gave me and Charlie came out and paid the taxi (luckily, as I had only about tenpence left) and I came in and met Lucas again and we sat in the kitchen and talked and talked and it was really great. They asked me so many questions and it felt really good to be with family again who really care.

Lucas showed me around his house too and I also saw all the foxes I remember Ella talking about. But the main thing I saw was the mess. It really was the messiest house I've ever seen. It seriously didn't look like it had been tidied in this century. It's all surface mess, Lucas told me. He said Ella was an excellent housekeeper and that it was actually spotless underneath all the books and papers.

And then we went into his kind of private room downstairs that was also really messy but in a good way, and there was a fire and big armchairs near it, and a whole wall of photos including loads and loads of photos of Felix. It was a big shock to see them at first and I kind of had to hold my breath for a minute, because I was scared I was going to cry, but then Charlie and Lucas came over to the wall of photos too and the three of us looked at them all together and we even started talking about Felix.

And Lucas said to me, straightaway—I didn't know if he would mention it or even if he knew everything that had happened that day but he did—he just brought it up and said, "It must have been especially hard for you, Jess, being there when it happened." And he just said it like that, "being there when it happened," not "it was your fault" like everyone else always hinted at. It just did something to me, and I started to cry and it was different from when I'd had the champagne with Ben and Zach and told them and cried, because I was with my brother, Charlie, and with Lucas, who is really part of the family too, and they just gave me big hugs and told me it would be okay, that I had to stop blaming myself—all the things everyone said to me all the time, but even as I was crying I felt something change inside me. It was exactly as Lucas had said, that I had been there when it happened and it was a tragic accident but they also knew, I could tell, that I would have done anything in the whole world to stop it from happening.

Charlie looked like he was about to cry too, and even Lucas did. But we still kept talking about Felix and we even laughed at one stage, when I reminded them both how OBSESSED Felix used to be with brooms, and I acted out what he used to look like when he was pushing a broom around the kitchen, with this REALLY determined look on his face, and it just felt incredible to be able to laugh when we were talking about Felix. It made me feel kind of warm inside myself, where my heart is. It made me feel good.

Lucas said he would make us all some tea and we went back into the kitchen and I could see that Charlie was looking at the clock and I said, "Is Ella coming back soon?" They said they didn't know, that she was out meeting someone and they didn't know how long she would be. And I said "Who?" and they looked at each other and then Charlie said, "Aidan. Aidan's in London." And I said straightaway, "Can I go and see him too?"

And Charlie said, "I don't think so, Jess. I think we need to leave them alone for now." And I thought about it and I realized he was right. I don't know for sure, as Mum stopped talking to me about it, but I don't think Ella and Aidan have spoken to each other since she left him. It made me glad to think they were talking again. I hope they will get back together again. They were two of the happiest people together I've ever seen. They just got on really well, they talked all the time, and if I was staying with them in Canberra, I'd hear them laughing in their room—not at me, either. I listened in once to make sure. Aidan had been telling Ella a story about work and he just really made her laugh. Ella's always had a great laugh. It actually sounds like she is saying, "Hahahaha-hahaha." Felix inherited it. He had a really great laugh too.

So what we did next was Charlie took me to Ben's in a taxi and we got my bags and then we went to Covent Garden and booked me into the hotel again. Dad had already e-mailed them with his credit card details so my booking was all in place and I don't know how it happened (maybe Dad being extra sweet) but they upgraded me to a suite!!! That's where I'm writing this at the moment. I not only have a four-poster bed again and an amazing bathroom, but also a little sitting area and even the tiniest balcony. I'm on the fourth floor and I look down on a great, lively street in Covent Garden. It's (seriously) like being in a film this time. Charlie and Lucas said they would leave me to settle in because they wanted to be back at the house when Ella returned. "Have you heard from her yet?" I asked, and Charlie said, "No, not yet." Then Charlie gave me some money (five hundred pounds!!) and said to go and get myself a new phone PRONTO so that Mum and Dad could contact me whenever they needed to. So I did, and then I went to the box office place in Leicester Square where you get last-minute tickets and I went a bit crazy, if I do say so myself. I've booked a seat for *The Lion King* for next Saturday, *Matilda* next Tuesday and for *Les Misérables* the night after! I'm going to see as many musicals as I can over the next two weeks, which is how long Dad's booked me into the hotel for now. I've decided to call this a research trip rather than an audition trip. Which means I'll still have plenty to tell the others about if and when I decide to go back to college in Melbourne.

If I didn't think one of those nocturnal actors was in the room beside me, I would start singing now, I am so happy. Either "I Whistle a Happy Tune" from *The King and I* or "Happy Talk" from *South Pacific*. I don't know which one, maybe both!! See what I mean, Diary—wouldn't today make a great scene in a musical????

I'm going to send Mum and Dad an e-mail now, just to say another big thanks for coming to my rescue and being basically the world's best and kindest and most understanding and generous parents. And then I'm going to change into the white robe and order room service and hopefully it will be Ben who delivers it!!

Love for now,

Jess xxxxoooo

FORTY-FIVE

A idan had written the story of our lives.

He started at the beginning, at our first meeting, when he came into the kitchen while I was cooking and made up a story about his mother being Italian. He wrote about our first date, the drink in the summery beer garden. Our first kiss. Our next date. The next. And the one after that. The first time we slept together.

He wrote about our visit to Australia. His proposal. My visit to Ireland. Our months in London, nights sitting up with Lucas, talking, laughing. Our move back to Australia. Our early days in Canberra together. Our wedding day.

He wrote about the night I told him I was pregnant. How he felt when I came into the bedroom holding the pregnancy test and told him there was a blue line. How I had done another test. A third test. How all he had been able to say was, "Bloody hell. Bloody *hell*!"

He wrote about my pregnancy. How he had always thought I was the most beautiful woman in the world and now he knew it for sure.

He wrote about the day Felix was born. The drive to the hospital. Sitting by my bed as my contractions got worse, more painful. How helpless he felt watching me writhe with the pain. How useless he felt, feeding me ice chips and rubbing my back. How he wished he could take on half the pain, all the pain. How desolate he felt watching them wheel me into the delivery room, wanting to come too and feeling so angry with the nurse when she said he had to wait. How he wanted to order everyone else out when they finally let him join me. How he stood behind the bed, holding my hands, how my cries cut into him, how he wanted to scream, "Someone, do something, help her, please, now!" How the labor seemed to last for days, for weeks, how those five hours seemed like the worst time in his life because he wasn't able to help me. He had to just stand by and watch, but then everything started happening. Suddenly everyone was moving and people were coming in and out of the room and I was really screaming and then there was a cry, a different kind of cry, and a nurse or was it the midwife, someone said, "It's a boy!" And then there was Felix, with that extraordinary thatch of black hair. And the two of us had laughed. We laughed and laughed as if his being born was the funniest thing that had ever happened to us.

I had forgotten that laughter.

He wrote about the two of us becoming the three of us. How it felt to bring that tiny baby home from the hospital.

How we lay in our bed that first night, after Mum and Walter and Jess went back to their hotel. I lay on my side, he lay on his side, and Felix lay in the middle. We were both so tired and so happy and in a kind of shock. Aidan wrote about that shock, how even though of course we knew I was having a baby, that of course there was going to be a baby at the end of my nine-month pregnancy, still, look, here he was.

He wrote about our conversation that night.

"Hold on to your hat," I'd said. "Here we go."

I'd forgotten I said that.

He wrote about Felix's first week, first smile, first months, first tooth, first steps.

He wrote about Felix's family—his granny, Walter, Jess, Charlie and his family in Boston, his family in Ireland.

He wrote about us too.

About him and me. About our lives together. Our conversations. Our work—his job, my job. Felix was now the center of our lives but we still had our own lives. It was all there on the page, descriptions of the editorial projects I worked on when I first came out of the maternity-leave haze. Anecdotes that I'd told him about authors I was working with. He remembered everything.

He wrote about our first wedding anniversary. Mum and Walter came to Canberra and babysat Felix for the night. We had dinner in an upmarket, overpriced Italian restaurant where the portions were too small and the waiters snooty. They hovered around our table too much and whispered in Italian to one another. They didn't realize we could hear them and that Aidan spoke Italian. He translated for me, also in a whisper. They were insulting all their customers, including us. I was too skinny, one of them thought. I'd be much more attractive if I had more meat on my bones. They thought Aidan was Scottish. One of them had been to Glasgow once and hated it. It was the hole of Europe, he said. They weren't impressed with what we ordered either. Unadventurous. As boring as Canberra itself, they agreed. If Glasgow was the hole of Europe, Canberra was the hole of Australia. As we left, after we'd put on our coats and paid and were standing by the door, Aidan turned to the waiters and thanked them in flawless Italian for a memorable evening, adding that he would be sure to let his Italian friends in Canberra know all about this place.

I remembered their shocked expressions.

We walked down the street, laughing so much we actually had to stop walking. Then Aidan confessed that he was still hungry. I admitted I was too. So we went to McDonald's and had a burger each. And then we went home, even though Mum had told us she didn't expect us until midnight. It was nine thirty when we arrived. Felix was up. He had gone to sleep, Mum said, but he'd started to cry, so she'd got him up for a cuddle. She looked so guilty, we knew she hadn't even tried to settle him. If she had her way, Felix would have been awake twenty-four hours a day.

Aidan wrote about Lucas's surprise visit coinciding with Charlie's visit. He wrote about that afternoon when we'd all been together, the sunny afternoon when we'd laughed and I'd felt so happy and I had taken a photograph of them all together.

He had remembered every moment that I remembered.

He wrote about Felix's first birthday party. I made an orange cake in the shape of a sleeping fox. *F* was for Felix and Fox. It looked like a large baked bean. I was as good at icing as I was at knitting.

He wrote about the first time Felix shouted, "I'm Felix O'Hanlon!" in his toddler-babble. About Felix's love of brooms and vacuum cleaners, how he would happily spend an hour pushing a broom around and get very cross if we tried to take it away from him.

He wrote about Felix's laugh. His laugh that everyone said was just like mine.

He wrote about how tired we often were. How we were still in a bit of shock that the two of us were parents. That someone had put *us* in charge of a baby. But he also wrote about how much fun it was. What a surprise it had been to us both, amid the sleeplessness and the exhaustion and the mess, just how entertaining a baby was. We could spend hours looking at Felix, watching his expression change. Watching him yawn. Stretch. Crawl. Pull himself up to a standing position. Take his first tentative steps.

Aidan remembered things about Felix I had forgotten.

He wrote about the week Felix decided to eat only green things. Broccoli, green beans, green grapes. Before that he'd eaten most fruit and vegetables—pumpkin, sweet potato, ordinary potatoes, carrots. But for some reason, for that one week, it was green foods only. He actually screamed when we tried to get him to eat some banana. Until, one morning, exactly seven days later, he happily ate some stewed apple, and then for lunch, a full bowl of mashed carrots and pumpkin. His doctor said he'd never heard of a baby doing that. Aidan and I were very amused. It was his Irish heritage coming through, Aidan decided. The eating of the green.

I had forgotten that.

Aidan wrote about the day Lucas's first box of books arrived. He wrote about Felix's favorite toys, favorite clothes, favorite nursery rhyme, favorite TV show.

He wrote about me.

He wrote that his favorite thing was to make me laugh. How much he loved the way I laughed. The way my eyes lit up first and then I would smile and then I would laugh. He wrote about how much he loved to watch me editing. The way I would bite my lip while I was concentrating. The way I would tap a pencil against my chin. I didn't know I did that.

He wrote about how much he loved being with me. Talking to me. How clever I was. How kind I was. How patient and loving I was with Felix. How beautiful he thought I was. How much he loved me in a particular red dress I had found in an op shop in Canberra. How much he loved the perfume I wore. The way I could twist my hair up into all sorts of styles, but how most of all he loved it when it was down.

He wrote about our families. About how much he enjoyed hearing me and Charlie talking on the phone, how much he enjoyed watching me Skype Charlie's kids in Boston. The presents I would send them, not just for birthdays or Christmas, but parcels at all times of the year, filled with clothes and books and toys, that the kids wouldn't open until they were Skyping me, so I could watch them unwrap everything.

I'd forgotten they used to do that.

He wrote about our plan for a big family. About the night we decided to try for another baby. How hopeful we were it would happen again quickly. How great Felix would be as a big brother. How we'd just have to convince him to put the broom down for long enough to play with his little brother or sister.

He wrote about the day Felix died.

It was all there, all the detail I had made him tell me again and again. He wrote about trying to call me as soon as Jess had called him. He wrote about my arriving at the hospital in the taxi. He wrote about the meetings with the priest, the funeral director. About the funeral being delayed while a coroner's report was carried out, how it had to happen after an accidental death. He wrote about going to collect Charlie from the airport. The funeral. The cemetery. About how it felt to watch that tiny white coffin go into the ground. How everyone had left us alone, left the two of us there on our own with our Felix, at his grave, for nearly an hour afterward, while we stood there, holding each other and crying.

I had blocked that out of my memory.

He wrote about the days afterward, after Mum and Walter and Jess went back to Melbourne. When it was just us. When all we seemed to be able to do was cry. When all I could ask him was for the details of that day, again and again. He wrote about me shouting at him when I found him trying to put Felix's toys into a box.

He wrote about the day I left him, five weeks after the funeral. He wrote about coming home from work and knowing the moment he turned the key in the door that I had gone, even before he saw the note lying next to the keys on the kitchen bench.

He wrote about the following weeks and months. About Mum coming to Canberra to help him pack up not just

Felix's room but all the rooms. He wrote about going to Sydney. About going to the restaurant to try to talk to me.

He wrote about his own move to Sydney. His job there. He'd hated it. He wrote about visiting Mum and Walter in Melbourne. About seeing Jess. How bad she was. He wrote about Mum telling him she'd discovered Jess was hurting herself. That it had started after she'd had Felix's name tattooed on her leg, at the exact spot his head reached when she measured him against her.

I remembered her measuring him. She did it every time she saw him.

I hadn't known about the tattoo.

He wrote about sending me letters, e-mailing me, leaving phone messages. Hearing nothing back.

He wrote about the first anniversary of Felix's death. He spent it with Mum and Walter and Jess.

I hadn't known that.

I'd been in Western Australia by then. I didn't talk to anyone in my family that day, not even Charlie. I'd thought it would make it worse.

He wrote about his friend from college days contacting him, offering him a job in Washington.

He wrote about Washington. About his new apartment. About his work.

He wrote about me.

How much he missed me. How he talked to me, every night. How he talked to me about Felix. How each night he wished I was in bed beside him.

He wrote about how guilty he felt, every day, every night. How all he wanted to do was change everything that had happened. How he knew he couldn't. How he knew he could never fix it. How that made him sad, every moment of every day.

He wrote about Charlie getting in touch with him. Lucas ringing to let him know I was in London. About Charlie and Lucas wanting to convince him to come over and see me.

He wrote that he had canceled the meeting with Charlie. That this was between him and me, not Charlie and Lucas and everyone else. It was our marriage.

He wrote that he had asked his boss, his friend, to send him to this London conference, even though one of his colleagues had already been given the job. That after his boss said yes, he used the conference date as his writing deadline, so he could leave this manuscript in London for me.

He wrote about our wedding day again. How, on the morning of our wedding, he had gone for a walk on his own. We hadn't slept apart the night before our wedding. We'd wanted to be together. Our apartment had been full of people that morning: Mum, Jess, friends of mine from Canberra and Melbourne, the hairdresser, even the florist and the caterer at one stage. It was a gorgeous blue Canberra day. He went for a walk around the lake. He thought about meeting me, falling in love with me, asking me to marry him. About how sure he was that he wanted to be with me for the rest of his life, to make a family with me, our own family. He described coming back and everyone saying, "He's back! Call off the search party!" He wrote that I'd looked up from where the hairdresser was finishing styling my hair into a retro-style bun. I'd caught his eye in the mirror. I'd mouthed the words, "Are you okay?"

He said yes. He smiled and said yes. Twice.

I remembered that.

There was just one more page of his manuscript to read.

It wasn't about Felix. It wasn't about London, or Washington, about his work or my work, his family or my family. It was a story from our wedding day. Something that happened at the end of our wedding day.

I remembered every minute of it.

It was after midnight. We'd finally farewelled everyone and gone back home, to our own bedroom. We'd fallen onto the bed, holding hands, me still in my cream silk dress, him in his dark suit. We'd been so exhausted and so happy. It had been a day of talking, laughing and dancing. It had been perfect.

As we lay there, Aidan started to recite one of the readings we'd chosen for the ceremony. Charlie had read them so well that afternoon. I sat up, amazed. I stopped him.

"Did you learn that off by heart?"

"Of course."

"So you could prompt Charlie if he lost his place?"

He smiled and shook his head. "Because I loved it."

We'd each chosen a reading. Aidan's was a poem by W. B. Yeats, "Aedh Wishes for the Cloths of Heaven," with its beautiful final line, *Tread softly because you tread on my dreams.* I surprised myself with my choice. I'd heard it so many times before at friends' weddings. One year, I'd heard it five times. I'd said to myself that if I ever got married, I wouldn't have it. It was too commonplace. It was from the Bible and I wasn't that religious. But as the day grew nearer, I kept returning to it. It seemed to say everything I hoped for the two of us.

I showed the reading to Charlie when he flew in the night before the wedding.

As he read it, I waited for him to say something about my choice being corny, overused. He looked up and smiled. "Great choice. Lucy and I had it at our wedding too."

I'd forgotten. Their wedding had been twelve years earlier. That sealed it for me.

Charlie read it beautifully the next day. I was watching him, but as he came to the last line, I turned to look at Aidan. He was looking at me.

That night, in our bedroom, he recited it to me from memory.

It was on the page in front of me now. It wasn't typed, like the rest of it had been. He had written it out by hand.

> *Love is always patient and kind; it is never jealous, love is never boastful or conceited; it is never rude or selfish; it does not take offense, and is not resentful. Love takes no pleasure in other people's sins but delights in the truth; it is always ready to excuse, to trust, to hope and to endure whatever comes. Love does not come to an end.*

FORTY-SIX

I didn't cry. Not then. Not yet.

I put the manuscript back together neatly, securing the pages with the rubber bands again. I put it back in the envelope and the envelope into my bag. I left the hotel and I walked until I reached Hyde Park. I started running then. I ran until I was deep in the park, on my own, surrounded by nothing but trees. There was a bench, on its own.

I sat down. I held my bag against my body and I cried like I hadn't cried since the day Felix died. I saw someone in the distance, saw walkers heading in my direction, but I couldn't stop. I cried until I had no tears left.

Afterward, I was spent. I could have lain down and slept, there on the grass. I made myself sit still, as alone as it was possible to be in the middle of London. I made myself breathe properly. I made myself notice everything around me, the shafts of light through the trees, the sky with its shimmer of blue, the faint green haze of buds on the branches.

I made myself acknowledge what I had known in my heart for months.

I still loved Aidan.

I had never stopped loving him.

Felix was dead. Our beautiful Felix had gone. But Aidan and I were still here.

He'd written me a love letter. A one-hundred-page love letter. Not about the future. He'd shown me the past. The story of us. All that we had shared. The promises we'd made to each other. Not just on our wedding day but in different ways, every day we'd been together. To enjoy each other. To look out for each other. Make each other laugh. Understand each other. Make love to each other. Keep loving each other. Whatever happened.

Endure whatever comes. Love does not come to an end.

I sat there, thinking. I don't know how much time passed. Perhaps an hour.

I came out of the park, onto Bayswater Road. If I turned left, I would be on my way to Lucas's house. If I turned right, back to the hotel.

I turned right. I didn't check my appearance. I walked into the foyer, straight across to the desk. There was no queue now.

I asked the young receptionist if I could speak to a guest, Mr. Aidan O'Hanlon.

There was a click of computer keys. "I'm sorry, ma'am," she said. "He's checked out."

"Are you sure?"

Another click. "Yes, ma'am."

"But I saw him here today. This morning."

She looked at her screen again, clicked some more keys. "He checked out at eleven forty-five a.m. It was a group booking. They all checked out at the same time."

Something must have happened. Something to make them leave early. My hands were trembling as I reached into my bag. I took out his letter. His dates were there in black and white. I showed the receptionist. "He was supposed to be here for three nights."

"He was, ma'am."

She showed me a newspaper with today's date.

I hadn't only lost track of the time; I'd lost track of the date. I'd been like this for months. I didn't work in an office. I didn't read the newspapers anymore. I never needed to know what date it was.

I apologized to the young woman, thanked her and went outside. I thought about going straight across to Paddington Station, getting immediately on the train to Heathrow. I began walking in that direction and then stopped. How could I find him there? His flight might have departed already, or he could have left from another airport.

I didn't know what to do. I simply didn't know.

Then I remembered. I had his American cell phone number. It was on the front of the manuscript. I took it out. I dialed the number. I'd wanted to see him face-to-face, to say what needed to be said in person, but it was my own fault. I'd left it too late to come to his hotel. He would have been told that I had collected the envelope. But then he'd heard nothing from me. He would think I either hadn't read it or didn't care.

His phone rang once, twice, a third time. It went to voice mail. I hung up. I couldn't say what I wanted to say in a voice mail message. I did the only thing I could think of next. I went back to Lucas's.

I didn't know if Jess would be there, or if she had been and gone or if Charlie and Lucas would be with her in town. I couldn't think about that. Not now. Not yet.

As I let myself in, Charlie was coming down the stairs.

"Ella, we've been worried. Did you see him?" He stopped and looked at me. "Are you okay?"

"He's gone, Charlie. I missed him."

"He's gone?"

"He checked out today." I told him what had happened. "I was too late."

"He might still be in London. Maybe he's not flying out until later."

"I tried his phone. I just got his voice mail. Would you try him, Charlie? Please?"

Charlie took out his phone, scrolled through his contacts and pressed call. After a second he whispered to me. "Voice mail again. Do you want me to leave a message?"

"No. Yes. Yes."

"Aidan, hi, it's Charlie. Can you call me when you get this?" He hung up.

"He must be on a plane," I said. "He must be on his way back to Washington."

"Maybe he's gone to Ireland to see his family. Maybe he's in London for a few more days, staying somewhere else, and he's in a meeting at the moment, not taking calls. Do you want me to find out?"

"How?"

"I'll call his office in Washington. I've rung him there before. The receptionist is German. She might help me."

It took him only a minute at his laptop to get the Washington number. He dialed. He gave me the thumbs-up as it was answered. *"Carla, wie geht's? Ja, hier ist Charlie. Gut, danke. Und dir? Sehr gut!"* He switched to English. "Aidan and I were supposed to meet up in London today and I got held up. Is he still here or have I missed him? Thanks, yes, happy to hold." Four minutes later he had the answer. "He's left London. He was booked on the two thirty flight from Heathrow. He's got another conference tomorrow morning in Washington."

I must have been sitting in the foyer reading for hours. I must have been there reading when Aidan returned to the hotel and checked out. I hadn't seen him. Had he seen me?

Lucas appeared. Charlie told him what had happened.

"You didn't speak to him at all?" Lucas asked.

I shook my head.

"Do you want to?"

"Yes."

"Go and get your passport, Ella," he said. "Bring it down to Charlie and then start packing. Pack lots of warm clothes. It's freezing there this time of year."

"What do you mean?"

"Aidan's gone to Washington, Ella, not Mars. You're going to Washington too."

An hour later, it was organized. Charlie had done it all

online, from his laptop on Lucas's kitchen table. Flight, train ticket, hotels, even a US travel authorization. That had given us the most concern.

"Keep your fingers crossed," he said, as he filled out the details. "Sometimes you get it automatically; sometimes you have to wait a day or two." We sat, staring at the screen. The message appeared. I'd been approved.

My journey had taken him some juggling. He couldn't get me a direct flight to Washington. They were all full. He got me a seat on the last flight to New York instead. He booked me into an airport hotel at JFK, and reserved a train ticket from Penn Station in Manhattan to Washington DC, leaving at nine in the morning. I'd be in Washington by lunchtime.

I'd needed a return ticket to get my travel authorization. Charlie picked a date at random, a week away.

Lucas insisted on booking a taxi to take me to Heathrow. They both insisted on coming with me. We had just reached Marble Arch when I remembered.

"Charlie, did you see Jess?"

He nodded. "She came over to the house."

"How is she?"

"She'll be okay."

"Did you see her flat?"

"She's moved out. She's back in her very nice Covent Garden hotel."

My flight left in three hours. I had time. I told them what I wanted to do.

Lucas was concerned. "Ella, are you sure? Today?"

"Why don't you wait until you get back?" Charlie said.

It felt important to see her now. Before I left. Before I saw Aidan.

It took us twenty minutes to get to Covent Garden. The taxi driver double-parked in front of the hotel. I went in on my own. Charlie knew her room number. I walked in past reception as if I were a guest. I took the stairs up to the fourth floor. The hotel was luxurious, with original paintings on the walls, thick carpet on the floor. I walked down a long corridor, counting down the numbers, until I was there, in front of her door.

I knocked.

I heard her voice. "Who is it?"

"It's Ella," I said.

FORTY-SEVEN

Dear Diary,

Hi, it's Jess!

Something wonderful happened. Ella came to see me.

I was lying on the bed, and I'm not making this up, I was lying there thinking about Felix. And I felt so sad, the way I always do whenever I think about him, but then I also thought about this morning, when Charlie and Lucas and I had stood looking at the wall of photos and talking about him and remembering him. And I remembered that feeling I'd had, that warm, good feeling; even though our Felix wasn't with us anymore, we could still think about him and remember how much we'd all loved him.

I got up then and went into the bathroom. I was wearing the hotel's cotton robe and I stood in front of the mirror and moved the robe out of the way so I could see the tattoo of his name on the top of my leg and I held my hand beside it, remembering how tall he'd been. And then I got so sad because it made me wonder how tall he would have got. We'd all been waiting for him to turn two so we could measure him. Mum had heard that if you measure a little kid when they are two, they're exactly half the height they'll be when they are a fully grown adult. It's been proven thousands of times apparently. Dr. Rob told her about it. But we didn't get to find out.

I went and sat back on the bed and I was sitting there, not reading or watching TV or anything, just sitting there thinking about Felix, and there was a knock at the door and I hadn't ordered anything, so I said, "Who is it?" and then a voice said, "It's Ella." I kind of panicked. I felt my heart start to race and I ran to the door and I looked through the security peephole and it was Ella. Ella with short hair. I'd never seen her with short hair. It really suited her. But I thought, she's going to scream at me, I can't bear it, I can't let her in, but I looked again, only for a second, and she didn't look angry, she just looked really sad. She looked like she had been crying, like she was really tired.

I opened the door and there was a few seconds when we just stood there looking at each other. We hadn't seen each other in a very long time. Felix's funeral didn't count. I took a step back because she still hadn't said anything, she was just staring at me, and then she did come in and she shut the door but she still hadn't said anything.

So I said it. I said everything I had wanted to say to her since the day it happened. I didn't cry. I wanted to, but I didn't. I told her again how sorry I was, how I had loved Felix so much and that if I could do anything to fix it, to bring him back, to change what had happened that day, I would do it. And she spoke then. She said, "I know, Jess. We all would."

And then she stepped closer to me, and she hugged me. She pulled me in close. She's much taller than me, and she put her arms around me and she hugged me. And I don't know if she'd ever hugged me before, I couldn't remember, but she was hugging me now and it felt so good that I did start to cry then. She did too. We were both crying. I kept saying, "I'm so sorry," and she kept saying, "I know."

That's all that happened. She didn't stay any longer. She said she had to go, that Charlie and Lucas were waiting in a taxi downstairs, that she was going to Heathrow.

I said, "Are you going back to Australia?" and she said no, she was going to Washington to see Aidan. And I said, "You didn't see him today at the hotel?" and then I saw the look she gave me and so I quickly told her that Charlie had told me just the basics. She shook her head and said no, there'd been a mix-up, so she was going to go and see him in Washington instead. And I said, "Safe travels," and she said, "Thank you," and we didn't hug again and she didn't say, "I'll see you when I get back." I don't even know if she is coming back but it doesn't matter. I saw her today. I said sorry and she hugged me.

I'm going to ring and tell Mum as soon as I can, as soon as the time is right. I'm going to think about it myself first. I want to think about Felix and Ella and I want to think about Ella meeting Aidan. They used to really love each other. I hope everything will be okay between them again.

I'll write more later. After I've talked to Mum.

Love for now,

Jess xxxxoooo

P.S. I talked to Mum. I told her what had happened with Ella and she started crying, and that made me cry too, but the weird thing was we actually both felt happier afterward. Mum told me to hop into bed, and to order something delicious from room service and to watch the cheeriest film I could find on the in-house movies. And she told me how much she and Dad loved me and missed me and I told her how much I loved and missed her and Dad too. I'm really glad I'm going home soon.

FORTY-EIGHT

ess was only a kid.

She'd looked about fifteen years old. So young. So little. I don't know what I had expected. She'd become something mythical in my mind, I realized. Monstrous. She wasn't any of those things. She was just a kid. An unhappy kid.

I don't think I'd ever hugged her before. Maybe when she was really little. If I had, I couldn't remember it. But I hadn't thought twice about it, there in her hotel room. As soon as I saw her, I wanted to forgive her. I did forgive her. As I'd walked up the four flights of stairs, I hadn't been sure what I would say, what I wanted to happen, what would happen.

But then I saw her. And we didn't speak at first. We just stared at each other and in those five or ten seconds, I remembered her with Felix. All the times she played with him. All the dancing and clowning she'd done with him. How much she had loved him too. And as I looked at her, I understood something for sure. It had been an accident. A terrible, tragic accident.

She started talking before I had a chance to say anything. She told me over and over how sorry she was, how much she had loved him, how much she wanted to change everything that had happened. And I told the truth. I told her that I knew. I did know.

I didn't stay long. I don't know what else we could have said to each other. Not then. Not there. We'll have to talk again. I know that too. I will need to hear from her all the details that I'd needed to hear from Aidan. I'll need to be able to picture that afternoon through her eyes. I'll need to hear her say sorry again. I know that.

I didn't say much to Charlie and Lucas about it. There wasn't much to say. I told them exactly what had happened, what I'd said, what Jess had said.

The car was silent at first and then Charlie said thanks. Simply that. "Thanks, Ella."

I looked at Lucas. "Good girl," he said again.

I said good-bye to them in front of the airport. I told them I'd ring as soon as I could. I didn't know when that would be. I didn't know if I would be ringing with good news or bad news.

Charlie hugged me good-bye and told me he'd call as soon as he got back to Boston. "I love you, Ella."

I hugged him close and told him I loved him too.

"Say hello to Aidan from me."

I said I would.

"And from me," Lucas said, when he hugged me good-bye.

I thanked him. For more than he knew.

He just hugged me again and wished me a safe trip.

I was in the departure lounge an hour later, about to start boarding, when I remembered. Something I'd read in Aidan's manuscript. Something I hadn't known about. Jess's tattoo.

It was suddenly urgent that I ask her something. I got the number of her hotel and rang, just as my flight started boarding. I was put straight through to her room.

"Jessica Baum speaking."

"Jess, it's Ella."

"Ella! Are you okay? Have you missed your flight?"

"I'm about to board. Jess, your tattoo—"

"Did Mum tell you about it? Ella, I'm sorry if you're angry about it. I just wanted—"

"I'm not angry." I wasn't. One day perhaps I'd even ask to see it. "What does it say, Jess?"

"It's his name. Just his name. On the spot where I used to measure him, when I used to get him to stand beside me to see how much he'd grown. Do you remember?"

I remembered. "Jess, which of his names? Your name for him or ours?"

"Yours. Felix. It says Felix. I thought it had to be his full name. Was that okay, Ella? You don't mind? Would you rather I got it changed to Elix? I will if you want me to. It's just I was the only one who ever called him Elix, so I didn't think it was right—"

"You don't need to change it, Jess."

There was a last-call boarding announcement behind

me. She wished me a safe trip and told me to take care. I told her to take care in return.

The flight was seven hours long. I didn't read or watch a movie, have a drink or a meal. All I needed were my own thoughts. I landed at ten and went straight to the airport hotel. I was asleep by midnight, awake again by six, on a shuttle bus into Manhattan and at Penn Station thirty minutes before my nine a.m. train to Washington was due to leave.

I'd been to New York only once before, on a weekend trip while I was first living in London. I'd loved it. This time, I was in a hurry to leave. I forced myself to notice details: yellow cabs and NYPD cars, newsstands selling the *New York Times* and *USA Today*. The skyscrapers. The crowds of people everywhere. I heard the honking of horns, the sirens. In Penn Station itself, there were commuters, homeless people, a hubbub of different accents and languages. I was in New York but I was thinking about Washington.

I was thinking about Aidan.

I'd never been to Washington. I couldn't imagine him there. I couldn't picture the two of us meeting somewhere in the city, sitting down in a bar or restaurant. Where would we meet? My hotel? His apartment? Somewhere neutral? I'd seen films and TV programs set there, seen dozens of photographs of it in newspapers and magazines, seen it on TV news bulletins. I knew its landmarks, the White House, the Capitol, Arlington Cemetery. I'd heard it described as the most European of American cities, with long boulevards and majestic buildings. The Paris of America. But I couldn't imagine being there myself.

During the flight, I'd made a decision. I was going to

ring Aidan before my train left. I wanted our first conversation to be in person, not over the phone, but I'd missed that
opportunity in London. I'd tracked his movements. He'd
have arrived home from London yesterday afternoon, Washington time. He probably started work at nine or ten in the
morning. Even if he had slept late after his flight, he would
be awake by now.

I stood on the platform, beside my carriage. I dialed his
cell phone number. My hand was shaking.

He answered after three rings.

"Aidan O'Hanlon."

"Aidan, it's Ella."

There was a long pause. "Where are you?"

"In New York. I'm about to get the train to Washington."

He didn't say anything. I thought for a moment I'd lost
the connection.

"Aidan?"

"I'm here, Ella."

I wanted to tell him that I'd got his manuscript. That I
had read every word. That I had got back to the hotel too
late to see him. But I couldn't say any of it when I couldn't
see his face.

"Aidan, would you meet me? Anywhere that suits you.
Whatever time that suits you."

"I'll come to you. Where are you staying?"

I didn't know the name of the hotel. The booking form
was at the bottom of my bag. I thought of the only place in
Washington I knew I could easily find. I couldn't risk missing him again.

"Could we meet in front of the White House?"

THE HOUSE OF MEMORIES | 455

He gave a soft laugh. "Fine. In front of the White House. At four?"

I'd forgotten how beautiful his voice was. "Four is great."

"Great. See you then."

"See you then."

My heart was beating faster as I made my way to my seat. My palms felt clammy. It had been either the hardest phone call of my life or the easiest; I didn't know which. I didn't know if he'd talked to Charlie or not. But it was done. We'd spoken. The arrangements were in place. As if it were a business meeting. Or as if we were two people who had once known each other very well.

I spent the journey looking out the window. Spring was slower in coming here. The trees were still bare. As we made our way toward Washington, there were even signs of snow on roadsides, in fields here and there.

His manuscript was in my bag. I could have read it again. I didn't need to. I'd already known every scene, every conversation, every moment he described. His story was my story.

I arrived at Union Station in Washington at one p.m. It was like entering a classical museum. I stopped in the main concourse, looked up, turned around. The building was three stories high, with sweeping arches and a soaring roof. There were marble busts and statues around the walls, decorated with gold leaf. I felt like I'd been transported back in time. I expected to hear classical music playing, to see women in long gowns, men in dress suits.

Outside the station it was very cold. The sky was a bright shining blue but there was a wind so icy my coat barely felt warm enough. I took a taxi to my hotel on Ninth Street. I checked in and went up to my room. I couldn't sit quietly. I couldn't settle, couldn't keep still. I would go out for a walk instead. Just around the block. I'd stay close to the hotel. Any sightseeing could wait. I just needed to keep moving.

I walked until it was three thirty p.m., until it was time to go to our meeting point. I'd checked my map three times. I made my way along the city streets until there it was. The White House.

It was different from how I'd imagined. Smaller. It surprised me that tourists were allowed to get so close. There was security—cameras, guards with guns—but I was able to walk right up to the fence and look through the rails at the building itself. I'd seen news footage of state cars pulling up in front, the president and his entourage walking in. It was less grand in real life.

I was early. It was only a quarter to four. I made myself take deep, calming breaths. I watched tourists come and go, heard other people also remark that it looked smaller than they expected. There were all nationalities, but the majority were Americans. A woman and her husband came close to me to take their photos, first her in front of the railing, and then him. I asked if they wanted me to take a photograph of them together. They accepted. I was glad. Another few minutes filled.

"It looks different on TV, doesn't it?" the woman said as they took up their pose.

"That's because they don't usually show it from this angle," the man said. "They show the front of it on TV."

I froze. "This isn't the front?"

"No, ma'am. The front's, well, at the front. This is the back."

I thrust their camera back at them, apologizing. I checked the time. It was three minutes to four.

I ran. I ran faster than I'd run in years. I was wearing boots with heels. It didn't matter. Aidan had waited long enough. I couldn't make him wait any longer.

I ran down Fifteenth Street. I ran past the souvenir vans selling T-shirts, the food vans selling drinks and hot dogs, the tour buses lined up in a long row. I ran past the boundary fence, turned right onto another path, saw another long fence, a big fence this time. I saw the view of the White House I recognized. The curving front window, the pillars, the big fountain, the sweeping driveway.

Hundreds of people were standing in front of the fence, posing for photographs. Tour groups, family groups, pairs of travelers, single visitors. I couldn't see Aidan. Had I got it wrong again? Had we said the back of the White House?

I couldn't make another mistake. I was breathless but I had to phone him. He answered after one ring.

"Aidan, it's me. I got it wrong. I'm so sorry. I went to the back of the White House first, not the front, and now I can't find you."

"Turn around, Ella," he said.

I turned.

He was standing five meters away from me. He was in a long dark coat, wearing a dark blue scarf.

I had given him that scarf.

He wasn't smiling.

I dropped my phone. I dropped it and I ran to him. I ran right into his open arms.

FORTY-NINE

Of all the photographs of the White House taken by tourists between four and four thirty that afternoon, a quarter captured a couple standing on the edge of the crowd. They had their arms around each other. They were holding each other tightly.

Video footage would have shown the couple talking. Talking over each other. Stopping. Starting. Interrupting. As though they both had so much to say, so much to hear.

If there had been sound, the first words heard would have been from the woman, tall with short dark hair, saying, "I'm sorry, Aidan. I'm so sorry." And the man, dark-haired, in a dark coat, saying, "It's okay, Ella, it's okay. It's okay."

If a film crew followed them for the rest of the day, it would have recorded them walking, arm in arm, through the city. Not to any of the landmark sights. They went home. Back to his home.

Inside, they took off their coats. He offered to make tea, and she said no, thank you, she was fine, and then she said, "I'm not fine, Aidan." And he said, "Nor am I, Ella."

And he cried then, in his wife's arms, for a long time. And she soothed him, again and again.

They held each other, arms tight around one another. They kissed, slow kisses, coming-home kisses. There was the slow removal of their clothing. They moved into his bedroom. They made love slowly, tentatively, as if they were getting to know each other's bodies again. They were.

She didn't sleep in her hotel room that night. She canceled the rest of her booking. He called his office, spoke to his friend and was given a week off. As much time as he needed.

They spent most of the next week in his apartment, staying close. They talked and cried and they even began to laugh again. Small remembered jokes found their way into their conversations, funny stories about their son that made them smile, that even made them laugh out loud once or twice. They had always laughed a lot, before it happened. They learned they could still laugh together now.

They didn't mark an anniversary that passed. An anniversary of twenty months of loss and heartbreak. They'd marked those feelings every day already.

The day before her return flight, she rang the airline and postponed it for another week. After that, another week. She stayed for a month, until they both decided to make a journey back to London, to see her uncle Lucas, his friend

Lucas. They spent three days in London, in her old bedroom, in the house where they had met.

Her half sister wasn't there. She'd returned to Australia. Her stepbrother was back in Boston with his family too. Ella and Aidan were planning a trip to Boston soon.

They were also planning another trip, a week away, somewhere warm, somewhere sunny. Spain perhaps. Or Italy. They were spoiled for choice, with Aidan and his languages.

They were both looking forward to it.

They were looking forward to many things again. Together.

EPILOGUE

Dear Felix,

I know I said I wasn't going to write to you anymore but tomorrow is the two-year anniversary of you leaving us and I need to mark it somehow. Actually, I just felt like writing to you again.

    I am in Spain at the moment. With your mum. With Ella. I wondered for a long time if I would ever feel happy again after you left us, but I am the closest thing to feeling it again. I missed your mum so much, Felix. I never stopped loving her. But we were both so sad and hurting so much that we needed to be away from each other for a while. I always hoped we could be together *again one day, once we had both done all the thinking and crying we needed to do.*

We are on holiday in Barcelona, a beautiful city full of great buildings and a long treelined street called Las Ramblas. I've taught your mum how to order tapas and to ask for directions. As she said herself, it goes well until someone says something in Spanish in return. She says I need to stay close. I'm very happy to do that. I also got to teach her some French on this holiday. We spent a weekend in France (before we came to Spain) with your granny and Walter and your Ess. They are all in the south of France filming Granny's TV series. Your mum and I got to watch a day of it. Between you and me, Felix, your granny is a terrible cook. She was trying to make a traditional French fish soup and I'm sure I'm not the only one who thought the final product looked more like dirty dishwashing water than a French delicacy. But she laughed a lot while she was making it, and tried to speak a bit of French, and before long all the crew were laughing too, not to mention the poor bewildered French people watching. Jess—sorry, Ess—joined in, trying out a bit of French as well as a bit of cooking. I'm sorry to say she takes after her mother on the cooking front. They make a very good comedy double-act. You just wouldn't want to eat their food. They are going to Germany to do some filming next (Walter is looking forward to that) and then on to England. Your granny said she can't wait to cook (or should I say try to cook) that great English dish toad-in-the-hole. Unfortunately, I can already imagine some of the jokes she'll make about that.

Your mum and I are here in Spain for a week and then it's back home to Washington. We both like living there very much. It's a beautiful, interesting city and my job there is very interesting too. (Last week I had to translate a document about the impact of pollution on the lizard colonies of the Nevada desert from American English into Spanish, German and French. I am now a lizard expert.) Your mum is working as an editor again, for a publisher she used to do some work with in Australia. It's an amazing world, Felix—she is editing on-screen these days, rather than sitting surrounded by piles of paper as she used to be in Canberra. If you were still with us, going to school soon, probably already comfortable on a computer, you would take this for granted, but old fogies like us think it's incredible.

It's June here in Spain, and the weather is perfect, warm, not hot. All the old stone buildings seem to glow in the sunshine. The Spanish people love their kids as much as the Irish and Australians do—we often see families out together in restaurants. And we think about you all the time, of course, and wish you were here with us. But you know that. That will never change.

I like to imagine that you are keeping an eye on us wherever you are, Felix. We think of you with as many smiles as tears now. I never thought that day would come. Some days are still harder than others. But your mum and I talk about you so much and that helps.

We are planning another trip soon, not as far as Spain this time, just a few hours away to Boston, to see your uncle Charlie and auntie Lucy and your cousins.

They miss you too. Your mum often talks to them on Skype and says she'll be surprised when she meets them again to find they're full-size, she's so used to seeing tiny versions on a computer screen.

Felix, we miss you every day. We are different now. All of us. In the same way your coming into our lives changed us in so many ways, your leaving us did too. But we are learning to live without you. Your mum is laughing again. I always loved her laugh and loved making her laugh. It was amazing that you laughed the same way, as though you were both saying "Hahahaha." When she laughs now, it's another great excuse to think about you.

Your auntie Ess is much better. She is still very sad too, and fragile, we know that, but she is back singing and dancing again, and seems to be entertaining all the crew filming with her in Europe. Your mum didn't spend a lot of time alone with her when we met up in France, but they did talk about general things, like the weather and the filming. I also know Jess showed her the tattoo of your name. Your mum found that hard, I think. But she said afterward that she was glad to see it and glad that we would always know what height you were. All those little reminders of you help us: the photos, the stories about you that we like to share.

We're hoping your great-uncle Lucas will come and visit us in Washington soon, for a week or two. He's about to get a lot of work done on his big and very messy fox-filled house in London (where your mum and I met), so he'll come over while that's happening. On his own, your mum hopes, not with his girlfriend. Her name is

Henrietta and your mum doesn't approve of her at all. I've met her, and between you and me, she's not that bad. Your mum is just very protective of her uncle Lucas.

Felix, your mum and I are talking about having another baby. We would love it if it happened and we hope it will happen soon. No one will ever replace you. But one of our secret hopes is that because a new baby will be half your mum and half me, as you were, it will be similar to you in some way. Maybe he or she will get that same look of mischief that you used to get. Maybe he or she will also have an obsession with brooms. Maybe he or she will shout his or her name out loud too. I know we will love that new baby and I know he or she will also help us to remember you. Not that we could ever forget you. Not our little Felix O'Hanlon.

I love you and miss you so much, Felix.

Dad xx

ACKNOWLEDGMENTS

My big thanks to all the people who shared family stories with me, especially Lisa Houatchanthara, Andre Sawenko, Xavier McInerney, Marie McInerney, Mikaella, Ulli, Ruby and Raf Clements, Jane Melross and Lizzie and Joe Arnold. For their help in many different ways, my thanks also to Lee O'Neill, Austin O'Neill, Max Fatchen, Brona Looby, Ethan Miller, Sabine Brasseler, Michael Boyny, Clare Forster, Sarah Duffy, Rosie Duffy, Kristin Gill, Bonnie Gill, Catherine Foley, Carol George, Mary Connolly, Rob McInerney, T. Bella Dinh-Zarr, Robert Zarr, Karen O'Connor, Bart Meldau, John, Bonnie and Stephanie Dickenson, Maria Dickenson, Ciaran McNally, Noëlle Harrison, Sinéad Moriarty, Noelene Turner, Helen Trinca, Robin Trinca and Hollie Blakeney.

This book is dedicated to my nieces and nephews in Australia, Ireland and Germany: Bernard, Nicholas, Patrick, Sam, Mikaella, Ulli, Ruby, Raf, Hannah, Dominic, Xavier, Callan, Mia, Catherine, Domhnall, Hannah and Thea. My love and thanks too to my two families, the McInerneys in Australia and the Drislanes in Ireland.

Many thanks to my publishers and agents around the world: Ali Watts, Arwen Summers, Saskia Adams, Gabrielle Coyne, Louise Ryan, Sally Bateman, Chantelle Sturt and everyone at Penguin Australia; Trisha Jackson, Natasha Harding, Jodie Mullish, David Adamson, Sophie Ransom of Midas PR, Gráinne Killeen and all at Pan Macmillan UK; Ellen Edwards, Elizabeth Bistrow, Michele Alpern and all at New American Library/Penguin; Fiona Inglis and the team at Curtis Brown Australia; Jonathan Lloyd, Kate Cooper and all at Curtis Brown London; Gráinne Fox at Fletcher and Company in New York and Anoukh Foerg in Germany. Thanks very much also to James Williams, Justin Tabari, Sarah Conroy and Ashley Miller for their Web site and photographic help.

Finally and as always, my love and thanks to my sister Maura and my husband, John, for all they do to help me write each novel.

MONICA McINERNEY

THE HOUSE OF MEMORIES

A CONVERSATION WITH MONICA McINERNEY

Q: The House of Memories *is a bit of a departure from your previous books in that the catalyst for the story is a tragedy. What inspired you to write it?*

A. The starting point was the idea of a blended family. All of my novels are family comedy-dramas, and I wanted to explore the ties and tensions within a family group when the blood links are more complicated, with half sisters, stepbrothers, stepparents, etc. I wondered how a family like that would react to something seismic, whether it would be possible to forgive someone if you were never sure how much you'd loved them in the first place.

I spent a lot of time deciding what that seismic event would be. Then, one night, I attended a crime writers' conference (as an observer) here in Dublin. One of the writers said the starting point for her novels was thinking about her own greatest fears, and then putting her characters through them.

That struck a real chord with me. I realized one of my greatest fears is something happening to one of my nieces or nephews while I'm looking after them. More than a decade ago, it nearly happened, when the baby niece I was minding started to choke on a piece of fruit. I'd turned away for just a moment and in that time she had turned blue. I only just got to her in time. Even though that story had a happy ending, I've never forgotten the feeling of terror. What if I hadn't turned around when I did? The entire landscape of my family would have changed. Would my sister, the baby's mother, ever have been able to forgive me? Could I ever have forgiven myself? I know that memory was the seed for this novel.

Q. What do you hope that readers will take away from reading the novel?

A. I hope readers will be entertained, moved and amused, but I especially hope they'll feel as though they have been right there beside Ella and her family through their journey from the shock and sadness of grief to a kind of peace and understanding.

Q. Although the novel is about a family that is grieving a terrible loss, it never feels depressing. How did you manage that?

A. I'm sure it comes from my own experience of life after loss. When my father died of cancer in 2000, it was as if our family solar system had lost a planet. We had to find a new shape for our family, and we all reacted in different ways. But we also laughed so much together. I can remember being shocked about it at the time—how could we possibly be finding so many things so funny? I realize now it's because our feelings were so raw—everything seems so vivid at a time of deep sadness and emotion like that. We were all easily moved to tears but also the bright moments and the funny moments seemed to shine very brightly.

A lot of the humor in *The House of Memories* comes from Charlie's entries about his family, especially his four children. Again, I remember my young nieces and nephews being like rays of sunshine in our dark and sad household after Dad died. I tried very hard to portray that sense of light illuminating times of darkness in *The House of Memories*.

Q. You have a wonderful knack for creating characters that fascinate us, and arouse our empathy, even when they are behaving badly. Jess is a perfect example of that. What's your secret?

A. Thank you very much—I work very hard on making my characters as real and well-rounded as I can, so I'm so glad to hear that. I think it's from years of observing people around me with a (sometimes too) curious eye. I think we are all a mixture of traits—good, bad, generous, selfish. . . . Different events bring different parts of our personality to the surface. We also never show all of ourselves to one another. There are always at least two sides to every story, as I wanted to show with Jess, in particular. She drove me mad with her vanity and self-absorption, but my heart often broke for her too, knowing the guilt and anguish she was feeling underneath.

Q. As in The House of Memories, *the action in your novels often revolves around a wonderful, rambling, big old house. Can you share something about what big houses mean to you?*

A. I've only recently realized that so many of my novels have a big house at the heart of them! I am sure that comes from my own childhood. I grew up in the small country town of Clare in South Australia, where my father was the railway stationmaster. My family (Mum, Dad and my six brothers and sisters and I) lived in the stationmaster's house just meters from the station, beside rolling hills and in sight of the railway tracks. It was a large, rambling house, set high on a hill, with terraced gardens and fruit trees all around, and a shady veranda spanning all four sides. It was like an adventure playground to us all. We played games of hide-and-seek and chase up on the veranda, to the great alarm of my mother many meters below! I also spent hours alone up on the roof, leaning against one of the chimneys, hiding and reading.

The house made me feel safe and special, all at once. I always loved coming home to it, as a child and as an adult. My parents ran an open house—apart from the nine of us, there were always so many visitors coming and going. I never knew who might be there when I opened the squeaky side gate or walked in through the (never locked) front door. Those memories of a big house filled with constant action, comedy and drama, the sense that you never know what might happen next or who might walk through the door with a shocking announcement, definitely feeds into my novels now.

Q. The House of Memories has already been published in Australia, Ireland and England. Is there anything in particular that you'd like to share about the response you've received to the novel so far?

A. I've been overwhelmed by the response to this story. I've had more e-mail and letters about it than any of my books to date. It has moved me so much to hear from readers, and to realize that so many people in the world have sadly experienced the raw grief that Ella feels. One e-mail in particular touched me very much, from a mother who had recently lost her daughter to illness. She thanked me for giving her "permission" to feel all that she was feeling: wanting to run away as fast as she could, the anger, the endless sorrow. She told me my book had given her hope that one day in the future, like Ella, she might be able to feel life has some joy to it again.

Q. You divide your time between Australia, where you were raised, and Ireland, where your husband is from. What do you most like about moving back and forth between the two countries? What are some of the cultural similarities and differences?

A. I think I'm spoiled to have two of the best countries in the world to call home. I do think of them both as my homes too—if I'm in Australia I talk about going "home" to Ireland and vice versa. I think moving so often is good for me as a writer—it keeps me observant, watchful for details and also in the role of "outsider" to an extent, all of which feeds into my plotlines and characters in some way. I also have big families in both countries (my husband is one of six), so there is always plenty of inspiration waiting in each country too!

Irish and Australian people are very similar, with a ready sense of humor, love of a chat, a disregard for too much authority. The links between the two countries are so strong; one in five Australians claim Irish heritage, and there are thousands of young Irish people living and working in Australia at the moment, for adventure and to escape the recession on this side of the world. Irish people often question my sanity, choosing to live in Ireland's damp climate compared to Australia's bright sunshine. The truth is I love cold, gray weather—I think I had enough of blazing summers and 104-degree days as a child!

Q. Can you share a little about how you go about writing each novel? I'm interested in where you write, and for how long each week, in addition to how you go about developing your plot and characters.

A. I generally get the idea for a new book about halfway through the writing of the "current" one, sparked by a minor character, a subplot or sometimes even a line of dialogue that I want to explore further. I think about each book for about six months before I physically start writing it. I imagine the characters, the dilemma that will be at the heart of my new family, how the plot will twist and turn. When I begin writing a book, I never know what will happen at the end. I like to be taken by surprise. I also spend a lot of time deciding on my characters' names and can't start work until their names feel right.

Once that basic foundation is in place—back to the house image again!—I choose a starting date and from that day on, I don't stop until I reach my ending, generally at the stroke of midnight on deadline day. I write a minimum of two thousand words a day, and won't leave my office unless I have done that. A story comes together like a house (yes, there it is again!). I build it brick by brick. In the early stages I write Monday to Friday, but usually about a third of the way in, it takes over my life completely and I am writing or editing seven days a week. I also usually develop insomnia about three-quarters of the way through. With *The House of Memories*, I started waking every night at 3:14 am, on the dot. I'd lie there for an hour or two untangling plot knots, thinking of dialogue, sleep again for an hour or two and then get up, make a cup of coffee, go straight to my desk and write down all that I'd imagined in the night.

My office is in the attic of our house in inner-city Dublin. I have two skylights that let in plenty of light (on the days when we get sunshine here) but more often there is rain pattering against the glass. It's a beautiful place to write, high up, warm and peaceful.

Q. What kinds of books do you enjoy reading? Who are some of your favorite writers? Have certain writers particularly influenced your work?

A. I read all and everything, and have done since I was a child. I learned to read as a four-year-old, encouraged by my mother, who worked in the local library, and then by great teachers at school. I read fiction and nonfiction, poetry, biographies, guidebooks, cookbooks. . . . My favorite writers include Charlotte Brontë, Jane Austen, Curtis Sittenfeld, John le Carré, Kristan Higgins, Laurie Graham, Benjamin Black, Tana French, Roald Dahl, Garrison Keillor, David Sedaris, Maeve Binchy, Elinor Lipman, Rosamunde Pilcher. . . .

All writers influence me in some way; I'm sure of it. I learn from good books, trying to discover why a plot has gripped me so much or why I care about a character so much—how has the author made me feel so connected to the story? If another book hasn't captured me in quite the same way, I also try to work out why and then do my best to avoid that in my own writing.

Q. Although this is your first novel published in the U.S. by New American Library/Penguin, you've previously written nine novels and a short story collection. How did you originally come to be a writer? How long have you been doing it? And can you tell us a little about what you're working on now?

A. I wrote my first book as an eight-year-old. It was called "The Smith Family Goes to Perth on the Train." I've since realized I don't have to sum up the entire plot in the title. I know that I'm a writer because I'm a reader. As a child, I read everything I could and it really felt like a natural progression for me to try to make up my own stories. I wrote plays for my family, poems, little songs, limericks, bad jokes. . . . My sister, brother and I also produced an annual family magazine called *The McInerney Report*, an issue a year for ten years, filled with scandalous stories about one another.

I began seriously writing short stories in 1997, submitting them for publication to magazines in Australia. I wrote in every genre I could think of: crime, fantasy, comedy, high drama. Looking back now, I realize I was trying to find my own voice as a writer. I was rejected many times, but I loved the writing process so much I kept going, and kept sending them out for publication. I was like an air traffic controller—I knew exactly where all my stories were at any given time, coming in or going out. Eventually, three were published in quick succession—all of them family stories with plenty of humor and a twist at the end—and that gave me the confidence to start my own first novel.

Again, it was a labor of love—I would write a chapter, send it to my sister Maura, who would read and encourage me to keep going, because she wanted to find out what happened next. The day I finished that story, I heard about a Write a Bestseller competition being run by an Irish publisher and newspaper. I entered, came runner-up, and that was the start for me. Since then, I've written many more short stories and nine novels. The first three were romantic comedies with a family background, but since then they have been more family comedy-dramas, with a romantic element.

I'm in the early stages of my new book, thoroughly enjoying the thinking, the plotting and the research. It's too early for me to say too much, but I know it's going to be filled with lots of misbehaving characters and plenty of family secrets and surprises. . . .

QUESTIONS
FOR DISCUSSION

1. *The House of Memories* is a novel about an extended family and their journey through grief. Does this necessarily make it a bleak story?

2. There are moments in the novel when we feel deep sympathy toward Ella, but are there also times when it's not so easy to understand her actions?

3. Is Ella's decision to distance herself from the rest of her family justified, do you think?

4. Lucas and his wonderful house are described in colorful detail. Discuss the importance of the setting for the novel.

5. Why do you think the author changes to first-person narration for Ella's chapters? Did you find this an effective device?

6. The complexity of blended-family life is acutely examined here. Why is it that Ella can have such a wonderful relationship with Charlie and such a vexed one with Jessica?

7. Did you love Jess or hate her?

8. There are many different parenting roles portrayed in the book. For example, Meredith, Charlie, Ella, Aidan. Does anyone strike you as being a "better" parent than another?

9. Discuss the theme of communication throughout the novel. In what major and minor ways does it play out in the story?

10. The Fox family is fabulously unique. Why, then, does this story resonate so profoundly with people whose families are nothing like theirs?

Photo by Ashley Miller

International bestselling writer **Monica McInerney** is the award-winning author of nine previous novels, one short-story collection, and numerous stories and articles. She grew up in Australia, one of seven children, and has split her time between Australia and Ireland for twenty years. Monica and her Irish husband currently live in Dublin, Ireland.

CONNECT ONLINE

monicamcinerney.com
facebook.com/monicamcinerneyauthor